She made her way along the path to the centre of the garden, which grew darker at every step as she moved farther from the street lamps. She looked back, and saw through the trees the faint glow of the window behind which Adrian was working. Theirs was one of the few houses in the square where a light still showed. In most of the others, the street lamps were reflected in blank dead windows. Bloomsbury, on the whole, kept early hours.

In spite of the stillness of the night, little rustles came from the bushes. A leaf fluttered down on to the path in front of her. The sky was the same ashy – *cendré* – colour as the trees. Under the scent of leaves and earth lurked the pervasive London smell of soot. She imagined for a moment how the night would be at Churston: the sky darker, the scent untamed.

Ahead now was the dim shape of the little summer house that stood in the very middle of the garden. From the darkness around it, a white triangle emerged, moved towards her.

'Henrietta?' His voice low.

'Yes. It's me.'

Also by Emma Cave

Bluebeard's Room
The Blood Bond
The Inferno Corridor
Little Angie

Cousin Henrietta

Emma Cave

CORONET BOOKS
Hodder and Stoughton

Copyright © 1981 Emma Cave

The right of Emma Cave to be identified as the Author
of the Work has been asserted by her in accordance with the
Copyright, Designs and Patents Act 1988.

First published in Great Britain by William Collins Sons &
Co. Ltd.
Published as a Coronet paperback in 1996 by Hodder and
Stoughton
A division of Hodder Headline PLC
A Coronet Paperback

10 9 8 7 6 5 4 3 2 1

British Library Cataloguing in Publication Data

Cave, Emma
Cousin Henrietta
1. English fiction – 20th century
I. Title
823.9'14[F]

ISBN 0 340 63255 0

Typeset by Hewer Text Composition Services, Edinburgh
Printed and bound in Great Britain by
Cox and Wyman Ltd, Reading, Berkshire

Hodder and Stoughton
A division of Hodder Headline PLC
338 Euston Road
London NW1 3BH

For Anne, and for Ethel

My thanks to G.G., R.H. and,
most especially, to P.S.

❦ *Part One* ❧

❧ One ❧

1924

As so often, late in the evening, in the house in the quiet square, the stillness was so absolute that it distracted her. Sitting in her accustomed position on the sofa, body turned sideways, book resting on the sofa's arm, she looked up. She shifted her feet, which were planted neatly side by side on the floor. Nanny's maxim – 'A lady never crosses her legs' – still influenced her, though her cousin Julia had discarded it long ago. Julia had even been photographed in *Vogue* ('Witty and chic – the Hon. Mrs "Algie" Thornton') with one bony little knee crossed over the other, narrow foot in arrow-pointed shoe aimed at the camera. *Bullseye!* Julia had such a passion for publicity.

How hot it was, the heat as distracting as the stillness. But she was easily distracted this evening. She wasn't reading a novel: she was making another of her desultory attempts at Freud, skimming the pages, her eyes and attention caught, from time to time, by some odd little episode in one of the case histories. But actually *reading* Freud was less interesting than her idea of him: the *idea* of the peeling away – as one might peel off the smooth skin of a ripe peach – of that unwrinkled life-surface which, in Aunt Louisa's world, it had always been of such supreme importance to preserve. According to Freud, everything that was really important happened *under* the surface. (Under the fruit skin, messy juice and pulp.)

Everything. She smiled, thinking of the room she was sitting in, lit by two reading lamps, one at her side on a small table, the other throwing a circle of light on the desk at which Adrian sat, making notes for the article he was writing.

The surface of the room was pleasant, soothing: the hand-blocked material in which the sofa was covered – so different from the brocades and velvets of Belgrave Square; the furniture painted at the Omega workshop; the Duncan Grant drawing over the fireplace.

She looked at her watch, with its diamond-encircled face – her wedding present from Uncle Harry. Five to eleven. She glanced towards Adrian who, at that moment, put down his pen and, raising his right hand, ran it over his hair. Then he picked up his pen again, dipped it in the ink-pot, and leant forward to copy something from one of the books that surrounded him. His narrow shoulders were hunched over the desk.

If his eyes had been fixed on her, as hers now were on him, she was sure that she would have become aware of it, would have looked up. But nothing broke into the closed circle of his concentration, a concentration which, he had often told her, with a note of reproof, was the result not only of a proper education, but also of a self-disciplined approach to work.

She stood up, went over to the window, lifted the edge of one of the curtains, and stepped behind it, seeing for a moment, before it fell back into place, Adrian's reflection in the window, position unaltered, concentration undisturbed by her movements.

Outside, the square was silent and deserted. In the square garden, the early summer leaves, so bright a green by day, were ashy – *cendré*, as Aunt Louisa, who liked to use French words, would have said – in the gaslight from the street lamps.

Pushing the curtain aside, she turned back into the room, feeling a bizarre impulse to break its stillness with some outrageous word or gesture. (Splash went the peach against the wall!) But how stupid that would have been. She looked at her watch again. Past eleven now.

'Adrian,' she said quietly, 'I think I'll go for a walk around the square. It's so hot tonight. I'd like some fresh air before I go to bed.'

He looked up. 'Hmm?' It took a moment for what she had said to sink in. Then he nodded, smiled perfunctorily.

'Right,' he said. He looked at his watch. 'Think I'll work for another hour or so. Bolt the front door when you come in, will you, Henrietta?'

She nodded, but he didn't notice. He had started writing again.

Downstairs, in the hall, she put on her coat, her hat. The house was silent – Vera and the kitchenmaid had gone to bed hours before. She remembered how, at Belgrave Square, Collins, the maid whom she and Julia shared, had waited up, however late it was, to help them to undress after dances. *The little buttons down the back of her dress had been fastened wrongly. Collins had said, 'I can't understand it.'*

Where, upstairs, it had been hot and airless, outside, the June night was soft, balmy. An incandescent halo of light, in which insects madly circled, surrounded the street lamp on the pavement in front of the house. She crossed the road, and in a moment was at the gate into the square garden. It was unlocked as she had known it would be. Opening, it creaked, as it always did. At the sound, loud and harsh in the silence, she glanced sharply from left to right. But there was no one about. She entered the garden, shutting the gate behind her.

She made her way along the path to the centre of the garden, which grew darker at every step as she moved farther from the street lamps. She looked back, and saw through the trees the faint glow of the window behind which Adrian was working. Theirs was one of the few houses in the square where a light still showed. In most of the others, the street lamps were reflected in blank dead windows. Bloomsbury, on the whole, kept early hours.

In spite of the stillness of the night, little rustles came from the bushes. A leaf fluttered down on to the path in front of her. The sky was the same ashy – *cendré* – colour as the trees. Under the scent of leaves and earth lurked the pervasive London smell of soot. She imagined for a moment how the night would be at Churston: the sky darker, the scents untamed.

Ahead now was the dim shape of the little summer house that stood in the very middle of the garden. From the darkness around it, a white triangle emerged, moved towards her.

'Henrietta?' His voice low.

'Yes. It's me.'

They met, they touched. He was in evening dress. His stiff white shirt front was hard and cool against her cheek. His mouth was fresh from the night – though it was always fresh; he was always so extremely clean. But here in the darkness, where touch, scent were all, she was particularly aware of it. She smelt the Euchrisma he always used on his hair.

She shivered. He took a step back, said with concern, 'You're cold? However warm it seems, the night air's treacherous, you know.' That had been another of Nanny's maxims, she remembered.

She said, 'Oh no. No, I'm not cold at all.'

He said, 'While I remember – the key of the garden.' He tossed it in the air, caught it, handed it to her. She put it in her pocket.

Now, together, they moved into the summer house. Side by side on the wooden bench, they embraced. She drew in her breath with an avid gulp of pleasure. Why, she wondered, did these hurried secret encounters in the garden at night hold such particular excitement for her?

'Missed you,' he said. 'I sat between two such dull girls

at dinner. Plain, too. Kept thinking of you, wondering what you were doing.'

She laughed. 'I was reading Freud,' she said.

'Freud – who on earth is he? Not that I care,' he added. Then he started to kiss her again.

❧ *Two* ❧

1925

She let herself into the house, and handed the little parcel of escalopes to Vera, who was dusting the hall. At Belgrave Square, she remembered, all the downstairs housework had been completed before the family got up. And when one handed a maid anything, she had given a little bob, a miniature curtsey. But those days were over, thank goodness.

Vera went down the passage to the kitchen. Henrietta took off her hat and coat, and went into the little cloakroom off the hall to hang them up. Looking at herself in the mirror, she patted her coiled hair. She had never cut it. She had always known that with her height, her figure, the effect would be ridiculous. And anyway, wasn't her hair one of her best features – so thick, so dark, with such a glossy sheen? Affectionately, she smoothed it with her hands.

Carrying the books Adrian had wanted, she crossed the hall to the stairs. Half way up, she halted, hearing voices coming from the drawing-room. Adrian's, and a woman's. Who could it be? Then an unmistakable laugh informed her that it was Julia.

Julia again? Why, it was only a week since she had last called. Julia was definitely forming a habit of dropping in.

How she wished that they had never met her at that

cinema. Before that, she had hardly seen Julia in years – once or twice at Belgrave Square when she had been visiting Uncle Harry. But outside the cinema, Julia, getting into her car, had said, 'I shall come and see you delicious creatures *very* soon.'

'I do hope she doesn't, don't you?' Henrietta said to Adrian as Julia drove off.

He gave a little shrug. 'I must admit,' he said, 'that I found her quite amusing.'

'Really?' was all she replied. What was the point of disagreeing? She had felt sure that Julia would never turn up. But she had been wrong.

How could someone so clever find Julia amusing? That was what she couldn't understand. Yet apparently others did too. In the reports of her doings which appeared in the Press, she was often in the company of artists, of playwrights and novelists.

When Julia had married Algie – ridiculous man with a ridiculous name – Henrietta had foreseen that she would follow undeviatingly into Aunt Louisa's footsteps. Town house, country house, two or three children; Ascot, Cowes, Henley Regatta.

But, over the years, something curious had happened. Julia had one son, but then no other children. And now, though they weren't legally separated, Julia and her husband virtually lived apart. He ran his father's estate, he hunted and shot; she had moved into a new block of flats in Knightsbridge – her husband's house in Grosvenor Square, described by Julia as 'pompous' and 'stuffy', was let furnished to rich Argentinians. And now Julia was always 'in the news'. *Witty and chic!* Henrietta shrugged as she went on up the stairs.

Yet, as she opened the door of the drawing-room, and the first thing she saw was Julia curled – quite an achievement! – in an uncomfortable Omega chair, she had to acknowledge the 'chic'. Everything about Julia expressed it: the close, white blonde crop of hair, the long slim neck, the little, brightly made-up face with the green eyes. And then there were her clothes: the green tube-like coat and skirt, the cream silk scarf, tied in a large cat's bow at her throat, the single vast barbaric metal ring on the middle finger of her left hand (she didn't wear a wedding ring), the green snake-skin shoes and bag.

Now, in one smooth movement, Julia uncurled herself (snake neck, snake shoes, snake-moving Julia) and darted towards Henrietta. She kissed her cheek, pricking her nostrils with a sharp scent – how different from Aunt Louisa's lily of the valley.

'Hitty Pitty!' Julia was exclaiming. 'Too divine! I've been praying like mad that you'd be back before I had to rush away. Not,' she added, 'that I haven't been enjoying myself. Darling Adrian has been entertaining me enormously.'

Henrietta couldn't resist a glance at 'darling Adrian'. To her irritation, he was looking pleased, though slightly sheepish.

'And what have *you* been doing, Hitty Pitty?'

'Oh,' she said, 'I went to the library for Adrian.'

'Such a perfect wife you have, Adrian! And what else?'

'Oh, a little shopping.'

'Something delicious to wear? Do tell.'

'No, just some meat.'

'Ah – your amusing little hobby! Too clever it sounds. I can't boil an eggy-peggy, but Adrian tells me you're becoming a positive chef. Do you wear one of those tall white hats?'

At this, Julia laughed, and Adrian smiled. Suddenly Henrietta saw, and was sure that they were seeing, just how ridiculous she would look in a chef's hat.

'You must let me taste some of these marvellous things you make,' Julia went on. 'I can see how delicious they must be, because you're looking so *well* on them. Isn't she, Adrian?'

Now, as Adrian murmured some kind of assent, Henrietta was sure that he was seeing her as *fat*, particularly because, at that moment, Julia put an arm about her waist, and stood beside her – so thin, so tiny, light as air. Towering above her, Henrietta felt larger than life-size. *Nymph and statue.*

Julia took her arm from Henrietta's waist, moved quickly – how fast she did everything – over to the sofa where she had left a small cloche hat, the same colour as her scarf. Going over to a mirror – its border of flowers and fronds looked suddenly muddy coloured in contrast to her reflection – she tugged the hat down over her ears. Julia, Henrietta decided, had the face for that kind of hat – she herself would have looked almost as ridiculous in it as in the chef's head-dress.

'What I came about,' Julia said, turning round, 'was to ask you to a great big party I'm giving next week. On Friday. Cocktails, and lots and lots of amusing people. You will come, won't you?'

Henrietta looked at Adrian. She would leave it up to him to extricate them. If there was one thing she knew he despised, it was cocktail parties.

'That sounds splendid, Julia,' he said.

'Wonderful! Any time after seven.' Now Julia was moving towards the door. Henrietta followed her, but Julia put a hand on her arm, gave her a little pinch – not like the pinches of the old days, but it still nipped her flesh.

'No, darling. Don't move. I'll see myself out. You must be exhausted after all those butchers' shops of yours. I really don't think I could *enter* one – that terrible smell of blood and sawdust. Just like a bullfight. Though I must admit I rather adored the one I saw in Pamplona.'

She gave a kind of wave – the hand movement used in a dance that Henrietta had never attempted, the Charleston. She was gone. The room suddenly felt very quiet and empty.

'Ugh. Bullfights!' Henrietta exclaimed. On *that* she was sure that Adrian would be in agreement with her.

'Mmm,' he said, but his back was turned. He was wandering over to the window. The front door slammed, and Henrietta realized that he had moved in order to be able to watch Julia's departure.

She heard a taxi draw up. Julia, she thought, was the sort of person for whom a taxi always seemed to be available. When the taxi started up again, Adrian turned from the window with a little sigh.

Why did she feel so angry? After all, she herself . . . And anyhow she didn't care about Adrian *in that way*. But really, she knew the cause of her anger quite well – that it should be Julia he was *sighing after*. She was sure that she wouldn't have minded if it had been anyone else.

Part Two

❧ Three ❧

1909

The butler opened the door ('Good afternoon, your lord-ship,' – 'Good afternoon, Hobart,') and Henrietta followed her uncle into the house in Belgrave Square. The first thing she noticed was the flowers massed in the curve of the stairs. Lilies she recognized, and carnations, but others, spotted like snakes, or hovering over the pots that held them, like flights of butterflies, were unknown to her. The scent of so many flowers was the scent of the funeral she had just been to, was the scent of the wreaths and sprays – almost all provided by her uncle – which had been piled on her parents' coffins.

Her uncle came to the funeral alone. Her aunt, he had told her, was suffering from a migraine – whatever that was. 'Your Aunt Louisa is in her boudoir,' he said now, opening a door at the back of the hall.

The butler had taken her uncle's hat and coat. Now he took hers. She followed her uncle through the open door.

Like a garden under the sea, she thought. A mass of greenery, lit from behind, filled a small conservatory which opened off the back of the room. The room itself seemed an extension of the conservatory, crowded as it was with plants and flowers, like those in the hall – but many more of them. Here the scent was positively overwhelming. In the grate a fire burned brilliantly. It was strange, she thought, to see a fire in a garden.

There was only one light in the room, a light with a green pleated silk shade which stood – a vase of tuberoses beside it – on a black shiny table decorated with gold dragons.

Next to the table was a piece of furniture which Henrietta's
mother had told her was a *chaise longue*, and which was
made of gilded wood. Green was the brocade in which the
chaise longue was covered. Green were the ribbons on the
creamy garment that frothed and foamed around the lady
who lay on it. Henrietta had never seen so much green
before. Elsie, their maid at home, had said that green was
an unlucky colour. This lady evidently didn't think so.

'Here is Henrietta,' her uncle said. 'Henrietta, this is your
Aunt Louisa.' Then he asked, 'Are you feeling any better
now, my dear?'

'A little, thank you,' the lady said. She had a tiny
lace-edged handkerchief in her left hand, with which,
now, she dabbed once or twice at her forehead. Languidly,
with her other hand, she beckoned to Henrietta. Moving
towards her with slow, careful steps – the room was so
crowded with plants and little gilt chairs and small tables
covered with ornaments and photographs in silver frames
that she was afraid of bumping into something – Henrietta
saw that even the lady's eyes were green, under lashes which
were strangely dark in contrast to the golden hair, puffed
and coiled around her face. She reminded Henrietta of
someone, but who was it? Then she remembered. It was
the mermaid with long golden hair and green eyes and a
green tail which her father had drawn and then painted in
water colour for her. Perhaps this lady had a tail under her
creamy dress, Henrietta thought, and, to her own surprise,
gave a little nervous giggle. Up rose the lady's smooth
rounded eyebrows, darker than her hair, but lighter than her
eyelashes. Immediately, Henrietta realized how *unsuitable* –
a word of her mother's – the giggle had been, and she felt
her face turn scarlet. In fact, she felt hot all over – the
room was so much hotter than the rooms at home, and
the thick black serge dress she was wearing was stifling.
She was aware that drops of perspiration had broken out
on her forehead, and the lady's – Aunt Louisa's – cold green

glance, she was sure, observed them. Suddenly she felt tears at the back of her eyes, but no, she wouldn't cry in front of this cold green lady.

'My poor child,' Aunt Louisa said in her low drawling voice. She leant forward a little, rested a soft cheek for a moment against Henrietta's. All the other flower scents were submerged in a wave of lily of the valley.

Henrietta stood stiffly, her arms at her sides. Her hands, hanging down uselessly, felt huge.

'Well, Henrietta, are you glad that you are coming to live with us?' Aunt Louisa asked.

Henrietta didn't know what to answer. She couldn't say 'Yes'; it wasn't true, and she also felt that to say it would be disloyal to her parents. So she simply stared at the golden hair, the green eyes, the white skin which, in the green light, had a greenish tinge. *I don't like green*, she thought.

Aunt Louisa turned to someone on her left whom, until then, Henrietta had hardly been aware of. This gentleman, thin, not tall, sat very upright on a small chair, his top hat, gloves and walking stick beside him. He was all black and white – his face, with small neat features, pale; his hair and moustache so fair that they were almost white – except for his grey eyes, and his grey silk tie which was fastened with a turquoise pin in the shape of a bird. To this person, incomprehensibly, Aunt Louisa said, 'Brahms or pure carpet, do you *think-ar-ay?*, Or that was what it sounded like. The gentleman gave a tiny shrug, smiled faintly.

'Must be off to the club,' Uncle Harry suddenly broke in. Where the other gentleman was black and white, Uncle Harry, despite his dark clothes, was warmly coloured, with reddish skin and very blue eyes. Uncle Harry, Henrietta had decided, was quite a kind man, and now she didn't want him to go.

But he was on his way to the door. 'Goodbye, Henrietta. I shall see you tomorrow. You'll be in bed when I get back.

The child must be tired,' he said to Aunt Louisa. 'Goodbye, my dear. Goodbye, Setty,' he added to the black and white gentleman.

When he was gone, there was a silence. At Aunt Louisa's feet, something, submerged in the frothing flow of her dress, moved. A little silky head with fluffy ears and two brown eyes like marbles emerged.

'Oh!' Henrietta exclaimed, stretching out her hand. But the little dog snapped, and quickly she pulled her hand back. It gave a high pitched yap-yap-yap.

'Ming doesn't like strangers,' Aunt Louisa said, and then, '*Naughty Ming!*' But she stroked the dog as she spoke, and she didn't sound at all angry.

At that moment, the door opened, and a tall fair young man came in. Did a sudden frown appear on his face because he had seen the black and white gentleman? Henrietta didn't have time to wonder about that because suddenly, astonished, she realized that she had seen him before, had seen him *at home* only a few months ago. Her eyes met his, and from a flicker of his eyelids she felt that he did not want her to refer to that. She became absolutely certain of it when he said, 'So this must be Henrietta.' He smiled at her. It was a really friendly smile.

'Yes, Edmund,' Aunt Louisa said, 'this is your cousin, Henrietta.' Then she said, 'And what have you been doing with yourself?'

'I've been looking at some pictures, Mother.'

'On such a fine afternoon?' Up went the rounded eyebrows. There was a coldness in her tone. 'I should have thought you could have found something better to do than that.' There was a pause. Then she said, 'Do you know where Henry is?'

'As far as I know, he was going to ride in the Park.' Edmund half closed his eyes, gave his mother what Henrietta thought of as a narrow look. 'Always so energetic, old Henry,' he said in a drawling voice.

Aunt Louisa's lips tightened. 'Very natural in a young man, I should have thought. Edmund, ring the bell for me, please.'

Moving slowly, Edmund went over to the fireplace, and tugged at the tasselled bell-rope that hung beside it. Standing with his back to the fireplace, he leant one elbow on the chimney-piece.

When, a moment or two later, the butler appeared, Aunt Louisa said, 'Hobart, please send up for Tebbins and Miss Julia.'

Edmund followed the butler to the door. 'Well, goodbye, Sir Richard,' he said, without warmth, and it was without warmth that the black and white gentleman replied, 'Goodbye, Edmund.'

'Goodbye, Henrietta,' Edmund said in quite a different tone. He smiled, and when she smiled back, he gave a little wink. She *liked* Edmund. 'See you later, Mother,' he said, and was gone.

As the door closed behind him, Aunt Louisa sighed. 'I worry so much about him, Richard,' she said. 'So different from his father, and so very different from dear Henry. It is hard to *believ-ar-ay* that they are twins.'

'Yes,' said Sir Richard. That was what Edmund had called him. Uncle Harry had called him something else – she couldn't remember what – and Aunt Louisa called him Richard.

He looked as if he were going to say something more, but then the door opened again. The faces of both Aunt Louisa and Sir Richard brightened.

'Here's Julia,' Sir Richard exclaimed, as a little figure danced into the room.

'Mama!' – and she was over by the *chaise longue*, kissing her mother. 'And here's my dear Sir Richard.' Now she was by his chair, and he was putting his arm around her, kissing her cheek. Julia's hair, which hung in ringlets, was white-fair, just like his.

Julia wore a white dress, with masses of frills down the front – her best dress, Henrietta supposed. In her own funeral black serge frock, she felt heavy and dull.

'Julia,' Aunt Louisa said, 'come here at once, you barbarous creature, and be introduced to your cousin, Henrietta. As you know, Henrietta has come to live with us because her parents have – have gone to Heaven. You're going to take care of her, aren't you, darling?'

'Mmm,' said Julia without enthusiasm. 'Hullo, Henrietta.' Then she said, 'Oo, what a lot of Henrys! There's Papa – people call him Harry, but his name's really Henry, isn't it? And then there's *our* Henry. And now there's this Henrietta. *I* shall call her Hitty Pitty.

'That's from a riddle,' Julia went on. 'I wonder if you know the answer to it, Mama.

> *'Hitty Pitty within the wall,*
> *Hitty Pitty without the wall,*
> *If you touch Hitty Pitty,*
> *Hitty Pitty will bite you.*

'Do you know? Do you know?'

But Aunt Louisa and Sir Richard, who were both smiling, shook their heads.

'It's a nettle. Hitty Pitty is a nettle!' Julia jumped up and down.

Aunt Louisa and Sir Richard were laughing as if Julia had said something funny, and the Nanny who stood in the doorway was smiling.

'Tebbins,' Aunt Louisa said, 'this is Miss Henrietta. Henrietta, this is Nanny Tebbins who is kindly going to look after you as well as Julia.'

Nanny Tebbins was small and dumpling-shaped. But though her figure was cosy looking, her face wasn't. It was a yellowish colour, and she had little bright black eyes.

Julia was back at her mother's side, nestling against her

shoulder as if she were going to have her photograph taken. There was a silly little smile on her face. Henrietta just stared at her – *she* wasn't going to smile. Julia's expression changed. Her face, invisible to anyone but Henrietta, clouded. Then, like a snake, she shot out a narrow pink tongue. Horrible Julia – how rude! And how strong the flowers smelt, and how very hot the room was. Henrietta felt a swirling feeling in her head, and then a lurch in her stomach. Suddenly, violently, she was sick on the Persian rug in front of the *chaise longue*.

Four

Lying in bed that night, she was free to think about the hateful day's events. She listened to horrible Julia's even breathing, coming from the other side of the pitch-dark room.

She wasn't used to falling asleep in the dark. At home she had had a night-light – at Papa's suggestion. 'Why should children have to be afraid at night?' he had said. And though Mama had murmured something about 'spoiling her', as usual Papa had got his way. The door of her room had always been left open, too. She had been able to hear the murmur of her parent's voices in the drawing-room downstairs.

The cottage in Kensington had been so tiny – only two storeys, and the basement where the kitchen and Elsie's room were. Elsie's room had one small window which looked on to a little area, roofed with bars, below the level of the minute back garden. The room smelt damp. Henrietta had wanted to play Prisoner of the Bastille in it, but her mother said she mustn't go in there.

This house was so huge. Doors into big rooms on the ground floor, off the vast hall. And then, on the first floor, as

Nanny hurried her upstairs, she had seen into an enormous drawing-room and along a passage with doors all the way down it. On the next floor, more and more doors. As they went upstairs, the house became colder and colder. The top floor was very cold indeed. That was where the night nursery, which she had to share with Julia, was.

'I used to share with Nanny, didn't I, Nanny dear? But now I've got to share with *you*,' Julia said. Julia couldn't be any more sorry about that than she was. How she wished she had a room of her own, as she had at home. Why couldn't Nanny and Julia have gone on sharing the night nursery? Then she could have slept in the little room next to it that Nanny had moved into.

How ashamed, what an *outcast* she had felt, after she had been sick on the rug. ('Outcast' was one of Papa's words; he often joked to Mama about having made her 'a social outcast'.) Aunt Louisa had wrinkled her nose and given a little shiver of distaste. Sir Richard had looked in the opposite direction. Julia had shouted, 'Mama, Mama, she's been sick on our carpet.' As if everyone didn't *see*.

At once, Nanny had taken her away upstairs, followed by a protesting Julia.

'But Mama, can't *I* stay a little longer? It's so *early*.'

'No darling, not this evening. Run and help Nanny to look after your cousin.'

'But I don't *want* to.'

'Now darling, don't whine. Do as I tell you.'

'I always stay much later. It's just because *she's* here, being sick on our carpet,' Julia had muttered on the stairs.

In the night nursery, Nanny took off Henrietta's black dress which had sickness all down the front of it. And she had to stay in her petticoat until one of the footmen brought up the trunk with her clothes in it.

'Nanny,' Julia said, 'Henrietta hasn't got lace on her petticoat.'

'Hush now, Miss Julia, do,' Nanny said, but Henrietta

saw a sour little smile on her face – a smile which reappeared when she unpacked Henrietta's trunk. She hadn't many clothes, and they were all made by Mama in the very bright colours which Papa liked.

'A *red* dress!' Julia said. 'I've never seen a little girl in a *red* dress, have you, Nanny? And what's *this?*' *This* was a blue velvet tunic in which Papa had painted her – she had worn dark green tights with it – as a medieval page. 'Is it your party dress, Henrietta?' Julia asked, giggling. 'It's very *short*, isn't it?'

When they had washed and brushed their teeth, and Julia was wearing a white nightgown with lace on it, and she had put on her own flannelette one, Nanny gave her a spoonful of a horrible grey powder, with a little jam on top of it, which almost made her sick again. From the grim look on Nanny's face, it almost seemed as if the powder were a punishment, not a medicine. 'Ugh, Gregory Powder. Henrietta's having Gregory Powder,' Julia chanted, and Nanny said, 'Now do hush, Miss Julia.'

Then it was time to say their prayers, and Nanny told Henrietta to say hers first. She knelt down, and said the one that Mama had taught her – 'Gentle Jesus', and 'God bless Mama and Papa, and make me a good girl.'

'And God bless my uncle and aunt and my cousins and Nanny,' Nanny had added, so she repeated it after her.

'What baby prayers you say, Henrietta,' Julia exclaimed. 'I gave up "Gentle Jesus" *ages* ago. I say the "Our Father" now.' And she said it in a high gabbling voice.

When Julia's prayers were finished, Nanny told Henrietta to get into bed, and then she took Julia off to the day nursery. 'Just for a very short time, Miss Julia, and only because it's earlier than your usual bedtime.'

How glad she was to be alone. But the grey powder had left a horrible taste in her mouth. How different it had been when she had felt ill at home – Mama putting a handkerchief, damp and cool with eau de cologne, on her forehead, and bringing her glasses of barley water; Papa sitting by her bed, doing wonderful drawings of fairies and animals, and making up stories about them. Oh how she missed Mama and Papa.

She cried a little, then, but stopped when she heard Nanny and Julia coming back. She shut her eyes and pretended to be asleep, though she looked quickly under her eyelashes at Julia jumping into bed. Who wanted lace on their underclothes, anyway? Nobody could see it. And Julia was wearing *curl papers,* screwed tightly all over her head.

When Nanny had kissed Julia – ugh, *she* wouldn't want to kiss Nanny – and had turned out the gas light, she lay in the dark waiting to hear when Julia fell asleep. Until she did, Henrietta felt she wasn't really free. To think. That was what she wanted to do, and, thank goodness, Julia fell asleep very quickly.

If only she could have said goodbye to them, at least, but she hadn't even been allowed into their room because the fever they had was so catching. And now they were dead – *how could they be dead?* – and she had to live with Uncle Harry and Aunt Louisa. There was nowhere else for her to go. That was what Elsie had said. 'Couldn't I come and live with *you?*' she had asked Elsie, but Elsie had answered that 'it wouldn't do'.

Although she had never seen Uncle Harry before, he was Mama's brother. When Mama had married Papa, her family had 'cut her off without a shilling', as Papa put it. What Henrietta couldn't understand was that they had done that because he was an artist. She thought an artist was a wonderful thing to be.

'Your Mama's relations don't think it is at all wonderful,' Papa had said, laughing, but Mama had shaken her head rather sadly. 'Harry isn't really a bad man,' she had said. 'It's Louisa.' 'Ah, the beautiful Louisa,' Papa had said, laughing again, but Mama had frowned.

Some of Papa's friends were at the funeral, but only one

or two of them came over to speak to her afterwards. She felt that they were put off because she was standing with Uncle Harry who looked so rich and grand.

She didn't cry at the funeral, but she cried afterwards when she had to say goodbye to Elsie outside the cottage. The driver was putting her trunk into Uncle Harry's carriage. She wondered what was going to happen to all the other things that were in the cottage: the furniture, and Mama's things and Papa's pictures. She didn't have the courage to ask her uncle, though she could see that he was trying to be kind.

'You'll come and see me, won't you?' she whispered to Elsie. Elsie kissed her and told her to be a good girl. Why hadn't Elsie said that she would come?

She heard Julia move, and she lay quite still, but then the steady breathing started again. She didn't like Julia, she didn't like Aunt Louisa, and she didn't like Nanny. And though she didn't dislike Uncle Harry, she couldn't imagine ever getting to know him well, or sitting in his lap as she used to do in Papa's. (Did Julia sit in Uncle Harry's lap? Probably she did. After all, he was her father.)

Of course, there was Edmund. One thing she was really glad about was that Edmund hadn't seen her being sick on the rug. He was the one person in the house she *really* liked. He had been so friendly – and quite different from how he'd been when he came to see Papa. Then, he had looked so miserable.

She sighed. She turned over, facing towards the wall, away from Julia. *That* was what she wanted to think about before she fell asleep: the time when Edmund had come to see Papa.

Running into Papa's studio, she stopped short at the sight of a stranger, but Papa called out, 'Come in, Henrietta. Come and meet your cousin.' Then he said, 'This is a rare occasion indeed. It's not often that we are honoured by a visit from your mother's relations.'

Not often? Papa must have meant never. The fair young man – Edmund – turned quite red.

He had brought a big black leather portfolio with him, full of drawings which Papa picked up, one by one, quickly glancing at each. The movement of his hand reminded her of Mama sewing, as he raised each sheet of very thick rough paper – the kind of paper he himself only used occasionally, because it was so expensive – held it for an instant, then put it down, and picked up the next.

When he put down the last one, he didn't say anything. He went over to the big north-facing window (artists' windows always faced north, he had told her), and stood staring up at the sky. How worried Edmund had looked, with his eyes fixed on Papa's back. At last Papa turned round and came back.

'Quite nice,' he said. 'Very pleasant amateur work.' But how disappointed Edmund's face was.

'You asked me for the truth,' Papa said, 'so I am telling it as I see it. No, I couldn't recommend your taking up art professionally.'

Edmund didn't say anything for a minute. Then he gave a sort of smile – but he still looked miserable, really. 'I see,' he said, and then, 'Well, thank you very much, sir.'

'I'm sorry,' Papa said. He put his hand on Edmund's shoulder, and Edmund jerked his head and made his shoulders stiff.

'Come and have a cup of tea in the house,' Papa said. 'I'm sure my wife – your aunt – will be delighted to see you.'

'The cab is waiting,' Edmund murmured.

'I'm sorry you don't feel you can keep it waiting a few minutes longer,' Papa said. 'Your aunt will be disappointed.'

Edmund turned red again. 'Oh well, of course . . . if you feel . . . Then I shall be delighted.'

Papa smiled. 'Come along then, my dear fellow.' He waved Edmund ahead of him through the door into the garden, and followed, taking Henrietta's hand.

Henrietta thought that it was a very uncomfortable tea party. Elsie hurried in and out, bringing the best thin china, which had violets on it, and cucumber sandwiches and a seed cake which she must have run out to buy from the grocer. Mama frowned when she saw the sandwiches, and Henrietta knew that she didn't think they were thin enough. When Mama poured the tea, Henrietta saw that her hand was shaking, but she didn't spill any. She asked Edmund lots of questions about his father, how was he, and what had he been doing lately, and so on. Edmund's answers to the questions were very short, and Papa hardly said anything.

Edmund drank one cup of tea, and ate a sandwich. He refused the seed cake – Henrietta didn't blame him; she hated seed cake herself. Then he stood up, saying thank you, and something else about the cab which was waiting outside the front gate.

'Well', Mama said, 'I'm afraid I can't ask you to give your father my love, as I imagine your parents don't know that you are visiting us.'

At that, Edmund turned redder than ever. He had been edging towards the door, and now he reached it. He nodded to Henrietta, gave a little bow to Mama, shook Papa's hand and said 'Thank you, sir,' again.

Henrietta watched him from the window as he went down the little path to the gate. How sad he looked. His shoulders were hunched as if a wind were blowing. Outside the gate, the cab horse jerked its head just as Edmund had done when Papa patted his shoulder. She turned round. 'Oh Papa, how could you be so cruel to him?' she said.

Papa looked very surprised. Then she felt surprised, too, at what she had said. 'Henrietta, how dare you speak to Papa like that!' came from Mama.

But Papa said, 'Don't be cross with her, Ella. She's quite

right. I was cruel.' He turned to Henrietta. 'I was cruel to be
kind,' he said. 'You must try to understand that. It would
have been much worse if I had lied to him. That was why
he came here, you see – to learn the truth.'

Cruel to be kind. No, she wasn't sure that she understood
that. Though of course she knew how important it was to
tell the truth. That was something Papa and Mama always
agreed about.

'His drawings were – very bad then, were they?' Mama
asked.

Now Mama and Papa were looking at each other. They
seemed to have forgotten about Henrietta.

Papa shrugged, hesitated. Then he said 'Oh, they showed
a certain facility. One or two of them were quite – graceful.'
Why did Papa make being graceful sound so awful? She'd
always thought that it was a compliment. 'Such a graceful
girl,' she remembered Mama saying approvingly about
someone.

'Essentially amateur,' Papa went on. 'Dilettante stuff.'

'What does dilettante mean, Papa?' Henrietta ventured.

'Dabbling,' Papa said. 'Dabbling instead of plunging.
Like paddling instead of swimming.' He turned to Mama
again. 'Only to be expected, I suppose,' he said, 'coming
from that background.'

He had spoken in what Henrietta thought of as his
'teasing voice', but Mama sounded cross when she said,
'*My* background too, Arthur, don't forget.'

'Ah but my dearest,' he said, 'you are a *woman*, not
an artist.'

Now Mama smiled. But couldn't a woman be an artist?
Henrietta wondered. Why, *she* wanted to be one. She nearly
said something, but Mama was speaking again.

'Poor boy,' she said. 'I feel rather sorry for him.'

'Yes, something of a misfit at home, I should imagine,'
Papa said.

'Imagine what Louisa would say! The very idea of

their son and heir wanting to be an *artist*!' They both laughed.

'From that point of view,' Papa said, 'I have it in me to wish that I could have encouraged the lad.'

'Now that's very shocking of you, Arthur,' Mama said, but she didn't sound at all shocked.

So this is *that* Louisa, Henrietta thought. It made her feel that she had been quite right not to like her. She must be a very stupid person to hate the idea of Edmund becoming an artist. But of course Papa had said that he couldn't be one. *Paddling instead of swimming*. She remembered the day that she had spent with Papa and Mama at the seaside. *She* had paddled. The cold water had flopped over her toes, and she had jumped back with a little scream.

The sea had frightened her. Of course she had been quite young then, only seven. Now that she was nine, it probably wouldn't frighten her at all. Perhaps, if she went to the seaside again, she might learn to swim. Ladies bathed from a bathing machine, Mama had told her. But did ladies swim? Perhaps only men swam, just as only men were artists. Was that really true? She must ask Papa. But no, she would never be able to ask Papa anything again. She was so tired. She mustn't think about Papa. She didn't want to cry again. Better to think about the sea. Paddling instead of swimming. Girls paddled . . .

A sharp pain in her arm woke her. Daylight was coming in through the curtains. There was something very near her, which turned into Julia's face. She blinked. The pain in her arm had been a pinch; Julia had pinched her. And now Julia was singing in her high, silly voice.

> *'Hitty Pitty within the wall,*
> *Hitty Pitty without the wall;*
> *If you touch Hitty Pitty,*
> *Hitty Pitty will – bite you.'*

On the word 'bite', Julia leaned forward and pinched her again. What should she do? But there were footsteps coming along the passage, and by the time the door opened, Julia was by the window. As Nanny came in, she was drawing back the curtains, saying, 'Good morning, Nanny dear. Isn't it a lovely day?'

Though the weather was fine, for Henrietta it wasn't a 'lovely day' at all. It seemed to go on for ever, without anything nice happening.

First came washing and dressing, and she had to put on her black dress again. It had been sponged, but it still seemed to smell of sickness. She was glad to wear one of her white pinafores on top of it. Julia wore a pinafore too, but Julia's had ruffles on the shoulders.

Breakfast, which they ate in the day nursery, was horrible – porridge and bread and butter. At home she had always had a boiled egg – except on Sunday when there were sausages – and toast and butter which Mama cut into little fingers for her to dip in her egg. Here there was only milk to drink. At home, Papa had always poured coffee into her milk. He had just laughed when Mama once said that it might 'stunt her growth'.

It was Saturday, so they didn't have lessons. On weekdays, a governess – 'silly old Miss Mackenzie,' Julia said, with a quick glance at Nanny, who pretended not to hear – came to give them lessons. Lessons were boring, Julia said, which made Henrietta feel quite sure that *she* would enjoy them.

After breakfast, Nanny was 'busy', so there were two hours to fill before they went to the Park. Julia played with her dolls and with things from her toy cupboard. Henrietta came over to look at them, but when she picked up a kaleidoscope, Julia said, 'Don't touch that – it's *mine*.' Anyway, she had never been very fond of toys. There was a bookcase in one corner of the room, and Henrietta went over to it. Julia didn't seem to mind her touching the books. She took one out – it was called *A Little Princess* – and sat down with it at the nursery table. The book was wonderful, and she would have become lost in it, except that, from time to time, Julia came buzzing round her like a wasp – a wasp with a sting, as she knew from that morning – and she had to keep an eye on her. She found that if, when Julia came near her, she just stared at her without smiling, it put her off and she went back to her toys, but it was a nuisance.

Nanny came back from whatever she had been busy with, and it was time to go to the Park. When Henrietta took off her pinafore, and put on her black coat, Nanny said to Julia, 'I must remember to speak to her ladyship about Miss Henrietta's clothes.' Why did Nanny say it to Julia instead of to her? It was almost as if she wasn't there.

Though the sun was shining, it was cold in the Park. The Nannies walked up and down together – some of them pushing babies in perambulators – and the children played ball, and skipped, and bowled hoops. Julia didn't introduce her to the other children, who stared at her. So she hung about near the nannies, until Julia's nanny – she couldn't think of her as *her* nanny – told her to 'run along and play'. After that she just walked up and down by herself.

She wished she didn't have to wear black clothes. She felt they made her look different from the other children. She would have thought that, at least, they would make people feel sorry for her, but they didn't seem to. It was strange that no one seemed to feel sorry for her about Mama and Papa. 'My poor child,' Aunt Lousia had said when she arrived, but no one else had said anything.

She had read lots of books about children whose parents had died, and everyone had felt sorry for them. Except in this one she was reading now, *A Little Princess*. Sarah, the heroine, had just heard that her father was dead, and no one was showing her any sympathy at all. The only thing that the horrible headmistress of her school was worried about was that Sarah's father hadn't left any money. Henrietta was sure that Papa hadn't left any money either. She had always known that they were poor.

Anyway, she felt ugly in the black clothes. She had never worn black before. She suddenly thought of the blue velvet tunic that Julia had laughed at the night before. When Papa painted her, she had worn a little gold-embroidered skullcap with the tunic. She was glad Elsie hadn't packed that, and that Nanny and Julia hadn't seen it.

At last – she was *freezing* – it was time to go back to Belgrave Square, walking one on each side of Nanny. (Julia held Nanny's hand.)

Lunch was even worse than breakfast. Slices of mutton – and they weren't hot, because they had been brought all the way up from the basement, so they left a sticky coating inside her mouth. When she left fat and gristly bits at the side of her plate, Nanny told her to eat them up, so she did, though she felt she was going to choke.

With the mutton, there were boiled potatoes with hard bits in them and a soft squashy mat of cabbage. Papa had always said that the English couldn't cook greens – Elsie had thought it was 'ever so funny' the way Papa liked cabbage, 'not cooked proper at all', only boiled for a minute or two. Now Henrietta knew how right Papa had been.

Afterwards there was rice pudding, not creamy like it had been at home, but thick and dry. Even at home she'd never liked rice pudding very much, though Papa had always taken off the skin she hated, and had only given her a small helping. Here a big skin-covered lump of the stuff was dumped on her plate by Nanny. Oh! Papa and Mama would never have expected her to eat such horrible food.

Papa didn't believe that children ought to be forced to eat things they didn't like, though Henrietta wasn't sure that Mama had quite agreed with him. Anyway, there had been hardly anything she didn't like at home. The food had been quite different there: not slabs of meat and awful stodge. They had eaten lots of fruit and eggs

and cheese, and sometimes Papa would cook Italian things
that he had learnt to make when he was an art student in
Rome. Elsie used to 'get the giggles' when Papa cooked,
and she would never taste the 'messed up' foreign food.
When Papa jokingly tried to persuade her, there would be
more giggles, at which Mama would frown. Mama didn't
believe in being 'familiar' with servants.

'What are you grinning at?' Julia said.

'Oh, nothing. I don't know.'

'Grinning isn't a very nice word to use to your cousin'
Nanny said. Henrietta almost felt grateful, but then Nanny
added, 'Funny not to know what you're smiling at, all
the same.'

After lunch, Henrietta and Julia had to rest on their beds,
with the curtains drawn, so that she wasn't able to read. At
home she had rested, but with a book. Papa had said, 'If
she needs to sleep, she will. If she doesn't, why should she
be bored?' Today she was sure that she wouldn't be able
to sleep, but she did, and was woken just as she had been
that morning by Julia pinching her and singing that awful
'Hitty Pitty' thing.

'*Hitty Pitty will – bite you.*' How she would have liked to
bite Julia, but once, at home, she had nearly – not quite –
bitten Elsie, and Mama had been horrified, and had recited
a poem that began, 'Let dogs delight to bark and bite'. But
how wonderful it would be to dig her teeth into Julia's
pinching hand and bite her till she screamed and screamed.
Surely pinching was as bad as biting?

After the rest, came nursery tea: bread and butter and
jam, and a plate of little rock cakes. She wasn't very
hungry, though she would have liked one of the little
cakes. But before you were allowed one of those, you
had to eat two slices of bread and butter, and one slice
of bread and jam. Henrietta only managed the two slices
of bread and butter.

'Not much of an appetite, have you, for such a big girl,'

Nanny said. Papa had always said what a good appetite she had. And was she really 'such a big girl?' She supposed she was, compared to Julia, though Julia was six months older than she was. When, after tea, all the fuss started, the getting ready to go downstairs, Nanny said it again. 'If you weren't such a big girl, you could have borrowed one of Miss Julia's dresses.'

'Nanny, I don't want Henrietta to wear my dresses.'

'Now Miss Julia, don't be so silly. You should be glad to lend your cousin one of your nice dresses, but I'm afraid they're all much too small for her.

So Henrietta had to keep on her black dress. Julia wore another frilly white one. Yesterday's hadn't been her party dress; there was a whole row of them in the cupboard.

Their hair was combed and brushed by Nanny – how she tugged at the knots – and then *polished* with a piece of silk. 'We must put your hair in papers tonight. It's that straight.' Nanny shook her head disapprovingly.

Henrietta didn't say anything. Elsie had once curled her hair at home, for fun, but it was so heavy that it was straight again in no time. Not before Papa had seen it, though – and hated it. 'Just like a doll,' he had said, and then that he didn't like children to look artificial.

Going downstairs was obviously the part of the day that Julia liked best. She kept jumping up and down, and was quite pink in the face with excitement. Henrietta could see that Julia was really quite pretty with her pink cheeks and her pale ringlets. 'Handsome is as handsome does,' Elsie used to say. If one went by that, Julia wasn't really pretty at all, because she was so perfectly horrible.

The drawing-room was the huge room on the first floor that she'd caught sight of the day before. Though it was so enormous, it was almost as full of things as Aunt Louisa's little boudoir downstairs. So many chairs and tables and screens and glass-fronted cabinets full of ornaments. There was a grand piano, covered with more silver-framed photographs, and lots and lots of pictures on the walls.

Two footmen were taking away the tea things when Nanny brought down Henrietta and Julia. Uncle Harry wasn't there. Nor was Edmund. Aunt Louisa was on another *chaise longue*, but sitting instead of lying on it this time. There were a lot of ladies, all beautifully dressed up, and almost as many gentlemen, including the black and white Sir Richard.

When Nanny opened the door, Julia ran to her mother right away. Henrietta hung back, and Nanny gave her a little push. She felt that all the ladies and gentlemen were staring at her. At that moment Aunt Louisa beckoned to Nanny, who came up to the *chaise longue*. In front of everyone, Aunt Louisa said something about 'getting the child a new wardrobe next week'. Though she didn't speak very loudly, Henrietta was sure that all the ladies and gentlemen heard her. Everyone looked at Henrietta again, as Nanny left, and murmured things to each other which she was sure were about her.

Julia really did love it downstairs, dancing from one visitor to another. She never stopped *showing off* – but nobody seemed to see how awful it was. The gentlemen patted her head, and the ladies smiled at her. Henrietta stayed near the door, and wondered how long it would go on for. It was ages and ages before Nanny came to fetch them. And then Julia said, 'Oh just five minutes more, Mama, *please*.' Sir Richard was showing her some kind of trick with a handkerchief. 'Well, then, just five minutes,' Aunt Louisa said, but it seemed much longer to Henrietta.

At last it was time. 'Go and kiss her ladyship goodnight,' Nanny said to Henrietta. Julia was kissing everyone, but apparently she didn't have to do that – thank goodness.

The lily of the valley cheek touched hers. She said, 'Aunt Louisa?'

'Yes?'

Now nobody seemed to be talking, though a moment before, they all had been. But she must say it. 'Aunt Louisa, do I have to have my hair put in curl papers? My papa didn't like me to have my hair curled.'

When she spoke the first sentence, a lot of the ladies and gentlemen laughed. When she finished the second one, they were all quiet for a moment. Aunt Louisa had a surprised, rather irritated look on her face. Then she shrugged, and called out to Nanny, 'Tebbins, I suppose Miss Henrietta *needn't* have her hair curled if she doesn't want to.'

Then everybody laughed. (Why? What was so funny?) And Nanny said, 'Very well, your ladyship.'

Out in the passage, Nanny marched across the landing ahead of Henrietta and Julia. As they reached the stairs, she turned and said to Henrietta, 'What did you want to go and ask her ladyship that for, and in front of all those ladies and gentlemen, too? You never said a word to me. I don't know I'm sure. Well, if you *want* to look like a board-school child, instead of having pretty curls like a young lady . . .' Then she muttered something about 'quite a little madam'.

Julia took it up. 'Little madam, little madam,' she chanted. But Nanny really sounded cross when she said, 'Now *will* you be quiet, Miss Julia.' It was in silence that they completed the journey to the day nursery, where Nanny told them to play quietly until she came to get them ready for bed, and stumped out of the room.

When she had gone, Julia gave Henrietta an unfriendly look – she was sulking, Henrietta thought, because of what Nanny had said to her – and went over to her dolls' cot, where she started talking to the dolls – 'Hullo, my dear little darlings' – in that high silly voice of hers. Surely, at nearly ten, she was too old for that sort of thing?

Henrietta fetched *A Little Princess* from the bookcase, and was at once lost in it. The horrible headmistress, Miss Minchin, now that Sarah's father was dead, had taken away all her nice clothes, and made her sleep in an attic. There was a very nasty girl called Lavinia at the school. Henrietta pictured her as just like Julia.

She didn't know how much time had passed when a sound made her look up. Edmund was standing in the doorway. 'Edmund, it's Edmund,' Julia called out.

'Hello, Julia,' he said, not very keenly, Henrietta thought. He came over to the table.

'How are you today, Henrietta?' His voice was kinder, she thought, than it had been when he spoke to Julia.

'Very well, thank you.'

'Henrietta doesn't want to play with me,' Julia said. 'She just sits there *reading*.'

'You're fond of reading, then?'

She nodded.

'You're like me,' Edmund said. 'Julia's like Henry – my brother. He thinks reading is a dreadful waste of time.'

'I'm like Henry. I'm like Henry.' Julia jumped up and down, clapping her hands. 'Henry thinks books are silly old things, too.' She picked up one of her dolls – 'My sweet little Effie' – and rocked it in her arms.

Edmund sat down opposite Henrietta, at the table. 'Well,' he said, 'how are you finding it here?'

She didn't know what to say.

'I'm so sorry about your parents,' he went on, in a low voice, 'and everything must seem so strange to you.' He paused, then he said, 'It was nice of you, yesterday, not to say anything about that time when I came to see your father.'

'I knew you didn't want me to,' she said.

'That was very clever of you, Henrietta. Well, we'll keep it as a secret between us, shall we?'

She nodded.

'We shall be friends then, Henrietta. Only friends have secrets.'

She gave him a smile of pure joy. With a friend, surely things wouldn't be so bad? She looked down at the table, then up at him again.

'Edmund,' she said, 'what does Brahms mean?'

Edmund looked surprised. 'Brahms?' he said. 'Brahms was a musician, a famous composer.'

'Oh,' she said. She frowned.

'Why are you looking so puzzled, Henrietta?'

'It was something Aunt Louisa said. She said "Brahms or pure carpet, do you *think-ar-ay?*'

Edmund laughed. 'Oh, it's a ridiculous kind of slang they all talk – my mother and her friends. Brahms means condescending. Pompous. Sort of pretending to be grand. Carpet – well, carpet just means dull. And they put "ar-ay' on to lots of words, to give them an Italian sound. Dinn-ar-ay, dans-ar-ay—' He broke off. 'Why are you looking so upset, Henrietta?'

She could feel how red her face was, and that tears were coming into her eyes.

'Aunt Louisa was talking about *me*,' she brought out after a moment.

'Oh!' he said. 'Oh heavens. Oh how perfectly appalling.' He stopped. Then he said, 'No, I'm quite sure you're wrong about that. Really, you mustn't be upset. You see the words can mean quite different things, too. Now, *I* see Brahms as meaning absolutely excellent. And carpets – carpets are splendid things. They look pretty and they keep one warm.'

But of course she knew that Aunt Louisa had meant the horrible things, not the nice ones. How nice *he* was, though. He was smiling at her, but looking worried at the same time. She forced the tears down, and managed to smile back. Over his shoulder, she saw that someone else had come into the room. *Edmund?* she thought, but Edmund was sitting here, at the table.

Then, at once, she realized that it wasn't Edmund. This young man was the same height as Edmund but his shoulders were broader. His eyes, like Edmund's, were blue, but they were bigger, rounder. Edmund's nose had a bump in it, and his face was thin. This other person's nose was straight, and his face was wider.

'Henry!' Julia ran to him, was lifted up, clung to his shoulders. Julia, she saw in that moment, really loved Henry. But Henrietta was quite sure that he couldn't be as nice as Edmund.

The thing that she looked forward to all that first Sunday at Belgrave Square – one had to have *something* to look forward to – was the coming of the governess on Monday.

Sunday was even worse than Saturday because of the long, boring time they spent in church. She had hardly ever been to church, at home, because on Sundays Papa always liked to take them to visit friends of his, or to go on expeditions to the country. Lunch was better, in a way: roast chicken and roast potatoes, but there was cabbage again, and thick brown gravy poured over everything. Afterwards there was apple pie, but Nanny covered it with lumpy yellow custard. So even when the food wasn't actually nasty, they still managed to spoil it. At home, where she enjoyed food, she hadn't thought about it half as much as she did here, where she hated it.

On Sunday, they weren't allowed to read ordinary story books. There was a special Sunday shelf. She chose something called *Parables from Nature*, which turned out to be very boring. But, anyway, she didn't have much chance to read because Julia kept buzzing around her, especially when Nanny was there. 'Henrietta, why don't you come and play with me?' she said. Henrietta did try once, but Julia wouldn't let her touch anything – really only wanted her to watch. Even *Parables from Nature* was better than 'playing' with Julia.

She had hoped that Edmund might come to the day nursery again, but he didn't, and when they went down to the drawing-room, he wasn't there either.

Monday morning was the first on which she woke before

Julia. So there wasn't any 'Hitty Pitty' – she must try to wake first every day. *What was she going to do about Julia?* She thought that Papa would have told her to fight back, but she didn't think that Mama would have. Anyway, Julia was so *quick* – a quick pinch, and she was off – though Henrietta was bigger and stronger. And, being bigger and stronger, say she did get hold of Julia? – would she be able to stop herself kicking and hitting and shaking her? Or even biting her? If she really hurt Julia, what a terrible fuss there would be. And how ashamed of her Papa, as well as Mama, would have been. Besides, she had this funny feeling that Julia *wanted* her to lose her temper. That was the very best possible reason for not doing so. She sighed. But something nice was going to happen today, wasn't it? Then she remembered. Lessons.

She had enjoyed lessons at home: reading, writing and French with Mama; drawing (her favourite), arithmetic, history and geography with Papa. All lessons with Papa were great fun. Arithmetic was a very fast game of questions and answers. And when they did history and geography, he used to draw the things he told her about: maps and jungles and wild animals, and Alfred burning the cakes, and Canute sitting on his throne at the edge of the sea, and Sir Walter Raleigh laying down his cloak for Queen Elizabeth to walk on. Whenever she read about any of those things she imagined them looking just like Papa's pictures.

At that moment, Julia woke up, yawned, raised her head from the pillow. Her eyes turned towards Henrietta at once, and when she saw her sitting up in bed, her fists clenched on top of the sheets, how disappointed she looked. Henrietta felt pleased.

A minute or two later, Nanny came into the room. 'Now then, Miss Julia, Miss Henrietta – hurry up,' she said. 'That Miss Mackenzie will be here before I know it.'

Nanny was looking cross this morning. Julia, as she had done before, with the same quick sideways glance, said

'Silly old Miss Mackenzie.' Again, Nanny pretended not to hear, but Henrietta thought she had – and that suddenly she looked less cross, rather than more.

After the usual horrible breakfast, they had to go and wash their hands again – goodness knew why, because they hadn't had anything nice and sticky, like jam or marmalade. When they came back to the day nursery, Annie, the nursery maid, who never said anything, had just finished clearing the table, and Miss Mackenzie had arrived and was laying out books on the dark blue cloth with bobbles round its edges.

Henrietta felt a pang of disappointment at the sight of Miss Mackenzie. She wore a muddy coloured tweed coat and skirt, and a mauve blouse that looked terrible with it. She was very thin, and awfully old, and her nose was bright red. But perhaps she was better than she looked.

'One should never judge by appearances,' Mama had once said, reprovingly, when Henrietta had said that someone was ugly.

Papa had roared with laughter. 'Absolute nonsense,' he had said. 'The sheerest hypocrisy. Judging by appearances is instinctive to all of us.'

But Mama hadn't smiled. 'We aren't here to follow our *instincts*, Arthur,' she had said.

Papa had laughed again. 'What a Puritan you are, my dear,' he said, and Mama had frowned.

Puritans were those dreadful gloomy men who had murdered King Charles and destroyed beautiful statues and windows in the churches. (When Papa had told her about them, he had sounded much crosser about the statues and the windows than about the King.) So no wonder Mama looked annoyed. Why had Papa called her such a rude name? Yet a minute or two later they were talking happily away as if he hadn't said anything wrong. Mama never stayed cross with Papa, and nor did he with her. Sometimes his voice would get rather loud, and he would march off to his studio, but when he came back again, everything would always be all right. Henrietta wondered if Uncle Harry and Aunt Louisa ever got cross with each other. She could imagine Uncle Harry, with his red face, talking in a loud voice. But if Aunt Louisa got cross, she would probably talk very quietly, and give the sort of look from her green eyes that she had given Henrietta when she had been sick on the rug.

Miss Mackenzie turned out to be quite as bad as she looked – worse, if anything. She had a bad cold, and she kept dabbing at her red nose with a tiny handkerchief, instead of blowing it properly. That was why she gave maddening little sniffs all the time. But the really bad thing about her was that the lessons she gave were so boring.

First they did arithmetic – 'while our minds are fresh,' Miss Mackenzie said – and instead of Papa's questions which were like a game, it was all learning tables and writing down sums. History came next, and that was all dates. Julia knew tables and dates far better than Henrietta did.

At quarter to eleven, they had milk and biscuits – Miss Mackenzie had tea – and then she took them for a walk around the Square. When they came back into the day nursery – which Miss Mackenzie called the schoolroom – it was time for English composition.

Henrietta liked writing compositions, and, for the first time that morning, she felt happy. The subject Miss Mackenzie gave them was 'A Day in the Country', and Henrietta decided to describe one Sunday when she had gone with Papa and Mama to Shoreham in Kent where the painter Samuel Palmer had lived. Samuel Palmer, like William Blake, had been a visionary, Papa had told her. She had asked him what a visionary was, and he had said that it was someone who saw the world quite differently from the way that ordinary people did.

Miss Mackenzie was looking over her shoulder, which she hated. Now Miss Mackenzie exclaimed, 'But, child, what terrible writing you have.'

Mama hadn't liked Henrietta's writing either, but Papa had always said not to worry about it, that it would correct itself. Now she shot a glance at Julia's book. Julia's writing was very round and tidy, and sloped slightly to the right instead of leaning backwards, as Henrietta's did.

Miss Mackenzie was saying, 'But of course your writing is bad. Why, you are using your *left hand*. Oh, we shall have to do something about that.' Mama had worried about her being left-handed, too, but Papa had insisted that it didn't matter. 'Look at Leonardo da Vinci. He was left-handed,' Papa had said.

At that moment, the door opened, and Aunt Louisa came in.

Miss Mackenzie leapt to her feet. Henrietta and Julia stood up, too. Julia ran across the room to kiss her mother.

'Oh, good morning, Lady Allingham,' Miss Mackenzie was saying. She didn't call Aunt Louisa 'your ladyship' as the servants did.

'Good morning, Miss Mackenzie. Good morning, Henrietta,' Aunt Louisa said, and Henrietta murmured, 'Good morning.'

Aunt Louisa, like Miss Mackenzie, was wearing a tweed coat and skirt, but her coat and skirt were quite different from Miss Mackenzie's. Though they weren't tight, she looked as though she had been poured into them. And what a beautiful white blouse she was wearing!

'Well, Miss Mackenzie,' she said, 'and how are the children getting on? How do you find your new pupil?'

'Oh Lady Allingham,' Miss Mackenzie said, 'I'm afraid that Henrietta is terribly *behind*. She doesn't seem to know any dates or tables. Of course, systematic training will correct that. And really her handwriting is disgraceful. Though there is an explanation for that. You see, the child has been allowed to write *with her left hand*.'

'Oh dear me, that won't do at all, will it?' Aunt Louisa

said. 'We shall have to do something about that. Or rather, *you* will, Miss Mackenzie,' and she gave a little peal of laughter.

The thought of writing with her right hand – why, she could hardly do anything with her right hand – filled Henrietta with such dismay that she felt she had to say something. What she came out with was, 'But Leonardo da Vinci was left-handed.'

Up went Aunt Louisa's eyebrows. 'Leonardo da Vinci? Indeed! Are you by any chance comparing yourself to Leonardo da Vinci, Henrietta?'

Miss Mackenzie gave what Henrietta thought of as a soapy laugh ('soapy' had been a favourite word of Papa's), and Julia tittered. Henrietta could feel herself blushing scarlet.

'No,' she said. 'No, of course not, Aunt Louisa. But Papa said—'

'Your father was talking about a famous artist,' Aunt Louisa broke in, not letting her finish the sentence. 'Not about a little girl with bad handwriting.'

'But—'

'Don't argue please, Henrietta. It's very unbecoming for a child to try to argue with grown-up people.'

Aunt Louisa picked up Henrietta's exercise book from the table. ' "The visionary, Samuel Palmer",' she read aloud. 'Goodness me! What, pray, is a visionary, Henrietta?'

'Someone,' she said, 'who sees the world differently from how ordinary people do.'

'You shouldn't use words you don't understand, Henrietta.' Aunt Louisa's voice sounded sweet, but, Henrietta thought, it wasn't really sweet at all. 'A visionary is someone who sees visions. Like the saints, and so on,' she added briskly. 'Anyway, Miss Mackenzie is quite right – your handwriting is a disgrace. But you will soon learn to use your right hand, Henrietta, and then of course, your writing will improve.'

'But I *can't*,' she said.

'Can't is a very silly word, Henrietta. Why, you haven't tried. Surely you've heard the old proverb. If at first you don't succeed, then try, try, try again. It is your duty to try, Henrietta, and, of course, duty is the most important thing in all our lives. Duty to God, to King and country, to those who are put in authority over us. If you don't know that already, Henrietta, then you will have to learn it. And children must do their duty in little ways, so that when they are older, they can do it in bigger, more important ways.'

Aunt Louisa moved towards the door. Miss Mackenzie followed her, murmuring, 'How true, Lady Allingham.' They stood in the doorway for a moment.

'Spoilt, you know,' Henrietta heard Aunt Louisa say. 'An only child.'

'I'm sure that dear Julia's society will do wonders for her,' Miss Mackenzie said. She was being soapy again.

'Henrietta, you're all red in the face,' Julia said. 'And you're a show-off,' she added in a low voice, as Miss Mackenzie came back to the table. 'Isn't Henrietta red in the face, Miss Mackenzie?'

'That will do, Julia,' Miss Mackenzie said, quite sharply. Then she said, 'I think we will continue with our compositions tomorrow. Now we shall learn a poem.' She handed each of them a copy of *The Golden Treasury*. 'Henrietta shall choose,' she added in a kind voice.

Henrietta knew a lot of poems from *The Golden Treasury*. Now she turned the pages, and picked one which she had already learnt by heart from Mama.

' "I wandered lonely as a cloud",' she said. 'Could we learn that one?'

'Ah, *Daffodils* – a delightful choice,' said Miss Mackenzie.

Julia, finding the place, groaned. 'But it's so *long*,' she said.

'Four verses? Twenty-four lines?' Miss Mackenzie said briskly. 'That isn't long, Julia. Now I understand why you always choose sonnets. Little girls mustn't be lazy, must they?'

Henrietta didn't see the words on the page. The words in her head were 'spoilt' and 'an only child'. If ever anyone could be called 'spoilt', it was Julia, she thought. And really, Julia was almost 'an only child', in a way. After all, Edmund and Henry were grown up.

It was funny that she and Julia should be the same age. She was so young because Mama had been quite old when she had married Papa. If only Aunt Louisa had had Julia at the same time as Edmund and Henry, then she wouldn't have had to put up with 'dear Julia's society' for ever and ever. Well anyway, until she was grown up, which seemed like for ever. When she really was grown up, and could do whatever she wanted, she decided that she would never see Julia again.

Next day, the writing torture began. Miss Mackenzie made her go right back to the beginning again. Using her right hand, she had to copy the letters over and over, row after row of them – 'just like a baby,' Julia whispered. She *had* to do it, because grown-ups *made* children do things, not because of that silly 'duty' Aunt Louisa had talked about.

It wasn't only her writing that she was forced to change. Aunt Louisa spoke to Nanny, and Henrietta had to do everything – eating, drinking, washing, brushing her teeth – with her right hand. Now Julia had a new game – catching Henrietta out, and gleefully proclaiming it.

The worst thing of all was that she found she couldn't draw anymore. Her right hand *wouldn't* draw; it just refused. As if it were her enemy.

If thine eye offend thee, pluck it out, and cast it from thee. The vicar preached a sermon about that one Sunday. The sermon was as boring as usual, but the idea stuck in her mind. If only she could cut off her right hand – then they would have to let her use her left one. She said that to

Edmund, and though he was sympathetic about her having to change hands ('It's rubbish,' he said. 'I wish I could get my mother to give it up, but I know she wouldn't listen to me!'), he smiled, and said, 'You wouldn't look very nice with only one hand.' That was true, of course, and, anyway, she knew she wouldn't be brave enough. Once she tried bending her wrist back to see if she could break it. But when it really started to hurt, she couldn't go on.

At first, sometimes, when she was alone – though that was hardly ever – she tried to draw with her left hand in the old way. But soon, as she began to get accustomed to using her right hand for everything else, that felt awkward, too. Besides, she couldn't concentrate. All the time she was afraid that someone would come into the room and stop her doing it. She imagined Julia triumphantly calling out, 'Henrietta's using her left hand again.'

So they had stopped her doing the one thing she really wanted to do. They hated her. Everyone hated her, and was cruel to her.

Everyone? Well certainly Aunt Louisa and Julia and Nanny, and usually Miss Mackenzie, though she wasn't as bad as the others. Not Uncle Harry or Henry – but then she hardly ever saw them. And not Edmund. Oh no – never Edmund.

Once she made a list of them in the order of how she felt about them.

1. Edmund – BEST OF EVERYONE
2. Uncle Harry
3. Henry
4. Miss Mackenzie
5. Nanny
6. Aunt Louisa
7 Julia – WORST OF ALL

When she had made this list, she tore it up. But writing it had helped her in some way, had, as she put it to herself, *tidied things up*.

✺ *Five* ✺

1913

A hot, blue and gold afternoon. The click of croquet balls, the cooing of doves. She sat by the window in the playroom at Churston Feverel, with her elbow resting on the sill, her chin cupped in her hand. Edmund and Isabel Pelham, one of the Saturday-to-Monday visitors, were walking slowly across the lawn to the cedar tree.

'Miss Pelham's pretty, isn't she?' Julia murmured behind her. 'I wonder if she and Edmund will get engaged.'

Horror? Astonishment? She didn't know which feeling predominated. Fiercely she exclaimed, 'What rubbish, Julia! What rubbish you talk.'

A quick pinch, with that little twist of her fingers which always made it so painful, and Julia jumped back.

'Hitty Pitty's jealous,' she chanted. 'Hitty Pitty's jealous!'

'I'm not. I'm not at all.' Henrietta sprang to her feet, whirled round. Her usual control was almost gone. Her hands, of their own volition, reached out to grab at Julia, grab at her long snake-neck. But, with a little laugh, Julia was at the playroom door. 'Hilty Pitty's *jeal*-ous!' – and she was alone, facing the door, which Julia had slammed behind her. Fists clenched, her breathing loud in the quiet room – dove cooing; click of mallet against croquet ball – she only stood there for a moment. Then she was back at the window.

Edmund and Miss Pelham had reached the cedar now.

They stood under its great spreading branches. She, dressed all in white (white dress, with a bodice of little tucks, white hat, white parasol, which, in the cedar's shade, she now closed, lowered, and twirled on its silver ferrule), glanced up at him under her lashes, under the brim of her hat. She smiled, said something. He looked away.

Now, staring straight ahead, towards the terrace, *he* was speaking. There seemed to Henrietta to be no expression on his face at all. Surely he couldn't be *proposing?*

He had finished what he was saying and, at that moment, the girl stilled her twirling parasol, a dove stopped cooing.

Henrietta realized that she was clutching the window sill with both hands. Was it a gaze she fixed on him that drew his eyes up to the window? As their eyes met, she experienced a wild impulse to step back, so guilty, almost naked – *caught spying* – did she feel. He gave the girl a quick sideways look, then cast his eyes up to the sky, at the same time turning down the corners of his mouth.

Miss Pelham was talking again. He looked briefly down at her, said something, gestured towards the house. She shrugged with a hint of petulance. Then she raised her parasol, opened it, and they started to walk back across the lawn.

Henrietta's hands relaxed. She turned from the window. *That look!* Absolutely certainly it wasn't the look that anyone who had just *proposed* would give, expressing as it had such cold contempt, such martyred boredom. Suddenly she was feeling so happy that she did a little dance in the middle of the room. Then, hearing footsteps in the passage, she stopped. Julia opened the door.

At the sight of Henrietta, facing her and smiling, Julia looked taken aback. She had, Henrietta realized, been expecting to find her at the window. A little nugget of triumph clinked on to the hoard of her happiness.

'Temper, temper,' Julia said, but without conviction, for

it must have been obvious to her that Henrietta wasn't angry any more.

Henrietta widened her smile. 'But Julia,' she said, 'I'm not in the least cross, not the least little bit.'

'You *were*,' Julia said sulkily.

'Oh well, you know, no one likes being pinched all the time. It's so *childish*'.

As, sullenly, Julia turned away, Henrietta saw a flush rise on her cheeks.

One of the best things about Churston Feverel was that, there, she had always had a room of her own – as, on their return to London this autumn, she would have (at last!) in Belgrave Square.

Henrietta guessed that this decision of Aunt Louisa's had been prompted by Julia – probably during one of the visits she now made to her mother's bedroom each morning after breakfast. At first, Julia had tried to make Henrietta envious of these visits – 'Mama and I have such lovely grown-up talks together' – but had desisted when she got no response. (The last thing Henrietta wanted was to spend an extra half hour with Aunt Louisa and Julia each day.)

It would be wonderful to have a refuge in London, like the one she had at Churston: somewhere where she could think at ease, free from the superstitious fear she always felt, sharing with Julia. It was absurd she knew, but she couldn't overcome it – the dread that Julia, awake, might in some way manage to *read her thoughts*: her fond thoughts about Edmund, her hate-hate-hating thoughts of Julia. At Churston she had never been troubled by that.

For instance, sharing with Julia, she would never have dared to think what she thought, for the first time, that night. Croquet, doves cooing, the two figures on the lawn – '*I wonder if she and Edmund will get engaged*'. And the shock, the horror, the feeling that she had been – hollowed out. Lying in bed, she thought: *I am in love with Edmund*, and then, *But haven't I always been?*

Why, in a way, she had realized it three years before, when she was only eleven, though she hadn't put it into words. Christmas at Churston. The carol service in the village church. They had been singing *Good King Wenceslas*.

> *'Sire, the night is darker now,*
> *And the wind blows stronger,*
> *Fails my heart, I know not how;*
> *I can go no longer.'*

> *'Mark my footsteps, good my page,*
> *Tread thou in them boldly,*
> *Thou shalt find the winter's rage*
> *Freeze thy blood less coldly.'*

She had thought, *But that is just like Edmund and me!* Edmund – the only person who made life bearable, the only person she ever really listened to or believed.

> *'In his master's steps he trod,*
> *Where the snow lay dinted;*
> *Heat was in the very sod*
> *Which the Saint had printed'.*

It had begun with the books. It hadn't been long before she had read all the books in the schoolroom at Belgrave Square. (Everyone called it the schoolroom, not the day nursery, except Nanny. And Julia when she was talking to Nanny – soapy Julia!) So then she had to start reading them all over again. She must have read *A Little Princess* at least seven times. Sarah, the heroine, had always behaved like 'a little princess', even when she was treated like a servant and was nearly starving. Thinking about that helped Henrietta in her resolve never to get angry with Julia, however horrible she was. Oh, she *felt* angry of course – sometimes almost dizzyingly angry – but she didn't show it, because she knew that was what Julia wanted her to do. Julia wanted her to lose her temper, wanted *Hitty Pitty to bite her*. Then – what a fuss she would have made!

In books she could escape from Julia. 'Henrietta's always *reading*,' Julia would whine. 'It can't be good for your eyesight, I'm sure,' Nanny would say sourly sometimes. Then Henrietta would hastily put aside her book for the time being. *Suppose Nanny stopped her reading!* But Miss Mackenzie encouraged her. She herself, she said, had always been 'a great reader'. Poor old Miss Mackenzie – really she hadn't been too bad. Though when they had said goodbye to her this year, after the summer term – she and Julia were going 'to classes for young ladies' in the autumn – she hadn't managed to cry. Miss Mackenzie had cried and, astonishingly, so had Julia. *Crocodile Julia*, Henrietta had thought, noticing how touched Miss Mackenzie was by Julia's tears and how hurt at Henrietta's own dry eyes. Perhaps she should have tried to cry for Miss Mackenzie – as she wouldn't have dreamed of crying when Nanny had left the year before. Julia, of course, had cried buckets then.

In the early days, Miss Mackenzie had lent Henrietta some of her own books – the ones she had read when she was a child – but most of them were as dull as the books on the Sunday shelf in the schoolroom. Anything that happened in them seemed to be an excuse for someone to preach a sermon even stupider than the ones she heard in church, and nearly as stupid as what she thought of as 'Aunt Louisa's sermons' – those little speeches she was always making about Duty.

Then Edmund had come to her rescue. He had started to bring her books from the library downstairs, a room which he said that no one but he ever went into. Dickens, Thackeray, Scott, the Brontës, Trollope, Jane Austen – Henrietta had devoured them all.

It was odd that it was always the 'bad' characters who aroused her sympathy: the ones who didn't belong, or who were cast out. How sensible she thought it was of Little Em'ly to run away with handsome, dashing Steerforth instead of marrying that stupid lout, Ham – she couldn't see why there was such a fuss about it. Apart from Sarah, in *A Little Princess*, Jane Eyre was the only actual *heroine* she liked. How splendid it was when she hit her dreadful cousin and defied the horrible aunt who expected her to be grateful because she had taken her in when her parents died. But Becky Sharpe was her favourite character. Becky's father had been an artist, like her own. She wanted to clap her hands when Becky threw the dictionary out of the window at Miss Pinkerton, and it was wonderful later when everyone admired her, including boring Amelia's first husband. Anyhow, Becky won in the end. She was well-off and independent. Even if her life sounded a bit drab, it was better than Amelia's – married to clumsy, ugly Dobbin.

Then there was *Dr Jekyll and Mr Hyde*, that was the strangest book she had ever read – well, the book that gave her the strangest feelings. When Mr Hyde trampled over the little girl in the street at night – as if he were a force more than a person – she felt a blinding shock, as if she were reading about something she had seen, had known already. It was after reading that, that the dream started, the dream in which she – or was it she? – like a force passed over Julia, leaving her trampled, broken, crushed beyond all recognition. And the strange thing was that she didn't mind it – she who shuddered from the blood on the feathers of dead pheasants – didn't mind at all, woke from it with such a curiously peaceful feeling every time she dreamed it.

She didn't ever talk to Edmund about *Dr Jekyll and Mr Hyde*, though she talked to him about all the other books she read. When, last year, she had told him how she always preferred the villains (she couldn't have told anyone but Edmund; how shocked, for instance, Miss Mackenzie would have been), he had laughed.

'Naughty, naughty Henrietta,' he had said. 'How splendid!' And then, 'Of course, you're a born Romantic.'

'Romantic?' she asked, puzzled, for to her 'romantic' meant 'in love' and all that, and she couldn't see what it had to do with what she had been saying.

'Romantic, as opposed to Classical, I mean.' But she didn't understand that either, and was silent.

'Sorry,' he said, 'you're so intelligent that I forget how young you are.' (*That* was wonderful. *That* would be something to think about later, when she was alone.)

'Romantics love disorder,' he said. 'They love turning everything upside down. And they think they can get away with things. Why, they even believe that people can be happy.'

She still wasn't sure what he was talking about, but she said, 'And what about the Classical ones – what do they believe?'

'Oh, *they* believe in order. If you upset the order, if you break the moral code, they think you're bound to be punished. I'd like to be a Romantic.' He paused. He frowned. 'But I think the Classicists are probably right,' he said.

'Oh no, Edmund,' she said. 'I'm sure they aren't. It sounds so horribly dull.' And he had laughed again.

They had most of their fascinating conversations at Churston. In London she never saw enough of him. There was always something she had to do, or somewhere she had to be. Lessons, dancing class, horrible children's parties; out to the Park or down to the drawing-room.

But at Churston, where they spent Christmas, Easter and the summer holidays, there was more freedom. Even Nanny had been more easy-going. Mrs Dowsett, the housekeeper, was a friend of hers, and Nanny spent long hours in the housekeeper's room. Julia was with Aunt Louisa more, too, and Henrietta would often escape. She loved the house with its winding corridors, its mysterious attics, its vast library – far bigger than the one at Belgrave Square – where Edmund was often to be found. Even more she loved the gardens and the park where Edmund would take her for walks or paddle her down the river in one of the punts.

It was in the punt that they had had one of their most interesting conversations.

'It's such a tragedy for them all that I'm the eldest son, not Henry,' he said. Willows hung their branches over the water; pale wild roses rioted on the banks. They sat facing each other in the punt, which was moored outside the boathouse.

'The heir,' he went on, 'and only by half an hour.' She didn't understand about the half hour; she didn't know how babies arrived. She frowned and, glancing at her, he continued quickly: 'Henry is so ideal in every respect. So handsome.' (She wanted to interrupt, and say, 'But you're much better looking', for she thought so, but it would have been embarrassing.) 'Such a splendid shot – enjoys killing things almost as much as Father does. So good at games, so fond of parties, so much enjoying his spell in the Coldstream. And so ideally, blessedly stupid, of course.'

For a moment she was almost shocked – after all, Henry was his *brother* – but that was silly, and anyway she felt so pleased that he should confide in her.

She said, 'But why should they want him to be stupid?'

He smiled. 'My dear Henrietta, havn't you noticed? Isn't it obvious how they all hate brains? Well, not *brains* exactly. It's quite all right to "come top" in things. But *intelligence* – that's what they can't stand at any price. Look at the words they use. "Brahms", for instance.' They both smiled. 'And "Ibsen" for ordinary. Anything that demands sensitivity is so utterly "carpet". That's why they loathe the way I live.

Going to art exhibitions, and reading, and trying to write. "Hanging about" – that's what Mother calls it. When I used to paint, of course, it was even worse.' A shadow crossed his face. ' "Just like some foreign loafer", I remember her saying. "Soon you'll start wearing a beret and growing your hair long." Well, that's over now – but writing is almost as bad. Unhealthy. Never been anyone *literate* in the family before. They'd far rather I did nothing at all. Man about town, and all that. The social round. So gross, so boring. Those appalling, endless meals.'

He paused. He shrugged. He was staring past her. At the river, at the roses, but she didn't think he saw them. Then he exclaimed, in tones of extraordinary bitterness. '*The mixing bell!*'

'The mixing bell?' she said.

'They should call it the un-mixing bell. That bell that a maid rings up and down the corridors at six o'clock in the morning.'

Once or twice she had woken early in the morning at Churston, to hear that little bell tinkling on the lower floors. She'd wondered why it rang so early, when none of the grown-ups rose till so much later.

'Why do they ring that bell?' she asked.

But he gave a little start – and, yes, he looked positively horrified. He jumped to his feet. The punt rocked violently. 'Don't you worry about that, Henrietta,' he said. 'Time we were getting back. Come along.'

Regretfully, she followed him. They had been having such a wonderful talk, and she was sure it wasn't tea-time yet. What, she wondered, as they crossed the lawn, was the mystery about the oddly named mixing bell?

But Edmund *was* mysterious about things. Why wouldn't he show her his poems? She had begged him to, but he had refused. 'Wait till you're older,' he said said, laughing, and then, seeing her crestfallen look, 'or anyway until my poems are better.'

But one afternoon, she had found him alone on the terrace. He was sitting in a deck chair. His eyes were closed. There, next to him, open on the ground, was the notebook in which he wrote his poems. She looked down at him. His breathing was deep and slow.

Down she crouched, next to him. He didn't stir. She stretched out a cautious hand. Her fingers touched the book. She edged it towards her. Then, quickly, she picked it up, started to read the first lines that met her eyes:

> *Or like the harlot's livid mask*
> *at every corner: like the groan*
> *with which she does her harlot's task,*
> *the millstone round her neck to drown*
> *her nightly twelve men deeper down –*

'Sly, treacherous girl!'

She started violently, at the sound of his voice, at his hand coming down to snatch the book from hers. For a moment, horrified, she believed that he was really angry. Dazed, she stared into his face, and saw that he was smiling.

'Did you think I didn't know that you were there?' he asked. 'I can see that I shall have to buy a notebook with a lock on it, like those diaries that *young ladies* confide their most secret thoughts to. Do *you* keep a diary, Henrietta?'

'Oh *no*,' she said at once. The tone in which he had pronounced 'young ladies' had been so withering. And, anyway, it was true that she didn't keep a diary – although she had often wanted to. It would have been such a release to pour out her 'more secret thoughts' – yes, that was exactly what she would have liked to do, instead of keeping them bottled up inside her. How she would have liked to write them down: *fond thoughts of Edmund, hate-hate-hating thoughts of Julia.* But she didn't dare. Someone would be sure to discover it – the most probable person, of course, being Julia.

'You've got an unscrupulous streak, I see, Henrietta,' he said. 'Reading my private property when you thought I was asleep.'

'I *so* much want to see them,' she pleaded.

'Well, you mayn't. All the same, I don't really mind your having tried. *Very* unladylike, which is always a good thing.'

Afterwards, she had thought about the poem. It had sounded wonderful, but she hadn't had the faintest idea of what it was about.

Lying in bed, on the night after she had seen Edmund on the lawn with Miss Pelham, she thought about *being in love with him*. In love – it was such a very grown-up thing to be.

What would happen? Of course, she was only fourteen, so she couldn't possibly get married for at least four years. What a long time that was – why it was four years since she had arrived at Belgrave Square. That seemed to have been ages and ages ago.

Then there was the question of Edmund's age. He was twenty-three now. When she was eighteen, he would be twenty-seven. Of course she knew that girls did marry men who were older than they were. But surely most men were married by the time they were twenty-seven? Would Edmund wait for her?

That, of course, would depend on whether he were in love with her or not. Until now, she had always thought of him as her friend – and she was sure that he still thought of her like that. She certainly wasn't going to give him *silly looks*, as that girl had done this afternoon – under her lashes, under the brim of her hat. She was sure that, if she did, he would burst out laughing.

Once Nanny had heard Miss Mackenzie praising one of Henrietta's compositions. Afterwards she had said, 'It's not young ladies' *brains* that gentlemen are interested in: it's how they behave and how ladylike they are.' Henrietta

felt sure that wasn't the case with Edmund – look how he
talked about 'young ladies'. And he did mind about brains.
'So ideally, blessedly stupid.' When Edmund had said that
about Henry, he hadn't sounded as if he really thought it
was 'ideal' or 'blessed'. Though it wasn't exactly brains that
he admired. It was *intelligence*.

She must become as intelligent as possible. She must work
harder and read more, too, so that she would understand
the things he told her. Would that make him fall in love
with her? she wondered, as she fell asleep.

Next morning, after breakfast, when Julia was with Aunt
Louisa, and Edmund, as he sometimes did, came into the
playroom, she had to hold her book close to her face for a
moment, to hide the blush which spread over it at the new
idea of 'being in love'.

She looked up.

'You're very pink in the face, Henrietta,' he remarked
at once.

'It's rather hot today,' she said.

'Mmm.' He went over to the window, and looked out.
'Certainly it will be later on,' he said.

She stood up and, after an instant's hesitation – the new
situation again – joined him. The grey morning haze was
melting the blue. The fresh smell of cut grass rose from the
lawn which she had heard the gardeners mowing earlier that
morning.

'I saw you at the window yesterday afternoon,' he said,
'when I was with that idiotic girl.'

'Is she idiotic?' Henrietta asked with careful detachment
– but what a rush of happiness she felt. 'She's very pretty,'
she added politely.

'Pretty? You think so? Well possibly, if one admires
soulful eyes and an earnest expression, and if one can bear
talk about Ella Wheeler Wilcox's beautiful poems. I'm sure
that her copy of them is bound in limp lambskin.'

She glanced at him sideways. He was frowning. His
fingers were tapping restlessly on the window sill that she
had clutched so frantically the day before. 'God,' he said,
'oh God, how I wish they'd stop.'

'Stop?' she asked. How angry he sounded.

'Yes,' he said. 'Mother and Father. When will they stop
presenting these appalling females for my approval? Each
seems worse than the last. Though I'm not absolutely
sure of that. Wasn't the "pocket Venus" with the giggle
the worst of all? Blue eyes and ribbons to match. Or
what about the one that Father thought so splendid,
the dashing auburn-haired, bold-eyed one who took her
fences like a man? She asked me something about hunting
at luncheon, and I said, "I've always shared Oscar Wilde's
opinion on that subject." Deathly hush in the conversation.
Mother launching some new topic of infinite banality. A
tremendous row afterwards, with Father: "How dare you
mention that swine's name under my roof – and to a young
gel at that!" '

'Who was Oscar Wilde?' she asked, but now he was
looking just the same as when she had asked about the
mixing bell.

'Oh, a social outcast,' he said hurriedly, and then, 'Now
let me see. Let me try to remember what other ladylike
horrors have been dug up for me.'

'Dug up!' She laughed. 'You make them sound like
bodies.'

'That's exactly what they are,' he said. 'Bodies for sale.'
Again he hurried on: 'Well, dolls in a shop window. And, not
being a girl, I've never wanted to play with dolls. Not baby
dolls, not debutante dolls, and certainly not granny dolls.'

'Granny dolls?'

'Why, only the other day, Mother said to me. "You know,
Clara Revelston thinks you're *very* good-looking." "Clara
Revelston, Mother?" I said. "*Your* dear friend? Isn't she
about to become a grandmother? Though I admit that it's

hard to tell her age with all the paint she plasters on her face." '

Had he really said that to Aunt Louisa, and in that frightening voice? She would die if Edmund ever spoke to *her* in that voice. But why had he minded so much about Aunt Louisa telling him that Lady Revelston thought he was good-looking?

Now he glanced quickly at her. Then he shut his eyes tightly. When he opened them again, he said, 'My dear little Henrietta, it is unforgivable of me to pour out this nonsense to you. Excuse me – and forget it all.'

'But I *like*—'

He interrupted her. 'Not another word. It's time for me to go. I must go and have further words about Miss Wheeler Wilcox. Duty's summons, Henrietta, must never be disobeyed. Duty to King, to Country, to those in Authority over us. Ask my dear mother if that isn't true. She knows *everything* there is to know about Duty.'

More mysteries, she thought when he had gone. Oscar Wilde, whoever he was. Bodies for sale. Lady Revelston. And Edmund had almost sounded as if he hated Aunt Louisa. It was all right for *her* to hate Aunt Louisa – but Aunt Louisa was Edmund's mother. Could one hate one's mother? She sighed. Anyway, it was wonderful to know how much he disliked all those girls. She smiled.

When they returned to London in the autumn, Henrietta and Julia started to attend Miss Dettmer's classes in Mount Street.

To Miss Dettmer's classes came many of the 'young ladies' of Mayfair. Some were stupid, some were clever; it wasn't easy to tell which were which, because the fashionable attitude was to appear bored with lessons. Julia at once joined a group which always sat in the back row, where the current craze was squeezing orange juice into glasses under the desks.

At Miss Dettmer's you could acquire quite a lot of education – if you wanted to, but nobody pressed you. Miss Dettmer was well aware that the mothers of Mayfair took little interest in their daughters' studies. The girls were allowed to choose their subjects. English literature, languages and history of art were the favourites.

A few girls took the School Certificate examination. One or two even went to university, but this was considered extraordinarily eccentric. Perhaps, Henrietta thought, determined to be well educated for Edmund, *she* might go to Oxford. But when she mentioned it to him, he laughed.

'Oh, my dear Henrietta, you should see those girls. Such a grubby collection of frumps. No, I don't think that's at all a good idea. Take what you want from the classes, but don't bother about *exams*. After all, what on earth for?'

What for, indeed – if he didn't like the idea?

Anyway, she worked just as hard as if she had been going to write the now despised exams. She took voluminous notes. She toiled over essays, and was rewarded with high marks and praise. In the back row, Julia and her cronies fiddled with their long glossy pigtails, tapped – almost but not quite inaudibly – on the floor with their high cloth-topped boots, wrote acrostics, which had now replaced squeezing oranges as the craze.

Then, one afternoon, when Henrietta and Julia were waiting in the hall for a maid from Belgrave Square to collect them, Miss Dettmer, who was passing, stopped. 'Strange,' she said, 'that you two should be such close relations, Henrietta being so clever . . .' and moved on.

'Swat,' Julia hissed. 'If I wanted to, I could do just as well as you do.'

This time the pinch was as sharp as the ones Julia used to give before that day when she'd told her pinching was 'childish'. Henrietta nearly cried out, but she managed not to. She didn't say anything; she just smiled and raised her eyebrows, and indeed what Julia had said seemed ridiculous to her. Bored, lazy Julia, who hardly ever read a book.

The essay subject that week – Henrietta would always remember it – was 'A Journey around my Room'. An extraordinarily stupid subject, she thought – what did one say about *furniture?* In the end she wrote about the books in her bookcase, and the view from her window.

Before handing back the essays, Miss Dettmer, as was her custom, read aloud the essay that she thought the best. Henrietta waited eagerly for her to start.

But it wasn't her essay. It began, 'My green dress lies on the bed.'

How irritating. *Her* essay had been best the last two weeks. 'Green is the colour of the Spring and of emeralds,' Miss Dettmer was reading. 'It is also the colour of my mother's eyes.' That was when a doubt struck her, but she dismissed it – Julia couldn't have won. 'When my mother wears jewels, her eyes sparkle to match them. My mother sits in a green room. It is green with plants and leaves. The chair she sits on is covered with green brocade, and is rimmed with gold. Green and gold are beautiful together, as jewels are in their settings.'

On and on Miss Dettmer went. Everything was green, green, green. *Could it be Julia?* 'Green is not always good, for green is the colour of envy, the envy I see in the eyes of a girl I know well. But her eyes are *not* green, and so green is not spoiled for me. It remains the colour of true delight.'

The envy I see in the eyes of a girl I know well. That couldn't be her. She didn't envy Julia. If this were Julia's – but surely it wasn't?

Miss Dettmer was reaching the end now. 'My room isn't green. I admit that. But now I look round it and imagine it all green. For this isn't a real journey. It is an imaginary one. And I dream of the green room I shall live in one day, the room that is green as my mother's eyes.

'Julia, come and collect your essay. Congratulations, Julia, most fresh and original. Perhaps a little extra care with spelling and punctuation would have improved it – but all the same, a splendid effort.'

A buzz filled the classroom. Up the aisle came Julia, with her neat steps and swinging plait. Returning with her essay, as she passed Henrietta, she raised her eyebrows, she gave a little smile – just exactly as Henrietta had done in the hall the week before.

'Henrietta!' She sat up with a start. Miss Dettmer was announcing that her essay had gained the second mark. 'Well done,' Miss Dettmer said, as she handed it back. 'Just a little pedestrian perhaps, but nicely thought out.' Then she said, 'We shall have to look to our laurels, Henrietta.'

And when they reached home, whom should they meet in the hall but Edmund?

'I got the top mark for my essay today,' Julia immediately announced.

'Oh jolly good,' he said, and then, 'That's unusual, isn't it?'

'It was *easy*,' Julia said, tossing her plait, as she started up the stairs.

'Didn't you write an essay this week?' he asked Henrietta, as she hurried past him. Usually, she would have lingered, not wanting to lose a moment of his company.

She almost said no. But he would be sure to find out. Julia would be sure to tell him. She said, 'I came second.'

'Oh,' Edmund said, and then, 'You'll have to look to your laurels.'

She murmured something, managed to keep the smile fixed on her face until she was round the bend in the stairs. Then tears came into her eyes, tears of misery and rage. *If it had been anyone but Julia.*

It never happened again. Julia relapsed at once into the diversions of the back row. But now every time Henrietta came first, she was conscious that Julia – the little smile, the raised eyebrows – was thinking, 'Of course I could have, if I'd *wanted* to.'

❧ *Six* ❧

1914–1919

In the summer of 1914 the sun never seemed to stop shining. So many people came to stay at Churston. Friends of Uncle Harry, of Aunt Louisa, of Henry, but never any friends of Edmund. Did he have any – except her?

She and Julia spent more time with the grown-ups nowadays. They even had luncheon in the dining-room, though at a special table with the Mademoiselle who had come for the summer to improve their French.

There was croquet on the lawn; there were punts on the river; there was lawn tennis, with jugs of lemonade on a table at the side of the court. But many long afternoons were spent at a game which was the rage that summer. It was called the War Game.

Henrietta and Julia watched as the young men of the party lay on their stomachs on the terrace, lining up hundreds of lead soldiers, arguing over their strategies and campaigns. Always, the older men found the temptation to join in irresistible, leaning over the young men's shoulders and giving them advice.

To Henrietta's surprise, Edmund enjoyed the game. And he was very good at it. Though she herself felt no interest in the game, she liked watching him play it.

'You see, old boy, you should have gone into the army,' Uncle Harry said to him.

'Oh no. Not me, Father,' Edmund said. But then the real war was declared.

The long calm of the summer was shattered as if a great rock had been hurled into one of the quiet backwaters of the river. Henry hurried back to his regiment. Edmund joined the local yeomanry.

'Well, Henrietta,' he said, the day before he left, 'it seems that I am going to be a man of action after all. What a relief for my beloved mother.'

'Oh, Edmund,' she said. 'But it will be over very soon, won't it?'

'I have my doubts about that,' he said.

'But everyone says that by Christmas—'

'We shall see,' he said.

Three months later, he was in France. By that time, she was back at Belgrave Square.

With Edmund absent, everything had changed, although many of the things she did were the same. She and Julia still went to Miss Dettmer's classes. Somehow, doing well at them didn't mean so much to her now, though she still worked hard. When Edmund came on leave, she must have lots of things to talk to him about.

She learnt to knit. First she made a scarf, and then pair after pair of socks for Edmund. She and Julia also took part in the bandage-rolling parties which Aunt Louisa held in the afternoon, twice a week. It didn't seem much. How she wished that she were older. Then she could have become a VAD and have gone to France with an ambulance, as some of the daughters of Aunt Louisa's friends were doing – though many more who wanted to were not allowed to.

If *she* had been grown up, no one would have been able to stop her going. Some of the girls who weren't allowed to go to France worked in London hospitals, but she couldn't really see the point of doing that. She didn't want to nurse anyone but Edmund.

She imagined herself in France, in uniform – though the uniform wasn't very nice; she was sure that awful flat white cap wouldn't suit her. She would be working in a 'field hospital', which she pictured as a marquee full of beds in the middle of a green field. And one day, Edmund, with some injury that wasn't really serious, but which would keep him away from the Front (a broken leg would be ideal), would be brought in on a stretcher. She saw him, in his uniform, lying on a white bed, with his eyes closed. And then he would open his eyes and would see her sitting beside him. 'Henrietta,' he would say, and his face would light up, and she would bend down and kiss him. (Was a VAD allowed to kiss a patient? If he was her first cousin, surely she could.) With the kiss, the picture dissolved. Next time she imagined the scene, she started at the beginning again.

She wrote to Edmund every three or four days, and he wrote back each week. 'I enjoy your letters so much, Henrietta. I like to hear all about what you are doing.'

To her, the things she was doing seemed so boring, but she made the letters as interesting as she could. What she wanted was to tell him how much she loved him, but that was what she knew she mustn't do. She must make the letters lively and amusing. She told him catty stories about the 'young ladies' at Miss Dettmer's.

'Your letters make me laugh so much,' he wrote. 'I can't tell you how nice it is. There is very little to laugh about here.'

How she longed for his letters. Every time she came into the house, her first action was to look at the post on the hall table.

Aunt Louisa wrote to him, of course, but she didn't talk about him nearly as much as she did about Henry ... especially after Henry was mentioned in despatches.

Edmund didn't get any leave until September. When she heard he was coming, she couldn't suppress her excitement. She tried to seem calm but, inevitably, Julia noticed how she was feeling.

'You know,' Julia said, 'Edmund's going to be terribly busy when he comes home. After being in the trenches, all

the young men like shows and parties. They don't want to
hang around with little girls in the schoolroom.'

'Of course not, Julia,' Henrietta answered.

But Julia, as she had hoped, was proved wrong. Edmund
refused all invitations. In fact he only went out once – to
see an old Oxford friend, he said. 'Why on earth should
I want to go to stupid musical comedies?' he exclaimed to
Henrietta.

'The first time she was alone with him was rather disap-
pointing. She had specially learnt Brooke's *The Soldier* to
recite to him, and said it, all through, in the library. He
didn't say anything for a moment, and she saw that he
was frowning. But when he spoke, it was very kindly. He
said, 'Henrietta, please don't fill your mind with rubbish
like that. I shall give you a real poem to learn.' And then
he gave her a poem by someone called Ezra Pound.

> *There died a myriad,*
> *And of the best, among them,*
> *For an old bitch gone in the teeth,*
> *For a botched civilization*
>
> *Charm, smiling at the good mouth,*
> *Quick eyes gone under earth's lid*
>
> *For two gross of broken statues,*
> *For a few thousand battered books.*

What a sad poem it was, and so hopeless somehow. Not like
the 'corner of a foreign field' that was 'forever England'.
But she learnt it with the enthusiasm with which she would
have done anything he asked her. And was rewarded, when
she said it to him – 'That's better, much better. Say that to
yourself whenever you hear anyone talking rubbish about
the war.'

He spent most of his leave sitting in the library. She stayed away from Miss Dettmer's to be with him – no one said anything.

He read, but often his eyes would close, and he would fall asleep. Watching him, she thought how tired he looked. He was so pale and thin. All the bones of his face stood out, and there were new lines at the corners of his mouth. She sat near him, with a book in her lap, but she hardly read at all. Once, when he woke suddenly, starting in his chair, he extended his hand to her. She stood up and took it, and he immediately fell asleep again. She was standing there, holding his hand, when she heard footsteps in the passage. She had only just time to pull back her hand – very gently – and sit down, before Julia put her head around the door.

'Edmund and his faithful sheepdog,' Julia said in a low voice.

Henrietta was wearing her hair loose, because Edmund had said he liked it better like that than in a pigtail. It hung down in a thick heavy curtain on either side of her face. Did it really make her look like a sheepdog? she wondered, as Julia stepped back into the passage, closing the door with a click. Again, Edmund started awake. There were drops of perspiration on his forehead. He was shivering.

'Is it terrible out there, at the Front?' she asked him.

'Not too good. The rats sometimes run over one's face when one's sleeping,' he said, and then, when she gasped with horror, 'Oh there are worse things than that, but I don't want to talk about them.'

His leave ended two days later. He was going at six in the morning, by cab, to catch his train. She was the only one of the family who got up to see him off. He had told her not to, but when he came downstairs, she was waiting in the hall.

'I wish I could come to the station with you,' she said.

'What! Coming back alone in a cab without a chaperone! I can imagine what my mother would have to say about that!' He laughed. 'Anyway, I'd much rather say goodbye to you here than in that appalling *mêlée*, all whistles and khaki and weeping women. *You* aren't going to weep, are you, Henrietta?'

There were tears behind her eyes. She closed her lids to force them back, and heard the cab draw up outside. She opened her eyes, saw Hobart the butler, the only other person up except herself, opening the front door and going down the steps with Edmund's kitbag.

'Kiss me goodbye, Edmund.'

'Of course.' He stooped to touch her cheek with his lips. But she moved her face, closing her eyes again as she did so, until her mouth was under his.

She felt him make a small movement of withdrawal. Then, 'Henrietta. Sweet little Henrietta,' he murmured. His mouth rested on hers – how cool and firm his lips were. Up, of their own volition, came her arms to go around his neck. But lightly he drew them down, gently pulled away. She forced herself not to cling to him.

She opened her eyes, found herself unable to understand the expression on his face – was it sad or doubtful or surprised?

He pressed her shoulders. 'Goodbye darling Henrietta. Take care of yourself,' he said.

'Oh, and you, please, please take care,' she said.

He was gone, out of the door, down the steps to where Hobart stood, holding open the door of the cab. It was a misty autumn morning. The mist drifted round him, lit dimly by a blurred street lamp.

He pressed something into Hobart's hand. As Hobart shut the door, the driver was already flicking at the horse with his whip.

Clip-clop went the horse's hooves. Now the tears were brimming over, but she hardly noticed them, trying to retain the feeling of those cool firm lips.

Hobart was coming in, shutting the door. *Pas devant*

les domestiques – that was what Aunt Louisa would have said. She gave him a little fixed smile, and then turned and walked very slowly, keeping her back very straight, towards the stairs. She mustn't run. *Pas devant les domestiques*. Now she had lost the feeling. She licked her lips, trying to reclaim it, failed.

Now her back was to Hobart and she could let the tears run down her cheeks. But she wasn't wholly sad. *Sweet little Henrietta, darling Henrietta*. He had said those words. And he had kissed her.

She lived for the postman's visits even more than usual, that week. She tried to be down in the hall near the times that he came. The letter arrived by the first post, six days after Edmund's departure. She pulled it from the letter-box as the postman pushed it in. She could hear Hobart coming up from the basement. She was half way upstairs before he reached the hall.

In her room, she held the envelope for a moment or two, gazing at it, before she carefully slit it open with her paper-knife – she kept Edmund's envelopes as well as his letters.

'Sweet Henrietta,' it began. She gave a deep happy sigh. *Her first love letter*.

'How very kind of you to get up so early to see me off. As I predicted, the station was an inferno – you would have hated it.'

On she read, but apart from that 'Sweet Henrietta', the letter was like all his other letters – chatty, friendly. She reached the signature, 'With love from Edmund'. But that was what he always wrote.

The winter seemed so long. Everything dragged. Everything was khaki-coloured, like the socks she knitted. The sons of Aunt Louisa's friends – Henry's friends – were being killed one after another. Theirs seemed to be almost the only household that had not yet lost someone.

Henry got the DSO, and came home on leave.

When he saw her, he gave her a startled look. 'How you've grown, Henrietta,' he said, and then, to Uncle Harry, 'What a pretty girl she is now, isn't she?'

Uncle Harry looked surprised, shot a glance at her. 'Dashed pretty,' he exclaimed in the tone of one making a discovery.

'Henrietta is becoming quite a big girl,' Aunt Louisa said coldly. Trust her to pick on Henrietta's secret fear – that she would never stop growing. She was five foot seven now. But Edmund, like Henry, was six foot one. Surely she would never become *that* tall. However, she towered over Julia, so tiny, so delicate – well, delicate-*looking* for Julia was hardly ever ill.

How different Henry was from Edmund. He went out all the time, except when Aunt Louisa entertained for him at home.

Writing to Edmund, and waiting for his letters – that was really all there was. Now, at Miss Dettmer's, she found that her attention wandered. When she read, her thoughts strayed from the page. She was always yawning.

Edmund didn't come on leave again until May 1916. He looked even thinner and more exhausted than he had before. When he arrived in the evening, he said that he would like to have dinner in bed, and that he was going down to Churston the next day. She wasn't alone with him at all. How she cried that night. His letters had been coming less frequently lately – and now he didn't even want to see her.

He returned to Belgrave Square on his way back to Victoria. She and Julia had tea downstairs. Again she didn't have a moment alone with him. They all went into the hall to see him off – he wouldn't let anyone come to the station – and he kissed her cheek just as he kissed Julia's.

When he had gone, she almost hated him. But a few days later, a letter came. He said how sorry he had been not to see more of her. 'Now,' he said, 'I regret that even *your* company couldn't keep me at Belgrave Square. Do you know, darling Henrietta, that I actually felt my sanity was at stake? I trust you to understand. Is that presumptuous of me? I hope not. You are the one person I have always known I could rely on.'

How often she recited those words to herself. How often she re-read that letter. She needed to, for she only received three more letters before Christmas, and one at New Year, 1917. Then Edmund just stopped writing to her, though he wrote every week to Uncle Harry – brief perfunctory notes in which he sent his love to everyone.

She went on writing to him just the same, but her letters sounded stilted to her, and her 'little anecdotes' didn't seem funny any more. *I'm losing touch with him*, she thought, feeling a fierce pang.

Henry came on leave twice during that time – why didn't Edmund get leave, too? Didn't he want it?

It was the Thursday before Easter. They were at Churston. She came up to the house with a bunch of daffodils for her room. Hothouse blooms had, over the years, bred a fondness in her for what she thought of as natural flowers.

The postman was coming up the drive, which was strange. She looked at her watch. Quarter to twelve – he never ordinarily delivered letters at that time. He seemed to be walking faster than usual, too. As she came nearer, she saw in his hand one of the yellow envelopes which everyone dreaded. She started to run.

Aunt Louisa and Julia were strolling on the terrace. The thin Spring sunlight lit Julia's white-gold hair. At that moment Aunt Louisa's glance alighted on the postman. She stiffened; one of her hands rose, then spread itself on her chest, below her throat. 'Postman!' Her voice was as authoritative as ever, but a little higher, a little shriller than usual.

The postman turned from his brisk progress up the drive,

started across the lawn. Aunt Louisa ran down the steps
from the terrace, hurried over the grass to meet him.
Once she stumbled. Henrietta realized that she had never
before seen Aunt Louisa move awkwardly, move with all
consciousness of self forgotten.

They reached the postman at the same moment. Aunt
Louisa almost seized the envelope from the postman's
hand. Her hands shook as she tore open the envelope.
She was white, except for colour standing out in two hard
patches on her cheeks. So she did wear rouge, Henrietta
thought, and then felt ashamed of noticing such things at
such a time.

Aunt Louisa was holding the telegram, arm extended –
she was becoming increasingly short-sighted. She read it,
and her hand dropped to her side. She gave a sigh that
seemed to be one of relief. So the news, then, wasn't
very bad.

Aunt Louisa's eyes seemed to be looking through
Henrietta. 'Julia, Julia,' she called. Julia, standing absolutely still, all this time, on the terrace, skimmed down to
her mother's side. 'Mama?'

'It's *Edmund*,' Aunt Louisa said. 'Edmund is badly
wounded.'

The postman, who had taken off his cap, was muttering
something – words of condolence? Aunt Louisa made a
visible effort.

'Thank you, postman,' she said. 'You must be thirsty
after your walk. Please go round to the kitchen and get
something to drink.'

As he retreated, Aunt Louisa said, 'Oh, Julia.' Julia put
an arm around her mother. 'We must tell your father at
once,' Aunt Louisa went on. 'He must find out all the
details. Perhaps he will be able to go to France, and
to bring Edmund home. My poor boy!' Now tears were
brimming in the green eyes.

Henrietta stood on the lawn, watching Aunt Louisa and

Julia going up the steps to the terrace. *Edmund, oh Edmund.* And that sigh of Aunt Louisa's.

For it *had* been a sigh of relief. 'It's *Edmund*. Edmund has been badly wounded.' What Aunt Louisa had really been dreading was that something had happened to Henry.

Uncle Harry left for London that afternoon, to speak to people who could help. Next day – Good Friday – he telephoned Aunt Louisa.

'Edmund is paralyzed from the waist down,' Aunt Louisa explained to Julia and Henrietta. 'A shell exploded very near him. He was riddled with shrapnel, especially the lower part of his body. Apparently he is very fortunate to be alive. He may never be able to walk again.

Julia burst into tears. Henrietta was glad about that. It distracted attention from her. She felt so strange. Aunt Louisa and Julia looked huge, and then looked small, looked huge – and now they flickered as if they were under water. Things were sliding away from her, and she had to hold on to them. She rose from her chair and felt her legs collapsing. She tried to cry 'Help', but the word wouldn't come out. That had happened to her before, in dreams—

There was a pricking, stinging feeling in her eyes and nose. 'She's as white as death,' someone was saying. She opened her eyes. Sharply before her was the face of Ellis, Aunt Louisa's maid. She could see the pores in Ellis's skin, the little black hairs on her upper lip. The face receded. Now she could see the tiny stitches on the bodice of Ellis's black dress. 'She's coming round,' Ellis said. The stinging was making Henrietta cry, and she brushed away the little bottle Ellis was holding under her nose.

Aunt Louisa and Julia were standing behind Ellis. They looked like giants. Or like judges, she thought, and then didn't know what she meant by it. 'You fainted, Henrietta,' Aunt Louisa said.

Aunt Louisa made it sound as if that were a silly thing to do. Perhaps it was. She had never fainted before. Once in church, on a very hot day, she had had a similar strange feeling, but she had bowed her head against the rail of the pew, and it had ebbed away. Why on earth should she have fainted now? Then she remembered. *He may never be able to walk again.*

Ellis came up to her room with her, and helped her to take off her dress, and removed the counterpane from her bed. She got under the eiderdown, and Ellis drew the curtains.

She was glad when Ellis had gone. *He may never be able to walk again.* She was cold, in spite of the eiderdown.

She thought of her disgusting daydream about being a nurse, and Edmund breaking his leg. Could her wanting him to be wounded have made God angry? She didn't think about God normally – just rattled through her prayers at night. When it was cold, she said them in bed, now that she had a room of her own. But here she was babbling, 'I didn't *mean* it, God. I didn't mean it about the broken leg.'

He was alive; that was what she must think about. He was alive, and soon he might be coming home. Wouldn't he need her more than ever before? Perhaps she would be able to look after him, to help him to learn to walk again.

Mightn't marrying Edmund be *more* possible now than it had been before? He wouldn't be meeting other girls, and certainly not those beautiful French girls whom she had been thinking about so much lately – wondering whether one of them might be the reason why he never wrote. And if she were always with him, always doing things for him, surely he would fall in love with her?

She got out of bed, went over to her table, found a pencil and a sheet of writing-paper. She made a list:

1. Look after him
2. Make him love me
3. Marry him

It looked so simple, set out like that, that she gave a little sigh of happiness.

The list torn up into tiny pieces and dropped in the wastepaper basket, she lay down under the quilt again. She felt so much better. Now she could think about the most wonderful thing of all. He couldn't be killed. He would write his poems again, and become a famous poet. He couldn't be killed – as Henry could be. *It would serve Aunt Louisa right if* – no, that was too horrible. What mattered was that Edmund was alive and safe.

In church on Easter Sunday, the vicar asked for prayers to be said for Edmund's recovery. She prayed as hard as she could. *If Edmund gets well, I'll kneel down and pray every day*, she promised God.

Uncle Harry got permission to go to France. Ten days later, the news came that Edmund was better, that Uncle Harry was bringing him home in a private ambulance. Two days before he arrived, a trained nurse whom everyone called 'Sister' was installed in the dressing-room next to his room.

On the day itself, Henrietta arranged a vase of daffodils in his room. 'A lovely splash of colour,' Sister exclaimed. She had a very mincing sort of voice. Henrietta was glad that she was quite old and not at all pretty.

Edmund was not expected until the afternoon, but from the early morning Henrietta listened for the sound of the ambulance. She sat in the morning-room, with its view of the drive, knitting a khaki sock, so that Aunt Louisa couldn't complain about her doing nothing. She didn't know whom she was knitting for. As it wasn't Edmund, she didn't care.

During luncheon with Aunt Louisa and Julia, her ears strained after every sound. How she longed for the meal to end. When it was over, Julia went off somewhere, and Aunt Louisa went upstairs to rest.

She paced up and down the terrace. It was at ten past three that she heard the sound of a motor. She ran round the side of the house, reached the front door just before the ambulance came round the bend in the drive. She was waiting on the steps as it drew up. Might she be able to welcome him without Julia and Aunt Louisa?

The back door of the ambulance opened, and a man jumped out. The driver got out next, and Uncle Harry climbed down heavily from the seat next to him. 'Uncle Harry!' she exclaimed, though all she could think about was Edmund.

He kissed her. 'So you've been waitin' for us, Henrietta? Where's yer aunt?'

'Upstairs, I think,' she said. *Oh Edmund, Edmund.*

Uncle Harry was speaking to Hobart on the doorstep now, telling him to send someone to fetch Aunt Louisa. Henrietta's eyes were fixed on the back of the ambulance. The driver and the other man were lifting out a stretcher. She ran to it.

Edmund lay under a grey blanket. The moving of the stretcher must have been hurting him, for his face was all screwed up, and his eyes were tightly closed. How ill he looked – his face was almost the same colour as the blanket.

The men had levelled the stretcher now. Edmund opened his eyes. Then, 'Henrietta,' he said faintly. He smiled – a flicker of his lips, after which his face twisted up again as the ambulance men started to move towards the front door.

There were steps behind her. Aunt Louisa, with imperious hands, brushed her aside. 'Edmund, my darling boy,' she said in a quivering voice, 'you're here at last.'

'Hullo, Mother,' he said. Aunt Louisa was stooping to kiss his forehead, and to Henrietta it seemed that he winced away. But perhaps it was just another grimace of pain.

Now there was a great bustle going on behind her. The servants were massing on the steps, Julia ran out of the house and up to the stretcher, exclaiming, 'Oh Edmund.'

'Hullo, Julia,' he said.

His eyes travelled over the figures on the steps. 'So many people,' he said. Mrs Dowsett was sobbing, and Henrietta saw that there were tears in Hobart's eyes.

Sister came forward to stand beside the stretcher, as Edmund muttered, 'Sorry. Not feeling too good.'

'This crowd is too much for him,' Sister said to Aunt Louisa, who at once called out, 'We must all disperse now. Mr Edmund must be taken to his room.'

The servants melted away. Aunt Louisa, Uncle Harry and Julia, with Henrietta behind them, followed the stretcher – Sister at its side – into the house. Uncle Harry stayed in the hall, but the rest of them continued up the stairs. Henrietta couldn't see Edmund's face, but she thought how going up the stairs must be hurting him, although the ambulance men tried to keep him steady.

They reached the open door of Edmund's room. Sister bustled in ahead of the stretcher. Aunt Louisa followed. At the door, she turned. 'Later, girls,' she said. Then she closed the door. Henrietta and Julia were left in the passage.

'Oh!' Henrietta exclaimed, off her guard. She felt so bitterly disappointed at being shut out.

'Hitty Pitty trying to push in where she's not wanted,' Julia said. The door opened, but only for the ambulance men to come out. Sister closed it again behind them.

In the weeks that followed, she picked great bunches of the flowers she loved – bluebells, cowslips, sprays of mauve and white lilac (strange that such little crisp flowers should have such a heavy soft scent). She took them to Edmund in his room day after day.

'Well, I suppose if you like them, Mr Edmund, it's all right,' Sister said, 'as long as they're put out in the corridor at night. Though I do feel they tend to make a sick-room rather untidy. I prefer the cultivated growths, myself. I always say there's nothing like a nice carnation.'

When she had gone, they giggled.

'I always say there's nothing like a nice carnation,' Edmund repeated. 'Imagine always saying that.' He added, 'All the same, she's a splendid creature.'

Henrietta agreed. Sister nursed him so wonderfully, and Henrietta didn't feel at all jealous. Why should she want to nurse Edmund, when instead she could spend so much time just *being* with him?

He was better, although the local doctor still came each day in his pony trap to visit him. A specialist had been down from London twice, and had said that Edmund was making good general progress.

'Shrapnel is unpredictable of course,' he had said to Aunt Louisa. 'But for the present, it is my opinion that we should let sleeping dogs lie. The important thing, at the moment, is to build up the patient's strength.'

Three or four times a day, cups of strong beef tea were brought to him. Calves-foot and wine jellies were made. At meal times, the cook sent up delicate little dishes, especially designed to tempt his appetite: poached breasts of chicken, fillets of sole steamed with peeled and seeded grapes. He often couldn't finish them, and sometimes he would persuade Henrietta to – 'so as not to hurt the cook's feelings', as he put it. He enjoyed watching her eat. 'It makes me feel better,' he said. And to her, even if she wasn't really hungry, there was something special – she couldn't have explained it – about sharing Edmund's food.

She spent as much time with him as she possibly could.

'Are you sure Henrietta isn't tiring you?' Aunt Louisa (coming into the room, and finding her in her usual place, in a little chintz armchair near his bed) asked one day. Her voice sounded solicitous, but Henrietta thought she could detect an underlying irritation.

'Oh no, Mother,' Edmund said. 'Henrietta cheers me up. I sometimes think she is my best doctor.'

Henrietta wondered if Edmund noticed, as she did, the slight compression of Aunt Louisa's lips. Sometimes she felt that Edmund and Aunt Louisa were playing some curious game – but not a friendly one. The War Game?

Anyway, no more comments were made on her visits to Edmund. Thank heaven, Sister didn't mind them. Sister had told her one morning in the corridor that she seemed to be 'a real tonic' for him.

More than a month had now passed since his return. Normally, the family stayed at Churston for only about ten days at Easter. Term had long since started at Miss Dettmer's – but no one worried about that. What they worried about was that 'everyone' was in London. Henrietta could see that both Aunt Louisa and Julia were getting restless. Even Uncle Harry was making wistful remarks about his club.

'My mother has been trying to persuade me to move to Belgrave Square,' Edmund told her one morning. ' "Though of course the country air is wonderful, I'm sure you'd find life more *lively* there," she said. But I was adamant. I told her I was quite determined to stay here. They wanted to bring me to London in the first place, and I wouldn't let them, so why should I move now? "Why don't *you* go, though?" I said to her. "I shall be quite happy on my own." She muttered something, but I couldn't help seeing that she longed to jump at the offer.'

A few days later, Henry wrote to say that he was hoping for some leave in the near future.

Obviously Henry would want to spend his leave in London, though of course he would want to come down and see Edmund. The decision was made. The household would move back to Belgrave Square, leaving Edmund at Churston with Sister and the resident staff.

'Edmund,' Henrietta said to him that afternoon – she

spoke timidly because the idea was so important to her –
'couldn't you persuade Aunt Louisa to let me stay behind
when they go to London? That is – if you'd like me to.'

'Stay here?' He sounded surprised. 'On your own? Why,
you'd be bored to death wouldn't you? Though,' he added
– and she saw with joy how his face brightened – 'it would
be splendid for me, of course.'

'Oh Edmund, I wouldn't be bored at all. I'd simply love
it. You know how much I've always preferred Churston to
London. Don't you think she'd let me – if *you* asked? After
all, it's not as if I were out yet.'

'But I thought you were so keen to be well-educated,'
he said with a gentle hint of mockery. 'What about your
classes with the *young ladies?* You must have missed a lot
of them already.'

'Oh, but I could work just as well here,' she said. 'Reading,
and so on. You could help me a bit, couldn't you?'

'Yes,' he said, 'I suppose I could.' He paused. 'I *wonder*
if she would agree. No chaperone. Though there's Mrs
Dowsett here, of course. And Sister. Anyway' – and
suddenly he sounded so bitter – 'in the circumstances,
no one could imagine that you would need a chaperone.'

Because he was ill, did he mean? Quite unexpectedly, she
blushed. He was looking at her. Then he smiled warmly.
'Don't look so worried, my dear girl. There's nothing for
you to worry about. I'll ask Mother this evening, when she
comes to say good-night to me.'

In bed that night, she *really* prayed again, for the first
time since Edmund had come home. *Dear God, please let
her say yes. If she says yes, I'll do anything you want me
to.* Did Edmund believe in God? That was something she
wanted to ask him. If, as she suspected from one or two
things he had said, he didn't, how silly he would think these
one-sided conversations she had when she felt desperate.

Next morning, just before the time at which Julia usually
went down to see her mother, Ellis came into the playroom.

'Her ladyship would like to see you for a minute, Miss Henrietta,' she said.

Julia, who was sitting by the window, glanced up, surprised. 'What have you been up to, Henrietta?' she asked coolly.

'Up to? Why, nothing,' Henrietta said. But as she followed Ellis down the stairs, her heart was pounding as if she had done something dreadful and was expecting to be punished for it. She smoothed her hair nervously as she went along the first-floor corridor.

She had seen the room before, but it was the first time she had ever been into it when Aunt Louisa was in bed. Suddenly the scene – Aunt Louisa extended, waiting for her to approach – reminded her of her arrival at Belgrave Square. *I hope I won't be sick on the carpet, this time,* she told herself, in an attempt to raise her spirits. She realized that she felt remarkably queasy.

In the huge, curtained bed, Aunt Louisa lay surrounded by letters, newspapers, magazines. Ming's successor, Fan, was curled up at her feet. How pale Aunt Louisa looked in the morning. She was reading one of her letters, giving no sign that she was aware of Henrietta's presence. She turned a page, read the next one, then looked up.

'So, Henrietta,' she said, 'Edmund tells me that you wish to stay on here, when we all go back to London. It seems a very odd idea to me.'

Henrietta's spirits sank even farther. If Edmund had said only that *she* wanted to stay – and not that he wanted her to – she was sure that she didn't have a chance.

'However,' Aunt Louisa went on, 'Edmund tells me that he would enjoy your society. What a strange boy he is! He could have as much society as he wanted, if he were prepared to accompany us back to Belgrave Square. But as that, for some unknown reason, is apparently out of the *ques-ti-oh-nay*, I suppose that we must fall in with his wishes. In the circumstances, we must do everything we can for him.

Of course I feel concerned about your studies.' (Well *that* was something new!) 'But Edmund says that he will see that you keep them up, which is extremely kind of him. I never quite saw my elder son in the role of a private tutor but, I suppose, *c'est la vie.*' She gave her cold little laugh.

'So I can stay?' Henrietta burst out, happiness disarming her. 'Oh thank you, Aunt Louisa. Thank you so very much.'

'Don't thank me, Henrietta. Thank your cousin, Edmund. You seem extraordinarily *exaltée.* I would have thought that any girl would prefer the life of London, with all the advantages that we provide there, to mooning about in the country. Very *carpet*, I would have imagined. Of course, next year, when you come out, anything of this kind will be quite impossible. You will be far too busy meeting suitable young people of your own age. You are a very fortunate girl. I hope that you realize how much your Uncle Harry has done for you, bringing you up just as if you were his own daughter. He is even prepared to make some *provision* for you, if you form an appropriate attachment. Which is, of course, quite possible. You are not bad-looking.'

Suddenly she remembered Edmund saying 'Bodies for sale'. She flinched from Aunt Louisa's detached, measuring stare.

'It's a pity,' Aunt Louisa went on, 'that your *type*' – she pronounced it in the French way – 'is rather going out of fashion. Men seem to prefer something *slighter* nowadays, something more like Julia. Though Julia, of course, would have been considered a beauty in *any* era.'

Now she was blushing as if flames were licking her cheeks. She fixed her eyes on the carpet, working out the balance of its patterned squares at some level of her mind parallel with the one which was reacting to Aunt Louisa's words.

Silence prolonged itself. Hoping that the blush was fading, she raised her eyes. The chilly green stare was still directed at her.

'Your colour is very high, Henrietta. You must try not to become too excited about things. It gives you rather a *milk-maidish* look – and not, alas, that of *le Petit Trianon*.' There was the little laugh again.

How she longed to escape. Surely Aunt Louisa would release her soon. 'Thank you very much for letting me stay,' she said, but more quietly this time. She shifted her feet.

'Before you hurry away, Henrietta, and I can see that you are anxious to do so—'

'Oh no, really—'

Aunt Louisa made a silencing gesture. 'Before you go, Henrietta, there is just one more thing I would like to say to you, if you can restrain your impatience. Of course I have always been aware of this *culte* you have for your cousin, Edmund. It would really' – there was that frosty smile, and back went Henrietta's eyes to the carpet – 'hardly have been possible not to be. At one time, I even felt some anxiety about it. Not from Edmund's point of view, of course, though I imagine that it must have embarrassed him at times, but from yours. One never likes to see a young girl making a fool of herself in public.'

Four green squares within a red square. 'I didn't, I haven't—'

'Henrietta, I am sure that I am a better judge of that than you are. However, in these new circumstances, those anxieties of mine fall away. Naturally, now that your cousin is a permanent invalid, your *devotion* to him can be looked at in a different light. There is really nothing for anyone to *relever* about. I just felt that I should mention it to you, so that in any future *cultes*, you don't behave in quite such an *Ibsen* way. Try to show a little more breeding. After all, your *mother*'s origins might entitle one to expect that.'

The green squares were blurring into each other. She clenched her tongue between her teeth. She *mustn't* speak. *Think of Edmund*, she told herself.

'Very well, Henrietta, that is all I have to say. Ask Julia to come down now, would you please?'

'Yes of course, Aunt Louisa.' Keeping her back rigidly straight, she turned and set off across the carpet to the door. What a long way it seemed.

Out in the corridor, she stood still, dazed by a confusion of feelings. What horrible things Aunt Louisa had said. Edmund *a permanent invalid* – what rubbish! And then that other awful sentence: 'I imagine it must have sadly embarrassed him at times.'

Surely she had never done anything to embarrass Edmund? He had never given the slightest sign of it. He wouldn't have wanted her to stay at Churston if she embarrassed him. But even if she didn't, might Aunt Louisa have mentioned it yesterday evening – and put the idea into his mind?

Nothing else had been as bad. 'Your *mother*'s origins' – she had become accustomed, over the years, to little digs of that kind. And did she really care what Aunt Louisa and her friends thought about her? No let them gossip – *relever* – away to their hearts' content in their silly Edwardian slang that Edmund said was now so old-fashioned.

But the feeling that now overwhelmed her as she started to walk along the passage – Ellis had appeared at the end of it, and she couldn't go on standing by Aunt Louisa's door like a waxwork – was a lightness of joy. Like the last movement of Brahms' Second Piano Concerto (how typical of Aunt Louisa's world to think Brahms pompous!), which she had heard at a concert she had gone to with some other girls from Miss Dettmer's. (Lots of people thought it was wrong to listen to music by Brahms or Bach or Beethoven, because of the war with Germany, but Edmund said that that was 'philistine idiocy'.) That last movement had made her want to dance, as she wanted to dance now. For she had won. She could stay. She gave Ellis (who was watching her, she could see, with a curiosity inspired by Aunt Louisa's unprecedented summons) a smile of pure happiness which made Ellis look astonished.

In the playroom, Julia still lolled by the window. She turned as Henrietta came in.

'You're looking very pleased with yourself,' Julia said.

'Am I? Yes, I suppose I am.'

Would Julia report her high spirits to Aunt Louisa? The idea delighted her. Aunt Louisa would realize that all the horrible things she had said hadn't mattered to Henrietta in the least. There would be nothing Aunt Louisa could do about that. Or – would she find some way of stopping her staying on with Edmund? Impossible – *or wasn't it?* Better to be on the safe side.

'It's just,' she said, flattening her voice, controlling her smile, 'that I'm going to stay on at Churston. Isn't it kind of Aunt Louisa to allow me to?'

'Stay on your own here? How boring!' Then Julia laughed. 'Oh, I *see*,' she said. 'Hitty Pitty can be alone with her beloved Edmund.'

'Don't be silly,' Henrietta said, but she said it calmly, in the way she knew always irritated Julia.

'That's not silly. It's true,' Julia said. 'What surprises me is that Edmund can put up with it.'

'Aunt Louisa says she'd like you to come downstairs now,' Henrietta said.

'Why didn't you tell me that before?' Julia jumped up from her chair.

'You didn't give me a chance to,' Henrietta said sweetly.

Later in the day, when she saw Edmund, he seemed so very pleased that she was staying. Aunt Louisa couldn't have said anything about her *embarrassing* him.

He asked her what Aunt Louisa had said to her, but she only told him about her saying she should be grateful to Uncle Harry for bringing her up as if she were his daughter.

Edmund gave an extraordinary laugh when she told him that – savage was really the only word that would describe it.

'That's the *supreme* irony,' he exclaimed. And, yet again, she didn't know what he was talking about.

✥ *Seven* ✤

Later she would be sure that that had been the happiest time of her life; the long spring and early summer at Churston with Edmund.

Morning after morning, she awakened with the feeling of the promise of the day. When she had washed and dressed, one of the maids would bring her breakfast in the schoolroom. A boiled egg, buttered toast which she cut in fingers and dipped in the egg yolk; the hateful days of porridge and bread were over now.

After breakfast, she walked in the garden. She had never enjoyed the garden as much as she did that year. It was hers. No ladies sitting on the terrace, glancing at her, and murmuring to each other as she passed. No nasty little dogs yapping, and snapping at her ankles. No peals and brays of laughter, no click of croquet balls – croquet, Edmund declared, was the essence of triviality and tedium.

No Aunt Louisa to criticize her for 'mooning about'. Best of all – no Julia. Since she arrived at Belgrave Square, she had never been separated from Julia, and she found that Julia's absence transformed her existence. It was wonderful, yet it left a curious gap in her life. She was so used to hating Julia.

At half past ten, carrying her books, she went to Edmund's room. Always, before she knocked on the door, she paused for a moment, prolonging the anticipation of being with him as, after playing tennis on a hot day, she remembered pausing with the longed-for glass of lemonade not yet raised to her lips.

Lightly she tapped on the door. He called 'Come in'. He was the first thing she saw when she opened the door. Over by the window where, now that the weather was warmer, he had had his bed moved so that he could look out on the garden. He always looked so shiningly clean, newly shaved by Sister, wearing a little frogged jacket of maroon quilted silk. His hair was smoothy brushed – it was quite long. She liked that – she thought it made him look like a poet – though, just before her departure, Aunt Louisa had said, 'We really must get a barber to come and cut your hair.'

'I'll arrange it,' he had answered, but he hadn't done so.

Always, when she came in, he would be reading. And she would sit down in the little chintz armchair and read too. Edmund had decided that she should read school books in the morning, and save novels and poetry for the afternoon.

She seldom turned the pages, for it was possible – holding the book in front of her – to steal long looks at him which he never seemed to notice.

Sometimes, he would put down his book and ask her about what she was reading – though they often ended up talking about something quite different from her 'studies'. Then he would break off, laughing, and say 'Red herrings, Henrietta. I know all about them. We had a master at school who was famous for being distracted by them. Back to work!'

'You're a slave-driver,' she would sigh, reluctantly picking up her book again.

They had luncheon in Edmund's room. Edmund had ordered the meal after breakfast. He was eating almost normally now, and had refused to drink any more beef tea. He introduced her to dishes she had never tasted. Yes, the nursery days were gone with a vengeance. Best of all, she liked the fruit: the peaches and muscatel grapes from the hothouse; the cherries, the strawberries. In the nursery they had never had any fruit but the occasional apple.

After luncheon, Edmund rested, but he said he liked her being in the room. So, with a novel, she stayed in the armchair. He slept better in the afternoon than at night, he told her. While he slept, she could gaze at him as much as she wanted.

Sometimes she pretended that they were married. After all, they spent much more time together than most married couples did.

Of course, if they were married, he would kiss her. Now he was ill – that was why he didn't. She wanted him to kiss her. Every evening, when they said good-night, he kissed her cheek. But he never kissed her lips as he had done that early morning in Belgrave Square.

She had gone over that kiss so often in her mind, that it had lost every trace of vividness. The smell of London, the haze around the street lamp, the sound of the horse's hooves – as with the kiss, she could remember them, but could no longer bring them to life.

Apart from her pretence that they were married, she had another daydream. But, she told herself, it wasn't really a daydream. It could come true. She knew that Edmund was going to get well.

After all, hadn't the specialist said that shrapnel was unpredictable? Hadn't he said that Edmund might have an operation some day? – and surely an operation meant a cure. But perhaps an operation wouldn't be necessary. Why shouldn't *she* teach Edmund to walk again?

There they were, all gathered in the hall – Aunt Louisa, Julia, Uncle Harry, Henry, and the servants. She didn't know why they were assembled there, but she would work that out some time. And then – it was a sound at the top of the stairs that made them all turn round, in one single movement, like a line of dancers on the stage. After that, they were absolutely still, absolutely silent, as they gazed up at Edmund, standing at the top of the stairs, with his hand on Henrietta's shoulder. Slowly, side by side, she and Edmund began to descend. A great sigh was released from the mouths of all the watchers – but they didn't move. Only as she and Edmund reached the bottom of the stairs did Aunt Louisa come hurrying forward.

'Edmund, Edmund,' she exclaimed, 'you're well again.'

How quietly Edmund answered, 'Yes, Mother, I'm well.' Then he turned to look at Henrietta and said, 'It is all thanks to her.'

Sometimes when she came back from the dream to the reality of Edmund's pale, sleeping face, of the little shivers, the low groans he sometimes gave, she would feel a pang of sickness: sickness with herself as if in some way, she were making use of him for her own pleasure. But that was nonsense, absolute nonsense. And she would let herself be borne on again, on the tide of the dream, to the moment when the imagined scene always ended, the moment when, in front of everyone, he put his arms around her, he kissed her.

When Edmund awakened, tea was brought. Carefully she poured it from the silver teapot, never spilling a drop, adding the thin slice of lemon he liked in it, taking the cup over to the bedside table with the same absorbed care. Afterwards she plied him with tiny cucumber sandwiches, asparagus rolled in thin brown bread and butter – he didn't eat cake.

Her favourite time was after tea had been cleared away. The great shadow of the cedar extending on the lawn, the cawing of rooks, evening coming down. After tea, one of the maids lit the fire. He liked, he told her, to fall asleep by firelight.

She had learnt from Sister that he also slept with a night-light burning by his bed. He had such bad dreams that Sister had persuaded him that it was better not to wake from them in the dark. But he never mentioned the night-light to Henrietta, and she never told him that she knew about it.

How strange it was to love the time after tea so much. It was the time of day that she had always hated most, the time for the dressed-up visit to the drawing-room.

Now it was the time when Edmund seemed most free from constraint – rested, calm after his sleep. He read poems to her. Not his own. ('I destroyed all my old poems,' he told her. But she had noticed a black notebook on his bedside table. She wondered if he wrote in that.) He talked about himself, about his childhood, which sounded as if it had been happy until he was thirteen. 'Then everything changed,' he said once. His voice was so sombre, the expression on his face so closed, that she did not dare to ask him how.

But that things *had* changed came out in his stories. Until he was thirteen, he had won prizes, been top of his form. Then suddenly he was a rebel, lazy at school work, turning to painting and poetry.

At Oxford, he had been an isolated figure. He described the exploits of Henry and his friends, loosing rats from a sack in the chapel, putting aesthetes in fountains, and breaking up their rooms. 'They didn't do that to me, though,' he said. 'I suppose I was an aesthete, but I didn't look like one. And anyway, loyal old Henry would never have stood for it.' She tried to fathom the character of the laugh that followed. Affectionate, disdainful – both perhaps.

Sometimes he even talked about the war, usually of military idiocies – ten days spent gaining three yards of ground which were lost again the day after.

'But we're always talking about me, Henrietta,' he said one evening. 'Not at all a fruitful subject. We should talk more about you and your plans.'

'My plans?' she said, rising from the chintz armchair, and

going over to the window. Rooks were cawing loudly in the elms that bordered the drive.

'Yes, your plans, Henrietta. What you want to do with your life.'

'Oh, I don't know,' she said. 'I haven't really thought about it.'

It was true. She never did – except, of course, in the way she couldn't mention: in terms of him. Her daydreams. His recovery. Marrying him. Of course . . . if she had been able to draw. But she pushed that thought out of her mind as she always did.

'But, at one time,' he said, 'you were always talking about the things you wanted to do. I remember that you used to talk about going to Oxford. I feel rather guilty about that, I think I discouraged you by the way I spoke about the sweet girl undergraduates.'

She laughed. 'You said they were grubby frumps.'

'Now I feel guiltier than ever – at your remembering my very words. I shouldn't have said it. After all, *you* could never have been grubby. *You* could never have been a frump.'

She was blushing, and turned towards the window to hide it.

'You might have found it interesting,' he went on. 'And it would have been a means of escape from us.'

'Escape from you!' she exclaimed. 'But that's the last thing I want.'

A dry little laugh – had she sounded too fervent? 'Not from me perhaps,' he said. 'I know you like being with me – which is very flattering, of course. But I may not be here much longer.'

She met a look so stern, and a silencing gesture of his hands so final, that she did not dare to say anything.

'And without me,' he went on, hands relaxing at his sides, his expression softening, 'perhaps you wouldn't enjoy life here so much. Mother and Julia aren't really dear to you, are they?'

She hesitated, not sure what to answer. He continued, 'Of course you will be coming out next year. And you're such a pretty girl that hundreds of charming young men will be all agog to snap you up.' He laughed again, and made a snapping sound with his teeth, like a dog that has been thrown a biscuit.

'Oh no,' she said, 'oh no, I don't want to get married.' *Except to you*, she thought.

'You don't?' he said, sounding mildly surprised. 'I thought all girls wanted to get married. But if it's true, it's even more of a pity that you aren't going to Oxford.'

'No,' she said. 'Really – I've quite got over that idea. Honestly I have. Don't let's talk about it any more. Shall we play a game of chess?' (He was teaching her to play. He always won – but she didn't mind at all.)

'Putting me in my place – that's what I believe you're doing, you impertinent girl.' He smiled. 'Set out the pieces by all means,' he said.

When half-past seven came, it was time to say good-night to him. Soon he would have his glass of sherry, his light supper. Sister would get him ready for the night.

After the precious kiss on her cheek, she went upstairs to the day nursery where one of the maids brought her milk and biscuits.

Being alone, at this time, was almost a luxury. She sat by the window, the darkness deepening, the silence only broken by the little night sounds of animals, or the hoot of an owl. She was peaceful in the knowledge that she would be spending the next day – another perfect day – with Edmund.

But though most of the days were perfect, occasionally there was a bad one: a morning when he had obviously not slept, and looked white and haggard, when he was nervous, irritable and disinclined to talk. He had a way of rubbing his thumbs against his forefingers which told her when he was in that mood. Then she would sit very quietly, forcing herself not to look up from her book. For when he was 'like that', he didn't read; he just lay staring into space.

Anyway, even on the bad days, he usually revived at tea-time.

'I'm afraid I've been rather glum today.'

'Oh no you haven't. Not at all.'

'Dear Henrietta – always so sweet and patient. What would I do without you?'

A remark like that made everything worth while.

Henry's leave had been postponed. Thank goodness, she thought, that the family had been safely established in London before that happened. Otherwise they might have stayed on at Churston, though she doubted it. In the four weeks since their departure, Uncle Harry and Aunt Louisa had only been down once, for the day.

Henry eventually reached London at the beginning of June. Two days later, he came down to Churston to see Edmund. He arrived in the early afternoon. Quarter of an hour later, Henrietta made an excuse, and left him alone with Edmund. Surely they must have private things to say to each other? But, at tea-time, Sister came up with a message that Henrietta should join them.

She sat in the chintz armchair and poured out the tea. She watched them. Though Henry was thinner, older-looking than he had been the last time she had seen him, Edmund looked very fragile next to him.

Henry was talking about the war. It was a different one from the one Edmund described. It was a war of successful strategies, advances, acts of gallantry. Apart from one reference to 'idiots on the staff', Henry's war seemed like an old war in a book. Or like Brooke's poems, like the letters that people wrote to the newspapers, and which Aunt Louisa sometimes read aloud. He talked about the war, she thought suddenly, in the same way that Aunt Louisa did. Not *preaching* as she did, of course – but Henry's war, like hers, had heroes. Yet you could see that he wasn't lying. She frowned, puzzled.

Edmund hardly said anything. He nodded, and asked questions, but he looked more and more tired. She was glad Henry was going back to London early next day.

Sister, coming into the room, gave Edmund a sharp glance. 'My patient is looking worn out,' she said to Henry.

'Oh, most frightfully sorry,' Henry sprang to his feet.

'Nonsense,' Edmund said, but he sank back against the pillows.

'Thoughtless of me, terribly thoughtless, old chap. Talking my head off.' As on other occasions, his voice, his manner reminded her of Uncle Harry's.

'Well, good-night,' she said, preparing to go upstairs. But Henry turned and said, 'You'll come downstairs later and have dinner with me, won't you, Henrietta? Can't leave me all on my own – can she, Edmund?'

Edmund smiled. 'Of course not,' he said. She could see that he was already feeling better at the prospect of being, in a few minutes, alone.

She didn't really want to have dinner with Henry – what would they talk about? – but she couldn't refuse. Henry said that he would arrange it. 'Must go and see Mrs Dowsett. She'd never forgive me if I didn't go and have a chat with her.'

Up in her room, Henrietta wondered what to wear. It would be the first time she had had dinner downstairs. Her white party dress, she supposed, though it looked short and childish. Suddenly she wished that she were out, that she had something grown-up to wear – a long dress – and that she could put up her hair. She put on the white dress, she brushed her hair, she fastened around her neck the string of coral and seed pearls that Uncle Harry had given her ages ago. She went downstairs with a feeling of dread.

It wasn't nearly as bad as she expected. For one thing, the food was delicious. 'Like to see a girl with a good appetite,' Henry said at one point, and she blushed.

'No, I mean it. Can't stand people who pick at their food.'

He insisted that she have a glass of champagne. The bubbles pricked her nose and it didn't taste as nice as lemonade, but drinking it made her feel reassuringly grown up.

He didn't talk about the war. He talked about the shows he was going to see in London, told little anecdotes about friends of his. She was surprised by how easy it was to respond – to laugh and to ask questions, and so on.

It was when they had finished the savoury – a sort of scrambled egg and anchovy thing which was apparently his favourite, for he sent a message about it to the cook – that he said, 'I think it's most awfully jolly of you to stay down here and keep Edmund company like this. Know how fond of the old chap you are, but it must be dashed dull.' He paused, added, 'Especially for a pretty girl like you.'

Was Henry *flirting* with her? Nobody had ever flirted ('spangled' in Aunt Louisa's language) with her before. Henry never used to pay her compliments ('dewdrops'). Though she remembered his telling Uncle Harry what a pretty girl she had become. But that had been different – they hadn't been alone. Edmund sometimes said nice things to her – the treasures which she counted over, like a miser, in bed at night – but of course that wasn't *flirting*.

She said, 'Oh, but I like being here.'

'You do? You enjoy a quiet life, what?'

She nodded.

'Like the country, myself. But must say I prefer a bit more life about the place. A shooting party, a few people to stay, you know.'

'Mmm,' she said, and then, 'I expect you'll have a lovely time in London.'

'Oh splendid, I expect, perfectly splendid. Lots of parties lined up. After being in France, you know, one wants a spot of gaiety.' He cracked a nut. They were having dessert.

'Yes,' she said, 'I suppose so.' She was remembering Edmund's leave, the long days in the library. Edmund had liked to be alone with her then, just as he did now. He had always liked it – not only when he was ill. At the thought, she smiled with all her heart, and became aware of Henry smiling back at her.

'Dashed if I'm going to sit here alone, drinking port,' he said. 'Like to take a turn on the terrace?'

'Yes,' she said. 'All right.' There was something rather dashing about taking 'a turn on the terrace' so late in the evening, alone with a young man – even though it was only Henry. Surely it wasn't disloyal to Edmund to feel that?

They went through the french windows onto the terrace. The night was warm; it smelt of flowers and grass.

'Mind if I smoke?' he asked her.

'Oh no, not at all.'

He took a silver cigarette case, and a small green morocco match container from his pocket. He smiled. He said, 'I suppose you don't?'

'Oh *no*,' she said, astonished.

'Sorry. You look so grown up nowadays that I can't believe you're just a little girl.'

'Not a *little* girl,' she said indignantly.

He was still holding the cigarette case and matches in his hand. 'Wouldn't you like to try, Henrietta? Just a puff.'

'Oh – all right,' she said.

He opened the cigarette case. 'Proper Turkish ones on this side,' he said, 'and "gaspers" on the other – I've got used to them in France. Funny, I really prefer them now. But I'd advise the Turks for you. Most girls like them better.'

'Do a lot of girls smoke, then?' she asked him.

'Oh yes, especially the faster ones.' He laughed again. He was holding the case out to her. 'Come along. There's a brave girl.'

She took one of the oval Turkish ones, hesitantly put it between her lips.

He struck a match. She realized that her hand, holding the cigarette, was shaking a little.

He noticed it too. 'Not a very steady hand,' he said, and rested his left hand on her wrist. A strange feeling – like a shiver, only warm instead of cold – ran down her back, and she gave a little start, as he put the lighted match to the cigarette.

'Breathe in,' he said, 'or it won't light.'

She could feel her heart beating. Surely he could hear it? No, of course he couldn't. She could smell the stuff called Euchrisma that Edmund used on his hair, too, and that added to her feeling of confusion. She took a deep breath, and her mouth was filled with stinging smoke. Horrible! She began to cough.

He laughed. 'Easy to tell that you're a novice,' he said. Now he lit a cigarette for himself, dropped the match on the terrace.

Thank goodness she had stopped coughing. 'Oh,' she said, 'I don't like it at all.' She tossed the cigarette away, saw a little shower of sparks rise as it landed on the shadowy lawn.

'It's one of those things you have to get used to before you can really enjoy it.' He was smiling at her. 'We'll try again in a year's time,' he said. 'Perhaps you'll like it better then.'

He was teasing her, but she couldn't quite work out how.

'That cigarette has made me all dizzy,' she said.

'Has it indeed?'

She was feeling – out of her depth. What a strange phrase to come into her mind. 'I must go to bed,' she said. 'It's getting late.' She must escape – to safety.

'Not very late, really,' he said. He looked at his watch. 'Only quarter to ten.'

'That's very late for me,' she said. 'Goodbye Henry. I shan't see you tomorrow if you're going early. I hope you enjoy your leave.'

'Thank you, Henrietta. Look after the old chap, and keep him cheerful.'

'Oh I will.' She turned to go.

'Won't you kiss me goodbye?'

How could she refuse? It would look so silly. After all, he was her first cousin.

She took the two steps that brought her in front of him. She had to tilt her head back, and raise herself on her toes to reach his cheek. As she did so, he dropped his cigarette on the terrace. His hands came up, and cupped her chin. Now his mouth was on her. It felt quite different from Edmund's. It was so very soft and warm, and his lips were a little parted so that she felt his warm breath. More than that, his whole presence enveloped her. The warmth was all around her, for now he had released her chin, and his arms enclosed her. *She wanted him to go on kissing her, enfolding her.*

She shook herself free, sprang back. 'Oh!' she exclaimed.

'You don't like that?' he said. 'Perhaps it's the same as it was with the cigarette. We shall have to try again in a year's time.'

She turned. She ran away across the terrace to the side door that led into a passage. No one was about. Thank goodness.

At last she was safe in her room with the door closed. The curtains were drawn; the bed had been turned down. All was peace and order. But when she had undressed, and had turned out the light, she went over to the window, and slipped behind the curtains. He was still there, pacing the terrace in the dark. He was smoking again – she could see the lighted end of his cigarette.

What was the matter with her? She loved Edmund. So

how could she have enjoyed being kissed by Henry? She had never even *liked* him particularly. 'So ideally, blessedly stupid.'

Stepping back into the room, getting into bed, she decided that now she positively disliked him. '*We shall have to try again in a year's time.*' Well, he was quite wrong about that. She would never let him kiss her again – never!

She awakened early next morning. After a moment she looked at her watch. Seven o'clock. In quarter of an hour, Henry would be gone, off to the station to catch the early train. When she heard the trap outside, she couldn't resist going behind the curtains to watch the little stretch of drive she could see from the window.

A perfect morning, blue and sunny. The trap came into view. There he was, lounging in the back. In a moment, the trap had vanished behind the elms. 'Good riddance,' she said aloud.

She felt uneasy about facing Edmund this morning. When she knocked on his door, it wasn't with her usual feeling of delighted anticipation.

'Come in,' he called. She opened the door. There he was – darling Edmund.

'Good morning,' she said.

'Good morning, Henrietta.'

Everything was just as it always had been.

Book in hand, she was ensconced in the chintz armchair when he said, 'It's rather a relief that Henry's gone, I must say. Very nice of him to come down, and all that, but he's rather heavy-going, poor dear fellow.'

'Oh *yes*,' she agreed, so wholeheartedly that Edmund looked at her with surprise. Then he smiled.

'I suppose you spent a pretty dull evening with him,' he said.

'Oh *yes*,' she said again. 'It was very dull.'

❧ *Eight* ❧

Paradise ended when the Season did, when the family came down to Churston. Oh, she still saw Edmund every morning and every afternoon, but she was expected to have luncheon and tea downstairs. And when she was with him, she didn't feel quite at ease in the old way because, at any moment, her uncle, her aunt or Julia might come in. Though actually, they didn't do so very often. While that was a relief to her and, she felt, to Edmund, she also found herself resenting it. They *should* have paid him more attention; they *should* have wanted to spend more time with him.

Now that the shock of his disaster, the novelty of his invalid state were wearing off, it was almost as if they wanted to forget about him, except for one formal daily acknowledgement, a visit usually paid before dressing for dinner. People were coming to the house to stay again. These guests would pay a duty call on Edmund when they arrived and another before they left, but they seldom came to see him in between.

He was remote and monosyllabic with them – quite different from how he was when he was alone with her. If only they knew what he was *really* like! A moment later, she would feel a deep gladness that they didn't. If they had known – then she would have had rivals for his company, wouldn't she? Or was *the real Edmund* as alien to them as the shadow that nodded, shook its head, answered with 'Yes' and 'No'?

How much she loved him – as she told herself every night, every morning, and numerous times each day. The memory of Henry's kiss was beginning to fade. News came that he had been given the Military Cross. He must be very brave. How endlessly everyone talked about him – so much more than they talked about Edmund.

The household didn't move to Scotland that August. Because of Edmund, she heard Aunt Louisa tell a visitor. But perhaps she imagined the undertone of resentment that she thought she heard in Aunt Louisa's voice.

Autumn approached with ripe fruit and the sweeping of leaves. Soon it would be time to go back to London. She knew that she would have to return with them, that they wouldn't let her stay on at Churston with Edmund.

All the same, she spoke to Edmund about it, and he said he would ask Aunt Louisa. 'Mother says it's quite impossible,' he told her next day. 'You'll be coming out next year. You've got to mix with people of your own age.'

She burst into tears.

'Henrietta, my sweet!' he exclaimed. 'Come here.'

Dabbing at her eyes with her handkerchief, she came to stand at the side of his bed. He took her hand.

'Dear little Henrietta,' he said, 'does being with me really mean so much to you?'

'Oh yes,' she said, the 'yes' emerging in a long wail. Her sobs increased; she couldn't hold them back.

'Silly girl,' he said. His voice was so kind that she cried all the more. He stroked her hand.

'Henrietta,' he said, 'calm down and listen to me for a moment. Stop crying now, or I shall be cross with you.'

She made a great effort. She wiped her eyes, then blew her nose.

'That's a good girl,' he said, and suddenly she felt almost angry with him.

'You treat me as though I were a child,' she said.

He smiled 'But what else can I do when you behave like one?'

Henry hadn't treated her as though she were a child.

'I'm not a child,' she said. 'I'm not.' Unable to resist the

impulse, she snatched up his hand which was still resting
on hers. She covered it with desperate little kisses.

Violently, almost savagely, he tore it away from her. 'Oh,
Henrietta!' he exclaimed.

She raised her head, and was transfixed by the expression
on his face: horrified – no, more than horrified, *disgusted*.

Suddenly her face was burning hot. *He was repelled by her*.
Never had she felt so humiliated, so altogether abandoned,
deserted. At that moment, she hated herself – and, yes, she
hated him. Hated Edmund – was it possible?

She knew hate so well. It had been her familiar for so long:
hatred of Julia, hatred of Aunt Louisa, hatred nourished
over the years, fed with its daily ration of contempt and
insult, cherished, nurtured even in her dreams. There had
been times when she had almost felt that it possessed her,
but it had never done so entirely. Always there had been the
safe warm corner where the plant of her love for Edmund
flourished. And now – it was as if, within an instant, that
plant had scorched and shrivelled.

She watched the expression of disgust, revulsion on
his face slowly fade, to be replaced by a look of cold
remoteness.

He spoke. 'Surely you must realize that this kind
of nonsense is utterly impossible?' he said in an even,
detached tone.

'*Why?*' she cried out, in a surge of recklessness. Why
shouldn't she love him? But of course she didn't any
more.

He shook his head. He closed his eyes for a moment. 'You
must understand that it is altogether out of the question,'
he said. His tone was severe. Then he said, more kindly –
patronizingly, she thought – 'When you are older, perhaps
you will understand better. Now you must just accept my
word that it is absolutely hopeless to feel as you feel – or
as you think you feel.'

What could she say? There was nothing. The fire of hate

was dying down. A bitter chill was succeeding it – a cold wind blowing through a cold place.

Edmund said, 'I think that perhaps I have taken the wrong decision.'

'Decision?' she asked. How quiet and polite her voice sounded.

'Yes,' he said. 'I decided last night that since you can't stay with me, I would come with you to London. To Belgrave Square.'

A few minutes before, how joyful she would have felt. Now she said, 'Oh Edmund – really?' Why should he want to come with her, she wondered, when she *repelled* him so?

'But now I think I ought to change my mind.'

Belgrave Square without him – a desert. Life would be so empty. Even if she hated him, wouldn't she rather he was *there?*

He was talking again. 'I have probably been selfish. Because I enjoy your company so much, I haven't been thinking enough about you. Perhaps it would be better for us not to see so much of each other. I think it may be upsetting for you.'

Upsetting for her – how *dared* he? So he 'enjoyed her company'! Why, there would have been a time, before she had seen *that look of his*, when those words would actually have pleased her. How stupid she had been.

'Oh no,' she said, 'it doesn't upset me at all. I was just sorry – and a bit silly, too, I suppose – because of leaving you.'

She could see that the calmness with which she spoke had an effect on him. His face was relaxing from its cold stiffness. But he said, 'No, I'm not sure. Not sure at all.'

He thought of her as a child. So now she said, 'I promise I won't behave so stupidly again. I'll be good, I promise, Edmund.'

'Be good!' he repeated. 'How can you say you're not a child!' And now he was smiling.

She pressed her advantage. 'Really, I really will be

good,' she said, to make him laugh. And he did. *Fool*, she thought.

'All right,' he said. 'I'll stick to what I decided. I'll come to London – but only on one condition.'

She nodded. She waited in silence.

'You must promise me something, Henrietta. You must promise to stop feeling about me – in that silly way. We can only be friends, Henrietta. Never anything else. The best of friends, but only friends. Will you promise to think of me only as a friend?'

The best of friends. *Fool*, she thought again. But he must come to London. Oh yes, she wanted him to do that. So she would promise. What was a promise but words?

'I promise,' she said, and felt a thrill of icy joy.

'The best of friends, but only friends,' said he.

'The best of friends. Only friends – I promise.'

Lying in bed that night, she cherished her strange new power. The power to deceive him. Oh, how she would deceive him. Perhaps by deceiving him, she might even make him change his mind, make him love her. What then? She saw a picture of him, suppliant, rejected. He was ill. Mightn't he die of grief? Into her mind, exactly as in a photograph, came his face – that look on it. *He deserves to die*, she thought. She felt herself cold, stern, a judge delivering a sentence. *Invulnerable*.

Back at Belgrave Square, everything went on as it had always done. She returned to Miss Dettmer's classes, although she felt that Miss Dettmer was disappointed in her, had quite lost interest in her, in fact. But what did that matter? By the time next summer came, she would have left Miss Dettmer's for ever.

Yes, everything was the same at Belgrave Square – except that Edmund was there. And now she anticipated her daily visits to him as eagerly as she had ever done at Churston – though now the quality of her anticipation was quite different. Each time she opened his door, she felt that she was making an entrance on a stage.

He always seemed pleased to see her, glad to listen to her chatter. Her aim was to amuse him – just as her letters to the Front had done. But now, amusing him was her armour. She treasured and embellished stories about the idiocies of Miss Dettmer's 'young ladies', as well as any silly remarks she heard in Aunt Louisa's drawing-room. She was rewarded by his laughter. Oh yes, he 'enjoyed her company'.

He was getting better. She could see it, and so could the doctors. By the beginning of November, he was able to sit up in a wheelchair. Now, as well as Sister, he had a valet who dressed him, and helped to move him between his bed and the wheelchair.

'Well, Mr Edmund, you soon won't be needing me any more,' Sister had remarked cheerfully on his second day up.

The doctor had been present at the time. He had said, 'Indeed your progress is most encouraging. But more haste, less speed, you know. Let us not be rash.'

'How true,' Edmund had said, telling Henrietta about it afterwards. 'I certainly shan't do anything rash in this ridiculous chair.' All the same, she could see that he liked being able to sit at his table or to take books out of the shelves. 'When you ask someone to bring you a book, you usually find you don't want it,' he said with a smile.

Seeing him at his writing-table one day, the black note-book in front of him, she wondered if he were writing again. He was going to get well. She had been right all along. What did she feel about that? She decided to wait and see.

Aunt Louisa, she noticed, hardly seemed pleased at all that Edmund was getting so much better. He came downstairs for two meals, and then, after the third, she said how inconvenient it was to fit 'that awkward wheelchair' at the dining-room table when there were a lot of people to luncheon.

Henrietta saw how Edmund turned not pale – he was always pale – but white, dead white.

'Yes, Mother,' he said, 'I'm afraid I'm a dreadfully awkward fellow. I doubt if it is merely my wheelchair that has that quality. I do apologize. The obvious answer is for me to have all my meals upstairs. That should obviate the awkwardness and inconvenience.'

Aunt Louisa actually blushed and stammered, said that she hadn't meant it, that she hadn't been thinking, that she had a headache, but he would not eat downstairs again. Did Aunt Louisa really try to persuade him? Henrietta didn't think so.

'Of course,' he said to her afterwards, 'Mother has always found me unsatisfactory. Now that I am crippled *to boot*, whatever that means, it must be even more tiresome for her. How unobliging it was of me not to get killed outright. She might have mourned for a month or two – though black isn't her best colour. But dear Henry would have filled my position so much better.' He laughed. 'Anyway, all that she needs is a little patience – in the long run I'm sure she won't be disappointed.'

'Oh Edmund, you mustn't talk like that,' Henrietta said. How she detested Aunt Louisa. How could Aunt Louisa treat her son like that? What a horrible woman she was.

Henrietta drifted through her last term at Miss Dettmer's. Beyond Easter lay the summer, loomed the Season. She was dreading coming out as much as Julia was looking forward to it.

'How I wish I didn't have to,' she said to Edmund. But he was unsympathetic. *He didn't care*.

'Once you are caught up in the giddy whirl, you'll enjoy every minute of it,' he said.

She was sure she wouldn't. Sometimes, now, in the evening, young people came to the house, and they danced to the piano. She didn't enjoy it at all. All the young men were so boring, and she couldn't think of anything to say to them. In spite of so many years of lessons, she felt that she still danced stiffly.

At such gatherings, Julia was in her element. Chattering, laughing, floating about like a feather. Or gliding like a snake – long slim neck, darting eyes. A pretty little snake. For one couldn't deny that Julia was pretty.

Now she and Julia had a maid of their own, called Collins, to help them dress and to look after their clothes. Collins practised putting up their hair, and was present when the dressmaker came to fit them for their new wardrobes of grown-up clothes.

Summer was coming. Edmund, who had seemed to be making such steady progress, suddenly lost his appetite, and started to suffer from blinding headaches. When he had a headache, he just wanted to lie in the dark, alone – he didn't even want her, *best friend* or no, to sit with him. The doctor gave him medicine for the headaches, which put him into a drugged state that often lasted for a day or more. Days when she couldn't visit him were shapeless.

One thing was a relief – wasn't it? Henry hadn't been home on leave recently. He had had a few days in January, but had spent them at a shooting party in Norfolk, only coming to Belgrave Square one morning when she and Julia were at Miss Dettmer's. How sorry Julia had been to miss him.

It was during the week before their dance at Belgrave Square – Julia's and her coming-out dance – that Edmund developed a fever. His wounds were hurting him again.

'Oughtn't the dance to be cancelled?' Henrietta said to Julia. How she wished it could be!

'Cancelled?' said Julia. 'What *are* you talking about?'

'Don't you think the noise will disturb Edmund?' He used *her*, so she could use *him*.

'The noise? There'll only be some music. Edmund's fond of music, anyway. Really, Henrietta, how absurd you are. I can't think of anything that would upset Edmund more than the dance being cancelled on his account. He would feel he must be terribly ill, if we did that.'

Henrietta was silent.

'Anyone would think,' Julia went on, 'that nobody cared about Edmund except you. We all care about him – after all, we are his family. But you're quite dotty on the subject. Dotty about him – and longing to be a martyr.'

If Julia knew. 'What nonsense,' Henrietta said coolly.

'Oh, you're so sly, *Hitty Pitty within the wall*. Anyone can see you're dotty about Edmund. Anyway, we'd have to have the dance for Henry's sake. He has managed to get leave. Mama told me this morning.'

Henry! How absurd that she should suddenly have this hollow feeling when she didn't even like him much. Though perhaps she had underestimated Henry a bit, because of the way Edmund was always running him down.

'Oh, is Henry coming? How nice. When does he arrive?' But in her eagerness to sound natural, she sounded almost breathless.

'On the day of the dance. Goodness, it's unusual for you to seem keen about anything except your beloved Edmund. Are you thinking of replacing him with Henry?' Julia giggled.

'Julia, you make me sick.'

'Oo! *If you touch Hitty Pitty, Hitty Pitty will bite you!*'

How she wished she *could* bite Julia, sink teeth in her flesh, pound her head on the floor, put a foot on her face, and *grind down*. Quickly, she left the room.

Next day, Edmund was better. His temperature had fallen below normal. But he felt weak, and of course was not allowed to get up, though she was allowed to visit him.

'I shall stay in bed until after the dance,' he told her. 'Otherwise someone might suggest that I should put in an appearance. I wouldn't care to watch the proceedings from "that awkward wheelchair". Anyway, Henry will be here to do the honours.'

'Yes, Julia said that Henry was coming.'

'Trust good old Henry not to miss a party. Such a gregarious fellow – sometimes I can hardly believe that we're twins. You know, there's meant to be some kind of mystic bond between twins. Not between Henry and me, though. There's more *rapport* between him and Julia. And it's not even as if they – ' He broke off abruptly.

'As if they?' she prompted hopefully.

'Oh, nothing. Actually, I've quite forgotten what I was going to say.'

But she felt quite sure that he hadn't. *He didn't trust her.* Yes, there were still many mysteries about Edmund which she must solve. Edmund still fed her. *Not me – my curiosity*, she told herself.

❧ *Nine* ❧

On the day before the dance, a red and white striped marquee was put up in the garden behind the house, and fairy lights were strung from the trees. On the morning of the day itself, the catering men from Searcy's arrived. All was bustle and excitement.

Henrietta spent the morning in Edmund's room. His temperature was still below normal, but there was no question of his appearing at the dance. 'Anyway, Mother hasn't mentioned the subject,' he said.

Henry and the dance, the dance and Henry were all that the family talked about. She was sick of the sound of Henry's name, she told herself now, though she kept wondering when he would arrive. She hoped to be able to avoid him until the evening. If he didn't come until after luncheon, she would probably succeed, for it had been decreed that she and Julia must rest in the afternoon.

Emma Cave

He still hadn't appeared when they went up to their rooms. Lying on her bed, she thought about the dance. She was dreading it – and yet her dread was mixed with some excitement, an excitement which she had to recognize was centred on the thought of Henry. Would he ask her to dance? Of course she *hoped* he wouldn't – but, as it was her coming-out dance, he would be bound to, wouldn't he? It would be awful if no one asked her to dance. She had heard about the 'wallflowers' who huddled by the ballroom door, and made frequent unnecessary journeys to the cloakroom. It would be better to dance with Henry than for *that* to happen to her.

At least the dance was in their own house. She could always escape for a few minutes to Edmund, or even to her own room. But she mustn't stay away too long, with Aunt Louisa watching everything. Though in some ways Aunt Louisa was so stupid, she was very observant.

She wondered how she would remember who had asked her for which dances – if anybody did. So many young men looked so alike that perhaps she wouldn't remember which was which. She had heard that, at some dances, there were programmes on which your partners wrote their names. That would have helped. But Aunt Louisa said that programmes were dreadfully middle-class.

She fell asleep.

It was time to dress. Collins had laid out everything on her bed: the white underclothes, the pale pink silk dress with its draperies concealing the row of tiny buttons down the back, the 'Sam Browne' belt of deep pink velvet rosebuds, the long white kid gloves. On the floor were the silver 'Grecian' sandals with the criss-cross pink ribbons that tied at the knee. On the dressing table was the wreath of velvet rosebuds – matching those on the belt – which she would wear in her hair.

Yes, the clothes were pretty. But weren't they, in a way,

too pretty? Pink was a colour she had always thought
insipid. She would have liked to wear brown – the colour
of her eyes – but of course brown was unthinkable for a
debutante's dress. And Aunt Louisa had been absolutely
set on prettiness. 'Something *soft*. We want a *soft* effect,'
she kept saying to the dressmaker. Henrietta felt that she
wasn't 'soft', so what was the point of trying to make her
look it – but she had known that it would have been useless
to argue with Aunt Louisa.

She liked the silver sandals, although, when she had tried
them on, they had pinched a little. But Aunt Louisa had
said, 'Surely you don't need an even bigger size? Your feet
look quite large enough as it is.'

It was true that she usually wore a size 6, in contrast
to Julia's 3½. But after all, she was much taller than Julia.
Anyway, for better or worse, the sandals were 5½. It was
lucky, she decided, that when Aunt Louisa had forced her
to *change hands*, she hadn't also bound up her feet like a
Chinese girl's.

She put on the underclothes and the sandals, and then
sat in her dressing-gown, waiting for Collins, who was
attending to Julia, to arrive to do her hair and help her
into her dress.

Soon Collins came, bringing her tongs and little spirit
lamp. With the heated tongs, she waved Henrietta's hair,
arranged the two side curls on her cheeks, fastened it up at
the back with tortoiseshell combs. As she worked, she voiced
her usual protest: 'Your 'air's so '*eavy*, Miss 'enrietta.'

Now it was time for Collins to lower the dress over her
head, then kneel on the floor to do up all the tiny buttons.
And finally the 'Sam Browne' was draped over her right
shoulder and fastened round her waist, and the wreath
pressed down on her hair. Collins gave the side curls,
which formed a half circle on each of her cheeks, a last
little pat. She was ready. She stood looking at herself in
the cheval glass.

'Ever so nice you look, miss,' Collins declared.

'Thank you, Collins.'

'You do seem calm, miss,' Collins said. 'Now Miss Julia – she's ever so excited. She can't seem to stop talking. Oh she does look lovely!'

Studying herself in the glass, Henrietta decided that she didn't look too bad. The pink silk fell around her in becoming folds. However, despite the folds, and the flattening effect of her bust bodice, she felt that she still stuck out in front too much – how she envied Julia's flatness. But having her hair up drew attention to her eyes, and her hair shone almost like the black lacquer cabinet in the hall at Churston. She wasn't sure about the wreath, though. Didn't it look rather absurd, perched above her firm features? At that moment, the door opened. Behind her, reflected in the glass, stood Julia. *Nymph and statue.*

Julia sparkled. Points of light glittered in the blondness of her hair, in the pupils of her green eyes. White chiffon floated round her. She too wore a 'Sam Browne' and a wreath – of tiny lilies of the valley.

'Miss Julia, reelly, you look just like a fairy,' Collins exclaimed.

Julia giggled. 'I'm the queen of the fairies,' she said. 'But where is my wand, Collins? Where are my wings?' Collins laughed warmly, admiringly. Henrietta reflected that she could never have joked so naturally with her.

'You look very nice, Henrietta. Quite regal.' Julia's tone wasn't hostile, almost sounded friendly. (Was there to be a truce for tonight?) But Henrietta hated the word 'regal'. It made her sound old and stiff and boring. She managed to murmur, 'You look lovely, Julia.'

'I suppose we should be going downstairs soon,' Julia said. 'Shall we go and show Edmund how we look, first?'

Edmund had asked her to come to see him before she went down to dinner – she had never imagined that Julia would come to fetch her. Now, the thought of going to see him with Julia unnerved her – particularly as Julia looked so much prettier than she did. And she had planned to pretend that she was looking forward to the dance, after all – would she be able to carry that off under Julia's observant eye? But if she didn't go, Julia would go alone, and what might she say to Edmund about Henrietta's refusal to come? Besides, the prospect of going downstairs by herself intimidated her – Henry might be standing in the hall.

She said, 'Yes. What a good idea.'

As they approached Edmund's door, she hung back, letting Julia take the lead. Julia rapped on the door, and when Edmund called 'Come in', dramatically flung it open. *She* could never have done that, even in her new role as actress.

'Here we are, Edmund,' Julia said. 'Well, what do you think of us?' She pirouetted in the middle of the room.

Edmund was sitting up in bed, wearing his frogged jacket, his face lit by the bedside lamp. Now Julia posed on tiptoe, arms outstretched like a ballet dancer.

'Come in, Henrietta,' Edmund said. 'Why are you hanging about in the doorway? I can't see you properly.'

Hesitantly she came forward. Edmund looked from her to Julia, from Julia back to her.

'The rose and the lily,' he said. 'Oh, you will be the belles of the ball, I'm quite sure.' Was there a hint of mockery in his tone?

Julia perched on Edmund's writing-table, swinging her tiny feet in their gold sandals. Henrietta moved nearer to the bed.

'Well Henrietta,' he said, 'you must promise me to have a wonderful time.'

She said – she couldn't resist it – 'You're always asking me to promise things.'

He smiled. 'And you keep your promises. I know that. So if you promise to have a wonderful evening, I'm sure you will.'

'Oh, I'm sure I shall anyway,' she said.

He raised his eyebrows, 'I'm delighted to hear it. Henrietta, you are looking beautiful. There's just one thing. Stoop down, would you?'

It was unimaginable that he could want to kiss her. She bent her head towards him, and lightly he lifted the wreath from her hair. She raised her head.

'Yes,' he said. 'Perfect now. I herewith confiscate the wreath.'

'But what will Aunt Louisa say?'

'If she asks, tell her that I am responsible. Tell her that I dragged it forcibly from your head.'

'Ruskin wouldn't – couldn't – fuck her,
So Effie smothered Millais' art,'

Julia's clear little voice made Henrietta turn abruptly. Sitting on the table, swinging her legs forward and back, Julia was reading aloud from Edmund's black notebook. Now she looked up. 'What does it mean, Edmund?' she asked. 'What does "fuck" mean, for one thing?'

Edmund moved so violently, that Henrietta thought he was going to topple forward. She put her hands on his shoulders, and he sank back, but his face was furious. He shouted, 'Leave my bloody things alone, Julia. How *dare* you.'

Henrietta's and Julia's eyes met. Julia was looking as shocked as Henrietta felt. She had never heard Edmund shout – or *swear* like that – before.

Julia closed the notebook, put it down, slid hastily from the table.

'I'm awfully sorry, Edmund,' she said. 'I'd no idea I was doing anything so dreadful.'

Edmund was seized by a fit of coughing. At last, hoarsely, he said, 'Some water, Henrietta.'

She hurried to the table by the window where a tray with water and glasses stood. She snatched the beaded cover from the water-jug, hastily filled a glass and took it to him. He gulped from it, coughed again, then sipped a little more. He handed the glass back to her, rested his head on the pillow, and closed his eyes. Julia was looking horrified.

'I'm awfully sorry,' she repeated.

Edmund opened his eyes. With an obvious effort, he smiled.

'Don't let me spoil your evening,' he said. 'It's all right. I'm sorry I was so – ratty.' The word sounded forced to Henrietta – Edmund hardly ever used slang. 'It's just that my notebook is private,' he said. 'I'm probably too sensitive about it.'

'Oh, no, no. I quite understand,' Julia said, nodding nervously. Henrietta had never seen her so much at a loss.

'You must run along now,' he said. 'Go and enjoy your party.'

With alacrity, Julia headed for the door. Henrietta lingered. 'I could come up later,' she said, but he shook his head.

'Not tonight, Henrietta,' he said. 'I'm really very tired. I need to be alone. You can tell me all about it in the morning.'

Just because he was annoyed with Julia. How spiteful of him, she thought. *The best of friends*, indeed! He didn't sound friendly. But why should she care?

'Good-night, Edmund. Sleep well,' Julia called from the doorway.

'Good-night, Julia. Good-night, Henrietta.' How remote he sounded. Hateful! 'Good-night,' she said, following Julia through the door. Turning to close it, she saw him pick up a book from the bedside table, without another glance at her.

'Goodness,' Julia said in the corridor, 'what a fuss!' She was recovering her spirits, Henrietta saw. 'I still wonder what "fuck" means,' she went on, 'but we'd better not ask anyone. It's probably something dreadful.'

*　　*　　*

They were in the drawing-room. All the people who had
been asked to dinner before the dance had arrived.

Henry was standing near the fireplace, talking to Aunt
Louisa's great friend, Lady Revelston, the one who had
said Edmund was good-looking, and who was considered
such a 'great beauty'.

Henrietta could see that she must have been pretty once,
but really it was ridiculous to call someone of that age a
beauty. Why, she must be at least fifty. However, Henry
seemed to be enjoying himself, talking to her. Though it
was she who was doing most of the talking – smiling,
casting upward glances at him, rattling away in the style
of all Aunt Louisa's friends. It was amazing the way they
could keep it up; they never said anything interesting. All
they did was *relever* and *spangle*. Henry and Lady Revelston
looked as if they were spangling. She decided that Henry had
probably spangled with everyone. *She* would never spangle
with anyone, she decided, though Julia did it all the time.
It was a certain way of laughing and talking and, especially,
of looking at someone. *Stupid* she thought, and dragged her
eyes away from Henry and Lady Revelston.

Julia was chattering away to two young men with mous-
taches, obviously on leave. Henrietta, alone, was rescued by
Uncle Harry.

'Ah Henrietta, you look perfectly charming. Roses, roses
all the way – what?' Then he said, in what was, for him, a
low voice, 'So very glad everythin' has worked out so well.
Feel I've got a second daughter.'

Dear Uncle Harry – he sounded as though he really meant
it, though she had never, for a moment, thought of him as a
second father.

Hobart was announcing dinner. She was taken in by one
of the two young men who had been talking to Julia. Piers
Alverley his name was. He seemed very supercilious, and
was difficult to make conversation with. His eyes restlessly
roamed the table. On her left was a friend of Uncle Harry's

– very deaf, which also made conversation hard. Henry was on the other side of the table, not quite opposite her, between Lady Revelston and a pretty friend of Julia's called Anthea.

Courses came and went; a series of glasses was filled. Julia and Henrietta had been told that they could each have one glass of champagne. She drank hers too fast. The pricking of the bubbles reminded her of that evening with Henry at Churston. She glanced across the table at him, and he gave her a little private smile. Was he thinking of the same thing? She looked hastily away.

A footman refilled her glass. She cast a swift glance at Aunt Louisa – she seemed wholly occupied with the perennial Sir Richard. She drank the second glass but made it last longer. The first one had given her a slightly light-headed feeling.

At the time, under the stilted conversation with her neighbours, Edmund's refusal to let her visit him later nagged at her mind. Of course, it was Julia's fault. What did 'fuck' mean? she wondered. Ruskin and Effie his wife, who had later married the painter Millais – she knew who *they* were, but that didn't help her to understand the lines any better.

Even though it had been Julia's fault, she couldn't help feeling just a tiny bit annoyed with – no, disappointed in Edmund. She had been relying on a little break from the dance in his company to get her through the evening. Surely he might have guessed that, might have made just a small effort for his 'best friend'? As she finished the second glass of champagne, Aunt Louisa rose, the blessed signal for the ladies to leave the gentlemen to their port.

As the orchestra struck up in the ballroom, she worked out that about a third of her dances were booked. That had been largely Uncle Harry's work; he had brought a stream of young men up to her, and almost every one of them had

asked her for a dance. No one had asked her yet for the
supper dances, though. She hoped that someone would.
She was feeling intensely nervous; she suddenly became
aware that she was fastening and unfastening the buttons
on her long white gloves.

Aunt Louisa hadn't taken any notice of her, except
for a distant nod when she came downstairs. She hadn't
introduced anyone to her. She had left her to 'sink or
swim' in this alarming sea. And Henry hadn't asked her
for a dance.

In the ballroom, all the girls were clustered near the door.
Though they exchanged remarks with each other, it was
obvious that their minds were elsewhere, firmly fixed on the
young men who circled around them. Bees seeking honey,
she thought – and as far as they were concerned, Julia was
the sweetest of all the honeyed girls. She was surrounded.
What was it about her that all these young men found so
attractive? She was very pretty, but no prettier than other
girls who didn't seem to be nearly so much in demand.

Henrietta's first partner came up to claim her. He was very
young, and the monocle he wore, probably to make him look
older, she thought, just made him look silly. One thing about
dancing was that one didn't have to talk. Or should one? she
wondered, as Julia whirled past her, chattering animatedly.
Really, this young man – she couldn't remember his name
– was very clumsy; he had trodden on her toes twice. How
hot his hands were, too. She could feel their hot dampness
through two pairs of gloves, his and her own.

The dance ended, and he took her back to the group of
girls by the door. She had no partner for the second dance
– a quadrille. It seemed to her, as the dance started, that all
the other girls standing by the door were plain. Surely she
didn't look as bad as they did? They had spots, or peered
short-sightedly, or were fat and gangling. She felt as though
their unattractiveness were brushing off on her, as though
a damp fog which they exuded was enfolding her.

She saw Henry, dancing with a very beautiful dark girl, and stepped back a little, possessed by a sudden intense desire that he should not see her drooping among the 'wallflowers'. He was flushed, talking loudly; she could distinguish his voice on the other side of the room, above the band. Now he was coming nearer. *He mustn't see her.* Murmuring 'Excuse me', she pushed through the crowd of girls, slipped into the hall, and hurried upstairs to the first-floor landing where she waited until the music stopped. Then she came down. The young man who had taken her in to dinner had booked this third dance.

In the ballroom, the music started up again, and still he hadn't appeared. *Where was he?* She cast a desperate glance around the room, and saw him at once, down at the other end, waltzing with Julia. Had he muddled the dances? She was certain that *she* hadn't. She was sure that he had said the third.

It was Uncle Harry who saved her. Up he came, red-faced, smiling his jovial smile.

'No partner for this one? Don't know what's the matter with these young fellers. Would you take a turn with me?'

Gratefully, she said, 'I'd love to.'

Round and round they went; she held firmly to his bulky form. There was something comforting about its solidity.

"fraid I don't reverse,' he said. 'Hope you won't get dizzy.' Round and round and round they went. She did feel a bit dizzy when the music stopped.

Back by the door, Uncle Harry – a little short of breath – about to leave her, suddenly they were joined by Henry.

'Father! Can't have you monopolizing all the beautiful girls. Henrietta, have you got a dance left for me?'

'Yes,' she said. She realized that she, too, was a little breathless. 'Yes, I think so, Henry.'

'That's right my boy.' Off Uncle Harry ambled.

'You're prettier than ever, Henrietta,' Henry said. 'Each time I see you, I'm astonished.' He was slurring his words a little, in a way she had never heard him do before, and how flushed he was. The flush on his cheeks and the brightness of his eyes brought his face to life. He really was quite handsome.

'Not this dance, I think,' he said. 'Don't really feel like the Lancers. They always make a mess of it, anyway, except at Court. Next one's a waltz. Are you free for that?'

She felt a little humiliated at having to say 'Yes', but it would have been silly not to. She added, 'I thought you would have booked up all your dances by now.'

'Never do. Don't like running about like a hen. Prefer to take things as they come. If you book yourself up, suddenly you find you've missed something ripping. Some lovely girl like you, Henrietta. Don't you feel that's a fearful mistake?'

'Oh yes,' she said, and laughed. 'Yes I do.' As she said it, she almost believed that it was by her choice that all *her* dances weren't booked.

Someone had already done something wrong in the Lancers. Confusion was spreading. 'You see,' he said, and they both laughed.

'Wouldn't you like some refreshment?' he said. 'Thirsty work, this. We've just got time.'

'That would be nice,' she said, thought she didn't really feel thirsty. He ushered her ahead of him along the passage to the marquee.

There were only a few people in there. It wasn't nearly time for supper which was being arranged on a long table at the end of the tent. A young man and a girl were engaged in earnest conversation at one of the tables which filled the body of the marquee. Four or five young men stood together at the bar, and one glum-looking older man a little apart from them.

'Nice and peaceful in here now,' Henry said. 'Frightful crush there'll be later. Hardly ever eat supper myself. Food's always the same. Soup, quail, chaudfroids – I'm sure the caterers take those chaudfroids from one dance to another – lobster, strawberries, ices. You'd think they'd have something different sometimes, wouldn't you?'

Henrietta nodded solemnly, though she found it hard to imagine that one could ever get tired of lobster and strawberries.

A waiter had come up to their table. 'What would you like?' Henry asked her. 'There's champagne, there's cup – I don't advise that; it's always dashed insipid – and lemonade.'

'Oh, lemonade please,' she said.

'Nonsense. Come on. Have a glass of champagne with me. We must celebrate. Your first dance, and all that. Launched on society, don't you know. Ships are always launched with a bottle of champagne.'

She smiled. 'I don't know what Aunt Louisa would say.'

'What the eye doesn't see . . .' She couldn't help imagining how Edmund would comment on Henry's conversation. Defiantly, she put the thought out of her mind. She was *enjoying* herself.

She sipped her champagne, but Henry drank his quickly, and then had another glass. The music of the Lancers was coming to an end.

'Probably all finish up in a heap on the floor,' Henry said. She felt wonderfully happy and free. Her usual stiffness and shyness weren't troubling her at all. *What fun I'm having!* In her mind, she spoke the words to Edmund.

'Well,' Henry said, 'madam, will you waltz with me?'

As they went up the three steps into the house, he stumbled, and put his hand on her arm to steady himself. What was it going to be like dancing with him? Part of her positively longed for it.

Round and round they went – as she and Uncle Harry had done, but how different it was. He held her so tightly that her waist was bent back over his arm. Unlike Uncle

Harry, Henry did reverse – holding her tighter still. She could understand why, until recently, reversing had been considered 'fast'.

He was a very good dancer. Her own body seemed to float; she was in a daze. How bright the lights were, and the music swooped like a bird. Edmund crossed her mind. *Serve him right*, she thought, but didn't work out what she meant by it.

The waltz was coming to an end. As it did so, again he stumbled. Odd, when he had been dancing so beautifully.

'Oops,' he said. And then, 'Well, alas we can't dance together all evening. Much as I'd like it. But think of the steely eyes that would be fixed on us. That would never do. But I hope you'll dance with me again, later.'

'Mmm,' she said, wishing that he would book the dance now. But he was leaving her by the door.

This time, her partner did turn up. As they danced – he wasn't nearly such a good dancer as Henry – they exchanged remarks about the band and the weather. *I hope you'll dance with me again, later*.

She was worried that, although she was engaged for the rest of the dances in the first half, and again for some at the end of the evening, there was a terrible gap in the middle, around the supper dances – seven or eight dances were free, in fact. What was she going to do then? She couldn't hang about, waiting for Henry to ask her to dance – the thought of his seeing her among the wallflowers was awful. It would be better to slip away for the whole series of dances that was unbooked.

What she would have done, of course, if it hadn't been for what had happened earlier, was to visit Edmund. And that, she suddenly decided, was what she would do anyway.

Yes, she would sweep into his room, smiling. She would laugh and chatter. He was probably in a better temper now, and would actually be glad to see her. There was a curious fascination in the idea of going to visit him, still stirred by the feelings which Henry so inexplicably aroused in her. Inexplicably – for surely her view of him *as a person* hadn't changed? 'Ideally stupid.' That was what was so puzzling.

One partner succeeded another. She circled and bobbed and marched, round and round, up and down. The last dance that she had booked in the first half was a gallop, her partner a middle-aged colonel introduced to her by Sir Harry. Up and down the ballroom they raced – she couldn't help being captured by the speed and vigour of the dance. The other dancers, she noticed, were all flushed and bright-eyed – even old men with orders clanking on their chests, and dowagers with tiaras askew.

Henry and Julia, she saw, were dancing together, and laughing. Both so good-looking, and yet not in the least alike.

The dance was over. Her partner thanking her. People were starting to leave the ballroom for supper. She merged with the crowd. But when it continued down the passage to the marquee, she moved quickly across the hall, glancing around. No Julia, no Aunt Louisa in sight. She ran up the stairs, and then hurried along the corridor, with its closed bedroom doors to Edmund's room.

She bent down. A line of light showed under the door. So he was almost certainly awake. At that moment, a waltz, the first of the supper dances, started. It sounded very loud. Surely he couldn't be asleep.

She tried to rap on the door as imperiously as Julia had.

'Come in.'

He was reading. As she closed the door behind her, he put the book down, open, on his knees. He frowned.

'So it's you,' he said.

Standing erect, a fixed smile on her face, suddenly she was conscious of her face, flushed from the gallop. Her hair was probably untidy, too. She couldn't help patting it nervously.

'More a peony than a rose, now,' he said, and didn't sound as though he approved of the transformation. 'Have you been enjoying yourself?' he asked in a cool, polite tone.

'Oh, tremendously,' she said. 'But I thought I'd just drop in and see how you were.'

'In the peace of my monastic cell,' he said. Really, he sounded quite different from how he usually did. 'You know, Henrietta,' he went on, 'I did ask you not to bother me, this evening.'

It took a moment for the words to sink in. Then her heart started to thump. As tears came rushing into her eyes, she turned, pulled open the door, dashed out into the loudness of the waltz music. As she shut the door, the tears poured down.

This was even worse – well, as bad as – *that look*. How she hated him. Why was she crying? She must go upstairs to her room, calm down, wash her face, wait until it was time for her to return to the dance. She almost ran along the passage. A door opened. Then a hand caught her by the arm.

'Why, Henrietta,' Henry exclaimed – for it was Henry, the last person she would have wanted to see her like this – 'you're crying. What's the matter?' And without waiting for an answer, he pulled her into his room, and closed the door.

Her first feeling was one of absolute shock at being alone with a man, in his bedroom. Something quite unimaginable, except, of course, in the case of Edmund, who was ill.

'I must go,' she said.

'Hush. Who's been making you cry? Tell me, and I'll go and knock him down. If it's a girl, it may be more difficult.' He was smiling. He put a finger under her chin, and tilted it up, though she tried to turn her head away.

'Pretty, pretty Henrietta,' he said. 'Pretty even in tears. Most women look like "H" when they've been crying. All red and swollen.'

It sounded, she thought, as though he had seen a lot of women cry. She moved her head, glanced around the room, saw the turned-down bed, ivory and silver things on the dressing-table, an open flask and a glass on a table. He slid his arms around her, and began to kiss her. He smelt of something strong to drink.

The kisses went on for a long time. They were very soft, warm, moist. They made her feel far more limp and dazed than the waltz had. She ought to stop them, she knew, but somehow she couldn't summon the will to do so. She wanted them to go on and on. By the time he drew her over to the bed, first gently tugging at her hand, and then moving behind her, pressing more kisses all over the back of her neck, she was completely lost, enthralled.

He was so very gentle. Surely it couldn't be wrong? The long gentle kisses, the hand that moved gently over her, that later, still so gently, undid the buttons down the back of her dress. The expression on his face was so quiet and serious – not at all frightening. The pupils of his eyes were enormous. His mouth had a soft swollen look.

When he had taken all of her clothes off, she felt a moment's panic. *Edmund* – his name, his face, flashed through her mind, then vanished. But now the hands, the lips felt immeasurably more exciting. Gently they lulled her into a shivering, longing passivity.

His weight on top of her felt wonderful. But something very strange was happening; she couldn't understand it at all. Slow movements. Now it was hurting. 'Stop,' she called out. There was a sudden piercing pain which made her gasp. 'Sorry about that, darling girl, very sorry,' he murmured. More slow movements, and then an extraordinary involuntary contraction of pleasure. It frightened her. She heard herself groan. 'Wonderful girl,' he was saying. 'Knew you'd be wonderful.'

A silence, a stillness; his weight removed. Now panic was overwhelming; there was nothing else. She sat up. He was lying on his side, turned away from her. His eyes were shut. A sudden snore came from his lips, a little whistling sound.

She seized his shoulder, shook it. Downstairs they were playing a polka, and she didn't know how many dances had passed.

'Henry, Henry.' She shook his shoulder more vigorously. He gave a grunt, started up into a sitting position, stared around. As his eyes lighted on her – she pulled the sheet up in an instinctive movement – he said 'My God.' Then he gave a sort of groan, turned over, rested his head on the pillow again.

'Henry, you mustn't fall asleep. We've got to go back to the dance now. We've *got* to.'

Slowly, he sat up again. 'Yes,' he said in a dull voice. 'Yes, of course we must.'

He sprang out of bed then, and at once started to dress, turning his back to her. As she got up, she saw there was blood on the bottom sheet. It must be hers. It couldn't be the blood that came every month – that had appeared only last week. No, this must have happened when she felt that pain.

Anyway, the bleeding seemed to have stopped now.

Dressing was extraordinarily difficult. Her fingers shook, and things were hard to fasten. Henry was dressed long before she was. He brushed his hair with a pair of ivory brushes, one in each hand. Then he poured himself a big brown drink from the flask on the table, gulped it down. She had to ask him to fasten the little buttons down the back of her dress. Apart from that, neither of them spoke a word.

In front of the mirror, she wrestled with her hair. She thought she would never get it up properly, but at last the combs were somehow in place, the two side curls – though how limp they looked – were dragged forward on to her cheeks. It didn't look as it had when Collins had done it, but it would probably pass. After all, dancing gallops and polkas would have been bound to disarrange it to some degree.

She was ready.

'Right,' Henry said briskly. 'I'll go into the corridor and reconnoitre. If it's all clear, you can go downstairs. I'll follow in a few minutes.'

She went after him to the door, hung back as he stepped out and glanced from one side to the other. *Edmund* - face and name again. A strange feeling of triumph.

'Right,' Henry repeated. Just as he ushered her into the passage, Julia appeared at the other end of it, at the top of the stairs. She saw them at once, stood quite still, staring at them emerging from Henry's room. Henrietta was possessed by a wild terror.

'Don't worry,' Henry muttered in her ear. 'I can handle Julia. Off you go.' As she set off, he called softly: 'Julia!'

How long the corridor seemed with Julia slowly moving towards her. When she passed Julia, she couldn't look at her. When she reached the stairs, she didn't glance back, went straight down. The music wasn't playing. She wondered what stage the dance had reached.

A young man was standing at the bottom of the stairs. 'Ah, Miss Purvis,' he said. 'Just in time. I've been looking for you for our dance.'

As they went into the ballroom together, the band struck up. Another waltz. She felt like a clockwork toy, a dancer she had once seen revolving on the lid of a musical box. Round and round and round.

She didn't know how she got through the rest of the evening. All she knew was that she had to *stick it out*.

After the waltz, when she was waiting for her next partner, Aunt Louisa – passing with Sir Richard – gave her a sharp glance. 'I wondered where you were, Henrietta. I didn't see you for quite a long time. Visiting Edmund, I suppose?' she said with her sweet-sour smile – sweetness on the surface, sourness underneath.

Henrietta nodded, and they passed on.

Henry seemed to be everywhere: waltzing, galloping, talking and laughing loudly with a succession of partners. He had said that he wanted to dance with her again later, but she was quite certain that he wouldn't – *now*.

At least she didn't have to stand with the wallflowers. An earnest young man, dark and stocky, and wearing thick spectacles, called James Lecksley, attached himself to her, begging for any dances that she still had free. So she gave him all that there were.

They sat out most of them. 'I'm afraid I'm not much of a dancer,' he said – and he was right. He took her to the marquee where they both drank lemonade, and she had an ice. He told her all about himself and his plans. He was going into politics, standing as a Liberal candidate. He hadn't been able to join up, because of his eyesight – without his glasses, he was almost blind.

It was ideal. All she had to do was to nod and to produce an occasional query. On and on he talked, chiefly about the Irish question, about which she knew nothing, and which didn't interest her at all. Her attention always wandered when people talked about Ireland.

But at last, it ended. The band played *God Save the King*. The guests put on their coats and wraps and hats and scarves, and went out to their motors and carriages. She stood in the hall, with Aunt Louisa and Uncle Harry, and Henry and Julia, in a line, saying goodbye to what seemed to be an endless stream of people whose faces were red and shiny in the light from the chandelier. At last, Hobart closed the door on the last of them.

'Well gels, enjoyed yourselves?' Uncle Harry asked, looking from Julia to Henrietta.

'Yes, very much,' Henrietta murmured.

'It was simply wonderful, Papa,' said Julia. Extraordinary Julia – she still looked fresh and radiant, hair perfectly in place.

'Why, Henrietta,' Uncle Harry said, 'how tired yer looking. Yer so pale.'

She could feel all their eyes turning towards her. She avoided even a glance at Henry, met Julia's icy stare, and looked away.

'I – I am a bit tired. I've got rather a headache,' she said.

Uncle Harry patted her arm. 'Too much excitement,' he said. 'Why don't you run off to bed? Feel like turnin' in meself.'

'Perhaps I should. Thank you very much, Uncle Harry and Aunt Louisa, for the lovely dance. Good-night.'

Uncle Harry kissed her cheek. Must she kiss Aunt Louisa? She and Aunt Louisa hardly ever kissed each other.

No. 'Good-night, Henrietta,' Aunt Louisa said, going down the passage to the marquee, where Hobart was supervising the departure of the caterers.

Quickly, without looking at Henry or Julia, Henrietta went up the stairs.

In her room at last, the door closed, she sat down on the stool in front of her dressing-table. She realized that her feet, in the tight sandals, were hurting, undid the pink ribbons, and put on her slippers. Staring at her face in the mirror – Uncle Harry had been right; her eyes looked like dark hollows in its whiteness – she unbuttoned her gloves, pulled them off, dropped them on the dressing-table. She raised her hands to her cheeks, and pressed her palms against them. Although she was so pale, her face felt hot. The headache she had spoken of to Uncle Harry had just been an excuse for getting away, but a real one was beginning now. There was a throbbing over her left eye.

She found a *cachet faivre* in her dressing-table drawer, went over to the washstand and poured out some water to swallow it with. Then she poured water into the washbasin. She rested her hands, which felt sticky and constricted, in the basin. Then she splashed water over her face, dried her hands, and returned to the dressing-table.

Collins would be coming soon to help her to undress. She must take down her hair first – for Collins might notice that it had been put up by unskilled hands. She pulled out the tortoiseshell combs, feeling a sense of relief as her hair flopped down around her shoulders.

There was a tap at the door. 'Come in,' she called, standing up. Her mind was moving quickly. She didn't want Collins to undress her. There might be blood on her clothes.

As Collins came in, she said, 'Oh, hullo Collins. If you'll just undo my buttons, I'll undress myself. You look tired,' she added, and it was true that Collins's eyes were shadowed. It must be tiring, she thought now, with a feeling of surprise – for it had never occurred to her before – to have to sit up so late just to help her and Julia to undress.

'Why, that's all right, Miss 'enrietta.' Collins's smile had more warmth in it than usual.

'No,' Henrietta said, 'I insist.'

'Wouldn't you even like me to brush your 'air for you?'

'No, I'll do it myself. I'd like to. Just unfasten my buttons please.'

Collins was kneeling down behind her now, putting the draperies aside. 'Why, miss,' she suddenly exclaimed, 'two of them 'ave come undone, and one's fastened in the wrong loop. I can't understand it, 'aving done them up so careful, and the dress fitting so nice.'

'Oh,' Henrietta said, 'oh yes. I felt one come undone when I was dancing. A least I thought it was one, but it must have been two. Of course I couldn't see when I fastened it myself.'

'Don't know 'ow you managed to do it at all. You should 'ave come and found me, miss.' She had finished undoing the buttons. 'Can't understand it,' she repeated, 'the dress fitting, as you might say, like a glove.'

'Well, thank you very much, Collins,' Henrietta said. 'Goodnight.'

'If you're quite sure, miss. Did you enjoy the party, miss?'

'Oh yes, very much.'

'You do look tired, miss, and I think Miss Julia must be tired too. I've never known 'er so quiet.'

'Oh, really.'

'Well 'ave a good night's sleep, miss.'

'Yes, I'm sure I shall.' And, at last, Collins was gone.

She stepped out of her dress, and hung it over the back of a chair. In her petticoat, she sat down again at the dressing-table, picked up her brush, and started to brush her hair with long slow strokes. She couldn't put off *having to think* for another moment. Now, the thoughts came flooding in.

The very worst thing, of course, was that she didn't love Henry. Oughtn't she to love Henry now? But she didn't. And so – what explanation was there for what she had done? Did Henry love her? Surely he must. And yet, he hadn't said so – neither of them had said a word about love. She was sure, quite sure, that she didn't feel for Henry what she had felt for Edmund – before *that look*.

It was really Edmund's fault, of course. If he hadn't been so cruel, it would never have happened. She wondered momentarily how, when she saw him the next day – if she saw him – she would feel, how exactly she would face him. And how would she ever be able to face Henry?

Oh, if it had happened with Edmund – *before* – she was sure she wouldn't be feeling so awful. Vaguely through her mind drifted the thought that perhaps what Henry had done was something Edmund couldn't do because he was ill. But that wouldn't have made him look at her with disgust, with revulsion. Then, her next thought – and she heard her own quivering intake of break was that what Henry had done was what made women have children. Was it possible that *she* might have a child, even though she wasn't married? How did one know if one was going to have a baby? She had no idea, and she couldn't think how to find out.

Her arm was becoming tired. She put down the hairbrush. She felt utterly exhausted. Resting both hands on the dressing-table, she levered herself up. She stepped out of her petticoat. Undressed, she found one small bloodstain. Carefully, with her nailbrush, she scrubbed it out. It would be dry by morning. What would Henry do about the blood on his sheet? But she couldn't worry about that.

She put on her white nightdress with its *broderie anglaise* trimmings. She turned off the light by the door, and got into bed.

Almost at once, a feeling of physical content crept over her. She ached a little, but her body felt so slow, so warm – in such extraordinary contrast to her mind. But now that seemed to be slowing down, too. The *cachet faivre* had got rid of the headache, thank goodness. She gave an enormous yawn, and closed her eyes.

She was awakened by a sharp little tap at her door. She sat up, called 'Come in', but no one answered. She felt as if she had only just gone to sleep. Then 'Oh!' she exclaimed aloud.

Her eyes had a dry hot feeling inside them. A faint light was seeping in through the curtains. Who could have knocked? Whoever it was must have gone away again. Perhaps it had been one of the maids who had forgotten that she and Julia were to sleep late, and to have breakfast in bed, as a special treat. She had never had breakfast in bed before, except when she had been ill.

Slowly, she got up, went over to the window and drew back the curtains, smelling London air. It was very early in the morning, she was sure. The misty square was absolutely silent. There wasn't even the clang of the milkman's churns.

She went over to the dressing-table, where she had left her watch when she dressed for the dance. Only half-past five. Who *could* it have been?

Her mind was working very slowly this morning. Perhaps whoever it was – *Henry?* – was waiting in the passage. She turned towards the door, saw a white envelope, lying just inside on the carpet.

She hurried over, and picked it up. There was nothing written on the outside. Tearing it open, she carried it over to the window. Inside was a single sheet of paper.

Dear Henrietta,

I cannot tell you how sorry I am about my appalling, dishonourable behaviour last night.

I will not ask you to forgive me, because I am sure that is impossible.

I cannot offer any excuse except that I had too much to drink.

I think it is best that I should go away at once, and give you a chance to forget, if not to forgive. Accordingly, I am leaving a note for my parents, telling them that I have been called back to my regiment. I have asked Hobart, who I can trust, to say there was a telephone call.

Anyway, I would have been returning to the Front in three days' time. I will spend them somewhere where I know no one.

Again my sincere apologies,

Henry.

P.S. Julia will say nothing.
P.P.S. In the case of any *consequences*, let me know at once.

As she read, she felt a blush rising up her neck, covering her face. *I cannot offer any excuse except that I had too much to drink.* She remembered the champagne, the flask in his room, the way he had stumbled and how loud his voice had been.

So what had happened had nothing to do with *her*. And, of course, absolutely nothing to do with love. The letter certainly confirmed that – so cold, so formal. What must he think of her? For *she* had no excuse at all. Obviously he couldn't bear the thought of seeing her. How he must despise her.

That postscript: 'In the case of any *consequences*, let me know at once.' He had underlined the word consequences three times. What he must mean was *if she found she was going to have a baby*. Though how would she know? If she started getting fat, she supposed. Girls weren't meant to notice that ladies who were going to have babies got fat, but of course they did notice – what fools grown-up people were. Though of course *she* was grown up now; she was out. But one wasn't really grown up until one was twenty-one.

So, if she started to get fat, she must write to Henry. That was what it amounted to. *I'd rather die*, she told herself. What would he do if she did write? Ask her to marry him? She couldn't help smiling when she thought of how Aunt Louisa would react to *that*. No, if it happened, she would run away. But where?

Anyway, what was the use of thinking about that now? She wouldn't. She would get back into bed – bed was always a refuge. But first she must get rid of the terrible letter. She read it again. Then she fetched the box of matches that stood on the rim of the candlestick on her bedside table. She and Julia did not have electric reading lamps, as reading in bed was considered 'bad for their eyes'. The candle was there in case the electricity should fail – which it did quite frequently.

She took the matches over to the fireplace. Holding the letter by one corner, over the grate, she lit the bottom of it, held it, burning, until the flame was near her fingers. Then she dropped it. When it was all ash, she pushed it to the back of the grate. Birds were twittering now in the square garden.

Back in bed, she wondered if she would be able to go to sleep again. Breakfast would not arrive until nine. She picked up *The Oxford Book of English Verse*. Edmund had given it to her. No, she didn't feel like reading. She yawned.

She was awakened by the maid with her breakfast tray. She ate the boiled egg and the toast, wishing there were more. She got up. She bathed and dressed. Although she had slept, she still had that dry hot feeling at the back of her eyes.

She wanted to get out of her room. Where should she go? Normally, at half past ten, she went to see Edmund. But she wouldn't do that today – not after how he had spoken to her last night. She could go up to the schoolroom, but Julia would probably be there. She remembered the icy stare that Julia had given her in the hall.

What she would have liked to do was go for a walk, but of course she wasn't allowed out alone, in London. She couldn't stay in her room. The maid would be coming to do it soon, and anyway she was full of an intolerable restlessness.

The schoolroom it would have to be then. After all, she would have to face Julia some time; there was really no point in putting it off. Anyway, perhaps Julia would be downstairs with Aunt Louisa, *relever*-ing about the dance.

Julia will say nothing. It must be true if Henry were so sure of it.

Julia, neat and fresh, was in the schoolroom, writing a letter. When Henrietta came in, she looked up. There was that Medusa stare again – Medusa with her snake hair, Julia with her slim snake neck.

'Good morning,' Henrietta said, but Julia didn't answer, went on with her letter. Well, she didn't care if Julia wouldn't speak to her. Really it was almost a relief – war between them was much more natural than yesterday evening's brief truce had been. All the same, the silence, this morning, got on her nerves. She couldn't concentrate on her book.

When Julia, having finished her letter, and put it in an envelope, left the room, she felt relieved of a weight of oppression. All the same, she still didn't feel like reading. She stood up, wandered over to the window. *How she wished she could draw*. A wave of hatred, for Aunt Louisa who had killed her drawing, for her enemy, Julia, for beastly Henry, most of all for Edmund – last night had been *his* fault – battered her, drowned her. She felt quite weak when it ebbed away. A knock on the schoolroom door made her start violently.

It was Sister. 'Mr Edmund's been wondering where you were. He's been expecting you.'

Indeed! 'Oh,' Henrietta said, and then, 'I'll come now.' She followed Sister down the stairs and along the corridor. Past Henry's room.

Sister never knocked on Edmund's door. Now she popped her head round it. 'Here's your young lady, Mr Edmund,' she said brightly. Then she went off down the corridor. *Your young lady*. Slowly, Henrietta entered the room.

'Come in, Henrietta. How are you? Come and sit down.'

She shut the door, moved towards him. How pale and fine he looked. Suddenly she felt that Henry was coarse – wooden featured, wooden minded. What would *that* have been like with Edmund? She tightened her lips.

'Stop staring at me in that intimidating way,' he said, and laughed. He beckoned. 'Come over here.'

Slowly she approached the bed. *The bed* – this must be how Eve had felt after she had eaten the apple.

He stretched out his hand, took hers, held it. How thin his fingers were.

'You're angry with me,' he said.

'Oh no,' she said in a bright voice. 'No, I'm not at all.'

'Of course you are, and quite rightly too. I was horrible

last night, positively boorish. I've been wondering why. I think that perhaps I was jealous of those young men you'd been dancing with, when I saw you all peony-flushed with pleasure.'

Now he was trying to *get round her*, as Nanny used to say. She shrugged. 'Oh, I wasn't enjoying myself all that much,' she said.

'Nonsense. I could see it in your glittering eye.'

'You make me sound like the Ancient Mariner.'

'You didn't *look* at all like the Ancient Mariner,' he said. He was joking, but there was an underlying anxiety in his tone, she thought. Could he possibly be jealous? That was a fascinating idea. She couldn't imagine anything she'd like better than to make him jealous.

'Why are you smiling in that Mona Lisa way, Henrietta?'

'I'm sure I wasn't,' she said, and now, of course, he changed the subject.

'So poor Henry has been called back after only one day,' he said. 'What bad luck.'

'Has he?' she said. 'I didn't know.'

'Yes, he stuck his head in here at some unearthly hour, to say goodbye. He was looking awful. He said he had a terrible head from too lavish potations.'

'Poor Henry.'

'You don't sound very sympathetic. But I wouldn't have thought that he would have got tight under the paternal roof. Was he behaving badly?'

'I didn't notice.'

'Oh well, then it can't have been too terrible. Goodness, this morning has been busy. First Henry, then one of my mother's surprise visits. She floated round the room, swathed in chiffon, talking about the dance. By the way, she managed to suggest that you had paid me too long a visit last night. "You must encourage Henrietta to mix with other young people more" – and all that. Of course I didn't say anything. But what were you doing?'

'Oh, I went up to my room for a bit.'

'Because I'd upset you. What a swine I am.'

'Of course you aren't. Don't be silly. How are you feeling this morning?'

'Not too bad. Had some pain in the night. Thought I'd got over that, but it's back again.'

⚜ Ten ⚜

The Season went on and on: dances, luncheon parties, theatre parties, garden parties. Everyone, in that summer of 1918, was sure that the War was nearly over, and they were so weary of it. The survivors, the young men who came home on leave, were men with charmed lives. They must be amused; they must be given a good time.

In public, Julia spoke to Henrietta when it was necessary. When they were alone, she resumed her cold silence. But they were hardly ever alone now. Julia was surrounded by admirers. Henrietta had one too.

James Lecksley, the young man in thick spectacles who had talked about Ireland, called at Belgrave Square, then called again. It was evident that Henrietta was the object of his visits. He sought her out at all the parties.

Aunt Louisa, inevitably, noticed, commented.

'Not *handsome*, of course,' she said, with one of her sharp glances at Henrietta, 'but quite eligible. A good solid county family. Mother middle-class, though. The daughter of a plantation owner in India, I believe – but a lot of money there. I hear he will be offered a safe seat. A pity, of course, that he's a Liberal. All right in the old Whig days, but now so terribly extreme. That dreadful man Lloyd George – I really can't understand why they have any respectable supporters at all.' She paused. 'I understand that Mr Lecksley is very clever.'

The kind of 'clever', Henrietta thought, of which Aunt Louisa could allow herself to approve. Winchester-clever. Prizes at school for writing Latin verses. A First in Greats. A devil possessed her.

'I think he's rather *carpet*,' she said.

Aunt Louisa drew in her breath. 'Are you trying to be impertinent, Henrietta?'

'Oh no, Aunt Louisa. I was just using one of your words,' she said innocently.

Aunt Louisa decided not to pursue it. 'Anyway,' she said, 'I think you are being very foolish. After all, beg—' she cut herself off, but Henrietta knew what she had been going to say, was aware, too, that Aunt Louisa had meant her to know. *Beggars can't be choosers.* An instant reprisal for that 'carpet'.

'I shall be most annoyed if you are rude to him,' Aunt Louisa went on. 'You should at least make an effort to get to know him better. It is very silly to be guided by first impressions.'

She said, 'Oh, I won't be *rude* to him, Aunt Louisa.'

She wasn't, though not because of what Aunt Louisa had said. The truth was that James Lecksley was becoming useful to her. He was always there. At dances, she never had to fear being a wallflower, which she felt she might otherwise have done. For the fact was – she had now, in the course of the Season, confirmed it again and again – that many girls who were less good-looking than she was were much more popular. It was as if she belonged to a different race from the people around her; she just couldn't pick up their language, their tone. She was also aware that she had a reputation for being – horror of horrors – 'brainy', a reputation which she suspected had been fostered by Julia.

With James Lecksley, she didn't have to worry. He wasn't really 'carpet'. He was actually rather sweet, although he was

so earnest and plain, and wore those awful thick glasses.
(Once he had taken them off, to wipe them, and she had
been oddly touched by the soft, naked look of his eyes.)
He was always telling her how intelligent she was, as if he
thought it was a wonderful thing to be. She didn't know why
he considered her so intelligent. When they were together, he
did practically all the talking. She suspected it was because
she had read all Trollope's novels, of which, unfashionably,
he was a great admirer.

Also, now that he was always hovering around, it eased
the pressure on her from Aunt Louisa, who seemed no longer
to object to her spending time with Edmund. One afternoon
when Mr Lecksley had been having tea at Belgrave Square
she said casually to Aunt Louisa, 'You know I've decided
that he's really very nice.' Aunt Louisa smiled at her with
something almost approaching friendliness.

'My mother tells me that you have an admirer,' Edmund
said one morning, 'and that he's very suitable. Do you agree
with her?'

She nearly said, 'What utter rubbish. I'm not in the
least interested in him,' but then she remembered about
making Edmund jealous. She shrugged. She said, 'Oh, he's
quite nice.'

'High praise indeed from you who are always so critical.
I must meet this paragon. Why don't you bring him up to
see me one day?'

Caught in her own trap! She could just imagine Edmund
with a detached expression, listening to Mr Lecksley droning
on about politics. Edmund, so pale, so fine; Mr Lecksley,
square, almost stout, with his thin dry hair and the thick
glasses. She couldn't restrain an involuntary exclamation
of 'Oh no!'

'How vehement you sound. You have aroused my curiosity. 'I *insist* on meeting him.'

How could she avoid arranging it? If only something could
happen to prevent it. Well, something did – that very night.

She wasn't allowed to see Edmund next morning. When she went down at ten o'clock, she met Sister in the passage. The doctor was with him. He had spent a feverish night in dreadful pain. Even morphia hadn't seemed to help.

Later in the day, the specialist came. When he left, Henrietta waylaid Sister again. 'Sir George is very worried about him,' Sister told her. Aunt Louisa came down the corridor, passed Henrietta without a glance, went into the forbidden room – forbidden to Henrietta, though not to her.

A visit to the theatre was cancelled. After dinner, Aunt Louisa made one of her little speeches. They must all offer special prayers for 'our dearest Edmund'.

Henrietta no longer carried on her old one-sided dialogues with God. Edmund did not believe in God, he had told her recently, and she had decided that she didn't either. So it was absurd, superstitious for her to feel that she might be punished for having thought that Edmund deserved to die. How? She didn't know. When she fell asleep that night, she dreamed the 'Mr Hyde' dream. But this time it was Edmund, not Julia, whom she felled and trampled. She woke trembling, soaked in perspiration.

That morning Edmund was better.

'He had rather a restless night,' Sister told her, 'but now he's sleeping like a baby. You might even be able to see him this afternoon. I'll let you know.'

In the afternoon – Edmund being so much better – Aunt Louisa and Julia went to a tea-party to which they had been invited. Determined not to go with them, Henrietta pleaded a headache.

She paced up and down the schoolroom. She would have liked to go downstairs, to stand in the corridor outside Edmund's room. But sister might not like that. She didn't want to offend Sister – and Sister had promised to let her know if she could see him.

Why did she want to see him? Did she really hate him?

She only had to summon up the memory of that look to know that the answer was still 'yes'. So why? She was feeling terribly, extraordinarily depressed. She sat down at the schoolroom table, rested her face on the worn cloth. At a tap on the door, eagerly she raised her head.

It was Sister, who was looking worried. 'Mr Edmund's asking for you,' she said. 'He's feverish again – of course the temperature always rises in the evening. But he's set on seeing you. You won't tire him, will you?'

'Oh no, I promise,' Henrietta said.

He was lying back on the pillows, not propped up as he usually was. There was a flush of colour on his cheekbones, but it didn't mean that he was well – she could see that. His eyes were closed.

He opened them. They were very bright. 'Henrietta,' he said, 'Henrietta, come and sit by me. Sister, will you leave us alone for just a little.'

'Very well then, Mr Edmund, but only for a few minutes.' She turned to Henrietta. 'I'll be just next door. Call me at once if there's any change. And remember, you promised not to tire him.'

Sister went through into the dressing-room, closed the door. Edmund stretched out his hand, patted the upright chair that stood just next to the bed. She sat down.

'Henrietta,' he said. 'There's something I want you to do for me.'

'Yes,' she said.

'When I die,' he said, and then, ' – don't interrupt me, please – when I die, I want you to destroy my notebook. The black one on the table. I got rid of the others ages ago – all those dreadful old poems of mine, and so on. But I thought I'd keep this one, just in case I recovered. Actually, I've had – a sort of superstition about it. Anyway, I want to be quite sure that, when I die, you'll take it away, without reading it, and destroy it.'

'But Edmund, you're not going to die,' she said.

He raised his hand. His fingers looked transparent.

'Hush,' he said, and smiled. 'This is a last request, Henrietta. Last requests can never be refused. Surely you know that it's against all the rules?' He went on; 'It's going to be what they call a merciful release. A release for me. Certainly a release for my parents' – a hint of bitterness in that. 'And,' he said, 'a release for you.'

'Oh no,' she said.

'Oh yes, Henrietta. It will be. You shouldn't be spending your youth sitting around with a hopeless invalid. My mother's right about that, right for once. Don't deceive yourself – you must never do that, Henrietta. It was your father who taught me that, when I took him my drawings, all those years ago. He made me recognize that they weren't any good, and I destroyed them. It's the same with that notebook, Henrietta. I don't want people pawing over my pathetic relics. And it would never do to upset my mother. It's for her own good that we shall deceive her. Besides, she's always been a liar, and liars deserve to be lied to.'

As he spoke, his voice had become lower, hoarser, until it was almost a whisper. Now a spasm twisted his body. His hands went down to clutch at his stomach as if he were holding it together.

'I'll call Sister.' She stood up.

'No,' he said. 'No, not yet.' His hands relaxed. Under the feverish flush, his skin was waxy yellow. 'First promise me to do what I ask you.'

She felt frozen. She forced herself to speak. 'I promise, Edmund.'

'That's all right then. I trust you. You're different from the others. All false except you. You're not false, are you?'

'No,' said her lips.

'Kiss me, Henrietta. Sounds like the death of Nelson. But at least it's a woman I'm asking. No women on the *Victory*, of course. Otherwise he'd probably have said, "Kiss me, Emma", instead of "Kiss me, Hardy". Some people say he said "Kismet", not "Kiss me", but that sounds damned unlikely to me. Anyway, I say "Kiss me".'

She stood up, bent over him. His breath had a terrible rotten smell. She tried not to breathe in as she kissed his lips.

'Henrietta,' he said loudly. She stepped back. He gave a shudder, and then was absolutely still.

'Edmund,' she said. 'Edmund?' His open eyes stared past her at the ceiling, but they didn't see it.

'Edmund!' she called out, and then, 'Oh, Sister!'

There was Sister, rushing in, running over to the bed, lifting his dead hands, then hurrying into the passage, calling to one of the servants. And Henrietta was over by the writing-table, had picked up the notebook, was holding it behind her when Sister came back into the room.

'No place for you, dear. Off you go.' Sister spoke to her, Henrietta thought, as if she were a child. Now Uncle Harry, a dazed look on his face, stood in the doorway. Slowly he approached the bed. He didn't even see Henrietta.

She must get away. Uncle Harry was bowed over Edmund's body. He was sobbing. With the book held at her side, her skirt pulled across to hide it, she hurried out of the room.

As, clutching the book, she went along the corridor – past Henry's door – what did she feel? At that moment, she felt nothing – nothing at all.

Days ruled by death. The funeral. The black clothes. Aunt Louisa talking about Edmund.

On the evening after his death, she had gathered them together in the drawing-room. She had said, 'We must all stay very close together, in this sad but beautiful time.' (*Beautiful*, what was *beautiful* about it?) She had gone on to speak of Edmund's courage, of his sense of duty, of his loyalty to King and Country. Julia and Uncle Harry had shed tears.

On the evening after the funeral, she said the same things over again. Then she read them a poem.

> *'The fighting man shall from the sun*
> *Take warmth, and life from the glowing earth;*
> *Speed with the light-foot winds to run,*
> *And with the trees a newer birth;*
> *And when his fighting shall be done,*
> *Great rest, and fulness after death.'*

On, remorselessly, went the clear voice with the quaver in it. *Like a bad soprano*, Henrietta thought.

> *'And when the burning moment breaks,*
> *And all things else are out of mind,*
> *The Joy of Battle only takes*
> *Him by the throat and makes him blind –*
>
> *Through joy and blindness, he shall know*
> *Not caring much to know, that still*
> *Nor lead nor steel shall reach him so*
> *That it be not the Destined Will.'*

Oh, she could just imagine what Edmund would have said about that. She could hear his very words, his voice: 'Barbaric sentiments expressed in appalling doggerel.'

> *'The thundering line of battle stands,*
> *And in the air Death moans and sings;*
> *And Day shall clasp him with strong hands,*
> *And Night shall fold him in soft wings.'*

As Aunt Louisa finished, Uncle Harry shifted in his chair. He cleared his throat. 'Dashed fine,' he said, and Julia nodded seriously.

Silence, a religious sort of silence, was broken by Aunt Louisa.

'Etty Desborough published that poem of Julian's in *The Times*, you know. I have been wondering what has happened to Edmund's writings. I believe he used to keep some sort of notebook. Who knows, there might be some good things in it. Poems, thoughts about the War, and so on. I have looked everywhere in his room. I can only suppose that he left it at Churston. I must search when we go down there next week. There might be material for a little memorial booklet perhaps.'

Julia said, 'But I'm sure it must be here. Why, I saw it on the night of our dance.'

'How perfectly extraordinary. Can one of the servants have moved it? Or that nurse? I had better ask Hobart to investigate at once.'

'I destroyed it,' Henrietta said.

Now they were all staring at her.

'You did *what?*' Aunt Louisa said.

Though she was frightened, at the same time she felt a sort of triumph. 'I destroyed it,' she said. 'The night Edmund died. Without reading it. He asked me to. He said it was his last request.'

'You asked nobody? You said nothing? You smuggled his notebook away and destroyed it, without even mentioning it to *his mother?*'

'He asked me to, Aunt Louisa.'

'How did you destroy it, pray?'

'I burnt it in my fireplace.'

'I see. You never paused to reflect that obviously he was not himself when he made this – request? Why, he was feverish. He was *dying*. I think that your behaviour was quite outrageous.'

'I promised him.'

'You cared nothing for the feelings of *his mother*, of his family. You've always been an interloper, an outsider—'

It was Uncle Harry who broke in. 'I say, steady now, my dear. She promised the boy. Had to keep a promise – of course she had. You're upset, Louisa, quite naturally, but don't yer know . . . really feel, really think that there's nothing more to be said.'

It was seldom that Uncle Harry expressed himself so decisively. No more was said. Aunt Louisa tightened her lips. Henrietta could feel waves of hatred lapping towards her from Aunt Louisa and Julia. Well, that was fair enough – how she hated them. Some lines of Browning's. *If hate killed men, Brother Lawrence, God's blood, would not mine kill you!*

What was it Edmund had said? *She's a liar and liars deserve to be lied to.* Aunt Louisa deserved to be lied to – and she had been. The notebook, carefully wrapped in paper, rested in a recess a little way up the chimney in Henrietta's bedroom. No one would find it there. The fire was never lit. The chimney sweep would not be coming till the autumn. She would take the book to Churston with her, and when she came back would find another hiding-place for it.

That night, as on every night since Edmund's death, she locked her bedroom door. She took the parcel from the chimney, and unwrapped it. In bed, she opened it, read its few pages once more.

Do other men, I wonder, sometimes feel, as I do, that none of this is real? The guns, the mud, the bodies in no-man's-land. I wake from a dream of Churston, of my mother, floating down the stairs in some preposterous chiffon tea-gown, and feel, here in the dark, smelly dugout, old Henwood coughing his rasping cigarette cough, that this is the dream. This *moves me* so much less. Its darkness is so much lighter than the darkness of the heart.

Last night, in my dream, I loved her – loved her as I used

to do when I was thirteen. In those days, I listened when she told me that I must always be clean and straight and true. 'Do noble deeds, not dream them all day long,' as she was fond of quoting. How I strove to be what she wanted. To play hard and work hard. Yes, I did well at school in those days, for she always made it clear that, as well as being clean and straight and true, it was important to be top. To win the prizes – and I did. What a little beast I must have been with my shining morning face and, behind it, one impulse pumping through my twisted brain: excel, excel, excel.

I did it all for her. How I adored her. One evening when she and Father were going to some great gathering, she came up to say goodnight to Henry and me, glittering in all her diamonds like the Snow Queen in Hans Andersen. As she bent over my bed to kiss me, I wanted to hold on to her in all her beauty and never let her go. (I flung my arms around her neck, and she said, 'Be careful of my hair.')

Rivalry, of course, was always present. How I longed to believe that she loved me more than Henry. I was the elder son, and undeniably the cleverer. But Henry was better at games. I won the prizes, but he won the cups. I headed the class, but he was captain of the team. In that sense, it was a draw, yet didn't I always fear that she loved Henry the better, for some quite other reason? Because he was, by nature, all those things that she told us we should be. Henry was utterly sincere about all that straightness and trueness, and I don't think I ever was. Henry always believed in *Jackanapes* and all those other books about little heroes. Even then, that sort of piety, that sort of patriotism made me want to blush, though I didn't understand why, and thought it was because of some streak of madness or badness in me. How I longed to be able to yield myself up to *Jackanapes!* Until – *the bolt from the blue*. Death to deceivers! The candle is guttering. My eyes ache. I must try to sleep.

* * *

I have felt, during this leave, so exhausted that practically all I have done is to sit in the library with little H. Hers is the only company I can tolerate. How fond of me she is. Too fond? But I needn't worry about that yet awhile. I must admit I enjoy my Mother's disgust at my spending so much time with my little cousin – whom, with her unerring bad taste, she has never liked – instead of escorting some stupid, simpering debutante. But she has given up pressing girls on me, thank God.

Last night, the irresistible compulsion came on me again. I told little H. that I was going out to meet an old Oxford friend and, after dinner, out I slunk.

Though the kisses of her bought red mouth were sweet. Well, they weren't sweet last night. Her breath reeked of gin I had bought her when I picked her up. A great brute of an Alsatian dog lay in the corner of the room, growling. Kept to protect her from her customers, I suppose. There were dog's hairs all over the blanket. It was soon over. As always, I spent before I could enter her. Just as well, bearing in mind the danger of disease. *The expense of spirit in a waste of shame.* Her neck was dirty – in fact she was altogether foul. But rather her than a 'good woman'. Better to pay for one's pleasure – if that's the word – with money than with one's life's blood.

Here, in the trenches, men form such intense friendships. Sentimental – and often something more, I know. But that has never tempted me. There is no strangeness in men and, without strangeness, what's to lure one? To lure and, of course, at the same time, to repel.

When I left, and little H. held up her lips to me, I could hardly bear to touch them, thinking of those other lips that mine had pressed so recently – though when I *kissed that one*, she turned her head away. I have noticed that *they* hate to kiss. Little H., on the other hand, was longing for me to kiss her. I suppose she will grow up to be just like the rest. A pity!

*   *   *

Most men are so damn matter-of-fact about things. They seem to be able to split their '*love*' – for want of a better word – into two quite separate compartments. There are the whores for fun (fun – my God!) and then there are the Young Ladies from whose number one is expected to select one's still unravished bride. A song I heard:

> *Little lady, I would love you, but alas I fear me,*
> *Every star that shines above you is about as near me.*
> *For your all-transcending beauty, chill as it is comely,*
> *Ties me to a mournful duty – just to worship dumbly.*

Yet they marry the 'little ladies' – and what then? Why then, they fuck them. And is *that* fun? Or does the bride 'lie still and think of England'? That's one school of thought – 'ladies don't move', as George Curzon is supposed to have said. Only the whores are believed to enjoy it – though I've seen no sign of that. Yet obviously some 'good women' have a taste for it. (*She* had/has . . . or *why else?*)

It is weeks since I last wrote in this notebook – no, not weeks, months. I doubt if, in hell, the impulse to write is very strong, and this war is hell – *nor am I out of it*. I've hardly been able to bring myself to pen the weekly bulletin to Father, but I have forced myself to do that. (Why? Have all those exhortations of Mother's about Duty lodged somewhere in the cellars of my brain?) I haven't been able to bring myself to write to little H. though I know I ought to. Her letters keep on coming. Last year, her artless effusions used to touch and amuse me, but now I can't respond to them at all. They're a babbling brook, and one can scarcely be expected to concentrate on a babbling brook when a tidal wave is breaking over one.

This morning, early, when I stuck my head out, a strange thing happened. It is only the beginning of March and, until now, the weather has been bitterly cold. Yet this morning, the air was the air of spring or even of early summer. There happened to be a pause in the firing, and the only sound I could hear was a bird singing. Suddenly I was back at Churston on that morning. The experience was so intense, so overwhelming that I wanted to write it down. Of course I couldn't do so then. I was on duty. But this evening the impulse persists.

I see myself, aged thirteen, woken that morning by the mixing bell. (I never knew, don't know now, why it's called that.) But every morning, at half past six, when we had house parties, a maid would go along the corridors, tinkling this little bell. Usually I slept through it. But not that morning. I jumped out of bed. Such a beautiful day that I thought I'd go out for a run in the park, on my own – Henry was fast asleep on the other side of the room. I got dressed quickly, and went down the back stairs, but I didn't want to bump into any of the servants who might ask me what I was doing up at that hour. So, when I reached the first floor, I decided I'd go along the main corridor, and down the stairs and out through the front door. I was tiptoeing along the corridor, when I saw my mother's door opening. I had just reached the little passage almost opposite her door which leads to the bathroom. Quickly I stepped into it, and pressed myself against the wall. I heard her door close, and then he came past me.

'Setty' – that beast, in his Afghan dressing-robe. Slinking off back to his own room.

I had always disliked him – been jealous of the way he hung around her. But I didn't think all that much about it. Until then. My brain was darting, whirring, like a bird trying to escape from a net. I wanted to escape, like the bird. I wanted not to understand, but it was no use. *I knew.* The fatal knowledge.

Julia was only four years old then. I had thought that it was rather jolly to have a sweet little baby sister. It wasn't for another two years that I understood about that. One day in the drawing-room after tea, she clambered on to Setty's lap, and I saw that she was what they call the spitting image of him. I've never cared for Julia since.

But – Father? Does he see? Can he be *so* stupid that he doesn't? He has never given a sign. And if he isn't so stupid, if he sees – then what? What does he *feel*? I shall never know. And Henry – does *he* guess? Indubitably, it's a subject he and I will never discuss.

It was the hypocrisy that, from the first moment when I knew, disgusted me as much as the thing itself – well, almost. Ugh, those *Edwardians*. Still spouting the Victorians' pious moral precepts: God, Duty, the whole paraphernalia. But not believing a word of it, not a word. Just living the form – with no trace of any quickening spirit.

The King is dead. Fat old Kingy, with his women and his greed, is dead. And very glad of it I am. His world, their world, is going, going, gone. This war will sweep away the last traces of it – and I say Thanks be to God – the God I don't believe in. The God that nobody is going to believe in any more.

They are all getting so old – however much they plaster themselves with paint. If Mother goes on layering it on as she does, one of these days her face will crack, and the worms will come crawling out from under the enamel. Imagine that at a tea-party! But I suppose everyone would pretend not to notice. Death to deceivers!

The mixing bell! It should have been called the un-mixing bell. (Ha-ha!) Ringing for one purpose – to get them out of each other's beds, and back into their own. In time for the tray of tea and thin bread and butter, the can of shaving water, the bath sprinkled with Hammam Bouquet, the ceremony of dressing. A Regie cigarette from a Fabergé case, and down to breakfast where perfect gentlemen bid good-morning to perfect ladies.

Did the servants know what the mixing bell was for? Surely they must have – and most of them good Christian souls! I can only suppose that they – honest Hobart, dear old Mrs Dowsett – believe the gentry are in some way above morality, not bound by the rules that fetter ordinary men. But can they really believe that? Surely, to some extent, they must be shocked, disillusioned. As they should be. Then, at least, 'their betters' won't be able to lie any more, won't be about to spout the Duty rot.

You see it in this war. Only the bad poetry is full of courage and glory. When little H. started spouting the rubbish of that idiot, Brooke – easy to guess that *he* had never seen a day's action – it was all I could do not to burst out in rage. But I was patient with her – she couldn't help it, having been fed with pap by people like Mother. *An old bitch gone in the teeth, a dead civilization* – I told H. to learn that instead. That is the message of all the good poetry this war has produced. There is no glory any more. Everyone knows that, in their hearts, except, I sometimes think, my brother Henry. (Henry would probably still be moved by *Jackanapes*.) No, the age of chivalry is dead, and the age of the poets that hymned it. From now on, a poem can be a laugh, a smile, a sneer, a tear, a fart. But never, never again a hymn to glory.

This is the first time I've written in this notebook since the shell exploded. The months at Churston, and now – back in Belgrave Square. I never thought I'd see this house again. I wouldn't have come here if it hadn't been for H. I was going to miss her so much. All the same, I nearly changed my mind. The poor sweet girl is – or thinks she is – in love with me. She obviously doesn't understand anything about what has happened to me – dear innocent that she really is. I really believe that she knows nothing of the act of love or why I shall never be able to perform it again.

And – if I could, what then? Would I want to do it with her, would I want to sully that purity which is, after all, what's so magical about her? Darling little H. It is probably as well that I shall never have to face that temptation. For, if I were able to yield to it, I know that everything would be spoilt between us. Spoilt, spoiled, dragged down in the dirt. But – to see her someone else's, sold on the marriage market, as she is sure to be, degraded! I don't think I could stand that either, so it is just as well that I'm going to die. Nobody else seems to realize that. Certainly, little H. doesn't. But I *know*. Know, know, know that I am going to die, die.

I don't think that I had better write in this book any more. I suppose that I should destroy it. And yet I feel an odd reluctance to do so. It is almost as if it were my last link with life.

> *Ruskin wouldn't – couldn't – fuck her,*
> *So Effie smothered Millais' art.*

Totally unbidden, that couplet gave birth to itself in my head this morning.

Of course I have often brooded on those three. Pretty little Effie – and poor Ruskin, so horrified by the *reality* of her. It was not he, it was pure, pretty little Effie that *wanted it*. So enter the third character – Millais. Soon caught in her toils. A talented painter until then, but once he was Effie's – what rubbish, what slop he churned out, to keep her and her brood.

Yes, they are all succubae; they drain us of life, they suck our strength from us. Even little H. could become a succuba. No, H. – get thee to a nunnery, go, farewell. Or if thou wilt needs marry, marry a fool: for wise men know well enough, what monsters you make of them.

Will H. marry, marry and then stray *feeling hunger*, like my mother's hunger for Setty? Will H. *have a taste for it*? Oh surely not. Surely not she.

Will H. have a taste for it? Surely not she. She closed the book, got out of bed, wrapped it in its paper, replaced it in the chimney. She unlocked the door, turned off the light, and went back to bed.

'*Will H. have a taste for it*? She smiled – calmly, gently. How terrible Edmund made 'it' sound, when really it was . . . pleasurable, wasn't it? Edmund made it sound more like torture than pleasure. He had felt like that, of course, because he had been so horrified by what Aunt Louisa had done.

She supposed that *she* ought to feel more shocked about Aunt Louisa. Oh, she was astonished, yes. How *extraordinary* it was – and how *extraordinary* was the truth about Julia. But what she secretly felt was – overjoyed. That Aunt Louisa, with all her sermons, should turn out to be a wicked woman. And Julia! How could Aunt Louisa dare to call *her*, Henrietta, an interloper.

Now, every time that Julia was horrible to her, she would be able to think about what she knew, and just smile. She smiled now, and then another thought made her giggle aloud in the darkness: 'Material for a memorial booklet'.

She had promised Edmund not to read the notebook – and she had read it. She had promised to destroy it – and she hadn't. But she knew that she had done what Edmund had *really* wanted her to do. No, it was only from *their prying* fingers that he had intended her to keep it.

The truth was that he had left it for her – as food for love and for hatred. Food for her rediscovered love for him: death and the notebook had given him back to her. Food for her hatred of Aunt Louisa and Julia. The book was his token.

For of course he had loved her. *Sweet girl . . . dear innocent . . . darling little H.* – what were those except words of love?

All the rest – that look; she could hardly remember it now – was easily explained. It was all jealousy. He had been jealous – darling Edmund – because he had known that he would never be able to marry her. Of course, if he hadn't been wounded, he would have married her, and everything would have been quite perfect.

In the circumstances, it had been inevitable that he should die – that was the only way he could be truly hers. 'Edmund, I love you,' she murmured, touching herself in the darkness until *that* happened, as she had learnt to make it happen. 'Edmund, I love you.' Such a feeling of peace.

Henry. 'So clean and straight and true.' *If Edmund had known*, but he hadn't, so it hadn't mattered at all, really – didn't matter at all now, as long as she didn't have a baby. Surely she wouldn't. Surely she was safe in Edmund's care. 'I love you, Edmund.' She slept.

✺ *Eleven* ✺

At Churston, she re-lived all their old times together, as she walked in the park or sat in the punt, a book – unread – in her lap. All the same, time passed slowly, but it passed, until soon, in August, they would be going up to Scotland for the grouse shooting. In Scotland, there would be a very small house party – 'just a few friends' – because they were still in mourning! What hypocrisy! The house party included two admirers of Julia's, and, at Aunt Louisa's suggestion, James Lecksley.

She mustn't just sit and think of Edmund, and ache for him sweetly – for he was hers. She must work out her plans. In her mind a resolve was being formed, a resolve to escape – Edmund had helped her to form it. When they returned to London in the autumn, when the social round started all over again, she must find something to do.

She made a list. What a pathetic little list it was:

1. *Teacher*
2. *Nurse*
3. *Charity*

She thought of the conversation she had had with Edmund, when he had said that perhaps she should go to university after all. But she couldn't face the thought of going back to Miss Dettmer's – she would be so much older than the other girls – and ploughing away at the school certificate. After all, what would be the point? She was certain that she didn't want to be a teacher.

It was conceivable now, that Uncle Harry and Aunt Louisa might allow her to be a nurse – so many of their friends' daughters were VADs. But the War was sure to be over soon, and she wouldn't want to nurse in peacetime. She had heard, too, that VADs were given all the dirty work to do. No, her earlier dream of nursing had been only part of her love for Edmund.

So what else was there? *Charitable work.* That sounded worthy, but so dull. She decided that she wasn't a ministering angel. She would have liked to do something *for herself* – but what? When they went up to Scotland, she still had no idea.

James Lecksley didn't shoot. When the other men went out shooting, he stayed with Henrietta. They went for long walks on the moors. There was no talk of chaperones, as there always was in London. Aunt Louisa positively encouraged the walks.

She was really quite fond of Mr Lecksley nowadays, but the idea of marrying him was unthinkable. Though she could understand how, in desperation, girls married men they didn't love, in order to get away from home.

He wasn't so boring as she had thought at first. When he wasn't talking about Ireland, she even found what he had to say about politics fairly interesting. She was astonished by his passionate support for women's suffrage and for social benefits for the poor – regarded with such horror in Belgrave Square. It was when he was talking about votes for women that she burst out, 'Oh I so long to do something.'

'Do something, Miss Purvis?'

'Yes. Some work. You can't imagine how I hate the life we lead in London. It's so trivial. It's such a waste of time.'

'How entirely I agree with you,' he said. 'Your presence was, of course, the only reason for my going to all those dances. As it is the only reason for my coming here.'

She must try to steer him off *that* track. Say he proposed? If she said no, then he would vanish from her life, and she didn't really want him to. How Aunt Louisa would pester her!

'Yes,' she said. 'Dancing, shooting, and so on. They're so useless. I so much want to do something different.'

'Have you any idea what sort of thing, Miss Purvis?'

'I know that I don't want to teach or to nurse. I know that they're very worth while, but I don't feel I'm really suited to either of them.'

'Have you ever thought of learning to typewrite and to write shorthand?'

'No,' she said. 'No, I hadn't thought of that. Anyway, Aunt Louisa would never allow me to.'

'I cannot see why not. Why, the most respectable young ladies' – involuntarily, she smiled; 'young ladies' always made her think of Edmund – 'a cousin of my own amongst others – are taking what are called secretarial courses nowadays. The establishment in Queen's Gate that my cousin goes to is above reproach in every way. It is run by a most excellent woman, a Mrs Harrington. I really cannot see what objections your aunt could raise to your going there.'

'You don't know Aunt Louisa. She's be horrified. She thinks that the only thing for a girl to do is get married.'

'Well,' he said, smiling at her, his eyes anxious, friendly, behind the distorting glasses – really they were quite nice

eyes, kind and brown, even if he couldn't see with them
– 'I can't think of any reason why working should disbar
a girl from matrimony. Many men, and I number myself
amongst them, admire independence in a lady.'

Danger was looming again. 'If I suggested it, I know
she'd say no. Feeling about me as she does.' A plan was
forming.

'As she does?' he repeated, sounding puzzled.

'Oh, she doesn't like me, you know.'

'Doesn't like you?' He sounded shocked. 'My dear Miss
Purvis, I am sure that you are quite mistaken. She always
speaks of you most warmly.'

She would – to you, Henrietta thought, but of course
couldn't say.

She shrugged. 'Oh, well,' she said, and then, 'If *you*
suggested it, she might listen. If *you* told her you thought
it was a good idea.'

'You overestimate me,' he said – but how pleased he
looked. 'I can't believe that my opinion would be likely to
influence your aunt.'

'Oh, she has the greatest respect for you and your opinions
– I know that,' she said confidently.

'Well,' he said, looking even more pleased – were all men
so easy to guide? – 'that is very flattering. But I hardly
think—'

She ventured further, put a hand on his arm, quickly,
timidly withdrew it. 'Oh please, Mr Lecksley,' she said,
tilting her head sideways. That was the only way she could
look up at him, because they were exactly the same height.
'Wouldn't you, please?'

Now there was a sentimental look on his face. 'Well
of course, if the opportunity should arise . . . How can I
refuse you anything, Miss Purvis, when you look at me
like that?'

The 'opportunity arose' two days later. Again, all the
other men were out shooting. James Lecksley and Henrietta

were sitting in the drawing-room when Aunt Louisa, in her elegant tweeds, came downstairs. The three of them, and Lady Revelston and Julia, were going in the pony cart to join the guns for luncheon. Two footmen had left, in the trap, some time before, with the equipment for the immense picnic which they would lay out in a farmhouse high on the moors.

James Lecksley sprang to his feet as Aunt Louisa came into the room. She smiled approvingly at them, sat down in an armchair, looked at her watch.

'We should be leaving in about ten minutes,' she said. 'Have you two been having an interesting talk together?'

'Oh most interesting,' he said, and then, loyally plunging, 'Your niece tells me, Lady Allingham, that she wishes to pursue an avocation.'

'Pursue an *avocation*?' Aunt Louisa sounded puzzled. As if, Henrietta thought, an avocation were some strange variety of furred or feathered creature. She repressed a nervous giggle.

'Yes, to learn shorthand and typewriting.' He hurried on before Aunt Louisa could have a chance to comment. 'An excellent idea, don't you think? I do feel that in the modern world, the world which will follow the War, it will be an excellent thing for a young lady to acquire professional qualifications.'

But Aunt Louisa was frowning.

'Even if she should decide not to pursue a career,' he continued, 'it would be useful if her husband should, let us say, be engaged in any kind of public work.' He laughed. 'So much easier to read a speech that has been typewritten than one which is written in longhand.'

Aunt Louisa's frown, as she listened, had gradually melted away. 'Yes,' she said now. 'Yes, I suppose so. I have never really given the matter any thought.' Turning to Henrietta, she said, 'Why, what a secretive girl you are!'

But she didn't sound annoyed. 'Why haven't you mentioned this little scheme of yours?'

'It – it only just occurred to me,' Henrietta said.

'I see. And how would you acquire these – useful arts?' Aunt Louisa's tone was faintly mocking.

'I know of a school,' James Lecksley said. 'It is in Queen's Gate. It is run by an excellent woman. A widow. A Mrs Harrington. My cousin Cynthia is a pupil there.'

'Indeed! This plan seems very far advanced for something that has only just occurred to you, Henrietta.' Now the mockery held a familiar hint of acid. 'I suppose,' she went on, 'that your attendance at this *excellent widow's* establishment wouldn't interrupt your normal social life too much.'

'Ah, Lady Allingham,' James Lecksley said, 'I am sure that it would not. But I suspect that Miss Purvis, like myself, is not a whole-hearted devotee of society's revels.'

'Revels, Mr Lecksley? Why, you make our innocent activities sound positively *bacchanalian*.'

'Such was not my intention, I assure you,' he said earnestly.

Aunt Louisa gave a little sigh. 'I was only joking, Mr Lecksley.'

'Oh yes, I see. I have been told that my sense of humour is not my strongest point.'

Again, Henrietta felt like giggling. Really he did sound extraordinarily pompous – quite Victorian. How could Aunt Louisa imagine that she would marry a man who talked like that – *she who was used to Edmund*? The ache throbbed dully.

'Oh, I'm sure that's not true at all,' Aunt Louisa said easily. At that moment, Julia and Lady Revelston came into the drawing-room. Aunt Louisa looked at her watch again. 'Well, we must be on our way to luncheon,' she said. 'Henrietta, we shall talk about this scheme of yours later.' She stood up.

*   *   *

'Mr Lecksley, you were wonderful,' Henrietta said to him when they were next alone. 'Positively Macchiavellian!'

'Oh hardly that,' he said deprecatingly. Perhaps he disapproved of Macchiavelli, just as the lecturer who had taught them about him at Miss Dettmer's had seemed to. It had puzzled her. What Macchiavelli said was surely just common sense?

'I meant it as a compliment,' she said.

'I see. But I was not aware that I was following in the footsteps of the wily Italian. How did I resemble him?'

'Oh, all that about marrying a man in public life. Just the right approach for Aunt Louisa,' she said blithely. The moment she had spoken, she knew she had made a mistake.

So it proved. 'But Miss Purvis, I really meant that.' He sounded hurt. The sentimental look was on his face again.

'Dear Mr Lecksley,' she said, but briskly. She hurried on: 'Anyway, it worked like a charm.'

Two days later, Julia became engaged.

Was Aunt Louisa pleased? Henrietta suspected that she had hoped for a more brilliant match for Julia – a duke at least. But really there were no reasonable objections to Algernon (everybody called him 'Algie') Thornton. Only son of an immensely rich twelfth baronet with vast estates in Yorkshire, good-looking in a wooden way, a true-blue Tory with an excellent war record, a superb shot – Uncle Harry thought him a 'perfectly splendid feller'. In the circumstances, what could Aunt Louisa do but express enthusiasm?

But what could Julia see in him? That was what Henrietta wondered. He was the kind of man that she most dreaded being seated next to at a dinner party. Utterly conventional, extremely stupid – dull, dull, dull. The engagement gave her a curious feeling of satisfaction – Julia, whom everyone thought so dazzling, so fascinating, ending up with – this!

And Julia's engagement made things so much easier for *her*. Aunt Louisa was preoccupied with it to the exclusion of everything else. She had her 'talk' – a very brief one – with Henrietta, and went to see Mrs Harrington at Queen's Gate. Aunt Louisa, Henrietta was convinced, was sure that she would soon become engaged to James Lecksley.

By the end of September, she was at Miss Harrington's, sitting behind a typewriter. Next to her sat James Lecksley's cousin, Cynthia Chanter.

In appearance, Cynthia was a pre-Raphaelite girl, red-haired, white-skinned, dreamy-eyed. But there was nothing old-fashioned about Cynthia. To Henrietta she seemed the epitome of modernity – an ardent suffragette, a Fabian, even a sympathizer with Pacifism.

Cynthia was the first friend Henrietta ever had. (Apart from Edmund, though he had been so much more. *Will you promise to think of me only as a friend?*) Daughter of a successful barrister and an 'advanced' mother who entertained writers and artists, the freedom of her life astonished Henrietta. She travelled about London alone, went to meetings, had tea, *tête-à-tête*, with young men.

Cynthia referred to her cousin James with patronizing affection as 'a dear old thing'.

'He's potty about you, isn't he?' she said to Henrietta soon after they met.

Henrietta, unaccustomed to female exchanges of confidences, responded to this enquiry with a little, noncommittal shrug.

But Cynthia prattled on: 'Don't expect you feel the same, somehow. Wouldn't have thought he was your type at all.'

'What would you have thought *my type* was?' Henrietta asked, smiling. Yes, she liked Cynthia.

'Oh something *much* more exciting. Tall, dark and handsome. Terrible blasé and aristocratic.'

'You're quite wrong,' Henrietta said. 'I'm absolutely sick of the aristocracy. I think they're terribly boring.' *Except Edmund.*

She was invited to tea at Cynthia's house in Bayswater – 'on the wrong side of the Park,' as Aunt Louisa put it. Aunt Louisa was not enthusiastic about Henrietta's visiting the Chanters but, as Cynthia was James Lecksley's cousin, did not actually object. 'Connections on his mother's side, I imagine. Quite middle-class people I should think. Goodness knows what extraordinary acquaintances you might pick up there,' she said, making 'acquaintances' sound like some disgusting disease. 'Do be careful not to encourage anyone to become familiar, and try to worm an invitation here.'

Cynthia's father was so handsome, so easy-going, her mother so emancipated and 'artistic'. (How horrified Aunt Louisa would have been by Mrs Chanter's loose-fitting clothes, and the coronet of braids in which she wore her hair.) Certainly the Chanters weren't in the least interested in 'worming' an invitation to Belgrave Square.

The first question Mrs Chanter asked her was whether she was any connection of 'Purvis, the painter'. No one had ever asked her that before.

'Yes,' she said. 'He was my father,' and was drowned in the flood of Mrs Chanter's enthusiasm.

'Such a wonderful artist. Such colour sense, such *feeling*. There's a revival of interest in his work, you know.'

Henrietta nodded. She hadn't known.

'Have you got any of his pictures?' Mrs Chanter asked eagerly.

She shook her head. 'No,' she said. 'My uncle put all the things from our house into a sale when my parents died.'

'Awful, quite awful,' Mrs Chanter said. 'Do you paint yourself?'

She shook her head. Then suddenly she found herself telling Mrs Chanter about *changing hands*.

'How appalling,' Mrs Chanter said sympathetically. '*Psychologically*, it could have been disastrous.' Henrietta hadn't heard of psychology. She decided to ask Cynthia about it.

Though the Chanters' house was bigger, and they had four servants, in some way their household reminded her of her childhood home. People dropped in instead of 'calling'. Tea was a casual affair. There was a single rose in a glass on the chimney-piece – no flower arrangements, no banks of potted plants.

After tea, Henrietta went up with Cynthia to her room. How unusual it was! The bed was heaped with cushions covered in Oriental-looking materials, and there were framed posters of the Russian Ballet on the walls. There were two big comfortable armchairs, and a proper desk with a revolving chair. Cynthia lit the gas fire, and turned on the bedside light, and a modern-looking reading lamp on the desk.

'What a lovely room! It's more like a sitting-room than a bedroom,' Henrietta exclaimed. How uncomfortable her room at Belgrave Square seemed, in contrast.

She sat in one of the armchairs, and Cynthia sprawled on the bed. ('Don't sit on the beds' had been one of Nanny's sternest injunctions.) They talked and talked. She was quite startled by how quickly the time had passed when the parlourmaid came upstairs to say that the motor had arrived to take her home.

'Well,' Aunt Louisa asked that evening, 'how did you enjoy your excursion to *Bayswater?*'

Oh, it was quite nice, thank you,' Henrietta said, without enthusiasm. *If Aunt Louisa saw how much she had enjoyed it, she might stop her going again.*

'I suppose that you had better ask the girl to tea here sometime, since she is your friend Mr Lecksley's cousin. Not the parents. That would be *too* much. But the girl.'

Cynthia came to tea, and was very quiet and polite. Sir Richard was there, and Lady Revelston who, as usual, kept up a stream of chatter. Aunt Louisa insisted on the chauffeur's taking Cynthia home in the motor, though she protested that she could easily catch an omnibus.

'Travelling alone on an omnibus with all the common people. What can her mother be thinking of?' Aunt Louisa said as soon as Cynthia had gone. 'But a nice enough little girl. Rather shy isn't she? Quite pretty, though a trifle *arty* looking.'

Next day, at Mrs Harrington's, Cynthia said, 'Goodness, how *grand* your house is! Honestly, Henrietta, I don't know how you put up with all those butlers and things.'

Henrietta laughed. 'Nor do I,' she said.

With Cynthia, she found herself able to talk as she had never done with anyone but Edmund – and she and Cynthia spoke of subjects which she could never have discussed with him, subjects like birth control and Free Love. From a conversation with Cynthia, she was able to extract the information that she definitely wasn't going to have a baby.

Cynthia was in favour of Free Love, though she had no experience of it. *What would Cynthia think if she knew about her?* But that was one thing she wasn't going to tell Cynthia. It was rather satisfying, though, that she, so backward in many respects, was ahead of Cynthia in this.

In November, the War ended. She couldn't share the hysterical joy and relief of everyone around her. The War had taken Edmund, the only thing she had ever wanted – there had been nothing else it could have done to her. Of course she was glad that people weren't being killed any more. But soon Henry would be coming home. She dreaded that.

Meeting Cynthia had made going to Mrs Harrington's worthwhile, but she found the course very boring. Shorthand and typewriting didn't interest her at all. Would she enjoy them more, she wondered, if she were actually working? She imagined herself in an office, in a dark skirt and a neat white blouse, and found that the picture didn't appeal to her at all. In her darkest moments, she wondered about marrying James Lecksley. *If she did, she would have to let him do what Henry had done.* No, the idea was impossible, unthinkable.

It was at the Chanters' that she met Adrian Wheeler. He was a new protégé of Mrs Chanter's – 'an absolutely brilliant young man,' she told the girls. Cynthia smiled. 'All your young men are "absolutely brilliant", Mummy,' she said. (How wonderfully easy Cynthia and her mother talked to each other.) But Henrietta was sure that Mrs Chanter was right about Mr Wheeler. He was a writer. He had actually had things published.

She liked his tallness, his thinness, his aquiline features. She admired the fluency, the sharpness and dryness of his conversation. He had a quality of austerity which reminded her, just a little, of Edmund. Unexpectedly, he also had a weatherbeaten, outdoor look – she thought of him as an indoor person. She mentioned this to Cynthia.

'Oh, he's been working on the land for years,' Cynthia said. 'He was a conscientious objector. Don't tell your uncle and aunt,' she said with a giggle.

Tell Uncle Harry and Aunt Louisa! Why, if she did, she would never be allowed to visit the Chanters again. A 'conshie' like 'that swine, Russell – a traitor to his country and his class'. If Uncle Harry and Aunt Louisa had had their way, 'conshies' would all have been shot. But what, she asked herself now, were her own feelings on the subject?

Until now, she had always believed that 'conshies' were cowardly. After all – you couldn't get away from it – Edmund had 'died for his country', though not in the sentimental way that Aunt Louisa thought of it. '*For an old bitch gone in the teeth, for a botched civilization.*' But she knew that he couldn't *not have fought*. Why? Because of the way he had been brought up? If that was why, hadn't his fighting been conventional, even cowardly? No, no, no. It couldn't be cowardly to *die* for something, even if one didn't believe in it. Yet now, in a way, thinking about it, she could see that 'conshies' were brave. To dare so much hatred and contempt. And surely the fact that Aunt Louisa hated and despised them, meant that there was something worthwhile about them? *A botched civilization*. Yet everyone in the Chanters' circle seemed to believe that a new, better, more just society was going to follow the War.

'I think Adrian's got rather a crush on you, Henrietta,' Cynthia said. That was what first made her really pay attention to him.

Was Mrs Chanter match-making? Was Cynthia? Certainly she and Adrian – as he had asked her to call him – often found themselves alone together in the Chanters' drawing-room. They walked up and down the rather gloomy back garden, where suspicious cats lurked in the laurels. Adrian enjoyed talking to her.

It was easy to escape from Belgrave Square that winter. Everyone was so absorbed in the preparations for Julia's wedding, which was to take place in February. And there was also the excitement of Henry's return.

His presence at Belgrave Square wasn't as distressing as she had feared it would be. He was out so much – and she was so often at the Chanters'. He had kissed her politely on the cheek when he came back from France. They hardly ever said more to each other than 'Good-morning' and 'Good-night.'

She told Aunt Louisa that James Lecksley was always at the Chanters'. Well, he did go there quite often. She found it a little awkward when he and Adrian were there together. One afternoon, she made a slip, and called Adrian by his Christian name. Afterwards, James had said to her, 'If you call that man, Wheeler, by his Christian name, surely you could do the same for me, Miss Purvis. Or may I call you Henrietta?' So now she and James were

on Christian-name terms, which Aunt Louisa duly noticed.
She made no objections to Henrietta's visits to Bayswater.
The chauffeur took her there and fetched her several times
a week.

She and Adrian started going for walks in the Park, and
having tea in little tea-rooms together. Provided that she was
back at the Chanters' when the motor came to collect her, it
was really quite safe. None of Aunt Louisa's friends walked
in the Park on midwinter afternoons, and the tea-rooms
were not places that they would ever have patronized. Mrs
Chanter smiled benevolently on these expeditions.

It was so wonderful to be with someone who knew
so much. She read the articles he wrote for the reviews
that lay about in the Chanters' drawing-room. They were
alarmingly learned. But the important thing was that he was
also writing a novel – he was what she thought of as a 'real
writer', too.

She welcomed a mentor, he a pupil. He made a long list
of all the books she ought to read. Most of them were what
Julia would have called 'heavy', and sometimes she skipped
and skimmed, lighting on ideas here and there to discuss
with him. She had found when she was at Miss Dettmer's
that she was quite good at doing that.

She wasn't 'in love' with him. She knew that. She knew
that she would never be in love with anyone but Edmund.
Edmund was perfection, was something apart. What would
he have thought about Adrian? *No, H., get thee to a nunnery,
go, farewell. Or if thou wilt needs marry, marry a fool.* Adrian
certainly wasn't a fool. But Edmund hadn't really meant
that. It was just that he had felt possessive about her. And
she was sure that he would have wanted her to escape from
Belgrave Square – he had said so.

When she applied the test that James Lecksley failed so
dismally – she just didn't know. Certainly, he didn't repel
her, as James did. And she had the oddest feeling that doing
that with him would not be an act of infidelity to Edmund

– as doing it with Henry had been. When Adrian first kissed her, in the Chanters' garden, she was reminded of Edmund's cool, closed lips. Henry – heat; Edmund, Adrian – coolness.

She imagined life with Adrian in a cottage in the country. A life, she decided, like the life which Papa and Mama had lived in Kensington. She even created a rustic version of Elsie to do the housework.

And she – what would *she* do? She would type Adrian's writings. She would read – really, properly read – all those books on his list. His interesting, intelligent friends would come to visit them.

Sometimes she caught Adrian looking at her with a kind of surprise. And surprise was mixed with pleasure in his tone when he said one day, 'You know, you're the first girl I've ever been interested in. Until now, I've never really cared for – girls.'

She remembered Edmund, and his withering comments on the 'young ladies'. But then there had been those awful women. *Dog's hairs on the blanket*. Had Adrian been with women like that? She hoped not. Though of course she knew now, from her talks with Cynthia, that many men did. It was part of something called the 'double standard' which made Cynthia very indignant.

'Why shouldn't they allow us the same freedom they have?' Cynthia said.

'But surely, one wouldn't want . . .'

'That's not the point. It's the principle that matters.'

So, though she hadn't realized it at the time, when she had gone to bed with Henry, she had simply been *being emancipated*. That was a consoling idea.

When Adrian asked her to marry him, she said yes. That was five weeks before Julia's wedding.

Reluctantly, Julia had asked Henrietta to be one of her bridesmaids, and reluctantly she had accepted. Really, the only alternative would have been for Julia not to have any

bridesmaids at all. If Julia hadn't asked her – or if she had
refused – how everyone would have *relever*-ed.

If only she could have avoided it by running away and
getting married to Adrian. (*That* would have been something
for them to *relever* about!) But she was only nineteen. Until
she was twenty-one, she could not marry without Uncle
Harry's consent. Unless, of course, they eloped to Gretna
Green. But when she had suggested that, Adrian had said
it was quite out of the question. She thought it would be
romantic, but he thought it would look silly.

'My friends would all laugh themselves to death.'

'But why?' she said.

He shrugged. 'So terribly old-fashioned.'

He also said that he felt it would upset his parents. His
father was a professor at London University.

Adrian couldn't seem to understand why she thought that
Uncle Harry and Aunt Louisa would object to the marriage
so much.

'It's not as if I were a Jew or anything,' he said.

She couldn't help laughing at the idea – though Kingy had
had friends who were Jews. But it was impossible to convey
to Adrian what they would feel about his middle-class
background. He had been at what he called a public
school, somewhere called Leamington College – could
it really be a public school? Eton, Harrow, Winchester,
Rugby – she had never known that there were others. He
had been at Cambridge, of course, at King's – that was all
right. The insurmountable obstacle was his having been a
'conshie'.

She tried to explain, in terms of Edmund's death, and
Henry having gained so many decorations.

He said, 'Oh they'll get used to it. After all, so many
people are pacifists. Look at Bertrand Russell.'

Exactly, she thought. *Traitor to his country and his class.*
No, she was sure that they would never 'get used to it'.

'Anyway, you don't have to raise the subject immediately.'

But she knew they would find out. One of the first things they would want to know would be what regiment he had served in. She could just imagine the spotlight that would be turned on every aspect of Adrian's life.

Then, of course, there was the question of money. If she married Adrian, surely Uncle Harry, kind though he was, would never give her that dowry? Adrian's family wasn't at all well-off, and Adrian wasn't earning much from his journalism yet – though of course, when his novel was finished, he would probably make lots of money from that. Royalties – a new word to her, which had nothing to do with kings and queens.

'You would probably have to do some secretarial work, to begin with,' Adrian said. That was rather a depressing thought. And, if they were living in the country, where would she find it? (How shocked Uncle Harry and Aunt Louisa would be. An unmarried girl working was bad enough – but a married woman!)

She talked a lot about their cottage in the country, and Adrian sounded enthusiastic. 'Though it might,' he said, 'be difficult to arrange, just at first.'

There was a possibility of his being made assistant editor of some new magazine, which meant that he would need to be in London. But as soon as he could support them by his own writing, they would go to the country. He said it would be wonderful; he would be able to get so much work done. Well, until then, she supposed she could put up with London. They would find a flat – something small and *cozy* (a word which appealed to her, though she could imagine how Aunt Louisa would sneer at it). And they would be seeing interesting people all the time, not stuffy boring ones.

Adrian's friends – it was with mixed feelings that she looked forward to meeting them. They all sounded so extremely well-educated and clever – would she ever be able to keep up with them? She really must concentrate harder on Adrian's reading list. The difficulty was just that her mind sometimes wandered, especially when the books were about politics or economics.

So far, she had only met one of his friends. Adrian had brought him to their favourite tea-shop – 'to inspect me,' as she had teased him afterwards.

Really, she hadn't known what she thought of Lancaster Tyrrwhitt, with his high voice, almost like a woman's, and the long white hands which he waved languidly in the air as he talked.

She hadn't said much. For the most part, he and Adrian had talked about old Cambridge friends. She could see that Lancaster was very witty, but how malicious he was – after all, he was talking about people who were meant to be his friends.

She dreaded what he might say to Adrian about her, afterwards. When she asked Adrian, the next time she saw him, he looked embarrassed for a moment, before replying, 'He said that you seemed to have all the necessary female impedimenta in abundance.'

She hadn't liked that much, but Adrian added, 'You should take it as a compliment. You saw how scathing he can be.'

With that she had to be content, though she couldn't help wondering if Lancaster had said anything else. Anyway, if he had, Adrian didn't tell her. She did hope that all Adrian's friends weren't going to be as chilly (yes, that was the word she wanted) as Lancaster.

She would have to break the news at Belgrave Square some time. *When?* That was the question. Should it be before Julia's wedding or after it? she wondered, when there were only three more weeks to go.

There would be advantages of doing it before. Everyone was so wrapped up in Julia that they wouldn't have time to focus their attention on her. And then, by the time the wedding was over, they would have had a chance to cool down a bit. (Though she couldn't put much faith in that.) But, after the wedding, they would have undistracted attention to give her; she shivered at the prospect.

Not telling was making her so nervous. She attempted to explain her dilemma to Adrian, who laughed and said, 'Try a *sortes Vergilianae*.'

He had to explain what that was. The ancient Romans, apparently, had dipped into the works of Vergil for guidance when they wanted to make an important decision. She wasn't a Roman. And couldn't read Latin. Perhaps she should try it with a different book?

The notebook. Of course, that was the answer. She would look in Edmund's notebook. He would tell her what to do. That evening, she took the book from its hiding-place, unwrapped it, sat down, holding it in her lap. She closed her eyes, she opened the book, ran her finger down a page.

I wanted to escape, like the bird. Yes, Edmund had spoken to her. Telling her that she must go away. 'I wanted to escape, like the bird.' She said it aloud. That was what she must do as soon as possible. She would tell them at the first opportunity.

Circumstances made it easy for her. Next evening, she and Aunt Louisa and Uncle Harry were alone at dinner – something which hardly ever happened. Julia was at the theatre with Algie, and Henry was out. It was fate, she decided.

She couldn't tell them at dinner, because of the servants. But afterwards, Uncle Harry, alone, did not linger over his port, but joined her and Aunt Louisa in the drawing-room after a few minutes.

They were drinking their coffee when she said, 'I'm engaged to be married.'

'Mr Lecksley – I suppose I must call him James now – has proposed,' Aunt Louisa exclaimed. 'Henrietta, I am delighted for you.'

Uncle Harry said, 'Young man with a future, they tell

me. Bit of a radical, but he'll soon settle down, I dare say.' He smiled. 'Under your good influence, Henrietta.'

'But it isn't James,' she said.

'Isn't James?' Aunt Louisa repeated. '*Isn't James?* Don't be ridiculous.'

'If it isn't him, who is it then?' Uncle Harry was frowning now.

'His name is Adrian Wheeler.'

'Wheeler? Wheeler? Never heard of the feller. Who is he? Where does he come from? What does he do?'

It was as bad as she expected it to be. 'He's a writer, Uncle Harry,' she said.

'A *writer*,' Aunt Louisa broke in. 'Where could you have met such a person? Oh, I can guess. With those terrible people you've been visiting all the time. I knew I should never have allowed it. It was only because they were connections of James Lecksley's. Well, of course we absolutely forbid it.'

'What regiment was he in during the War?' Uncle Harry asked.

She steeled herself. 'He wasn't in the army.'

'Oh. Navy I suppose?'

'He didn't fight in the war.'

'Didn't fight? What's the matter with him? Sickly, is he?'

'No, he's perfectly healthy.'

'Well, what did he do in the War then, for heaven's sake?'

Get it over once and for all. 'He was on the land. He's a pacifist. He was conscientious objector.'

Uncle Harry reacted first. 'A damned conshie? A man who hadn't the courage to fight for his country? How could you think of marrying such a feller? Your aunt is quite right. We forbid it.'

'I'm going to marry him.'

'Bad blood will out. I've always said so.' Aunt Louisa spoke almost triumphantly.

'How dare you speak about my father like that?' Suddenly she felt possessed by a wild, reckless daring.

'Now Henrietta,' Uncle Harry interposed, 'can't have you talkin' to yer aunt like that. Steady, Louisa,' he added.

An angry flush rose on Aunt Louisa's cheeks. She pressed her lips together. 'Anyway, this really has nothing to do with what we're talking about,' she said. 'The point is that Henrietta is not going to marry this man. We can prevent her – at least until she is twenty-one. By then she will have forgotten this idiocy.'

'If you try to stop me, I shall run away with him. Just imagine the *scandal*, Aunt Louisa! How people would *relever*.'

'You disgusting, degraded creature.'

'Steady Louisa,' Uncle Harry said again. He turned to Henrietta. 'You don't understand what you're sayin'.'

'The ingratitude – after all we've done for you. Bringing you up as a second daughter. I always said that it was a mistake. I only thank heaven that my sweet little Julia has escaped contamination.'

'Must say' – Uncle Harry's voice low – 'I'm a bit disappointed in yer, Henrietta. Goin' off behind our backs, and gettin' yerself entangled with this brute.'

'He's not a brute, Uncle Harry. He's a very intelligent man.'

'*Intelligent!*' Aunt Louisa exclaimed with scorn. '*Intelligent!* Some shabby Bohemian, I suppose. If you're looking for brains, what's the matter with James Lecksley or some other decent young man of your own class?'

'Because they're all boring.' After so many years of self-control, she was really letting go! 'Boring and stupid – however many exams they've passed. They just aren't interesting!'

'I see. And this young man is *interesting*. What is so *interesting* about him, pray? Who are his family? *Wheeler*. What does his father do?'

'He's a professor. A professor of History.'

'A don?' Uncle Harry said. 'Oxford or Cambridge?'

'At London University.'

'London University!' Aunt Louisa said. 'And where did he go to school?'

She couldn't help feeling embarrassed. 'Leamington College,' she murmured.

'Leamington College? What is that? A *grammar school?*'

'No, Aunt Louisa. It's a public school.'

'What absolute nonsense you are talking, Henrietta. I have never even heard of it. And after this whatever-it-is college, I suppose he went to London University.'

'No, he was at Cambridge.'

'What college?'

'He was at King's.'

'King's. Well, yes. And what about money, Henrietta? Having always had everything your heart desired, I don't suppose that you have given the subject very much thought. Does his family have money? They don't *sound* as if they have.'

'No, they aren't well-off.'

'I thought not. And what, pray, does this *Adrian Wheeler* earn, himself? Can he afford to support a wife?'

'He earns – oh, quite a lot from journalism. And soon he will have finished his novel.'

'His *novel!*' Even Leamington College had not provoked quite this degree of contempt from Aunt Louisa. Though the only books she ever looked at were novels – the 'daring' ones that 'everyone was talking about'.

'Anyway,' Henrietta said, 'I would work, myself, to begin with. I've always wanted to work.'

'Wanted to work, indeed. As a common little typist in some office. One thing is certain – you are going to leave that secretarial college immediately. I should never have listened to that dreadful Mr Lecksley. I suppose he knows all about this. What a betrayal of our kindness and hospitality.'

'But I thought you liked him so much? I thought you wanted me to *marry* him, Aunt Louisa? Anyway, you're quite wrong. He doesn't know anything about it.'

'What a deceitful girl you are, Henrietta. Sly. Sly and secretive – I have always been aware of that. There's no openness about you, none of that lovely frankness and innocence of Julia's.'

Henrietta said nothing, but her thoughts must have been evident on her face, for Aunt Louisa's voice was shrill when she spoke again.

'You think you're so clever, so *intelligent*, and you haven't a quarter of Julia's brains. Yet you presume to sneer at her, just because she hasn't always got her nose buried in some stupid book. I suppose that it is from *books* that you have picked up your absurd ideas. Life is very different from what you find in cheap and common story books, I assure you. I suppose that you are dreaming of love in a cottage, for of course, you realize that you would not receive one penny from us.'

'Cut off without a shilling, like my mother? Well, at least she was happy.'

'Happy. Happy. It isn't happiness that counts in life. It is doing one's duty.'

'And you have always done your duty, Aunt Louisa?' Henrietta spoke suddenly so meekly that Aunt Louisa frowned, narrowed her eyes. Then she said, 'Yes indeed I have, Henrietta. I have always done my duty – to God, to my country, to my family. By the way, I cannot imagine what your cousin, Edmund, whom you always pretended to be so fond of, would have had to say to this. Or rather, I can. He would have been disgusted, utterly disgusted. Only a few months since he died for his country, and you are proposing to marry a filthy conshie. Conscientious objector, indeed – *coward* is the correct word.'

'Think we've talked enough about this business.' Caught from their deadly hatred (open at last), almost dazed, they both turned towards Uncle Harry. He went on, 'Henrietta, go away, and think about all this. Young gels are headstrong. It's well known. But I'm sure, if you think about this quietly, you'll realize that marryin' this feller is quite out of the question.'

'I won't, Uncle Harry. I won't realize anything of the kind. I've thought about it already, and I'm going to marry Adrian.'

'We shall prevent you.' Aunt Louisa's voice was cooler now. 'We shall – and we can. And also I shall go and see this Wheeler's parents. They are probably quite respectable people. They will doubtless be anxious to dissuade their son from marrying a young girl from quite a different sphere, in total opposition to the wishes of her family.'

'I'm sure they won't,' Henrietta said, 'when they understand that we are in love.' As she spoke, she almost, for a moment believed that she loved Adrian. *No, Edmund – it's only you I love.*

'You are an exceptionally foolish girl, Henrietta. There is really no point in trying to treat you as a grown up person. You behaved like a child and you should be treated as one.' Her voice rose. 'You should be *whipped*. But I suppose that it is too late for that. Go to your room, and stay there.'

'Do you think you can keep me locked up? Are you going to feed me on bread and water?' Henrietta could hear her own voice rising. 'This isn't the Victorian age, you know. I shall escape. I promise you I shall.'

'Now don't be deuced silly, Henrietta,' Uncle Harry said. 'No one's going to lock you up. What a dashed stchoopid idea. I'm putting my faith in yer good sense. You've always been a sensible gel until now.'

Aunt Louisa clicked her tongue in disagreement, but she didn't say anything.

'Think about it. That's what we want you to do,' said Uncle Harry. 'Sure you'll change yer mind. I've got a lot of faith in you, yer know.'

If there had been any chance of her changing her mind, how much more she would have been influenced by his kindness than by Aunt Louisa's viciousness. *If.* But, whatever happened, she wasn't going to change her mind.

She didn't.

Next morning, life began again, just as usual. As usual, she went to the secretarial college, but she didn't visit the Chanters' afterwards – she gave Cynthia a note for Adrian. Nobody at Belgrave Square said anything. Aunt Louisa was cool – but then she always was. Uncle Harry behaved as if nothing had happened. He was giving her time to think it over, as he had said.

On the next day, James was waiting for her when she came out of college. She brought him back to Belgrave Square and took him up to the schoolroom where she told him about herself and Adrian. Stiffly she wished her happiness, but she could see how upset he was. When she invited him down to tea in the drawing-room, he shook his head. Then – the only sign of bitterness he gave – 'You don't want me to persuade your aunt to sanction your engagement, I trust?' he asked.

'Oh James,' she said.

'Forgive me, Henrietta. My very best wishes. Must go now.'

He blundered out of the house and, she knew, out of her life, and she went into the drawing-room for tea.

Julia's wedding took up more and more of everybody's time. Then it was upon them. Down the aisle after Julia she went in a dress she didn't like, and with an unavoidable wreath jammed down on her forehead. How quiet the house seemed when all the guests had gone.

It was two days later that Uncle Harry sent for her. He was in the library, where he never normally went. He was by the window, fiddling with one of the curtain cords.

'Been thinkin',' he said. 'Hope you have, too. Well, have you changed yer mind about this feller?'

'I never shall,' she said.

'Hmm. That's what Henry said. "Henrietta's got the bit between her teeth," he said.'

'*Henry?*'

'Yes. Been talkin' to him. About all this business. Had to talk to someone. Yer aunt—' He broke off, then began again.

'Henry seems to think we've been a bit hasty. That we ought, at least, to meet the feller. "Henrietta's never really cared for our sort, you know," he said. "Perhaps this chap'll suit her better".'

Uncle Harry sounded dejected. At Henry's viewpoint? At the idea of her rejection of 'our sort'?

'Told him about this Wheeler bein' a conshie. Henry just laughed. "The War's over now, Father," he said. "If Henrietta wants a chap like that, if she doesn't mind, who are we to argue?" Then I got to thinkin'. Didn't do any good that I can see when we all got so angry with yer mother. As one gets older, things . . . look different. And if Henry, after all he's been through, doesn't object, don't really see why we should.' He sighed heavily. 'Henry's havin' a word with yer aunt. She'll listen to him, if she'll listen to anyone.'

Two weeks later, Adrian was asked to tea. Aunt Louisa was chilly. Uncle Harry was gruff. Henry was out.

It went off better than she could have expected. Adrian was quiet and deferential. It was agreed that they could see each other, that she would finish the secretarial course, that the whole subject would be discussed again later in the year.

She noticed a change in Aunt Louisa's attitude, as the weeks passed. Not that she disliked Henrietta any the less – oh, not at all – rather that she was beginning to see the advantage of 'getting her off her hands'. Then Uncle Harry said that he would give her an allowance after all, if she married Adrian. Four hundred a year – she didn't *have* to work, though probably she would.

The wedding was arranged for July, when her course ended. It would be quiet, but she would be married from Belgrave Square. The night before, she read right through Edmund's notebook again before putting it in the bottom of her suitcase before going to bed.

Why had Henry helped her? she wondered, as she fell asleep, to dream that he was making love to her. How extraordinarily vivid, exciting the dream was. She awoke feeling full of a lazy joy which slowly ebbed away as she ate breakfast, bathed, dressed for the wedding. Coming downstairs, she saw him standing in the hall – the dream seized her by the nape of the neck, and she shivered, felt colour rush into her face.

'Henrietta, you're looking radiant, a radiant bride,' Uncle Harry said, stepping forward, taking her hand.

Part Three

❦ Twelve ❦

1925

The bed was heaped with garments which she had discarded. Normally she didn't behave like this. But tonight, with the prospect of an evening at Julia's ahead of her, she had felt unhappy with everything that she had tried on. Finally, in a brown dress, the string of pearls that Uncle Harry had given her round her neck, she thought she looked drab, pale – 'wanting animation' as Aunt Louisa might have put it. But she wasn't going to change again.

Surely Aunt Louisa wouldn't be at the party? Henrietta imagined that Julia kept her 'breathlessly smart' life in London separate from her family. Anyway now, since Uncle Harry's death two years ago, on that – unwise at his age – big game hunting expedition, Aunt Louisa spent most of her time at Churston, though she rented a house in Brompton Square. When Uncle Harry had died, the family had found that he hadn't been quite as well off as everyone had imagined – he and Aunt Louisa had always lived extravagantly, of course.

How annoyed Aunt Louisa had been when his Will had disclosed that he had left a substantial sum to Henrietta. The capital, of course, was in trust for her children – if she didn't have any, it would revert to the Estate. But the income was quite enough to have made the Morris motor and the cottage in the country possible. Anyway, the bequest had added – if that were possible – to Aunt Louisa's dislike of her. When the house in Belgrave Square had been let to an embassy, and Aunt Louisa had moved to the pretty little house in Brompton Square which she referred to as 'my

rabbit hutch', Henrietta had paid her a 'duty' visit (a duty
which she had felt that she owed to Uncle Harry's memory
rather than to Aunt Louisa herself). Aunt Louisa had been
so cold and acid that she had not called again – and had
never been invited. That hadn't worried her at all; she only
wished that Julia had also remained absent from her life.
She sighed. *Why had Julia reappeared?* Could her frequent
visits have anything to do with the reputation Adrian was
beginning to acquire as a journalist?

Julia, of course, was a 'lion hunter'. Though surely,
Henrietta thought, raising her eyebrows – the statue's
face, reflected in the dressing-table mirror, briefly moved
– Adrian was a very small lion, indeed hardly more than
a cub. She wondered what other larger lions would be
at Julia's tonight, roaring at each other, or devouring
lesser animals, or doing whatever lions did at parties. She
was smiling – the statue smiled coldly back – as Adrian
came into the room. He was looking tidier than usual,
she noticed.

'Ready?' he asked.

'As ready as I'll ever be, I suppose.'

'Henrietta, you really are extraordinary,' he said. There
he was, looking at himself in the mirror, running a hand
over his hair. 'You're always complaining,' he went on,
'about what a dull cooped-up life we lead—'

'Oh, I haven't done that for a long time,' she interjected.

'Well, anyway, about how boring my friends are.' He
raised an admonitory finger to prevent any further inter-
ruptions. What a *schoolmaster* he is, she thought. 'And
now when we're invited to a "smart party" ' – he gave the
words a humorous, deprecatory stress – 'you do nothing
but grumble.'

'But my dear Adrian, I'm not grumbling at all,' she said
lightly.

He shrugged. 'Anyway, shall we go?'

'By all means,' she said in the same light tone. Really,

she did dislike him so very much at times. This was one of them.

As Henrietta parked the car outside the new mansion flats in Knightsbridge where Julia lived, she could hear party sounds, even though Julia's flat was on the top floor. A reminiscent shudder – those gatherings of her brief season – ran down her spine. One thing could be said for evenings in Adrian's circle, she thought. They couldn't provoke a shudder in anyone. Though of course there were those timid undergraduates who came to attend with awe at the intellectual (certainly no other) feast. Perhaps *they* shuddered on the doorstep – but probably with delightful anticipation, a very different sensation from her own this evening.

As the porter took them up in the lift with its large mirror, on which she turned her back, and its green painted walls, picked out in gold, the noise of the party grew louder.

Julia's was the only flat on the top floor. The maid who opened the door to them took Adrian's coat and hat, and Henrietta went into Julia's room to remove her own. Other garments were piled on the vast bed with its crème-de-menthe satin cover. At the dressing-table, a girl with Dutch doll circles of rouge on her cheeks gave Henrietta a sharp glance in the mirror, before adding more powder to the layer on her nose. The look seemed to Henrietta to say as plainly as words, 'Oh well, *she's* no competition.'

She really couldn't see any point in fiddling with her hair or putting on more powder (she never wore any other make-up; it didn't seem to look right on her), when she had only got ready so recently, at home. Ignoring the mirror (there seemed to be mirrors everywhere), she joined Adrian who was waiting in the hall, looking impatient.

The huge drawing-room was so crowded that it was difficult to cross it. Slowly they managed to make their way over to a bar behind which a man in a white coat was mixing cocktails. (A bar in a drawing-room! What would

Aunt Louisa say? But perhaps she'd accept even *that* from her beloved Julia.)

The cocktail was sweet, delicious, tasted strong – Henrietta was glad of that; she felt she needed something strong. Perhaps this White Lady would make her feel more at ease. She and Adrian stood by the bar with their drinks. Henrietta couldn't see anyone she knew, even Julia. Over in the corner, a Negro was playing the piano. A *nigger*, Aunt Louisa would have said. Aunt Louisa would have found that even worse than the bar.

Everyone was so *modern*, especially the women. Really, some of them did appear rather curious. Not curious like 'the scarecrows', the women Adrian knew, with their long purple skirts and black shawls. Absolutely the opposite, in fact, with their very short dresses – all bodice and no skirt – and so many tassels, so many fringes, so many strings of beads. Such short hair and so much make-up – not feminine, but no, not at all masculine. Bracelets clattered together as thin arms were raised – how did they all manage to be so thin? – and the contents of tiny glasses were gulped down. A man and two maids with trays wove through the crowd, refilling the glasses from cocktail shakers. There hardly seemed to be anything to eat – a few dishes of nuts and little biscuits. How very different from 'entertaining' at Belgrave Square.

'Darlings! Adrian and Hitty Pitty – how too delicious!' Suddenly, there in front of them was Julia, wearing a narrow, narrow dress, more like a tube than anything else, of vividly pink satin. Heavy ivory bracelets, carved all over, covered her arms right up to her bare shoulders – shoulders as smooth as ivory though they were hardly wider than her wrists. Were they beautiful, those arms? Henrietta wasn't sure. Certainly they were chic. Thinking of her own arms, 'beautiful' in the style of Aunt Louisa's generation, indented at wrist and elbow, rounded above and between, she felt that they were dowdy and old-fashioned – yes, positively Edwardian.

'Darlings, there are so many people who are simply dying
to meet you.' Julia's thin, predatory little hand clutched at
Adrian's sleeve. When she is old, Henrietta thought, she
will have hands like claws. Then she thought: But she isn't
old *now*.

'Adrian,' Julia said, 'there is a tremendous admirer of
yours here. He adores everything you write. You must meet
him *at once*. Ah, there he is.'

Julia's hand slid down Adrian's sleeve. When it reached
his wrist, she took his hand. She started to lead him away
through the crowd.

Henrietta wondered if she should follow like a dog,
uninvited and probably unwelcome. No, she would stay
where she was. She half turned, and put her empty glass
down on the bar. The man in the white coat immediately
filled it up again. Oh well, perhaps another drink would
make her feel more cheerful, or at least more lively,
more able to contemplate the possibility of entering into
conversation with someone – but with whom?

The little cold glass clutched in her hand, she turned back
to the room, took a sip. Over by the window, Adrian was
talking to a man with long grey hair who was gesticulating
with thin pale fingers. Adrian was smiling. They both looked
as though they were enjoying themselves. She took a swallow
from her glass, then a gulp, and realized with some alarm
that it was empty. She mustn't have any more. She never had
more than two drinks, and she wasn't used to cocktails.

'Henrietta, good evening.' At the sound of the familiar
voice, she swung round. Henry was standing beside her.
She had wondered if he would be there, had thought that
probably he wouldn't, that it was unlikely to be his kind
of party.

'You two haven't met, I think. Henrietta, let me introduce
Miss Mallerby, Caroline Mallerby. Caroline, this is my first
cousin, Mrs Wheeler.'

Miss Mallerby was certainly very pretty: slight, slender,

but not at all in Julia's style. Where Julia was all angles, all brilliance, with her glittering green eyes, her startling clothes, this girl was delicate, flowery, dressed not to startle but to 'look nice'. A lady – that was the immediate impression one formed. And how pleasantly she was smiling.

Had Henry brought her to the party? Now he was asking her what she would drink.

'A lemonade,' she said, 'if there is such a thing. I rather doubt it.' She laughed but not at all maliciously.

'Henrietta, your glass is empty. Can I get something for you?'

'Another White Lady please, Henry,' she said.

A siphon of lemonade was discovered behind the bar. Drinks were poured. Henry had a whisky and soda. 'Can't stand concoctions,' he said.

People had rolled back a rug at the other end of the room, and were dancing to the piano. One of those new dances she had never attempted – not that she had had many opportunities – because she had always felt that she would look ridiculous doing them.

She turned to Miss Mallerby who was saying what a lot of people there were at the party. She was looking about her with an air of innocent surprise. These were obviously unaccustomed surroundings to her, as they were to Henry, but neither of them looked ill at ease. Miss Mallerby's expression was quizzical, Henrietta decided.

'Henry!' Julia was upon them. 'And you've brought sweet Caroline. I'm delighted.'

Miss Mallerby's smile *was* sweet. 'Unspotted from the world' was the odd phrase that came into Henrietta's mind now, looking at her. She couldn't remember where it came from, but it certainly suited her, particularly as she was standing next to Julia. Beside Miss Mallerby, Julia, for all her chic, looked almost tawdry: her make-up too bright, the glitter of her eyes too feverish, the colour of her dress – yes, definitely garish.

'Hitty Pitty *still* lurking by the bar,' Julia said. 'Now, who can we introduce you to?'

'I'm perfectly happy, thank you, Julia,' Henrietta said. *Lurking by the bar*, indeed!

'But darling, there must be *someone* here you'd like to meet. After all this is a *party*.' Now she spoke to Miss Mallerby: 'Hitty Pitty – oh forgive me; that's my old pet name for Henrietta – has always rather despised parties, I think. Or anyway she tends to stand about *looking* as if she despises them.'

With a quick, friendly glance in Henrietta's direction, Miss Mallerby said coolly, 'I've always thought one should do whatever one feels like doing at parties. Anyhow at very big parties like this.'

Julia gave a petulant little shrug. A second later, she darted aside. Imperiously she tapped the shoulder of a small man who was standing near her, engaged in animated discussion with another, younger man. Both of them looked, Henrietta thought, as they might have something to do with the stage.

He turned. 'Julia, my sweet!' he exclaimed. Yes, his manner was distinctly theatrical. But then, of course, so was Julia's.

'Rupert, you simply must be introduced to my cousin, Henrietta Wheeler. She's longing to meet you.'

He looked faintly surprised as, Henrietta thought, he might well do. He was wearing a blue shirt.

'Henrietta,' Julia said, 'this is Rupert Midgeley. As you know, he designs the most divine hats.'

Now Julia swung round to face Miss Mallerby and Henry. 'Henry, Caroline – I insist on your *mixing*. Come with me.'

The mixing bell, Henrietta thought, as Julia led them away. She and Rupert Midgeley gazed at each other blankly.

'You admire my work?' he said.

'Oh yes, well . . . I don't really know it.' A faint gleam of professional interest faded from his face. 'You design Julia's hats, do you?' she asked.

'*Most* of them, except when she's a perfect *beast* and buys them in Paris.'

'I like some hats very much,' Henrietta said. She paused, then added, 'Mostly large ones.'

'Ah yes, the garden party ones, all aviaries and orchards and herbaceous borders. Too quaint. I can imagine that those might be your – style.' He hesitated before the last word, as if he weren't really sure that she had a style. 'Too sad that they're so completely *out* nowadays. But one must be *à la mode*, of course, whatever the personal sacrifice involved.' He surveyed her. 'If you *pop in* to my little *boîte* one of these days, there might just be something I could do for you. A cloche, of course – *de rigueur* – but perhaps with a great big bow or something at the side. *Not* a bird, though. I can't possibly allow you a bird.'

'I don't *want* a bird,' she said. 'The last thing I would want on a hat is a bird.'

'Oh well, *that's* lucky, isn't it, dear?' His eyes, she saw, were getting desperate, fluttering towards the freedom of the party in a manner rather reminiscent of the forbidden birds. Now they alighted on an object in the middle distance.

'If you would excuse me,' he said, 'there's someone over there I just *have* to catch before he rushes off and is lost for ever.'

'Of course,' she said, and he was gone.

So there she was by herself again – though being alone was really better than talking to that silly hat man. How extraordinary of Julia to ask a man who made hats to her party. Again the shadow of Aunt Louisa crossed her mind.

She couldn't see Adrian anywhere. Her glass was empty again. She put it down on the bar. As the barman handed her her fourth – yes, it was her fourth – cocktail, Henry spoke behind her.

'I say, Henrietta, going it a bit, aren't you?' He laughed.
'Those things are stronger than they look, you know.' As
she had been at other times, she was struck by the way that,
though he didn't pronounce words as Uncle Harry had, his
speech was really closer to Uncle Harry's than it was to that
of most of the people she knew nowadays.

'I feel quite all right, thank you, Henry,' she said, aware
that she herself was pronouncing her words with unusual
care and precision. She took a sip – just a sip this time –
from the new drink.

'Of course you do.' He smiled. 'Just giving you a friendly
warning. Dreadful concoctions.'

'That's a very pretty girl you were with, Henry,' she
said.

'Caroline? Yes. Jolly nice girl. Her brother was at school
with me, and in the Coldstream.' There was a moment's
pause. 'As a matter of fact,' he said, 'I've rather got to rush
away now. She and I are expected at a dinner party.'

'Oh yes.'

'Been wanting to talk to you, Henrietta. Quite impossible
to talk here of course. Wondered if you could possibly come
round to Half Moon Street tomorrow afternoon.'

'Tomorrow afternoon,' she repeated. She felt an impulse
to say that she was busy. But she didn't. 'Yes,' she said. 'I
think I can manage that. About three o'clock?'

'Yes. Absolutely. Three o'clock.'

'Here's Miss Mallerby,' she said quickly, for suddenly
the girl was almost at his elbow, saying, 'Henry, we shall
be awfully late if we don't go now.'

'Yes, yes. Must be going. Goodbye Henrietta.'

'Goodbye Henry. So nice to have met you, Miss
Mallerby.'

'Oh yes, Mrs Wheeler. I do hope we meet again soon.'

When they had gone, she finished the drink. Then she
sighed deeply. *Henry tomorrow*. It was more than two weeks
since they had last met at Half Moon Street. They hadn't

arranged their next meeting – he'd been off to the country, he had said – and she hadn't heard from him. She had been wondering what could have happened. That was probably why she had been feeling so irritable. *Henry tomorrow*. Now she wanted to go home. She felt tired. She must find Adrian – she couldn't see him anywhere.

Putting down her glass on the bar, she set off round the edge of the room, under big paintings, many of which looked like the insides of engines, and staring African masks. She had to push her way past people sitting in chairs of chrome and pale wood, tables of the same materials, and other tables made of mirrors. There were big panels of mirror on the walls, too. She saw a figure coming towards her. 'What a stiff-looking woman,' she thought, before realizing that she was looking at her own reflection.

Glass on the tables, glass on the walls, and glasses everywhere. In people's hands, and on the floor as well as on the tables. Glasses full, half empty, drained. A maid was sweeping up some broken glass.

People, people, but no Adrian. The hat man gave her a nervous glance as she passed a group he was standing in, but she ignored him. Otherwise, all strangers. Over by the piano, a girl with fat calves who was wearing a very short dress was dancing the Charleston all on her own. A few people sitting on the floor nearby, were laughing and making comments. No Adrian – and no Julia either.

Adrian and Julia weren't in the room. By the time she'd circled it completely, she was quite sure of that. She would see if he were in the hall, and if he weren't, she would go home without him. Serve him right for deserting her all through the party. She smiled at the thought of how he would dislike having to pay for a taxi. She wasn't feeling happy, she realized, in spite of *Henry tomorrow*. In fact, as she marched out of the room, a tear welled up in her eye, and she had to wipe it away. Could her melancholy be something to do with the cocktails? She remembered someone saying that gin made people maudlin. Who could have said that? It didn't sound like one of Adrian's friends. They never drank gin. Tea and coffee mostly, but sometimes beer or a glass of sherry. Perhaps it had been Julia. A tall man came down the passage, looking very red in the face. As he passed her, he swayed, and put a hand on her arm. She pulled away. 'How now, proud beauty,' he said, and laughed and went on down the corridor.

No sign of Adrian at all. She was definitely going home. A door in the passage was open, and she glanced inside as she passed. There were no lights on, but the curtains were open, and pale bright moonlight poured through the window, under which two figures were embracing. She saw that they were Adrian and Julia.

Quickly she went on down the passage, and into Julia's bedroom. She put on her hat and coat. She had expected to look pale, but she saw in the mirror that in fact she was very flushed. *More like a peony than a rose.*

Outside the flat, as she waited for the lift, she noticed that the party was quietening down.

Driving home, she couldn't stop going over it in her mind. *Julia and Adrian. Adrian and Julia.* It was quite ridiculous. Julia must have had dozens of affaires. What could she possibly see in him? *Wait till she goes to bed with him!* she heard herself say aloud, and gave a little giggle. Perhaps she had? But no, Henrietta was quite sure she hadn't. If she had, she wouldn't have bothered to stand embracing him there in the moonlight. Embracing in the moonlight – what an old-fashioned thing for chic Julia to be doing, anyway. She giggled again.

Henry tomorrow. But – Henry and that pretty little girl this evening. Surely he couldn't be – involved? But if he were, would it really make any difference?

✤ *Thirteen* ✤

1922

She had never, ever, been so bored in her life. She couldn't
help smiling sometimes when she remembered how proud
she had been of escaping from Belgrave Square. She hadn't
really 'escaped' at all. Well, she had got away from Aunt
Louisa, but she hadn't escaped *to* anything. That had been
why she had started, of all things, cooking.

'Our food is as bad as the food in the nursery in Belgrave
Square,' she said one day to Adrian. The cook had sent up
a notably, though not exceptionally, repulsive luncheon of
stringy mutton and tapioca pudding. 'I can't think,' she
added, 'why one puts up with it.'

Adrian looked up, with an expression of surprise, from
his book. He had introduced the custom of reading at
meals gradually. Now it was habitual and she, perforce,
had adopted it too, though there was so much other time
for reading that she felt it might occasionally have been nice
to talk. Not that talking to Adrian was much fun.

'Hmm?' he said now, as usual, and then, 'I suppose it
isn't very interesting. But good cooks are expensive, you
know. Anyway, it doesn't really matter, does it?'

Two attitudes typical of Adrian, she noted, were summoned up in that speech. First his devotion to that
Victorian concept, 'plain living and high thinking'. Food
was something one absorbed four times a day to fuel the
body – and thus, of course, the all-important brain. Any
pleasure that might be involved in the process of absorption
was wholly incidental, not to say unnecessary. This was the
general view in Adrian's circle, she had found.

Secondly, there was his unvarying concern for economy – his *meanness*, she thought with a thrill of guilty pleasure. It was true that a good cook was expensive, and so were the rich ingredients that had made dining-room – as opposed to nursery – food so good at Churston and Belgrave Square. But surely one could have good food that wasn't so expensive? She *knew*, in fact, that it was possible. A distant memory of Papa, wandering from his studio into the kitchen, becoming as absorbed in pots and pans as he had been in paints and canvas, made her smile sadly. So – and as she voiced the sudden inspiration, the movement of Adrian's head made her feel as if she had physically dragged it up, by the hair, from his book – 'Why shouldn't *I* learn to cook?' she exclaimed.

'Learn to cook?' he said, blinking in the way she always found irritating. Then, raising his eyebrows, he said, 'I can't see any reason why you *shouldn't*, if, of course, you *wanted* to.' He made the idea of 'wanting to' sound more than eccentric: inexplicable.

'Of course,' he went on, 'Mrs Beale might well be annoyed by your "interferin' in 'er kitching".' Imitating cockney was not one of his talents, despite the cult of music hall, which he shared with so many of his friends. They praised its 'wonderful robustness' – how extraordinarily out of character *that* was if one thought about it – where *she* found it vulgar and boring.

'But,' she said, 'I would get rid of Mrs Beale.'

'Not have a cook at all, you mean?' Now he definitely sounded doubtful.

'I'd get a kitchenmaid to do the vegetables, and so on. And think how much we'd save on Mrs Beale's wages!'

The last lure she cast deliberately – as she had seen Uncle Harry cast a fly for salmon.

'Yes, *that's* true,' he said, rising to it – oh how *predictable* he was.

'So you'd plunge *in medias res*?' he asked. 'Wouldn't you

take lessons or anything? You could do that without Mrs Beale's knowing anything about it.'

'No,' she said. 'I shall buy a cookery book.'

'A cookery book. Yes, of course. Well, when one thinks of the people who *do* cook, you should be able to pick it up quite quickly.'

He bent over his book again. Then he looked up. 'Of course,' he said, 'you know I don't really mind *what* I eat.'

'I know,' she murmured, and could feel the little sneering smile on her face. But he didn't see it, of course. He was reading.

The idea of getting rid of Mrs Beale – something she hadn't even thought of until today – delighted her. An end to that awful quarter of an hour each morning, discussing the 'menus' – having to experience in anticipation, as well as, later, in fact, the day's horrors. And with what a wall of sullen and, she felt, deliberate incomprehension she had been faced with if ever she ventured to suggest some new dish: 'I'm afraid I haven't been accustomed to anything like *that*, madam.' Away with stringy mutton, with gluey tapioca, with a solid but tremulous pudding called 'shape', with that thick pink blanket which covered cod, and which always contained little lumps of uncooked flour. Away, in fact, with Mrs Beale.

She would be as glad to be rid of Mrs Beale's presence as of her cooking. She had always found servants a drag on her spirits – their perpetual presence, their constant attentions at Churston and at Belgrave Square. A legacy perhaps of what she had once heard Aunt Louisa refer to (she was sure she had been meant to hear) as her 'unfortunate early upbringing'. And, of course, there had always been a difference in the way the servants had treated her and the way they had treated Julia. They weren't rude – but they were remote, aloof, and she, in her turn had been stiff with them. So unlike Julia, prattling away to them, and 'adored' by every member of the staff.

Servants had been part of the weight of things that darling Edmund had hated so much. How he had detested that heaviness, that over-abundance. Marrying Adrian had been a rejection of all that. She had chosen simplicity.

'An artist's life.' For of course, in those days, Adrian had been writing his novel – and talking about it all the time. That unfinished novel – consigned to a cupboard long ago. And when she had persuaded him to let her read it, she had been able to see why. It wasn't at all what she thought of as a novel – just a series of long conversations between young men at Cambridge. The high point of the 'plot' had been when two of them went for a midnight swim in the river, naked, and 'felt a sort of strange communion'.

And now he wrote nothing but pamphlets and articles, though he was making notes for a book on politics. Really his writing was just one of a mass of things that occupied him; his writing, his lectures, his meetings, his discussions – all of them utterly uninteresting to her. Really his life was just as remote as life at Belgrave Square from what she had imagined. *An artist's life*.

Why, when they were engaged, she had actually imagined that they might live in the country, in a cottage. 'Ideal for a novelist,' Adrian had said. They had moved into the flat in the square only temporarily. For it wasn't really a house. The rooms on the two upper floors, apart from those in which Mrs Beal and Vera slept, were stacked with the landlord's furniture. The landlord had moved out of the house after his wife had died. Now he lived in an hotel. Sometimes in the evening, when Adrian was out, she would imagine creaks and footsteps overhead in the deserted rooms. 'Rats,' Adrian had said, and Vera had put down strychnine crystals, but she still heard the creaking sounds. And now Adrian had given up the novel, and all the things he did made it essential for them to live in London. The flat was cheap – she often felt they'd never move from it.

At first she had imagined that she would be able to help Adrian with his work. When Uncle Harry had given her the allowance and she didn't need to work in an office (to her relief she had to admit), she had thought that her typewriting and shorthand would be useful. But Adrian wouldn't dictate; he had to write everything out, and though she tried, she simply couldn't read his tiny squiggly writing.

Then she had wanted to do 'research' for him. He had asked her to look up things in libraries, and so on, but he'd never seemed pleased with the results. Really, he had said, he found it easier to do it himself. Her mind, he said in explanation, was 'untrained'.

She had struggled for some time with that course of reading he had given her. But she did find those 'great men' of his terribly heavy going. She really preferred simply getting an idea of them. Just as Freud said one acted for reasons hidden under the surface, so Darwin said one did things in order to survive, and Marx said one did them because one belonged to a certain class. Really, in fact, one wasn't responsible for anything. But when she had said that to Adrian, he had groaned and clutched at his forehead, and had exclaimed, 'Honestly, I give up!'

How rude he was. So *she* had given up, and now just read what she wanted to.

Adrian had closed his book, was standing up, ready to go back to his desk. 'You look deep in thought,' he said. 'Surely not still on the subject of cookery?' But he didn't wait for an answer.

First she bought Mrs Beeton's *Household Cookery*. She made a list of all the essential things: frying, boiling, roasting, making sauces, and tried them one by one. When she could do them, she found Eliza Acton's *Modern*

Cookery, which was much more fun. Soon they were eating food which she thought was really delicious. How absorbed she became in her cooking. People said cooking was an art, didn't they?

Sometimes she felt that Adrian had actually preferred Mrs Beale's boiled cod – pink blanket and all – to Miss Acton's Mackerel Stewed in Wine, and Mrs Beale's gluey tapioca to Miss Acton's Very Superior Whipped Syllabub. Often, when he tasted something she had cooked, he would look gloomy and say, 'It's very rich, isn't it?' Adrian had what he called a 'sensitive stomach', and he was always taking pills and powders for indigestion. She couldn't help feeling revolted, remembering Nanny's Gregory Powder. She should try to be more sympathetic, she told herself, but it was difficult as she herself never got indigestion. It was the same with his insomnia. She, who almost always slept for eight hours or more each night, couldn't understand why he had to take laudanum drops mixed in water two or three times a week.

Of course Adrian also remarked on the fact that the housekeeping bills had risen because of the cost of the ingredients required for the new dishes. But, as she pointed out, they were saving a cook's salary. Besides, she said, eating proper food – plenty of eggs, butter, cream and wine – was good for them, was an insurance against future bills from the doctor. But Adrian, particularly when he was suffering from his indigestion, didn't seemed to be convinced by that argument.

He seemed to become particularly indignant about her buying wine. He didn't like wine, said it 'didn't suit' him, and that, anyway, it clouded the brain. So, when she cooked with wine, which was quite often, she would have a glass or two with her meal, and leave him to his water or his (very occasional) glass of beer.

Often she wished that she had a more appreciative public for her dishes – after all, cooking was an art, and artists needed patrons. But entertaining, in Adrian's circle, was almost always confined to coffee and cakes or buns, handed round after the discussion of some 'paper'. That was another unfortunate thing. Although she loved cooking, she couldn't bring herself to take an interest in baking – there was something so drab about it. Once or twice she made cakes for 'evenings' but they never seemed to turn out quite right. Not that the circle cared; they didn't even seem to notice.

An unforeseen effect on the new *cuisine* was that – the food being so delicious, and Adrian's appetite so meagre – she began to put on weight. She had always been curved, but now her bosom and hips were almost opulently rounded. *Bosom. Hips.* Looking at herself in the mirror, she would sigh, for both, in terms of the fashions of the day, should have been non-existent. But after all, she was tall, and large-framed, and her waist retained its smallness. Really, she sometimes reflected, she should have lived in Aunt Louisa's heyday – would in fact have been very much to the taste of 'Kingy'. But everyone had eaten so much in those days – far more than she did – that it was amazing they hadn't all been much fatter than they were. She remembered how Edmund had complained about those Edwardian meals. Would Edmund have thought her too fat? Would he have preferred skeleton-girls like Julia?

Most of the women attached to Adrian's circle were also thin – though far from elegantly so. That was why secretly, in her thoughts, she called them 'scarecrows'. Just as they didn't mind what they ate, they seemed to take a pride in not caring what they wore. Such lumpy cardigans, such drooping skirts, such *shawls!* And surely their hats could only have been dug out of the 'jumble' in some church bazaar – except that all 'the scarecrows' were impeccably agnostic. Goodness, she herself wasn't all that interested in clothes, though she chose good materials and went to quite a good little dressmaker. But – how Aunt Louisa and Julia would have laughed – in Adrian's circle she was considered positively 'smart'.

Adrian's circle. She always came back to that. Never never hers. So circle was the right word for it – a circle, of its very nature, being closed.

A masculine circle. A Cambridge circle. And, at Cambridge, almost all of them had belonged to some club or 'society', as they called it, which seemed to be as important to them now as it had been when they were undergraduates. Extraordinary! It was almost as if they were still members of that secret, male society. 'Secret' because apparently no one knew officially of its existence until he was asked to join. And 'male', of course, because it had no woman members.

Weren't even the 'scarecrows', those earnest wives and sisters (although they were closer to the circle than she was, and actually sometimes read papers at meetings), still *outside?* Outside some magic ring that, though invisible, still gave a repelling shock to any stranger who approached? Yes, she felt convinced of it.

Of course, in Uncle Harry's and Aunt Louisa's world, men and women, if one thought about it, had spent most of their time apart: the women trying on dresses and chattering of 'spangles', 'dewdrops' and 'cultes'; the men slaughtering things – why, she remembered one day's shooting when her uncle and five of his friends had killed thirteen hundred pheasants. Yet, when they met, they had seemed genuinely to enjoy each other's company. More than that. Aunt Louisa and Sir Richard – and so many other affaires that she had read and heard of since. *The mixing bell.* When *they* met, there had been *sparks* between them.

But – sparks between 'the scarecrows' and the members of the circle? Never! The circle's members only kindled to ideas – and the ideas were dead ones. Morals – but they didn't believe in God, so why did they bother? Politics – yet none of them seemed to want to be Prime Minister. Personal relationships – but she had never heard them talking about love, which was the only personal relationship that really mattered, wasn't it?

How interesting it would be if, one evening, they would hold a discussion on love, real love. But they would probably manage to make even that boring. She remembered that evening when she had actually dozed off. Jumping awake, she had glanced hastily round the room to see if anyone had noticed – and had found Adrian watching her with an expression she couldn't fathom. And then, quick as a flash, he had looked away, as if he had observed nothing.

What did Adrian think of her? When they were engaged, he had told her that she was the first woman he had loved. And now, as she thought about that, a particular dry taste came into her mouth, a particular dry smell into her nostrils: the taste, the smell of his 'approaches', as she always thought of them – for wasn't 'advances' rather too strong a word? She knew so well the little dry cough he gave when he came into her room, and then the kiss he would place on her mouth with dry closed lips, and then the tentative journeys of his cool dry hands, which she had noticed always made a little jump of withdrawal when they touched her breasts. And she knew how, then, he would take his hands away from her and touch himself, and how she would wait until she heard his breathing quicken. And then, at last, he would flop – *like a fish on dry land*, she thought – on her body, coming, as often as not, before he was inside her, which, though it was messy, she rather preferred because she always found his entries painful.

She remembered the night of her wedding, and her hair, so thick, and flowing down below her waist, and how she had lain there, with her eyes closed, waiting for him to bring her to life.

Did most girls go through that? she wondered. If they did, then perhaps – ignorant, innocent – they thought that

was what it was always like. She however had once – only
once – known quite otherwise. She smiled.

✤ *Fourteen* ✤

1923

One couldn't spend all one's time cooking, and anyway,
she was beginning to find cooking every day rather
monotonous. She read a great many novels when she
wasn't cooking: good ones, bad ones and detective stories
for which she had developed a sudden passion.

She started walking, through the squares of Bloomsbury
at first, and then, when that became monotonous, farther
afield, through the parks of central London: the Green Park,
St James's and Hyde Park, 'the Park' of her childhood. She
walked as far as Kensington and went to look at the cottage
where she had lived with Papa and Mama. She found that
it had been turned into a public house, so of course it was
impossible for her to go inside. If there had been people
living there, she might have knocked at the door, and asked
if she could look around because she had lived there as
a child.

Sometimes she got into an omnibus and travelled as far as
it went. Then she got out, wandered around for a little, and
caught another one back to where she had started. She often
remembered how horrified Aunt Louisa had been at Cynthia
Chanter travelling 'alone with all the common people'.

She spent a lot of time in bookshops, opening one novel,
one volume of poetry after another, looking for 'the book',
though she didn't know what 'the book' would be except
that she was sure she would recognize it after a few sentences.
Anyway, she never found it.

It was outside Hatchard's bookshop in Piccadilly that she recognized him, walking towards her. Her first impulse was to turn back into the shop. Why, she hadn't seen him since her wedding. But something prevented her – boredom, curiosity; she didn't know. She hesitated – and he had seen her, was raising his hat. She started to move towards him. As they met, the expression of surprise on his face was replaced by one of pleasure.

'Why, Henrietta, how well you're looking.'

She had felt the same herself that morning when she was getting ready to go out. It was a June day, a strawberries and wild roses day, a day for drifting in a punt down the river at Churston. *No strawberries, no roses, no Churston for me*, she had thought, but she had put on a new summer dress, lilac coloured, matched with a lilac straw hat with grey velvet ribbons round the crown.

'Good-morning, Henry,' she said now, noticing the gleaming whiteness of his shirt, the glossy fairness of his hair, the brightness of his eyes, the scrubbed freshness of his skin. Adrian and his friends never looked as clean as that, as clean as Edmund and Henry had always looked. Oh, Adrian washed, his clothes were laundered, but somehow his skin, his linen had – in her mind anyway – a greyish tinge when she compared them now with Henry's. Indubitably, of course, Henry had a valet, a man whose life's occupation was making sure that Henry looked like this.

As she thought of these things, she was asking about Uncle Harry and Aunt Louisa. Both well, he said, and Uncle Harry preparing for a big game hunting expedition.

'Rather too much, at his age, I would have thought, but he's set on it. His last fling, he says, before he settles down to pottering round at Churston or sitting in the window of his club, reading the newspaper.' Henry laughed abruptly. 'And where are you off to, Henrietta?'

'I'm on my way home,' she said. 'I've been in Hatchard's,' and she gestured at the bookshop behind her.

'Ah. Never seem to go into a bookshop from one year to another. But you were always fond of reading, weren't you? Like dear old Edmund.'

A moment's flickering resentment that Henry, *the ideally stupid*, could speak with such easy affectionate patronage about Edmund. *It is easy to patronize the dead*, she thought. Just because one is alive, and dear old Edmund – not to mention dear old Shakespeare and dear old Beethoven – is not. 'Charm smiling at the good mouth, quick eyes gone under earth's lid' – yes, *she* felt sorry for them all on this perfect morning with the light breeze blowing her dress against her knees.

Henry looked at his watch. *He's going to say goodbye*, she thought, with a curious pang of regret. But what he said was, 'How about a bite of luncheon? Just the day for a lobster and a bottle of the Widow.'

A bottle of the Widow – Uncle Harry's expression for a bottle of champagne. It must have done wonders for the sales of Veuve Clicquot. Astonished by the invitation, she said, 'Oh I . . .' and found herself wondering if she could. Adrian was lunching with a friend. That was why she had dawdled in Hatchard's for so long. It was nearly one o'clock. There was no reason to hurry home. She had told Vera that she would lunch on bread and cheese, as she often did when she was alone, now that cooking was amusing her less. Bread and cheese – or lobster and champagne?

'Please don't refuse me, Henrietta,' he was saying with a teasing smile which suddenly reminded her—

'That would be lovely,' she said.

'Splendid, simply splendid. The Ritz? No, I think – Rule's. Have you ever been to Rule's? Wonderfully old-fashioned.'

As he called a cab, she thought: *Not the Ritz because someone might see us*. She dived into the cab to hide a sudden flush of almost guilty excitement. And Rule's? No, she had never been to Rule's, a place which she associated with Victorian 'swells' and actresses.

As they drove towards Piccadilly Circus, she was surprised by how extraordinarily happy she felt. She glanced sideways at him. He really was very good-looking – though of course not nearly as good-looking as darling Edmund. She wondered why he had never married. Why, he was nearly thirty-three. But he must have had lots of affaires – oh yes, she felt quite certain of that.

'Nowhere like London,' he was saying. 'Nowhere in the world. Especially at this time of year.'

And, at this moment, she felt inclined to agree with him. Everyone so well dressed. Everything looking glittering, polished, in the sunlight. The fresh paint on the buildings, the gleaming shop windows, the shining cars and glossy horses. London – normally the grey fabric of her life; why had she never seen it as bright and fresh and exciting?

The head waiter in the dark-panelled restaurant knew him well. *Who else did he bring here?* she wondered. Sitting opposite him, on a red velvet banquette, she realized that this was the first time in her life that she had ever had luncheon alone in a restaurant with a man. How delicious the lobster mayonnaise was, and the pale icy champagne. And what surprised her was that she didn't find him difficult to talk to.

He did most of the talking, chatted about the Season, about all sorts of people whom she had once dimly known; it was more amusing to hear about them than to meet them, she found. He mentioned Julia. 'Funny,' he said. 'Never expected her to go in for this sort of show.'

'Show?' she asked. 'I haven't seen Julia for ages.'

'Oh, all this Bright Young Things business, don't you know. Parties, parties, parties, with artists and other extraordinary people.' He had obviously entirely forgotten that her father had been an artist. 'But perhaps,' he said, 'you go in for that sort of thing yourself?'

She laughed. 'Absolutely not,' she said. 'I assure you that

no one could possibly be less bright, and I don't even feel young any more.'

'That's all rot, of course,' he said. 'Never seen you looking better. Marriage suits you,' he said. Did she hear the infinitesimal hint of a question in the way his voice rose on the word 'suits'?

'Mmm,' she said, drily, coolly.

Somehow the bottle of the Widow had vanished terribly quickly – he had drunk much more of it than she had. Now he ordered another.

'Oh Henry,' she said. 'I'm sure we shouldn't.'

He leant forward a little across the table. 'Shouldn't? Hmm? Henrietta, don't let's bother about "shouldn't".'

And the overwhelming attraction which, as she recovered it, she recognized she had felt to him all those years ago, which had, indeed, been bubbling away inside her ever since they met outside Hatchard's, suddenly gushed up inside her as – pop, the waiter opened the second bottle of champagne.

He felt it too – yes, she was sure of that. They drank the champagne, they followed the lobster with strawberries and cream, but all the time something else was happening. Both of them had been *caught up*, were being carried irresistibly along. Carried along to what? But she knew to what. How, when, where, were the questions.

To his rooms in Half Moon Street it turned out. Luncheon over, the bill signed, as they left the restaurant, he said, 'You'll come back with me, Henrietta, won't you?' Aside, to the doorman, he said, 'A cab.' Then, as the doorman moved to the edge of the pavement, 'You will,' he said. 'Can feel you will.' And she, dismissing from her mind the preposterous idea that they would be going 'back' to Belgrave Square, said, 'Yes.'

Sitting side by side in the cab, a few inches apart, not saying a word. The cab stopping in the middle of Half Moon Street. He getting out, putting his hand under her

arm as she followed. He paying the cab, opening the black
front door himself with a key. An elderly man in a dark
suit appearing at the back of the narrow hall. 'That will
be all right, Beedon.' The man retreating.

As she started up the stairs, she heard him call to the
man that he didn't want to be disturbed. Suddenly she felt
sordid, wanted to turn and run, hesitated, but Henry was
behind her now, and on she went. How she wished that
that man hadn't been there. Apart from what he must
be thinking, she imagined blackmail, scandal. *A divorced
woman*. But all that was absurd, surely. Henry must know
that it was all right – he wouldn't risk anything, wouldn't
want scandal any more than she did. They had reached the
top of the stairs. He gestured the way along the landing,
opened a door, ushered her into a room.

Walls papered in dark red. A mahogany glass-fronted
bookcase. A leather-topped desk. A leather sofa and
armchairs. A pipe rack – but surely Henry didn't smoke
a pipe? She gave a little nervous laugh.

'What's the joke?'

'Perfect bachelor chambers,' she said. 'As if they were in
a Victorian novel.'

He looked round as if he hadn't noticed the room before.

'Oh yes? Really? It suits me very well. Must have a
bolt-hole of one's own. Can't live at home all the time at
my age.'

Can't take women home. But she didn't say it. She gestured
to the pipe rack. 'Do you smoke a pipe now, Henry?'

'A pipe? Heavens, no. Can't stand the things or the people
who smoke them. Puffing away, preaching at you usually,
too. Like my tutor at Oxford. No, that thing was here when
I came. The rooms are furnished, you know. Beedon's a
retired butler, and his wife's a retired cook.' He paused.
'Suits me very well,' he said again.

In the course of this conversation, all the excitement she
had felt in the restaurant, and sitting next to him in the cab,

had ebbed away. Oh, she did wish she hadn't come. But suddenly he took her hands, clasped them between his.

'What on earth are we doing,' he said, 'talking about pipes? Horrible things.' He laughed. Then, all at once, his expression was completely serious. He took a step forward and began to kiss her.

Again, immediately, everything was all right. If 'all right' could describe dissolving utterly while concentrating entirely. This must be how it is, she thought, when there's something you really care about, something you really want to do. *How painters must feel about painting,* she thought, just before she stopped thinking at all.

When they parted, breathless, his eyes with a dazed lost look, that extraordinarily serious expression on his face, he said, 'Come, Henrietta.' His voice, so low, had lost all its mannerisms, as if only the words were real, not how he said them. He led her over to a door by the bookcase, and opened it. They were in a cool dim bedroom, the curtains, drawn to keep out the June sun, moving slightly in the air. Heavy furniture – a wardrobe, a chest, a big mahogany bed, with a white damask counterpane on it. He kissed her again, and then he began to undress her, with hands that shook a little, which somehow moved her extraordinarily, as did that utter seriousness of his regard.

When she was naked, he pulled the counterpane off the bed. 'Lie down,' he said, and she started to draw back the sheet. But he said, 'No. Lie down on the top. I want to look at you.' She felt shy, but she did as he asked.

He was taking off his clothes, dropping them on the floor, and all the time looking at her. When he was naked too, he sat down on the side of the bed. 'Beautiful,' he said, 'An odalisque.' What an extraordinary word for him to use, she thought. He lay down beside her, started to kiss her again.

So slow and so gentle – an extraordinary gentleness.

The difference between him out in the world wearing his clothes, and naked with her here, suddenly made her feel like crying. *And the difference in me*, she thought, the difference in me.

She fell asleep, and when she awoke, he was leaning with his elbow on the pillow, looking down at her. She started to sit up, saying, 'I must go,' with a vague little laugh, but he said, 'No, not yet, not now.' And it all happened again, the same but entirely different. Learning each other.

Afterwards, this time, she didn't want to sleep, though she was tired. She wanted to enjoy the tiredness. Such a wonderful tiredness, of the body not of the mind. The mind floating above the body, not floating as in water, but as in air, drifting, gliding.

'Have you ever been in an areoplane?' she said.

'An areoplane?' He laughed. 'What a funny girl you are. Yes, I have as a matter of fact. Twice. It was rather ripping.'

'Was it like being a bird?'

'Well, never having been a bird . . .' He laughed again. 'But no, I wouldn't have thought so. It's very noisy and rather bumpy.'

'Pity,' she said. She sat up, looked at her watch 'Half past five,' she said. 'Goodness. I must go. Can I have a bath?'

In the bathroom, there was an enormous white bath with a mahogany surround, and huge, thick dazzling white towels. Though she didn't feel like hurrying, she bathed quickly. Adrian – though he was never curious about where she was – would have reached home ages before. She would tell him that she had been to see Uncle Harry, and had stayed to luncheon and tea, she decided. When she had dressed, she put up her hair – 'your wonderful hair', Henry had said. She was glad that putting up her hair was so easy nowadays. Not like that time at Belgrave Square. Funny, but this time, she didn't feel a trace of guilt about what had happened.

An adulterous woman. Like Aunt Louisa, she thought, and smiled.

Back in the bedroom, she found him dressed again, smiling. He was his other self again. *Ideally stupid?* She didn't know. But in bed – oh there, no one could have called him stupid.

'I'll get you a cab,' he said, and then, when she murmured something about finding one herself, 'No, I insist!' They went through into the sitting-room where there was a speaking tube – 'Ah Beedon, would you find me a cab right away.'

'I shall say I was visiting Uncle Harry if Adrian asks me where I've been,' she said after a moment.

'Oh yes. Quite,' he said, averting his head as if she had committed some *faux pas*. Mentioning Uncle Harry? Or mentioning Adrian? She didn't know.

She went over to the window, and looked down into Half Moon Street. A brightly painted middle-aged woman in a very short skirt was tottering on high heels towards Piccadilly. What did *those women* feel? *'There were dog's hairs on the blanket.'* She thought, *Why, it could be the same one*, and shivered just as Henry's hands came to rest on her shoulders.

'Cold?' he asked.

'No.'

'You know,' he said suddenly, 'always, all these years, I've felt so frightfully sorry about what happened at Belgrave Square all that time ago. What an unspeakable cad I was. But you've forgiven me?'

'Apparently,' she said, and burst out laughing. She swung round. He was smiling, but a little stiffly.

'Henry,' she said, 'you amaze me. That was all wrong – but this isn't?'

He looked at her with surprise, thought a moment, was obviously puzzled at how to express what he was thinking. He plunged. 'You know,' he said, 'a married woman is meant to be fair game.' All at once he looked horrified, but she was laughing again.

'I see,' she said. 'Oh yes, I see.'

'Here's the cab, I think,' he said, looking out of the window. 'Yes. Henrietta, when am I going to see you again?'

'Again?' she said. She was feeling absurdly light-hearted.

'Surely you'll come again?'

'Oh why not,' she said.

'Next week? Tuesday?'

'Wednesday would be better. Adrian's going to Cambridge for the day.'

'Wednesday then. Luncheon?'

'Better not to risk being seen together.'

'We could have a cold luncheon here, if you'd like that.'

'It would be lovely.'

'One o'clock then,' he said.

Going downstairs with him, she said, making conversation, 'And what are you going to do now?'

'Oh, have a bath, get dressed, and so on. I'm dining out this evening.'

They had reached the front door, which Beedon was holding open. Henry went out ahead of her, and she saw him glance quickly up and down the street. *The corridor at Belgrave Square*. He opened the door of the cab, and she got in.

He smiled. 'I don't know your address,' he said. She gave it to him, and he shut the door. She saw him speaking to the driver, giving him money.

Through the window, she made a little gesture of protest which he ignored. He smiled and raised his hand. He stood on the doorstep until the cab turned the corner.

She sat back. Beautiful manners, she thought. Adrian and his friends didn't have manners like that. Perhaps because they believed that they treated women as equals. Which of

course they didn't. But how nice of Henry it had been to
get dressed just to see her out, when he was going to bath
and change as soon as she had gone.

She liked that. And, yes – she rather liked him. 'A married
woman is fair game.' She smiled. *The other Henry*, though.
She felt something different for him. That naked, serious
Henry. Not love, of course. She would never love anyone
except Edmund. But, as she couldn't have love, it was rather
wonderful having this.

❧ *Fifteen* ❧

1925

When she woke on the morning after Julia's party, she had
a nasty taste in her mouth and a feeling that a headache was
in the offing. She hadn't stayed up late. She wondered if it
might have something to do with the cocktails. A 'hangover'
didn't Julia call it? If it were, she was certainly never going
to have one again.

She got up. She had almost finished breakfast by the
time Adrian came down. His face was yellowish, and his
eyes looked tired.

'What on earth happened to you last night?' was the
first thing he said to her, opening *The Times*, propping
it on the table between them. 'I had a terrible time
finding a cab.'

'I looked for you *everywhere*,' she said innocently, 'but I
just couldn't find you.' *Or Julia*, she was tempted to add,
but she didn't.

'What nonsense,' he said. 'I was there all the time.'
Brazening it out, she thought coldly.

'Well, anyway,' she said, 'you must have been enjoying

yourself to have stayed so long. I'm surprised. I thought it was extraordinarily boring.'

'Yes, I gathered that you stood by the bar all evening, looking as though you despised everyone. You must learn to be more flexible, Henrietta. It's interesting to meet new people occasionally.'

'Except that I didn't meet anyone.'

'Julia told me she had introduced you to someone.'

'A little man who made hats,' she said.

'How snobbish you sound,' he said, and began to read the paper.

Really he was *stupid*, she thought. If he were having this thing, whatever it was, with Julia, what he should have done was to be nice and polite. It almost made her doubt that anything was going on. But 'the moonlight embrace', as she thought of it, in inverted commas, had happened – no doubt about that. Could he be trying a sort of double bluff? But she dismissed that idea immediately. Despite all his talk about personal relationships, he knew absolutely nothing about people. Why, he had been married to her for six years, and he still knew nothing about her. Of course, he wasn't interested in her. (Had never been?) And he had never shown an interest in any other woman since she'd known him. Until Julia. What was it he had seen in Julia that had led to 'the moonlight embrace'?

Perhaps its because she's so like a boy. This thought, springing as it had, fully grown, clothed in words, into her mind, astonished her so much that she put her teacup, which she had been holding in her hand, down on the table instead of in its saucer, and, resting her elbow on the table, her chin on her hand, stared across the table. All she could see of him above the newspaper was the top of his head – his hair was getting very thin on the crown – and a frown creasing his forehead. *So like a boy*. The cropped head, the breastless body.

She started. He had lowered the paper, and the frown was directed at her.

'Oh,' she said vaguely. 'Oh, I wasn't staring at you. I was just thinking.'

He raised his eyebrows, shrugged, took a piece of toast from the rack and put it on his plate, then poured himself another cup of tea. He liked tea for breakfast, and so, to save Vera trouble, she had it too, though she preferred coffee. The thought gave her a sudden sense of grievance.

Replacing her cup in its saucer, she stood up. He was reading the paper again, didn't look at her. Going upstairs, she thought: *But that would explain so many things*.

It wasn't a subject to which she had ever given much thought. Of course she knew, now, why Oscar Wilde had been an outcast – though she'd never known exactly 'what they did'. And there were men who were obviously effeminate, like the hat man at Julia's party. But she'd never though of anything like that in terms of anyone she knew (thought what about Lancaster Tyrrwhitt?), and certainly not in terms of anyone who was *married*. (Though Oscar Wilde had been married and had children, hadn't he?) Yet now she felt absolutely certain about Adrian.

The whole of Adrian's circle suddenly appeared to her in a new light. The sense she had always had that 'the scarecrows' were forever on the fringe. The feeling she'd had when she went into the drawing-room and Adrian was there with friends and the conversation suddenly stopped. It hadn't been, as she had thought, that they were engaged in some discussion in which they thought her incapable of participating. No – it had been a freemasonry. And so many little jokes and references which she hadn't understood – hadn't bothered to try to understand.

Yet he had wanted to marry her. Why? In order to escape *that*, or to conceal it. In either case, he had used her, used her ruthlessly. Yet – hadn't she, in a way, used him: to escape from Aunt Louisa, from Belgrave Square? But that was quite

different. Why, she had given him everything. She had even
learnt to cook! Everything but love. Well, thank heaven for
that. How terrible this discovery would have been if she had
loved him. As things were she just felt – cold, really. Not
even angry. But she was angry – oh yes – that if this were
true – and from that moment at the breakfast table she had
been utterly convinced of it – he should have chosen to have
an affaire with Julia. Why hadn't he chosen a *real* boy? For
a moment she was shocked that she should have had such an
idea. But one shouldn't be shocked by anything. Silly Julia
wasn't, so why should she be? Which made her wonder –
did Julia guess? About Adrian?

She went into her bedroom and drank a glass of water.
She was feeling better than she had when she got up. She
peered closely at herself in the mirror. She was rather pale,
did look a little tired. She would tell Adrian and Vera that
she had a headache, that she didn't want to be disturbed.
She would lie down on her bed, with pads of cotton wool
soaked in wych-hazel on her eyelids, and doze for an hour
or two. She must look her best in the afternoon, when she
went to see Henry.

Driving to see him. As always, she felt eager. Extraordinary
– there had never been a time when it hadn't . . . worked.
Inevitably, the way they made love had grown more
experimental, more elaborate, as time passed. That first
sweet simplicity couldn't have been expected to last for ever.
She wondered if this summer they would meet in the square
garden at night as they had done last year. That had been her
idea. They hadn't done it very often because it was so easy for
her to go to Half Moon Street. But there had been something
so exciting about slipping out of the house, making her way
to the summer house – the darkness, the night smell, the
rustling leaves – and something even more exciting, though
she would never have told Henry, about the thought of
Adrian so very near. Only just across the road.

Piccadilly was held in a Saturday afternoon quietness, the shops closed and hardly any people about. She looked at her watch. She was twenty minutes early. She remembered one of Aunt Louisa's maxims, 'A lady should never be early for an appointment'. Of course, Aunt Louisa hadn't been speaking about illicit assignations – though who could have been better qualified to do so?

She parked the car in Arlington Street, and walked under the colonnade of the Ritz to Green Park. She wandered down Queen's Walk. The trees, the grass still kept their spring freshness. It was cloudy, and the birds were making that special sound, throatier than their normal song, which she had often noticed at Churston, that they made before rain. She sat down on a bench, took her compact out of her bag, and powdered her nose. She was looking well after her rest that morning.

She sat on the bench until the moment when her watch told her that she would be five minutes late. Then she crossed Piccadilly to Half Moon Street.

She rang the doorbell, and Beedon answered it.

'Good-afternoon, madam. His Lordship is expecting you.' It still startled her to hear Henry called 'His Lordship'.

'Good-afternoon. I'll find my own way up,' she said, as she always did, and Beedon retreated with a bow. She still wondered what he thought, though she had stopped worrying about it long before.

Henry opened his door when she was halfway up the stairs. 'Hullo,' she said. 'Here I am for our *talk*.' She raised her eyebrows and smiled, but all he said was 'Splendid'.

Inside, with the door closed, she felt the familiar mixture of safety and illicitness. A hint of triumph, too, today – *so much for Julia and Adrian*.

She had thought about it in the car on the way – why somehow she knew she couldn't mention *Julia and Adrian* to Henry. Any more than she could have spoken to him

about Aunt Louisa and Sir Richard. Oh, that strange sense
of honour of his which she felt that she would never really
understand. '*My sister* – how dare you suggest such a thing!'
Yes, Henry was quite capable of a remark like that. But
what, then, about married women being 'fair game'? Why
was she so sure that that wouldn't apply to Julia, when it
applied to *her?*

Now she almost asked him. 'What do you think of *me*,
Henry?' He was standing by the window to which, instead
of embracing her, he had gone when she came in. Sitting
in one of the leather armchairs, still wearing her coat and
hat, suddenly she longed for a cigarette, though usually she
never smoked when she came to see him, because she didn't
want her mouth to taste of tobacco.

Turning from the window, he said, 'You know, I
really meant it when I said I wanted to talk to you
this afternoon.'

'Oh yes?' she said, and then, 'Well talk away, Henry, by
all means.'

He cleared his throat. 'Dashed difficult, as a matter of
fact. Don't quite know how to put it.'

'Put what, Henry?' Something was definitely, as he might
have said, 'up'.

He paced across from the window to the door, stopped
there. He was wearing country clothes. Perhaps he was
going down to Churston later. How she wished she were
going with him, in his fast motor, driving into a greenness
that would make the greenness of the park look like a
faded backcloth. But how very strange that he should have
changed . . . before.

'You see, Henrietta,' he said, 'I'm getting married.'

'Have you got a cigarette, Henry?' she said. 'I left mine
at home.'

'Oh yes. Yes, of course. Didn't know you smoked,
really.' He fetched a silver box from the desk, brought
it over to her. Turkish and Virginian – *Churston, so*

long ago – divided by a wooden barrier. She took a Virginian.

As he lit it for her, she said, 'Why Henry, congratulations! Is it that pretty girl I saw you with last night?' Which sounded, she thought immediately, just like a music-hall song.

He was looking relieved. Yes, that was definitely what his face expressed – relief. *Is it that pretty girl I saw you with last night?*

'Why yes,' he said. 'How clever of you to guess. It's Caroline. Awfully nice girl. Didn't you think so?'

'Oh yes,' she said. 'Awfully nice.'

'And really,' he said, 'time I settled down, produced an heir, and so on. Mother's frightfully bucked. And Julia.'

'Julia's pleased, is she?'

'Oh yes. Frightfully pleased. You know, in spite of all those racketty people she seems to know, and the parties and so on, she's really quite, well, a simple sort of chap underneath. Keen on the family, and all that. Rather like me in some ways.'

'Really!' And then, something in his look, something, for a moment, evasive where normally all was openness, made her pounce.

'Henry,' she said, 'Julia doesn't know about *us*, does she?'

His silence, his deep flush were her answer.

'Henry,' she said, 'How *could* you? I thought you believed in honour—'

'You don't understand,' he broke in. 'It wasn't like that. I let something slip one day that showed I'd been seeing you. I'm not much of an intriguer, don't you know. There was that awful Italian chap we had to learn about at Oxford.'

'Macchiavelli,' she said.

'That's the one. Anyway, never been any good at that sort of thing. But what was so extraordinary was that Julia had known all along. She didn't say anything for a moment, and then she said "But Henry, I've always known about you and Hitty Pitty." "But how?" I said, and she said "Oh well, call it woman's intuition".'

'She didn't know at all. She was just getting you to admit it.'

'Oh nonsense, Henrietta. Old Julia's not like that.'

'And then you *talked* to her about me?'

'But Henrietta, I've just explained.'

'All right. Yes, you've explained. What did she say?'

'Say?'

'About me. About us.'

He hesitated.

'Come on,' she said, trying to keep her voice calm, 'tell me, Henry.'

'Well, not very much.' He smiled nervously. 'She just said that she was surprised that you were – my cup of tea.'

'Oh, and why did that surprise her?'

'I say, look here, Henrietta, she wasn't criticizing you at all. I give you my word she didn't say a single word against you. It was just, well, don't you know, no interests in common, and so on. And then my not getting any younger. Needing to settle down. All that. Having children. Duty to the family. Strong on that, just as I told you a minute ago.'

'Ah yes.' And now her tone was entirely calm, absolutely cool. 'Anyway, Henry, I've always accepted that you'd get married one day.' She managed a little laugh. 'It would hardly be reasonable for me to object. In the circumstances.'

Again the expression of relief. She got up and, in her turn, went over to the window, looked out. It was raining, a light capricious shower that made the pavement glisten and, as she watched it, abruptly ceased.

She turned to face him. 'But I never really saw,' she said, 'why your getting married should make any different to us.'

Now his expression changed again – to one of shock.

Really it was like watching a film. So many changes of expression without words. And not even a piano hammering away in the background.

He took a step towards her. 'Yes. Well. You know.'

'But I don't know, Henry.'

'I feel,' he said, and paused again. How difficult he found it to say things. Why, she almost felt sorry for him. 'I feel,' he said again, 'that that wouldn't, well, be "quite the thing". A young girl, don't you know. Marriage – really meant to be a fresh start. No loose ends.'

'I don't really very much care for being described as a loose end, Henry.'

'Oh Henrietta, you know that isn't what I meant.' Another of his pauses. Then out it came: 'Apart from anything else, I rather think I love her.'

Yes, *that* struck home. Struck harder than she could ever have imagined that it would.

'I see.' How steady her voice sounded. 'Oh well, in that case, there's absolutely nothing more to be said.'

And now, yes, he was looking at her with admiration. 'Knew you'd understand when I explained,' he said. 'Henrietta, dear Henrietta, I can't thank you enough. For everything. I shall always remember it. And I hope you'll always let me think of you as a friend.'

Clichés. Edmund on clichés. And a game Adrian had told her that he and a friend at school used to play during sermons. 'Counting the clichés.' You had to memorize them, and the person who remembered the most won.

He said, 'You're the first to know, outside the immediate family.'

What was she to say to that?' She said, 'I'll send you a wedding present.' She came back to the leather armchair, and picked up her bag. 'Well,' she said. 'I think I must go now.'

The look of admiration on his face. She couldn't bear it. She was going to cry. She must say something. 'You're

dressed for the country, I see,' she said. 'Are you going
down to Churston?'

'Yes,' he said. 'Yes, taking Caroline down as a matter of
fact. A sort of family gathering. Caroline's parents, and her
brother. And Julia's coming.'

'A celebration,' she said.

'That sort of thing.'

'Henry,' she said, 'kiss me goodbye.'

He smiled. 'Of course,' he said, and held out his arms.
She came into them. His lips came lightly down on hers, but
it was so easy for her to slide her tongue between them, and
after only a moment, he was kissing her too. She dropped
her bag on the floor. She ran her hands over him, and on
and on they kissed, parting for only instants, to breathe,
then drinking again, drinking each other down. She pressed
herself against him, knew he wanted her. It was she who
drew back. She saw on his face that lost, that serious look,
and knew that the victory was hers.

'Henry,' she said, 'Henry, one last time.'

'No,' he said, 'oh my dear Henrietta, no.' But she
swayed forward and kissed him again. She knew he hadn't
a chance.

When they were in his bedroom, and their clothes were
scattered on the floor, and their naked bodies twined
together on the bed, then, oh then, she exerted every art
and skill that she had learned with him, from him. He was
her instrument.

But all the time, she was outside; she was seeing herself
'doing tricks'. For the first time ever, that was how she saw
it. Did he feel the same? In the silence, when it was over,
she was certain that that was exactly how he felt.

There was nothing to do but take her clothes into the
bathroom, and wash as quickly as possible, and dress and
do her hair. For some time, she had kept a toothbrush and
some scent in a sponge-bag in the bathroom cupboard. She
came into the bedroom with the sponge-bag in her hand.

He was still in bed, covered up, one elbow propped on the pillow.

'Henrietta,' he said, 'would you think it very rude of me if I asked you to see yourself out? I'd rather like to have a little rest before I go out.'

The first time that had ever happened – and, of course, the last. 'No, that's quite all right, Henry,' she said.

'You've got your motor?'

'Yes, down at the side of the Ritz.'

'I think it's raining,' he said. Yes, she could hear it. He sat up. 'I think I'd better go and bring it round for you,' he said.

'Nonsense,' she said. She was putting on her coat. 'What are a few drops of rain? It's only a minute's walk.' Now her hat, in front of the mirror.

'Goodbye, Henry. Be happy.' But he certainly didn't look happy now.

'Thank you,' he said. 'Well, goodbye.'

As she closed the bedroom door, she had a glimpse of him, turning over with a violent movement, burying his face in the pillow. *I've spoiled things for him*, she thought with an astonishing pang of fierce regret.

Through the sitting-room, down the stairs. She could hear Beedon ponderously ascending from the basement. She almost ran to the front door, tugging it open, slamming it behind her.

It was raining. 'Damn,' she muttered. 'Damn, damn, damn.' The rain was pouring down.

I've spoiled things for him. But she wouldn't think about that until she was safely in the car.

Safely in the car. She didn't start it, but got in, and sat, breathing rather fast after her dash through the rain. Her thin coat was soaking. She took it off, and put it on the seat beside her, with her bag and that ridiculous sponge-bag.

Her face was wet, and now a few tears trickled down it. *I've spoiled things for him*. Angrily she brushed at her eyes with her hand. What had she spoiled? His fresh start? Surely she didn't care about that? *Why should she?* No, it was something else she minded: his image of her, now clay-footed, tarnished, shattered. *Play the cliché game and take your choice*.

Why had she done it? If only, when he had been looking at her so admiringly, when she had been behaving with such dignity, such calm – if only, then, she had done what she had intended: kissed his cheek, taken his hand for a moment, and . . . gone. *Why hadn't she?*

Well, she knew, really, didn't she? If only she hadn't taken her tightrope walk that step too far, had jumped down gracefully, just before the end, like that girl with the parasol at the circus that Uncle Harry had once taken them to see. If only she hadn't asked him, with such polite interest, if he were 'going down to Churston'. Then she wouldn't have been confronted by the picture of that family gathering. Aunt Louisa so 'frightfully bucked', and Julia glowing with satisfaction at her triumph – oh, *what* a pinch for Hitty Pitty!

But if only, if only. She saw the scene so clearly: herself gliding so smoothly down the stairs, followed by Henry, that admiring look fixed on his face. He opening the door for her, watching her walk lightly down the street without ever turning her head. Oh then – wouldn't he have felt a pang? She gave a little gasp as the scene which she had been living, believing, was suddenly displaced by the vision of that violent despairing movement with which he had buried his face in the pillow. And that, in its turn, was succeeded – out of the blue – by the picture of that dreadful old creature she had seen long ago, tapping on her high heels down Half Moon Street. She was sure she knew now how prostitutes must feel – as she had felt in bed with Henry today.

It had almost stopped raining. She got out of the car and turned the starting handle. Driving up Piccadilly, she began to think about Caroline Mallerby. *That prunes-and-prisms*

Miss. But she had thought her nice at the time. Anyway, she didn't now. Now Caroline was Julia's ally, demure and scheming. *If Caroline knew . . .*

Dimly she was remembering some old story that she'd heard. Cynthia – yes it had been Cynthia Chanter who had told it to her. Daughter of excellent family, engaged to some – charming, altogether eligible – young man. The evening before the wedding. The bride called to the telephone. A woman's voice: 'You're marrying' – whatever his name had been 'tomorrow?' 'Yes, but who's speaking?' The name given – the name of a well-known musical-comedy actress. 'Oh yes?' from the girl. 'Do you want to know where he is now?' 'What do you mean?' 'He's here, in my house. Upstairs in my bed. Just as he was last night, and the night before.' Tears. Broken engagement. Scandal – hushed up as much as possible.

When Cynthia had told her the story, Henrietta's sympathies had at once gone out to the actress – to something extreme, reckless, dashing about her action. But quite out of the question in this case. More than unlikely, especially after today, that she would be able to lure Henry into bed on the evening before his wedding. And Caroline Mallerby, she felt, even from that one meeting, might not respond with tears and horror. Might even fight back – and win.

Cynthia had been on the other side, the girl's side. One of her lectures on the double standard. She hadn't thought of Cynthia for ages. The only girl she had ever been friends with. Cynthia who, unexpectedly, had married a civil servant and gone to India. She'd had a picture of Cynthia fanning herself with a peacock's feather. But E. M. Forster hadn't made India sound at all like that.

But why should Henry *love* this Caroline? Suddenly she was overcome by such a wave of misery that she wanted to stop the car, put her head down on the steering wheel, and sob. Words were in her head: Why has no one ever loved *me?* But that was nonsense. Absolute nonsense, *Edmund had loved her*. Darling Edmund. She drove on, up Shaftesbury Avenue.

❧ *Sixteen* ❧

At breakfast, three days later, Adrian looked up from *The Times*, and said, 'I see that your cousin Henry is engaged.'

'Oh really,' she said. 'Who to?'

'*To whom*, you mean. To someone called Caroline Charlotte Mallerby. She is the daughter of a Major-General who lives in a castle in Yorkshire. It all sounds extremely suitable.'

'Oh yes,' Henrietta said. 'I met her at Julia's party. I thought she was very pretty and rather nice.'

'Mmm,' Adrian said, sounding wholly uninterested, and returning to the paper. It was surprising, she thought, that he had mentioned the engagement at all. Perhaps the connection with Julia had aroused a fleeting interest. Now, without taking his eyes off the page in front of him, he said, 'You were complaining that you hadn't met anyone at Julia's.'

She didn't answer.

In the weeks that followed, she moved through the days somnambulistically. Getting up, dressing, cooking, eating, going for walks; all were mechanical. While, *underneath*, as she thought of it, round and round her mind went like an animal in a cage. It was the same at night. For the first time in her life, she slept badly; her squirrel thoughts scurried round and round. And when she did sleep, her dreams were so bad – chases down dark corridors, choking filth, falls from great heights, snakes that oozed through doorways – that she was almost glad to wake, crying out, and find herself back in the little cage. Once she had the 'Mr Hyde' dream – the dream of Julia, trampled and broken. She hadn't had that for years.

Living so much in her own head, it took her several days to notice that Adrian was behaving oddly. At meals, he sat just staring at his book or paper – nothing unusual about that, but now he didn't turn the pages – and hardly touched his food. She wouldn't have believed it possible that he could take less notice of her than he normally did, but now it was as if she simply weren't there.

When he was at his desk upstairs, it was the same; he would just sit staring in front of him for minutes at a time. Then he would come to himself, with a start, with a sort of shiver; his hands would fumble with his books and papers. He would make an obvious effort to read, or would pick up his pen, before lapsing again into that utterly abstracted immobility. Then he would suddenly leap up and say 'I'm going for a walk.' From the window, she would watch him, striding off down the pavement, hands in his pockets, head bowed. Then she would return to her current detective story, though even detective stories couldn't distract her as they usually did.

At night she heard him pacing in his room. His footsteps were regular as the slow tick of a clock. Then suddenly they would halt. In a prolonged silence, she would think that he had gone to bed at last. But next minute, the steady pacing would start again. Why didn't he take his laudanum drops? Adrian, she realized, was in his own private cage. Unhappiness was meant to 'bring people together', so she'd always heard. It certainly wasn't doing so in their case.

Then, after a week or two, Adrian changed – literally overnight. In the evening, he had gone out for a walk. He must have come in during one of her patches of sleep, for she didn't hear him. She looked into his room next morning, wondering if he were there, and he was in bed, fast asleep.

When he joined her at breakfast, he was whistling. She watched him tucking into his egg and toast and tea. He skimmed *The Times*. This morning, she felt, he was too happy to concentrate on it.

When he went up to Manchester, to lecture to a Fabian group, a few days later, she was glad of a day when she would not hear him bouncing about the house and whistling, or see him gobbling down his food – fuel for what? she wondered. Though he has been out a lot: walking, visiting the library, seeing editors. Each time he left the house, he gave an elaborate account of where he was going – something that he'd certainly never done before.

The day when Adrian went to Manchester was the day when Julia called.

It was late in the morning and, as usual, she was sitting on the sofa, reading a detective story, when she heard the doorbell ring. Then there was the sound of Julia's voice in the hall. 'Don't show me up. I know the way.'

What a cheek, Henrietta thought, pushing her book under the sofa cushions. For if Julia saw it, how she would sneer. Julia was such a *highbrow* nowadays. She leapt up, seized a book from the bookshelf – *Swann's Way*, yes that would do beautifully – sat down and opened it at random. She started to read ('a side which far more resembles a crushing burden, a difficulty in breathing, a destroying thirst') as Julia's neat little steps clicked up the stairs ('than the abstract idea to which we are accustomed to give the name of Death?'). She looked up as Julia came into the room.

'Hitty Pitty darling!'

'Oh hullo Julia,' she said, not getting up. 'Adrian isn't here. He's in Manchester.'

'Manchester – goodness, how terrifying! I can't really imagine anyone *going* to Manchester. I suppose the poor things who are born there have to make the best of it, though I would have thought that even *they* might make feeble efforts to escape. But actually *going* there, buying a ticket, and taking a train and so on, seems rather rash, don't you think, Hitty Pitty?'

Could this sort of thing be what people meant when they described Julia as *witty?* 'I wish you wouldn't call me that, Julia,' she said.

'Goodness, you seem rather gloomy this morning. Pining for your spouse perhaps? I agree that Manchester seems awfully far away. Much farther than the South of France, for instance. Well, I must do my best to cheer you up.'

'I'm not at all gloomy. I was just spending a quiet morning reading.'

'Reading what?' Julia plucked the book from her hand, glanced at it, handed it back. 'Ah – *cher* Marcel. But so much better in the original. You must try one day. Anyway, too much quietness is terribly bad for one, I think. You mustn't turn into a hermit, Hitty – I mean Henrietta.'

Julia took off her hat, put it down on the table. Paris rather than Midgeley, Henrietta guessed from the look of it. She was wearing one of her little suits – green again. Now she repeated her earlier feat of curling up in the Omega chair.

'Goodness, life had been a positive whirl lately. You heard about darling Henry's engagement?'

'Yes,' Henrietta said. 'I saw it in *The Times*. I thought the girl seemed charming when I met her at your party.'

'Caroline? Oh yes, we all adore her. And she's so absolutely right for Henry. Young, pretty, smart, interested in all the things he is. She'll make a wonderful *châtelaine*, as darling Mama would say, for Churston.'

'Yes, she sounds perfect,' Henrietta said enthusiastically. From Julia's petulant look, she guessed that she was doing well.

'I was getting quite worried about darling Henry,' Julia said. She took a black lizard-skin cigarette case out of her bag, opened it, extended it in Henrietta's direction. She would have liked a cigarette, but she wasn't going to stand up and fetch it. She shook her head. 'I had the feeling,'

Julia went on, lighting a cigarette for herself with a gold
lighter, 'that the poor sweet was having a long boring affair
with some quite unsuitable woman. The sort of thing that a
kind man allows to drag on because he hasn't got the heart
to take the plunge and cut loose.'

Loose ends, Henrietta thought. She said, 'Miss Dettmer
wouldn't have approved of all those mixed metaphors,
Julia.'

'Dear old Miss Dettmer. You were always so keen to
please her. Do you remember how cross you were when
I came top with my essay? Anyway, reverting to Henry, I
knew that whoever it was must be fearfully dull, because
poor Henry was beginning to get dull, too.'

*But I've always thought Henry was terrible dull to start
with.* How nearly she said it. She was sure that it would
have annoyed Julia. But of course she would have repeated
it to Henry at the first opportunity. Perhaps she should have
wanted Julia to do so. But she didn't.

She said, 'Perhaps Henry will run them in double harness.'
How had *that* extraordinary phrase come into her mind?

Certainly, Julia didn't care for it. She frowned. 'I'm quite
sure that would never occur to Henry,' she said. 'He's far
too honourable.' But the frown remained.

'Julia,' Henrietta said, 'what a terrible hostess I'm being.
Would you like some coffee? Or a drink? Surely you'd like
a drink?'

'No, thank you,' Julia said. 'I must be off in just one
moment. I'm going down to the country for a few days,
and I must get started.'

'To Churston?'

'No, home.' She laughed. 'You forget that I'm a wife and
mother.'

'Yes, that is rather hard to remember sometimes,'
Henrietta said, and smiled.

Julia's eyes widened, making her face look mask-like
for a moment. 'Must really dash away, Hitty Pitty –

Henrietta.' She uncurled herself, this time with particularly conscious litheness, from the chair, stood up, and stretched exaggeratedly. 'I would have fallen asleep if I'd stayed in that chair another minute.' She picked up her bag from the floor, put it on the chair, felt about inside it, and took out a powder compact and a lipstick. With her back to Henrietta, she carefully powdered her face, outlined and filled in her lips. Then she put the make-up back in her bag, whirled round – what a performance! – and advanced towards Henrietta, who slowly rose from the sofa.

'Goodbye,' Julia,' she said. 'Have fun in the country.'

'Well, I don't know about *fun*, but lots of *beauty sleep*, anyway. Do you remember darling Nanny telling us that the only real beauty sleep came "in the hours before midnight"? In London I never get a *moment's* beauty sleep, let alone *hours*. But at home there's really nothing else to do. Yawn, yawn, yawn by half past nine.'

Today, Julia didn't kiss her – thank goodness – perhaps because Adrian wasn't there. She picked up her hat from the table, jammed it down on her head, tugged at the brim.

'Don't ring for your little maid to see me out, darling. You must be longing to get back to *Du Côté de Chez Swann*. Or whatever that *much* more exciting book is that you're hiding under the cushions.'

Involuntarily turning her head, Henrietta saw that one of the sofa cushions had slipped, and that half the lurid cover of her thriller was revealed.

'Do give Adrian my love when the poor lamb gets back from mad magenta Manchester.' Over to the door she clicked, gave one of her Charleston waves, was gone.

Henrietta stood for a moment, looking at the half open door. Then she went over to the door and closed it. What, she wondered, had been the purpose of that visit? To plant darts? – *I adored the bullfight.*

Would Julia have ventured so far if she had been aware that Henrietta knew of her part in what had happened with

Henry? She was quite sure that Julia couldn't know about that. She was certain – yes, absolutely certain – that Henry would not have discussed their last meeting with anyone.

Yet, even if Julia had known, it would probably not have held her back. What was it that Julia wanted now, and had always wanted? *To break Hitty Pitty down.* And that was what she would never achieve.

It was at that moment that Henrietta's eye was caught by the piece of paper that was lying on the seat of the Omega chair.

Something that had dropped from Julia's bag? Slowly – she was conscious of moving as slowly as possible – she approached the chair, hesitated for a moment, before picking up the piece of paper folded in four. She held it in her hand for a moment – how extraordinarily reluctant she felt to unfold it. But then, very quickly – her fingers were trembling a little – she did so. What she saw was a letter in Adrian's writing.

Darling Julia,

As I am off to mad magenta Manchester tomorrow, and you to your country seat (what ho!) – a line to say that I live (no, that's too strong), survive, endure ('in durance vile') for Friday week, when we spin off to Sussex.

I'll be at your flat by five (on, or even before, the dot, you can be sure) – and then off we shall go a'maying to the cottage. As I warned you, you may find it a little rough (not, I fear, what you are accustomed to!), but we shall be alone (oh the bliss of it, past all envisioning), shall be together every moment. Oh Julia! (And Julia, your feet *are* like little mice, as Herrick – wasn't it? – poeticized, even though they don't creep in and out beneath your petticoat, but form a termination devoutly to be wished for, to your exquisite silken ankles.)

I shall tell H. that I am going to Cambridge. She, of course, suspects nothing.

Ton (truly) *dévoué*, not to say *obsédé*,
Adrian

She read it twice before going over to the sofa, and sitting down with it in her hand.

'Off to catch my train now, Henrietta. See you on Monday, what?'

'All right. Goodbye Adrian. Have a nice weekend. I hope your meetings go well.'

He kissed her cheek and, suitcase in hand, went bounding down the stairs, two steps at a time. Throughout the past ten days *in durance vile*, since his return from *mad magenta Manchester*, he had been in this hey-nonny-no mood from morning till night. It didn't suit him – and it didn't suit her. What had made it worse was that he had been at home all the time. *That was because Julia was away.*

A cab had drawn up a little way down the square. She went over to the window and looked out. Adrian was getting into it. She glanced at her watch. Only just four. He would be very early at Julia's (*on, or even before, the dot, you can be sure*).

Anyway, soon, they would be *spinning off to Sussex*. Spinning, she thought, was definitely the word. For Julia was a reckless driver, Henrietta was sure, remembering the way she revved up her Isotta Fraschini – seeing herself, probably, as Iris March in *The Green Hat*. And Adrian was such a nervous passenger. Well, certainly he was when *she* drove him, always telling her she was going too fast, though actually she was very careful, and she couldn't have gone fast in the Morris, even if she had wanted to. Adrian hated motors; it had annoyed him when she had learnt to drive so quickly and easily.

Off *a'maying* indeed! Perhaps they could join up with a

troupe of Morris dancers. She smiled coldly. For even if, extraordinarily, all this rustic nonsense was for Adrian, it certainly wasn't for Julia.

Really, she was quite astonished that, after reading that letter, Julia hadn't wanted to be off as fast as those little mice would carry her. Instead of *spinning off to Sussex* with Adrian. To Hitty Pitty's cottage.

She, of course, suspects nothing. What a fool Adrian was. Even if it had been true, which, of course, it hadn't, Julia would have remedied that. For, without doubt, Julia had left the letter deliberately – hence all that business with her bag, and turning her back, and whirling round, which had looked so silly at the time. She had been distracting Henrietta, had been determined to have gone before Henrietta saw the paper on the chair. Why, otherwise, she might have called out, 'Julia, you've dropped something.' What would Julia have done then?

Now Julia must be wondering how she had reacted. She would try to find out from Adrian. 'How has dear old Hitty Pitty been lately? When I dropped in the other day, she seemed a bit down in the dumps.'

Well, she would get no comfort from Adrian. Ever since he had come back from Manchester, she had been sweetness itself. Smiling whenever he looked at her, speaking when she was spoken to, never interrupting his work or his reading. She had even cooked nothing but the simple, boring food he liked best, and had drunk water at every meal. Why, only yesterday, he had commented approvingly on how much lower than usual the past week's housekeeping bills had been. And she had sacked the kitchenmaid after an argument – another economy, if only a temporary one.

No, he would have no tale of woe to tell Julia, when they were alone. (*Bliss past all envisioning* – would Julia really find it so?) 'H', 'suspecting nothing', had surely rendered his '*durance vile*' as 'survivable', 'endurable', as possible?

She never could have managed it without the notebook.

Again, as always in a crisis, she had turned to Edmund: to her counsellor, her guide, her only love. And he, coming to her from the past, bringing its magic aura with him, had comforted, strengthened, steeled her.

But she gave a deep sigh as she turned away from the window, through which, unseeingly, she had been staring. The long lonely weekend stretched ahead.

❧ *Seventeen* ☙

Sitting on the sofa, late on Monday afternoon, she had fallen into a doze when she was woken by the doorbell ringing. Hearing voices she couldn't recognize, down in the hall, she straightened up, rubbed her eyes, ran her hands over her hair. *Who could it be?* There was a sound of hurrying footsteps on the stairs. Vera almost rushed into the room. She was looking – startled or excited? Henrietta didn't know.

'Excuse me, madam, but there are two gentlemen downstairs to see you. They say they're from the police.'

'From the *police?* What do they want?'

'They just said they wanted to see you, madam.'

'Oh well, I suppose you had better show them up.'

The police, she repeated to herself. She had never spoken to a policeman before – except she seemed to remember that once she had asked one the way somewhere. Hearing heavy steps on the stairs, she got up from the sofa – so it was true; they walked heavily in real life as they did in detective stories.

'The gentlemen from the police, madam,' Vera said, showing two men into the room. They weren't in uniform. They both wore blue suits, with the buttons done up, and

brown shoes and collars that looked as if they were made
of celluloid – what extraordinary things she was noticing.
They were both tall, but the taller was the one who came
first. He was the elder of the two, had dark hair, and dark
eyes in a long thin face. The other one was gingery and
freckled, with big ears.

'Thank you, Vera,' she said, and then, as Vera still
lingered, 'Please close the door behind you.'

'You are Mrs Wheeler, madam?' the dark one said.

'Yes.'

'The wife of Mr Adrian Wheeler?'

'Yes.'

'I am Inspector Forman of Scotland Yard, and this is
Detective Constable Ames.'

'Scotland Yard?' she said, and then, 'I'm sorry, won't
you sit down?'

They did so, the Inspector in the Omega chair – *Julia's
chair*, she thought suddenly – and the other one on a
straight-backed chair which he pulled forward from the
wall, with a scraping sound which made the Inspector
frown, as he cleared his throat.

'May I ask you, madam, if you and your husband rent
a cottage at Little Evenham in Sussex?'

A lurching feeling in her stomach. 'Yes,' she said.

'Is it correct that your husband has been staying at that
cottage this weekend?'

Her mind was racing. One thing she wasn't going to tell
them or anyone about ever was that letter.

She said, 'No, he went to Cambridge for the weekend.'

'To Cambridge?'

'Yes, he had two meetings there – academic things. And
he was going to see some friends. He should be back
by now.'

'Mrs Wheeler, I am afraid that I have some bad news for
you. Your husband is dead.'

'*Dead?*' In the silence, the shock of the word was vivid.

She found herself clenching her fists, then raising her hands to cover her face.

'I'm very sorry to be the bearer of such bad news, madam.'

She raised her head, lowered her hands to her lap. 'An accident?' she said. In her mind was a picture of Julia crashing her car into a tree, just as Iris had done in *The Green Hat*. 'A motor accident?'

'Not really an accident.'

'What do you mean?' She heard her voice rise.

'Excuse me, madam, but do you think you could answer one or two questions?'

'Yes, of course. But I want to know what has happened.'

'Of course. I quite understand that, madam. Well, not to put too fine a point on it, it appears that your husband died from unnatural causes.'

What was he trying to say, this man? What did he mean? Did he mean that he thought that Adrian had been murdered? Her heart was thudding against her ribs so loudly that she wondered if they could hear it. 'What do you mean – unnatural causes?' *Why wouldn't he tell her?*

'Excuse me, madam, but before we proceed, would you just answer one question for me? Are you acquainted with a lady who, it would appear from her effects, is called the Honourable' – he said it with something of a flourish, pronouncing the 'h' – 'Mrs Julia Thornton?'

'Julia, why yes, of course. She's my first cousin.'

'I see, madam. *Your* cousin, you say, not your husband's?'

'No, mine. Her father was my mother's brother.'

'Yes, I see, madam.' There was a second's pause before he continued. 'Forgive me for asking you, but were you aware of any – special relationship between your husband and the Honourable Mrs Thornton?'

She couldn't tell them about the letter. What would

they think of *her?* If they knew she had known, had said nothing to Adrian. She would never be able to make them understand why.

'No, none at all,' she said. 'But please tell me what this is about.'

The lie had brought a shrillness to her tone. The Inspector said, 'Please try to keep calm, madam. I quite understand the distress you must be feeling.'

'I'm sorry,' she said, and then, 'I'm quite calm, really.'

'It appears, madam, from what facts are available to us – subject always to official confirmation – that at some time yesterday your husband took the life of the Honourable Mrs Thornton, and then took his own life.'

'Took Julia's life, took his own life?' It was as if the great shivering sigh that poured from her had carried with it all the breath from her body. A dizziness overwhelmed her . . . a feeling . . . years and years ago . . . Churston, when Aunt Louisa had said that Edmund . . . She felt herself sway, almost topple forward. Consciousness was sliding away. The Inspector had leapt from his chair. His hands were on her shoulders. Now he was pushing down until her head was almost on her knees. She was coming back again now. She heard him say, 'Water – fetch some water, Ames.'

'A . . . a basin, sir?'

'No, a glass, you fool.'

'Right, sir.' The tone was slightly reproachful, and she felt a hysterical laugh bubbling in her mouth. She gulped it down. If she had hysterics, they probably would pour a basin of water over her. She tried to raise her head, but his hands were still pressing on her shoulders.

'Take it slowly, madam.'

'Yes, yes. I'm quite all right now.'

He withdrew his hands, and slowly she sat up. She could see how pale she must be from the look of concern on his face. 'White as death,' Ellis had said in the drawing-room at Churston. Ellis had given her smelling salts.

Now the Inspector was moving the cushions behind her. She rested her head, for a moment, against the back of the sofa, raised it as Ames returned with a glass of water. He was carrying it on a silver salver, and looked so funny doing so, in his blue serge suit, that again she had to force down laughter.

'Thank you so much,' she said, taking the glass. He held the salver awkwardly in his hand for a moment, then went and put it down on a table that stood near the door.

She took a sip of water, and then, discovering that her mouth was dry, almost parched, a deep drink. Resting the glass on the arm of the sofa, curving her left hand round it, she leant back against the cushions. 'I'm so sorry, Inspector,' she said.

'Not at all, madam. It is I who should apologize. I shouldn't have broken it to you so suddenly.'

'No,' she said. 'You had to tell me. I wanted to know. It was just the shock. It was bound to be a shock, and I'm quite all right now. Please go on. Adrian – my husband – *killed* Mrs Thornton, you say, and then himself?'

'That is definitely how it appears, madam.'

'But why, and how? How did he do it?'

'Are you sure that this isn't too much for you?'

'Yes. Quite sure.'

'It would seem that your husband took the Honourable Mrs Thornton's life by suffocation, and then administered poison to himself.

Adrian. How unbelievable it sounded to her. The Inspector sounded quite matter-of-fact about it, but of course he didn't know Adrian.

'As to the motive, madam, that, of course, has not yet been determined,'

'Suffocated her, poisoned himself, but I can't believe ...' She halted. Then she said, 'I suppose it must be what they call a *crime passionnelle*, Inspector?' She looked down. Her thumb circled round and round on the side of the glass.

He said, 'I really don't think we should go into that now, madam. Not until we have the official findings. Of course I shall have to take a statement from you, but I think we can leave that until tomorrow. There will of course have to be a proper identification of the body. While the woman cleaner who found the deceased was able to recognize your husband, we really require someone who knew him well—'

She gave an uncontrollable shiver. 'Oh, I don't think I could,' she said. 'I really don't think—'

'I quite understand, madam. Perhaps there is some relative?'

'There's his father,' she said. Poor old man – how cowardly she was being. But the thought . . . 'Does he know?' she asked.

'I have as yet been in touch with no one but yourself. We were able to obtain your address from the cleaner.'

'And all this happened at the cottage?'

'Yes, madam.'

'Do please call me Mrs Wheeler.' She faintly smiled at him, and he smiled back. She took another drink of water, put the glass down on the table next to the sofa, and tried to sit up straight. But an overwhelming rush of weakness forced her back against the cushions again.

'You've had a very great shock, madam – er, Mrs Wheeler,' the Inspector said. He was looking at her with a grave, sympathetic expression. *Why, he likes me*, she thought. She never expected people to like her.

Now he said, 'Perhaps I might break the news to Mr Wheeler's father, and speak to him about the identification?'

'*Could* you? How very, very kind of you.'

When she had given him the address, he said, 'And now, if you will forgive my saying so, I really think that you should have a bit of a lie-down, madam. Are you alone here?'

'Oh no,' she said. 'There's Vera – the house-parlour maid.'

'I was thinking more of, say, a relative.'

'Oh there's no one,' she said. 'Only Aunt Louisa. And that wouldn't do at all. She is Mrs Thornton's mother.'

'Yes, I see. A friend perhaps?'

'No really. There's no one I want.' *Cynthia?* But Cynthia was in India, waving a peacock-feather fan.

He stood up. 'Mrs Wheeler, I really cannot leave without telephoning your doctor and asking him to come round and see you.'

'Oh but that's not necessary.'

'Excuse me, but I must insist. We see a great deal of the effect of shock in our job, you know.'

'Well, if you really think . . .'

'I do.' Again he smiled.

So she gave him Dr Emerson's number. She hardly listened to what he was saying: 'Mrs Wheeler . . . shock . . . as soon as possible.' The words echoed from the shore of a great sea of weariness in which she floated.

He had finished. 'Well, good-day, Mrs Wheeler. No, please don't move. Just you go and lie down in a minute or two. I'll tell your maid to come up and help you. The doctor says he'll be here in about half an hour. I shall be round tomorrow. About the statement, you know. Not too early. Would about eleven o'clock suit you?'

'Oh yes, that will be quite all right. Goodbye, Inspector. Thank you so much for being so kind and helpful.'

'It was nothing.' He hesitated. 'I admire your courage, madam,' he said.

They were gone. She closed her eyes. She felt she would never want to open them again. She was so tired. The thought summoned up an immense yawn. But what a kind man. She had never imagined that a policeman could be like that. The ones in detective stories weren't. So polite and sympathetic – and how wonderful of him it had been to volunteer to tell Adrian's father. Of course, she should have done that. His wife had died four years ago, and now he was all alone. How would he take it? She didn't know him well enough to guess – always so absorbed in his old Roman remains.

The Honourable Mrs Thornton. *Julia*. Everything had been Julia's fault; that was the one thing she was sure of. She sighed. The sigh turned into a yawn. And Adrian? About Adrian, at this moment, she just couldn't feel anything at all.

'Madam?'

She opened her eyes. Vera was standing half way between the door and the sofa. 'Excuse me, madam, but the gentleman, the gentleman from the police, 'e said as you should lie down because Doctor's coming, and that I should 'elp you. 'E said Madam as you'd 'ad a nasty shock?' Certainly all this was very exciting for Vera.

'Vera,' she said. 'It was about Mr Wheeler. He's had an – accident. He's dead.'

'Oh madam, oh madam, I *am* sorry. Oh, 'ow *awful*.' Vera's eyes were fixed on her with a wondering look. Vera probably thought that she ought to be crying.

'Vera, I don't want to talk just now. I'm so terribly tired. Could you turn down my bed and, yes, perhaps light the fire in my room?' For the early evening, though it was late in May, was distinctly chilly.

'Oh, yes of course, madam.'

Off hurried Vera, and Henrietta closed her eyes again. Now the weariness wasn't a sea in which she was floating. It was a weight pressing down on her: on her forehead, on her eyelids, on her whole body. A martyr she had once read about had been 'crushed beneath a heavy oaken door'. The phrase had stuck in her mind. That was how she felt now. She must get up from the sofa at once, though. The doctor would be arriving soon. With a great effort, she opened her eyes, sat up, and, with a hand on the arm of the sofa, pushed herself to her feet. How shaky she felt.

A hot bath? No, she might feel faint again. She would go straight to bed. The Inspector had been right.

She went down the passage to her room, hunching her shoulders involuntarily as she passed Adrian's closed door.

The bed was turned down – how welcoming it looked. Vera was on her knees before the fireplace, arranging paper, sticks and coal in the grate. 'I've put a 'ot-water bottle in your bed, madam.' And then, 'Oh madam, you look ever so pale.'

'Do I? It must be the shock. I feel terribly tired. And I didn't sleep well last night. I went to bed early, but I read for hours and hours.'

'Yes, madam. I saw your light on when I came in.'

'Ah yes.' She sighed. Vera would probably chatter on for ever if she didn't stop her. She collected her night things, and took them into the bathroom, and changed there. She washed her hands and face, and brushed her hair, though doing those things seemed to require an enormous effort.

At last, she was back in her room. Vera had gone. The fire was starting to burn brightly. Although it wasn't dark yet, Vera had drawn the curtains and switched on the bedside light. She got into bed. It was warm from the stone hot-water bottle, which she pushed down to just within reach of her feet. She closed her eyes again.

The doctor arrived a few minutes later. Vera brought him upstairs.

'My dear Mrs Wheeler, I hear that you have had bad news. Mr Wheeler. That Inspector, wasn't he? told me that he is dead. I cannot tell you how sorry I am. An accident, was it?'

Dr Emerson was obviously just as curious as Vera, though he expressed his curiosity with more restraint.

'Not exactly, but would you forgive me if I didn't talk

about it now. Another time. Perhaps tomorrow. I'm sorry,
but I feel so tired.'

'My dear lady, but of course. I quite understand.'

He took her temperature, felt her pulse. There really
wasn't much else he could do. Both were normal. He said
that he would come to see her next day, and talked of
prescribing a tonic. Then he summoned Vera, and asked
her to bring some water. When she came back with it, he
told her to bring whisky and hot milk when he had gone.

'I've never tasted whisky,' Henrietta said. 'I'm sure I
won't like it. I've always thought the smell was horrible.'

'It will do you good,' he said. He was mixing a powder
in water.

'I hope that isn't a Gregory Powder,' she said.

'My dear Mrs Wheeler! No, it is something that will help
you to sleep.' He handed it to her, and she drank it. A minute
or two later, he left.

Vera brought the hot drink, and put more coal on
the fire.

'Thank you so much, Vera. For the hot-water bottle and
everything. You've been such a help to me.'

'Oh madam,' Vera said, and looked pleased. 'Is there
anything more I can do for you?'

'No, thank you very much. The doctor has given me some
medicine. I'll try to go to sleep now. Good-night, Vera.'

'Good-night, madam.'

She was alone. She drank the whisky and milk, which
tasted strange, but was comforting. When she had finished
it, she turned off the bedside light.

The firelight flickered on the walls, reminding her of
Edmund's room at Churston, and how he had said
that he liked to fall asleep by firelight. Edmund! How
comforting it was to think of him. Far more comforting than whisky and milk, to lie thinking of Edmund,
and feel herself drifting so gently, so certainly towards
sleep.

❧ *Eighteen* ❧

Six weeks had passed, and at last it was all over: the interviews with Inspector Forman, the inquest, the reports in the newspapers.

Only on a few occasions had she ventured from the house. Otherwise she had stayed at home, sitting, hour after hour, in the drawing-room, sometimes reading, sometimes just staring into space. Often, she fell into sudden dozes, like an old woman – it was as if she simply couldn't get enough sleep.

Twice a day, she wandered down to the kitchen, and cooked an enormous meal. She felt hungry all the time. It was extraordinary, she thought: she would have expected to have lost her appetite, just as she would have expected to find it difficult to sleep.

Vera had been wonderful; she didn't know what she would have done without her. Vera hadn't minded at all about her not engaging a new kitchen maid – when she had explained that she simply couldn't face the thought of a stranger in the house. Vera had done everything except the cooking; she had even done that once or twice, when Henrietta hadn't felt like it, bringing her a cutlet or a poached egg on toast on a tray. Several times, Vera had shared her meals, though of course they had eaten separately. She had proved much more enthusiastic about Henrietta's cooking than Adrian ever had. And, best of all, she had kept the newspaper reporters away, repelling them ruthlessly from the doorstep.

Adrian's father had asked Henrietta to say, but she couldn't have faced it, though he had been so sweet –

and so utterly shattered by what had happened; she had
never realized quite how much Adrian meant to him.

Henry, almost inarticulate, had telephoned: 'Extraordinary. Quite horrible. Just wanted to let you know that I
feel for you, Henrietta.' He had asked if she would like him
to come to see her.

'No, no, Henry,' she had said. 'I don't think so. Not at
present.' He had said that he quite understood.

That was what everyone said to her: Adrian's father, the
doctor, the friends of Adrian's who visited her until she
asked them not to. 'I quite understand' – and she felt that
they said it with relief. For the fact was that they had all
been *embarrassed*. What could one say to the widow of a
man who had killed his mistress and then himself? *I quite
understand.* She sometimes thought that if she had declared
that she wanted to go to the moon or to a night-club, the
answer would have been the same.

How appalling the papers had been, with their crimes of
passion and aristocratic love nests. 'Wife's childhood friend
his mistress-victim' – that was one sentence that stuck in
her mind.

But Inspector Forman had been so kind, so helpful, and
the coroner had been kind and sympathetic, too. Everything
was so obvious. 'Intercourse had taken place', as they had
put it. Then Adrian had suffocated Julia with a pillow,
and had swallowed strychnine crystals dissolved in a glass
of beer.

Had the crimes been premeditated? The coroner had
spent some time on that. Where had the strychnine
crystals come from? Henrietta had been able to explain
that. When Inspector Forman told her that Adrian had
poisoned himself with strychnine, she had taken him at
once to Adrian's desk.

It had been after Vera had put down strychnine to get
rid of the rats in the unoccupied upper rooms, that Adrian
had locked away the crystals that were left, in a drawer of

his desk. 'They mustn't lie around in the kitchen – servants are so careless,' he had said to Henrietta at the time. (How *fussy* he is, she had thought.)

Now, the drawer was unlocked. The crystals were gone.

Both Inspector Forman and the coroner had asked her when they had been taken to the cottage, and she had told them that she didn't know. But she couldn't remember any occasion before *that* weekend when he could have taken them there. No, she couldn't think of any other opportunity he would have had in the recent past to go to the cottage without her.

It was hardly likely, the coroner had remarked drily, that a man setting off for an illicit weekend, would have planned to lay down poison for rats as part of it. (Laughter in court.) Had there been rats at the cottage? he had asked Henrietta. She had shaken her head. She had never seen any evidence of them. There had once been a mouse in the kitchen.

So the crimes had presumably been premeditated – the suicide, at least, and it was likely that the suicide was connected with the murder. *Adrian's motive for the murder* – that was the crux of the matter. But that was what nobody could explain or discover. Including Henrietta.

She had told the court about Adrian's changes of mood, during the weeks before his death, how he had swung from depression to exuberance. She told everything she could remember about him – except that she had known of his affair with Julia. And what difference could that have made?

Dr Emerson was called. He said that he was afraid that he couldn't be of much assistance, but he described Adrian as 'nervous' and told the court of his indigestion and insomnia.

In the end, the coroner's verdict had been that Adrian had acted 'while the balance of his mind was disturbed'.

All over. Except that it was today that she had decided that she must telephone Henry.

She rang up Half Moon Street. Beedon answered and said that his lordship was in the country. No use in putting it off, she decided, and made a personal call to him at Churston.

After some time, she was put through. 'Lord Allingham speaking.'

'Henry,' she said, 'this is Henrietta.'

'Oh. Yes?' he said. He didn't say her name. There was probably someone in the room with him. Then he said, 'How are you?'

'Not too bad. But Henry, I'm afraid I have to see you.'

'Oh. It's something important?'

'Yes. Very important.'

'I'll come up to London tomorrow,' he said. 'Would about noon suit you?'

'Yes,' she said. 'Half Moon Street?'

'Yes. I'll be there. Goodbye.'

'Goodbye,' she said, and he rang off.

So there she was, on the doorstep in Half Moon Street again. Beedon answered the door.

'Good-morning madam.'

'Good-morning.'

'His lordship is expecting you, madam.'

'Yes, I'll go up.' The familiar feeling of the banister under her hand. Henry wasn't in the passage today. She opened his door. He was standing by the window. One or other of them always seemed to be standing by the window.

He came towards her, took both her hands in his. 'Well Henrietta,' he said, and then, 'Never seen you all in black before. You're pale, but I think you've put on a little weight.'

'Yes, I'm afraid I have,' she said.

'No, it suits you.' He paused. 'God, what a terrible business this has been. For you more than for any of us, of course.'

'Oh I don't know,' she said.

He broke a long silence. 'You wanted to see me about something important?'

'Yes Henry,' she said. 'I had probably better come straight to the point. I'm going to have a baby.'

She had never seen anyone turn as pale as he did then, and his face became absolutely rigid.

At last he spoke. 'And it's mine?'

'Yes,' she said, and then, steadily, 'It couldn't be anyone else's.'

'Ah,' he said.

Would he ask if it could possibly be Adrian's? If he did, she would tell him the truth: that it had been months and months since she and Adrian—

'You're quite sure?' he said. 'I mean that you're going to have it.'

'Yes,' she said. 'I saw a doctor the other day. Not my own doctor. One I didn't know. I gave him a false name. He said that it was absolutely certain.'

'Yes, I see.'

Would he ask her why she didn't pretend that the baby was Adrian's? But somehow she couldn't imagine Henry asking that.

She murmured very quietly, 'I believe that there are ways of getting rid—'

But he broke in, 'No, no. How can you suggest such a thing?'

Over to the window he went, stared out. She sat down in one of the leather armchairs, and he half turned: 'I'm sorry. Should have asked you to sit down.' Out of the window he stared again. He leant forward, pressed his forehead against the glass. Suddenly he spoke in such a loud strange voice.

'She said, she said that we should have married at once when it happened, got married quietly and gone away. Her parents were so upset by it all. Really, I think, they wanted the engagement broken off, but of course she would never have agreed to that. She said, "Let's slip away. I'm twenty-one." But I felt I ought to be with Mother. I thought it wouldn't make any difference if we waited, let everything quieten down.' He started to cry, his shoulders shaking, his face still pressed against the window pane.

She sat very stiffly in the chair.

It only lasted for a few moments – that convulsion of sobs. Then he took a handkerchief out of his pocket, and blew his nose. He said in a blurred voice, 'Just as well we didn't, as things have turned out.'

He put his handkerchief back in his pocket, turned to face her. He was still very pale, his cheeks white under the red flush around his eyes.

'Sorry about that,' he said. 'Don't know what came over me. Strong man in tears, and all that rot.' He gave a choking sort of laugh.

He came towards her. 'Well, Henrietta,' he said, 'it seems that you and I are to be wed. Always owed it to you, really, haven't I? Ever since years and years ago.' But he didn't say it bitterly. He said it – sweetly was the only word she could think of.

'And then,' he went on slowly, 'Julia and your husband—'

Was she understanding him rightly? 'Oh Henry,' she broke in, 'you can't possibly hold yourself responsible for that.'

'No? I suppose not. Funny, but I do in a way. After all, she was my sister.' His tone changed. 'Well, Henrietta, I think that we have got to go into action rather fast. After all, the son and heir must be born at a respectable interval after the wedding. Though of course it could be a girl. Wouldn't mind a daughter, either. Anyway how many months do you make it?'

'Nearly three,' she said.

'Hmm,' he said. 'A special licence, I think. "Forward the Light Brigade!" But first I must go down to Churston.

Caroline's there. I must tell her everything's off, and so on.'
A look of pain, but controlled instantly. He said, 'Have to
do that right away. You understand, don't you?'

'Of course I do,' she said.

He stooped, took her hands, pulled her up from the chair.
'Now I know why you've put on weight,' he said. He put his
arms around her. She rested her head against his shoulder.
Her forehead was burning as if she had a fever.

'No reason in the world why it shouldn't work out,' he
said in a detached, measuring tone. 'No reason at all. We've
always got on very well together, haven't we? Seems like
fate, hmm? Henry and Henrietta.'

❧ *Nineteen* ❧

She looked at her watch. In less than an hour, Henry would
be coming to collect her. They were due at the register office
at three.

Beedon and his wife were to be the witnesses. (Henrietta
had never seen Mrs Beedon, the retired cook.) 'I can rely
on them absolutely. That's the main thing,' Henry had
said. Rely on them not to talk to the papers was what he
meant. Though of course the papers would find out. But
by then she and Henry would be in France. They were
going to remain abroad until the commotion died down.
For of course there would be a commotion. 'Murderer's
Widow Weds Victim's Brother.' She could just imagine the
headlines. Yes, the papers would make a meal of it, added
spice being provided by the fact of Henry's being a lord.
As she, of course, would now be a lady. 'Lady Allingham'
– she couldn't imagine that title belonging to anyone but
Aunt Louisa.

Then, when the fuss was over, they would return – to Churston. How extraordinary that she should end up living at Churston.

Aunt Louisa had announced her intention of moving permanently to Brompton Square. When Henry had told her that he was going to marry Henrietta, her fury apparently had been beyond all bounds. (Henrietta had managed to drag an account of the occasion out of Henry, though he had told her nothing of his parting with Caroline Mallerby, and of course she hadn't asked him about it.)

'That hateful, hateful girl – she has ruined all our lives now,' Aunt Louisa had declared, and had added, 'Of course, I refuse ever to see her.' But when Henry had answered, 'In that case, I'm afraid you will not see me either. After all, Henrietta is going to be my wife,' she had wept and weakened.

The eventual result had been a terrible lunch at Churston, two days ago. Aunt Louisa had looked dreadfully old, quite gaunt and haggard, her grey hair untidy – how unthinkable that would once have been. Her hands had trembled. Henrietta almost felt sorry for her. The atmosphere had been icy, but surface courtesy had been maintained. All the same, Aunt Louisa was moving to Brompton Square, and had firmly refused Henry's offer of the dower house – empty for forty years – though he had promised to refurbish it completely. Thank goodness she had, Henrietta thought. The idea of living half a mile away from Aunt Louisa was not one that appealed to her.

How quiet it was this afternoon, in the house in the square. Vera had just departed. She had begged to wait until Henrietta left, but Henrietta had said she wanted to be alone for a little. Vera had been so happy – as well she might be, for Henrietta was paying her wages while she was abroad, and then Vera was coming to Churston to be her personal maid.

How loud her footsteps sounded in the empty hall. Until

today, there had been a grandfather clock that ticked
there, but this morning everything had been taken away
– the furniture to be sold, Adrian's personal possessions
despatched to his father, her own sent down to Churston.

She went upstairs, and into the empty drawing-room.
There were dark patches on the walls, where the pictures
had been. The light that came through the uncurtained
windows was harsh and grey. She crossed the room – her
footsteps echoed more loudly up here than they had done
downstairs – and looked out towards the square garden.
Trees hid the summer house. She turned round sharply –
with a curious feeling of the presence of Adrian at his desk.
In her mind, as her eyes wandered round the empty room,
he faded, to be replaced by Julia. Julia curled in the Omega
chair. Julia the last time she had seen her here, but not the
last time she had seen her.

When she was lying there, on top of her, holding down the
pillow on Julia's face, she felt as if she were draining rather
than pressing the life out of her. *Yes, they are all succubae,
they drain us of life, they suck our strength from us. Even
H. could still become a succuba.* But when Julia stopped
breathing, when her pulse was still, it was she herself who
felt drained of life. Why, she could almost have lain down
at Julia's side and slept till morning.

> *How wonderful is Death,*
> *Death and his brother Sleep!*
> *One pale as yonder wan and horned moon,*
> *With lips of lurid blue . . .*

She could have fallen asleep next to Julia's body, but
she couldn't have lifted the pillow and looked at her
face. No, it would have been quite impossible for her
to do that. As it was, she didn't know how she was
going to face the horror in the next room. Edmund had

steeled her before – 'Edmund help me,' she heard herself murmur now.

Slowly she rolled over, sat up, swung her legs over the side of the bed, felt the floor beneath her feet. The palms of the gloves she was wearing were drenched in sweat – as young men's gloves, she remembered, had sometimes been at dances. But she couldn't take the gloves off yet. There was still so much to do. She stood up, looked down at Julia's body, the head covered by the pillow. Julia's hands, extended at her sides, were a dead bird's open claws.

The bed was chaotically disordered. The picture she had seen when she first came into the bedroom – Julia and Adrian, limbs entwined – was suddenly sharply before her eyes. When she had lain on top of Julia, Julia had smelt of sex.

She went through into the living-room, averting her eyes from Adrian's body, slumped in the armchair. For a moment, she stood quite still in the middle of the room, breathing deeply. Now – the list.

She went into the kitchen, picked up her bag from the kitchen table, opened it and took out the small piece of paper in the pocket at the side. She put down her bag on the table again, and, holding the piece of paper, went back into the living-room.

1. Bottles and Glasses. Tray. She put the list in the pocket of her cardigan.

Adrian's beer mug was on the floor, where it had fallen from his hand – a wet stain around it on the rug. No need to touch that. Julia's empty tumbler was on the little table by the sofa, and her own was on the big table, next to the tray on which was the wine bottle – still a third full. She poured some wine into a tumbler, gulped it down, felt an impulse to pour more. But it might 'cloud the brain', as Adrian used to say. Involuntarily, she glanced in his direction, quickly she looked away – his jaw, gaping, his face still that hideous blueish colour.

She took the tray with the bottle and the two glasses on it into the kitchen. She poured the wine that was left down the sink – out of temptation's way – and ran the tap. She removed the cork from the corkscrew which lay on the kitchen table, and pushed it into the top of the bottle. She put the bottle next to her bag, and the corkscrew inside it – they hadn't had a corkscrew at the cottage.

She washed the two tumblers under the tap, taking particular care not to get her gloves wet. She dried them with the clean cloth she had brought with her, and put them away with the other glasses in the kitchen cupboard. She washed and dried the tray, and put it on the table.

Bottles and glasses. Tray. Ah yes – now the beer bottle, which was standing by the sink with some beer still left in it, and its screw top next to it. She wiped the bottle and the top very carefully with the cloth. She wasn't looking forward to the next bit. Carrying the bottle and the top, she went through into the living-room.

She didn't look at his face. She kept her eyes lowered as she crouched down on the floor, and picked up Adrian's right hand which hung over the arm of his chair. It was limp and heavy, not stiff yet. Thank heavens, she couldn't actually feel it, because of the gloves. She wrapped his fingers round the bottle, pressed them against it, moved his hand up and down – he would have left more than just one clean set of prints. Then she put the bottle down on the floor, and pressed the bottle top into his palm. She took his thumb and forefinger and ran the tips of them round the rim of the bottle top. That should do the trick. She released his hand, which flopped limply down. She gave a sudden violent shiver. Then she stood up, picked up the bottle, and put it, open, with the top next to it, on the big table.

Well, that was *Bottle and Glasses. Tray.* She took the list out of her pocket.

2. Strychnine. She went through into the kitchen again, and opened her bag. She took out the small packet, which

had only a few crystals in it now. She took it into the
living-room, rubbing it as she went, with the cloth with
which she had dried the glasses. Over to Adrian – last time.
Picking up his hand again and pushing it round the packet,
pressing the finger-tips against the paper. There! She sighed
with relief as she put the packet down on the table next to
the beer bottle.

Back into the kitchen. In her bag was the small empty
bottle in which she had dissolved the strychnine crystals in
warm water before she left home. She rinsed it out under
the tap, and put it back in her bag.

List again, out of her pocket.

*3. Check (a) fingerprints before gloves (b) appearance of
room (c) lights (d) laudanum bottle in bag.*

She put the list on the kitchen table.

She'd been so careful not to touch anything she didn't
have to. There was the handle of the front door, of course.
She would wipe that on her way out. Otherwise there was
only the handle of the kitchen cupboard – she had been
wearing gloves whenever she turned on the tap. With the
cloth, she wiped the handle of the cupboard.

She went into the sitting-room, looked around it. She was
sure that there was no need to go back into the bedroom.
Everything seemed all right. Then she saw that a chair had
been pushed back from its normal position when she had
dragged Julia into the bedroom. She moved it back into its
accustomed place. Now everything was just as it had been
when she arrived. Except, of course, for Adrian's body in
the armchair, and the overturned beer mug on the floor
beside him.

Lights – that had been the next thing. Well, there was
only the oil lamp on the table. She would leave that
on. It would have burnt itself out by the time Mrs
Baker, the cleaner, came in next morning – and found
the bodies. Poor Mrs Baker! She hoped it wouldn't
upset her too much. But people of that class enjoyed

excitement, she had always heard. They led such drab lives.

As she went back into the kitchen, she gave a deep sigh of relief. Almost over now! She picked up the list. *Laudanum bottle.* Yes, it was in her handbag. She would put it in its usual place on Adrian's dressing-table when she got home.

The final item: *4. Destroy list.* She took the box of matches out of her bag, and went over to the sink with the list. She pushed the dirty dishes to one side, so that she wouldn't get ash on them. Then she burnt the list – it was awkward lighting a match with gloves on. *She had burnt Henry's letter at Churston in the fireplace.* She turned on the tap and swilled the ashes down the sink with her hand – it didn't matter now if she got her gloves wet.

She turned off the tap, and – at last – took off her gloves, rolled them up, and put them in the bottom of her bag. She wiped her fingers on the dish cloth, and then flexed them, with relief. She picked up her hat from the kitchen table, and put it on.

Now – her bag, the dish cloth and the wine bottle. That was everything, she confirmed with a last glance around the dim kitchen. With her bag over her arm, and carrying the wine bottle and the dish cloth, she went through the living-room – not a glance at Adrian – and into the little hall. She realized that she was dreading the walk down the unlit lane to where she had parked the car. She turned the front door knob with the dish cloth wrapped round her hand. Outside the night was black; there was no moon. She closed the door, wiped the handle on the outside thoroughly, with the dish cloth.

She walked as quietly as she could. There were little night noises in the hedgerows. Strange that this walk down a Sussex lane should be the most frightening part of the whole thing. At last she reached the car, put her bag, the dishcloth and the wine bottle on the seat next to the

driver's. Then, with the starting handle, she started the car.
Thank heavens, it started at once. She got in.

As she passed the cottage, she could see the glow of the
oil lamp through the curtains. She would never come to
the cottage again.

She looked at her watch, holding it close to her face.
Ten o'clock. As she had expected, the village was quiet
as a tomb. The cottages were all in darkness. Not a sign
of anyone about.

About five miles farther on, she stopped the car, and
hurled the bottle in which she had dissolved the strychnine
crystals over a hedge. A mile after that, just before she came
to the main road, she got out of the car and dumped the
wine bottle in the ditch. She got into the car again with a
little sigh, realizing how tired she was. But in less than two
hours, she would be back in London.

Before she left, she had switched on the bedside light in
her room, drawn the curtains and locked the door. Vera,
returning from her Sunday afternoon off – probably at about
nine this evening – would have seen it on, and would have
presumed that she was in bed. Vera would be fast asleep
by now.

What else was there? She couldn't think of anything.
Yesterday, she had left the car in a *cul-de-sac* off a street
near the square. She had told Vera that it had broken down,
so Vera wouldn't have wondered at its absence this evening.
She would park it in the same place tonight. Tomorrow she
would fetch it, and mention to Vera that she had managed
to start it again.

'All over – *thank you, Edmund.*'

She began to hum the last movement of the Brahms
second piano concerto.

Now, in the empty drawing-room, she heard that happy
music again in her head, and smiled. Music for her
wedding-day.

> *When her mother tends her before the laughing mirror,*
> *Tying up her laces, looping up her hair,*
> *Often she thinks, were this wild thing wedded,*
> *More love should I have, and much less care.*

The words made her smile. Edmund had thought *Love in the Valley* such a ridiculous poem. Darling Edmund. What would he have thought about her marriage to 'ideally stupid' Henry? Hadn't he said in his notebook, 'if thou wilt needs marry, marry a fool'? Last time, she hadn't taken his advice, and how badly it had turned out. Though, as Nanny used to say, 'all's well that ends well'. It was Edmund who had helped her to end it so well, so perfectly. Hadn't he put the idea into her head, when he wrote 'Death to deceivers!'?

It had been dark for about half an hour when she parked the car off the lane, by a five-barred gate into a field. Carrying her bag, the bottle of wine and bottle of beer, she approached the cottage. Julia's green Isotta-Fraschini was parked outside the fence. *Her* fence. And Julia was presumably with *her* husband inside *her* cottage – a lamp glowed behind the curtained window. For it had been she who had rented the cottage, looked forward so much to going down to it at weekends. Yet only three times had she managed to get Adrian down there. When *Julia* was involved, though, it was evidently quite a different matter.

How dedicated Julia was to taking away *her* things: *her* lover, *her* husband, *her* cottage. Her anger rose as she thought about it, just as she had intended. For she needed anger, she knew, in order to *carry it off, carry it through*.

She was by the front door now. She turned the handle. *She must remember, from now on, to touch as few things as possible*. Only the things she needed, in fact. Very gently, she opened the door, which gave a tiny creak In the little hall, she paused, listened, but couldn't hear anything.

A wide band of light came into the hall from the open

door of the living-room. She moved forward, looked in. No
one there. She advanced into the room. The door into the
dark kitchen was open – there was no one in there, either.
So they must be in the bedroom. She hadn't expected that
– though why not? After all, the bedroom was presumably
the object of the weekend. Her nerve almost failed her. In
flagrante delicto. But what an advantage it would give her.
She put the bottles down on the table, as she passed. The
bedroom door was ajar – she pushed it open with her elbow.
One of the beds was empty – hadn't been made up at all,
she noticed. In the other, a tangle of limb unwound in the
sudden light flooding from behind her. For a moment, she
felt quite weak. She clenched her teeth hard together.

'Well,' well,' she said, and was delighted by how cool she
sounded.

'Henrietta!' Adrian exclaimed. How ridiculous he looked,
with his mouth open like that, pulling himself into a sitting
position, and clutching at the sheet, which he dragged over
them. They were both quite naked. Julia, too, looked
astonished, really *taken aback*, which was amusing.

'Adrian,' she said. 'I've never known you so early to bed.
But you told me, Julia, you *always* go to bed early in the
country. I thought it was for *beauty sleep*, though.' She
laughed. Goodness, she really was *carrying it off*.

'Well, Hitty Pitty, *what* a lovely surprise,' Julia said, but
she didn't get the tone quite right.

'I thought this would be a good opportunity for us to
have a little talk. Away from the distractions of the big
city, and so on. But perhaps you'd like to put on a few
clothes first, and come into the other room? I find it just a
teeny bit stuffy in here. We'll have a drink. I brought some
very good Burgundy with me.'

'Darling Hitty Pitty, how civilized of you,' Julia said.
Evidently she was recovering.

'Burgundy?' Adrian said in a bemused tone.

'Yes, Adrian, that red stuff they make in France. From

grapes, you know. But the Burgundy's for Julia and me.
I brought a bottle of beer for you, since you like that
better.'

'Mm, isn't he a barbarian?' Julia said. '*I* brought a bottle
of champagne down. But he'd only drink half a glass, so I
had to drink all the rest myself. I was merry as a marriage
bell, as they say – though I don't think that's so terribly
merry. But goodness, *I* was, wasn't I, darling?'

Thus addressed, Adrian gave a sort of grunt. *Out of his
depth by miles*, Henrietta thought. She said, 'Right. I'll go
and open the bottles.'

She turned, and went through the living-room to the
kitchen, picking up the bottles on the way. Enough light
came through the living-room door for her to see quite
nicely. The kitchen was in a mess – the sink piled up with
dirty cups and plates. Broken eggshells on the table, and
a greasy frying pan on the cooker. The empty champagne
bottle stood by the sink, with a half-full bottle of gin and
a bottle of angostura – Julia had evidently felt in need of
Dutch courage. Anyway, *she* wouldn't have to clear up –
she wasn't going to touch anything they'd used. And now
– she must hurry.

She pulled off her hat, and put it down in a space on
the table. The kitchen tray was on the draining board.
She brought it over to the table, put the two bottles on it.
Then she fetched a beer mug and two tumblers from the
cupboard – they hadn't any wine glasses – and put them on
the tray, too. She opened her bag. She needed three things
– the corkscrew, the bottle of laudanum drops, and the little
bottle in which she had dissolved the strychnine crystals.

Open the bottles first. The screw top of the beer bottle
came off with a little hissing sound. Now for the wine
bottle. Carefully she inserted the corkscrew, pulled – was
it going to stick? But it came out, smooth as silk, with a
small pop.

She opened the bottle with the strychnine in it, poured

its contents into the beer mug, and put it back in her bag. Now the laudanum. She poured about a quarter of an inch into one of the tumblers. That was at least forty drops. Laudanum bottle back in the bag now. Close the bag. Then she filled both tumblers with burgundy – the glass that was farther away from her had the laudanum in it. Now the beer. Holding the mug tilted slightly, she poured the beer in slowly, so that it wouldn't form a head.

Well, that was everything wasn't it? On the tray were the full tumblers, the nearly full beer mug and the Burgundy bottle. She carried the tray through into the living-room, put it on the table, just had time to pick up the bottle, as if she'd that moment finished pouring, when Julia came through from the bedroom wearing a black satin dressing-gown, trimmed with marabou. Goodness!

'You've surprised me this evening, Hitty Pitty, really you have,' Julia said, sinking down on the sofa, crossing her legs – a white ankle, a black satin mule, also trimmed with marabou, appearing beneath her dressing-gown.

Now Adrian came through, fully dressed in shirt and jersey, trousers and shoes and socks. Sensible. He wouldn't have cut a very impressive figure in his striped pyjamas and carpet slippers. He stood by the fireplace.

'Why don't you sit down?' Henrietta said, waving a hand towards the armchair.

'Thank you, Henrietta,' he said stiffly, 'I prefer to stand.'

Julia laughed. 'Oh sweetie, you *do* sound pompous. Come on. Sit down – join the party.'

He shrugged irritably, but sat down in the armchair, upright, not leaning back.

'And now for this little talk of yours, Hitty Pitty. I'm dying to hear what it's all about. But even more, I'm dying for my tiny drinkie.'

Henrietta picked up Julia's tumbler from the tray, leant over the back of the sofa, and handed it to her. 'Goodness, not so tiny!' Julia said.

'I'm afraid we haven't any wine glasses here.' *Thank heaven*, she thought, for surely, in so much Burgundy, Julia wouldn't taste the laudanum.

She picked up her own glass. 'Well Julia,' she said, 'shall we drink a toast?'

'What about poor Adrian?'

'He can have his in a minute. This toast is for us. Julia, I give you *Adrian's ladies.*'

A grunt from Adrian. A peal of laughter from Julia: 'Hitty Pitty, I never imagined you had this Noël Coward streak.'

'No indeed.' How cross Adrian sounded. 'I really think this is all in the worst possible taste.'

Julia frowned. She raised her glass. '*Adrian's ladies,*' she said.

'No heeltaps!' Henrietta exclaimed. 'That's what I heard Uncle Harry say.'

'Did you? I don't remember that. But if you say so. No heeltaps!'

Her eyes met Julia's with a direct challenge, as she raised her glass to her lips. Then she blinked, started to drink. Yes, Julia was following suit. What a lot of wine a tumbler held. Finishing it, she felt quite sick for a minute. Julia put down her empty glass with a clink on the little table next to the sofa.

'Hardly the way to drink Burgundy,' Adrian said.

'Oh shut up, Adrian.' Now Julia grimaced. There was a puzzled look on her face, as if she were listening for something.

'Something the matter?' Henrietta asked.

'Tasted rather funny. Are you *sure* it's such a good burgundy?'

'Chambertin 1904,' Henrietta said.

'Hmm. Sounds wonderful. Give me a drop more.' She held out her glass. Henrietta poured a little wine into it, and then a little into her own.

Julia took a sip. 'No, you're right. It isn't bad at all.'

'Really,' Adrian said. 'I do think that you're both behaving in the most extraordinary way. Swilling vintage Burgundy—'

'Adrian,' Julia said, 'you're being extremely boring. Give him his beer, Henrietta.'

'I don't think I want it.'

'Give it to him, Henrietta.'

She picked up the mug from the tray, took it over to him. For a moment she thought that he was going to refuse. But Julia's eyes were fixed on him. Pettishly he shrugged, and took it. *How weak he is*, Henrietta thought.

Julia raised her own glass. 'No heeltaps, Adrian,' she said.

'I've never heard of anything so childish.' But he shrank from Julia's savage look, as she repeated, 'No heeltaps.' 'Perhaps,' he said, 'when this performance is over, we shall be able to talk some sense.' He didn't wait for Julia to reply, but hastily raised the mug to his lips, tilted his head back, and drank.

His back arched. Then his whole body contorted. The mug, seeming to jerk from his hand, fell to the floor. He held his breath and, as he did so, went white, then blue. He sank back in the chair. His face was twisted, and his mouth gaped open.

Julia was on her feet. 'Adrian!' Now she was over by the armchair. She put a hand on his sleeve.

Henrietta, still standing by the table, was shaking violently.

Julia turned, stared at her, stared, then, at the glass on the floor, swung towards Adrian. 'He's dead.' And she gave a shrill little scream, stumbled to her feet, and towards the door.'

But Henrietta leapt in front of it, barring the way. 'No,' she said in a loud clear voice.

Julia was tugging at her arms. Henrietta gave her a tremendous push, and Julia staggered backwards, fell to the floor.

'You're mad,' Julia said. 'Why you must be mad.' Then, 'The police,' she said. 'Must get the police.'

Henrietta moved towards her, stood above her. She could hear how soothing, how reasonable her voice sounded as she said, 'Of course you can go to the police. In just a minute. We'll go together. I'm perfectly willing. I just want you to tell me something first.'

'Tell you something?' Julia murmured dully. She rubbed her arm across her forehead. Sweat and powder made a smear on the sleeve of her black dressing-gown. 'Tell you what?'

'*Why?*' Henrietta said. '*Why*, ever since we were children? Hating me so. Trying to take everything away from me.'

'Mad,' Julia said vaguely, 'quite mad. Why, it was you that hated me. So cold and sullen from the day you came. So hard – the way you used to stare at me. And so sly – scheming about your precious Edmund. I'll tell you something – Edmund wasn't worth Henry's little finger.' She blinked, shook her head as if to clear it. 'I'll tell you something else. I wasn't going to let you get your claws into darling Henry.' She started to smile, then seemed to forget about it. The corner of her mouth twitched. Her lids came down for a moment. Then, with a visible effort, she forced them wide open.

'That's all nonsense, Julia. Why did you take Adrian? You couldn't have wanted him. Why, I don't think he even likes women.'

Now Julia did smile. She was looking blurred, dazed. 'Poor old Adrian,' she said. 'All Englishmen are a bit like that. A woman has to take the lead. Oh, I've heard about *you*. Lying there like a sacrificial lamb. *You* didn't want him. I felt sorry for him. Thought I'd cheer him up a bit.'

'How can you tell such lies? You know you only did it to hurt me. Leaving that letter for me to find.'

'Hurt you? Wake you up perhaps. So bloody smug. So cold. Inhuman. You can't *always* get your way, Hitty Pitty.'

She frowned. 'Feel so terribly sleepy. Can't understand . . .'
And then, '*You.*' Her snake-neck straining forward, the
green eyes staring, but then her lids came down. Her head
nodded forward. Her chin rested on her chest.

'Julia!' Henrietta was shaking her arm. 'You've got to
listen.' The *coup de grâce*. 'Henry will marry me. I swear
to you he'll marry me, swear it. Do you hear that?' But she
could see that Julia didn't hear. Julia was breathing with a
snoring sound. She pinched her arm, as Julia had so often
pinched hers, but Julia didn't stir. Julia, at the last, had
eluded her.

It hadn't happened as she had wanted it to. The anger
came over her in a wave. She was shaking again. The anger
carried her to the table where she drained her glass of wine,
then carried her into the kitchen, where she opened her bag,
took out her gloves, put them on. *Thank heaven for the
anger*, she thought, as she went back into the living-room.
Now she must pull Julia into the bedroom. *Thank heaven
for the hatred*. Yes, and her hatred resonated now, in the
empty room in the quiet square. 'Death to deceivers,' she
murmured. And Julia had died deceiving her. Julia hadn't
really answered any of her questions. Everything Julia had
said about it all being *her* fault – 'cold and sullen', indeed!
– had been nothing but a pack of lies. Well, she would never
know the real answers now.

She looked at her watch. Half past two. Henry would
arrive at any moment. Dear Henry, so upright, so honourable. 'Edmund not worth Henry's little finger,' Julia had
said. Stupid Julia. Of course *that* wasn't true. But all the
same, dear Henry.

She frowned. Still one more task ahead of her. Letting
Henry know that she wasn't pregnant. She would manage
it somehow. Should she say that it had been 'a false alarm'?
But then she had told him that a doctor had confirmed
it. No, that wouldn't do. Would she have to feign a
miscarriage? She sighed. She would work out something,

once they were abroad. Whatever she said, surely he – so upright, so honourable – would believe her? Oh yes, she was certain that she could make him believe her. After all, he had done so, implicitly, until now.

A car was coming down the square. Yes, it was Henry's. She raised her hands to the brim of her hat, patted the thick coils of her hair. She hurried from the room, with one backward glance. Dark patches on the walls where the pictures had been. Then – down the stairs, across the hall. The door opened, slammed behind her. The key turned in the lock.

❦ Epilogue ❧

1938
Henry had lingered longer than usual at the breakfast table that morning. In fact, she was beginning to feel distinctly edgy – *what if the telephone rang* – by the time he went off to the gun-room, where he did the business connected with running the estate. Ricky, the aged spaniel who followed him everywhere, had ambled after him, and she had been struck by the resemblance between them. But Henry shouldn't amble and look old at forty-eight.

He was drinking far too much, of course. Last night, as on so many other evenings when they were alone, he had stayed in the dining-room for more than an hour after dinner. He had drunk, as he so often did, a whole bottle of port. Eighteenth-century squires had apparently flourished on such a regime, but presumably they had sweated it out on the hunting-field next day. Henry took hardly any exercise nowadays. And when, eventually, he had joined her in the drawing-room, he had drunk three whiskies and sodas before going to bed.

It was wearing him down. It had been going on for such a long time. At first she hadn't noticed it, but it had started, she realized now, when they got back from their honeymoon. Steadily his intake had increased, and now he wasn't just drinking in the evening. Why, the other day she had gone into the gun-room at eleven o'clock in the morning, and he had had whisky in front of him, on his desk. She sighed.

He had been more shocked than she had ever imagined he would be by her 'miscarriage' – when she had bribed that awful little Italian doctor to back up her story. She still wasn't absolutely sure that Henry believed it. That strange expression on his face when he was sitting by her bed. And two days later, when she was up and about again – she probably should have feigned weakness for longer, but it had been so hot, and she had wanted to bathe – he had said to her, out of the blue. 'You have been quite straight with me about everything, haven't you, Henrietta?' He had seemed to believe her indignant 'What do you mean? Of course I have.' 'Of course, of course,' he had muttered in a shamefaced way.

She would have been glad to have a child. But it hadn't happened. And then that doctor in Harley Street had told her that it was impossible. Some internal malformation – though an operation, he had said, might put it right. But what would she have told Henry? So she had just left it – and, of course, had never mentioned her visit to the doctor to him. No children – that had been a blow to him. Yes, the drinking was probably connected with that.

And she still wasn't sure that he hadn't found out about her affaire with Guy. How long ago had that been? Nearly six years now. Her second affaire – she was quite certain that he had known nothing about her first one, with Paul. And now surely he didn't know about her and Simon? Though she had, perhaps, been going up to London rather too often lately. And there had been that little click on the telephone the other day – she had often wished that the telephone in the gun-room were a separate line and not an extension. But what possible reason could there have been for suggesting such a thing? Except the true one.

Anyway, she didn't think that he knew about Simon. But Guy – that was much more doubtful. At that time she had sensed a definite change in his attitude towards her. Well, of course she had – for that was when he had stopped making love to her. They had never discussed the subject – he had just given up coming to her room. She wondered what poor people, couples who had to share a room, did in those circumstances. If they had shared a room she probably would have been able to lure Henry back. But would she really have wanted to? Somehow, after they were married, sex had never been the same. Could it have been its illicitness that had kept her physical passion for him so alive, before? She gave the little smile that what she called her 'cynical thoughts' always provoked.

Sometimes, at dinner parties with 'the county', when they were all expressing their mortal outrage at everything on earth – well, everything *new*, anyway – and calling for more hangings, more floggings, tougher prisons, she would find herself smiling that little smile. A Justice of the Peace on one side of her, the Lord High Sheriff on the other. *We walk among them*, she would think, *and they do not know us*. Often, walking down a crowded London street, she would wonder how many she passed, unrecognizing and unrecognized. Members of her fellowship. The undiscovered. 'Criminals' the county would have called them. But that was all such nonsense, anyway. *Freud, Marx, Darwin* – her unholy trinity, all so morally repugnant to Henry's and her 'friends'. Oh yes, she had her own thoughts, thoughts which she could never express to any of them.

That was what was so nice about being with Simon – she could say what she liked to him. He kept her in touch with the modern world, though he did go on about capitalism and Fascism and Spain rather a lot. Dear Simon – he had been so horrified by Mr Chamberlain's trip to Munich last month. As, oddly, had Henry – it must be the only thing they had in common. Except her. She smiled again. Though she didn't say so, to either Simon or Henry, she hadn't been at all horrified by Munich – the last war had been quite enough for her. Darling Edmund. How she still missed him. How intensely he had felt about things. Simon felt intensely too, of course, but in quite a different way. Simon's poems were full of pylons and factories and classes and masses. They didn't really mean very much to her – but she didn't tell *him* that.

He was so young. Fourteen years younger than she was. She supposed some people would consider that disgraceful, though she couldn't see why. The French – and they were the experts on affaires, after all – thought it was a very good thing for a young man to have a relationship with an older woman. An older woman. She would be forty next year. Forty! When she was young, she had thought that so terribly old, and now she didn't feel it was at all.

She got up from the table, and went over to the mirror that hung over the fireplace. She had worn well. There wasn't any doubt about that. Her hair was still thick and glossy, with not a trace of grey. Simon found her long hair altogether amazing – she was the only woman he had ever known who hadn't cut her hair. She had kept her figure. It had meant rigorous dieting – and she had always loved food – but when it came to a choice she hadn't hesitated. She ran her fingers over her cheeks – thick, pale skin like hers survived so much better than those 'wild rose complexions' that had been so much admired when she was a girl. Poor Cynthia Chanter! When she'd seen her five years ago, on her return from India, she had looked so sallow and withered. And what a bore she had become – whining and disappointed with her life. If Julia were alive today, she would probably look awful. Tiny and dried up, with a neck like a chicken's.

One of the parlour-maids was peeping round the door. 'Come in, Margaret,' she said. 'You can clear away the breakfast now.' The girl was polite and pleasant, though not really what Aunt Louisa would have called well-trained. Good servants were so difficult to find, nowadays. When Hobart had been pensioned off, they hadn't been able to find a satisfactory replacement. All the butlers worked for rich Americans now. Vera of course was a treasure – she was so thankful that Vera had never married.

She went through into the morning room. *The telephone could ring at any moment.* It would be Simon, and she would arrange to meet him in London next week. She would tell Henry she was going to the hairdresser – and she'd fit that in first. She must remember to ring up and make an appointment with Antoine.

What day would be best? She went over to her desk, and opened the leather-bound engagement book that lay on the blotter. On Thursday, there was the Annual General Meeting of the Women's Institute. On Saturday she would be opening the autumn bazaar in the church hall. The new Chief Constable was coming to lunch on Wednesday. Tuesday or Friday, then. Monday would just be possible, but they were going to dinner with the Falconers – poor old Guy and that appalling new wife of his – which would make it a bit of a rush. She wouldn't be able to catch the later train, as she usually ended up by doing when she went to see Simon, No, it must be Tuesday or Friday.

She closed her engagement book, glanced round the room. The morning-room was her favourite room in the house. It was the first room the maids did each day, and it was in spotless order, the chintz cushions plumped out, the polished furniture gleaming darkly. The great vase of chrysanthemums she had arranged yesterday was beautiful. The bitter sharpness of their scent mingled with that of the brightly burning wood fire and the pot pourri she had made in the summer. No one could say that she didn't keep things going. And they had the best food in the county. She had been a good *châtelaine*, as Aunt Louisa would have said, of Churston. At that moment, the telephone rang.

'Hullo. Lady Allingham speaking.'

'Henrietta.' Yes it was he. She sank down in the chintz-covered armchair beside the telephone table. 'Hullo darling,' she said. *'Comment ça va?'*

'Fine,' he said, as he always did, 'but I'm in rather a hurry. I'm in a telephone box, and I haven't any more change. When am I going to see you? How about Wednesday?'

'No,' she said. 'I can't manage that. It will have to be Tuesday or Friday.'

A moment's pause. Then, 'Friday,' he said. 'A treat to look forward to at the end of the week.'

'Sweet,' she said, and then, 'At your flat at one? I'll bring a tiny picnic from Fortnum's.'

'You're so extravagant, Henrietta,' he said. She knew he felt he ought to disapprove of luxuries like picnics from Fortnum's, but she had noticed that that didn't stop him enjoying them.

'It's part of my charm,' she said, and then – she couldn't resist it – 'I *want* you.'

'Me too,' he said. The pips sounded. 'Must go,' he said. 'Friday. Goodbye.'

'Friday,' she said, and then, just before they were cut off, 'Goodbye, my darling. Kisses.' The dialling tone purred in her ear. She put down the receiver.

'Mmm.' She let out the sound in a long sigh. She stood up, stretched, then suddenly shivered.

She crossed the room to where sharp sunlight drained the colour from the fire. She held out her hands to the little pale flames. *Winter soon.* Click. Startled by the unexpected sound, she turned.

He stood in the doorway. The shotgun, cocked under his arm, was aimed at her, as she had so often seen it aimed at animals and birds. How grey his face was. He stared at her, but his eyes were blank and glazed.

She must do something. Ricky, the spaniel, ambled towards her, wagging his tail. A ray of sunlight dazzled her eyes. She must do something. How long had he been there? *I want you . . . Goodbye, my darling. Kisses.*

She must say something, but her mind was whirling, and the sun was in her eyes. She knew he was going to fire. *Death to deceivers.* She extended her hands in a little pleading gesture. Words wouldn't come. She made a last tremendous effort.

'Edmund,' she heard herself say. And then, the crack, the shock, the silence.